Princess of the Broken

Severed Kingdoms: Book 1

Jasmine K Swinburne

Fat Fox Publishing

Editing by Jess Lawrence

ISBN's:

Ebook- 978-1-7392995-0-7

Paperback- 978-1-7392995-1-4

For Scott,
my sun, my moon, my earth.

Gavaria
Sorrelle
Kignet
Jalendia
Quendore
Zenick
Faldova
Thezmare
Yendoth
Mirdoff

Aldros
The black mountains
The fire lands
Faldova
Bordorne
Yendoth
Thezmare
Challahan
Gavaria
Brendare
Handover mountains
Neith
Quater
Sorrelle
Nuval
Mirdoff
Quendore
Quendore
Kignet
Sorentine
Zenick
Handore
Jalendia
Xanth

A HISTORY OF ALDROS

Long ago, when the kingdoms of Aldros remained as one, twins were born bathed in blood and chaos.

They were born from great power and beauty. Beings with eyes of gold, feathers of white cascading down their backs in magnificent wings, and formidable magic coursing through their veins. A boy, Elio, and a girl, Aruna.

The children knew nothing but anger for each other, raw and venomous displeasure in one another's company. Their fights would last centuries, leaving nothing but destruction in their path. Elio would curse his sister, and Aruna would curse him right back. It did not matter who or what stood in their way, they would see nothing but that raging fire of loathing.

Their father grew tired, weakened by the very children he brought into this world. He tried to make it work, time and time again he would try to make things better. But it was no use.

Until one day he snapped.

He used his children's own game against them, cursed them both with all the power he could muster. If he could not bring them together, then he would separate them forevermore.

He banished Elio to the sun. It greeted him with warmth and love, showing him the greatness he could achieve. His daughter, Aruna, was banished to the moon. She was welcomed into the open arms of darkness, cold and utter despair.

The spell was stronger than their father had first thought; his power ripped from him, scattering away into a thousand stars. Left powerless and alone, he came to miss his children's bickering.

Time stretched by. Elio learned from his old ways, and as a gift to those below, he would grant powers to the ones he deemed worthy. Aruna didn't have such abilities; she grew more bitter and resentful of her brother as the years went by, waiting for the day that her moon would align just right with his sun, to take out her frustrations once and for all.

But something happened on that day, something Aruna could not quite explain. As the world was coated in darkness, and her brother sent down a piece of his magic wrapped in the sun's warmth, she found she could do the same.

She threw out her power, as much as she could gather, every last ounce of darkness in her bones. It collided with the power of the sun, writhing and fighting, and together they merged into a new-born child. Elio tried to stop it, but it was too late. There was nothing that could be done. Nothing except watch and wait to see what gift the child would accept for themselves.

To Aruna's dismay, the child chose the light, though he would not live to see the age of twenty.

It was another three hundred years before they collided again, and Aruna waited for that day with patience. Again, she sent down her gift with her brother's.

This time, the child succumbed to the darkness within.

Aruna again waited—three hundred years was nothing to her after all.

And that, that is where our story begins...

MANY MOONS AGO

Elisaria had never intended to marry a king.

The day she met Prince Orilius, he stole her heart. Their marriage was an arranged one, but every part of her belonged to him. She wished she could say the same for him, but she knew he strayed for a while, not truly accepting her love. It was painstaking, but she waited for him to return those feelings. Turns out it didn't take long at all.

She remembered the day it happened clearly. Saw it in his eyes the moment he fell head over heels for her. They stood on the parapet, waiting for his sister to arrive back in Gavaria. She had said something that made him laugh. His whole face lit up, then he looked at her as if it was the first time he had ever seen her. His face crumpled for a moment, something dawning on him, then he took her hand in his, his eyes fixed upon the horizon.

A year later, she fell pregnant with their first child.

Elisaria had always dreamed of having a large family, so a short while after Reed was born, they decided to try for another. This time they were not so lucky.

Thirteen years passed. Elisaria and Orilius had become King and Queen of Gavaria. Orilius' sister had sadly passed away. Reed had grown into a handsome young prince. And four children had been lost in the womb, never held, never kissed.

Elisaria's heart couldn't take much more. So, the night the travelling carnival came to their kingdom, her hopes soared when they sought out the fortune teller. She told them that with the help of an ancient witch, they would conceive once more, and a child would be born. But only with the crone's magic would this path come to be.

Another year passed, the king away most of this time, searching the Handover mountains for the crone the fortune teller spoke of. He did not recount much of his journey upon his return, only that the witch would not help. The queen's heart broke once more for the child they would never meet.

A week later, when the moon shone down on the castle, Elisaria woke with the urge to visit the gardens. There she found a hooded figure deep within the rose bushes. She knew without asking who this person was. The crone.

The witch told her she had decided to help. That she had had a vision of the daughter that would come to be, a vision of the power she would possess. That it was not down to her to deny the world that power. But she would only help her at a cost. She wanted the magic that would run through the child's veins.

Once the child had grown and her abilities had fully developed, she would come to collect what was hers. The queen agreed, not caring of the powers her daughter would possess, only of the child she would receive.

As the moon reached its peak in the sky, the witch whispered an ancient spell, holding a clear liquid vial to the skies. The liquid turned thick and silvery, sharing the brightness of the moon. The witch urged Elisaria to drink the vial's contents, every last drop, assuring her it would help the gods of the skies to find her when the time came.

Her blood burned, her skin glowed brightly. The torture of it was indescribable. The queen dropped to her knees, her eyes wide with pain and fear. Then, just as quickly, the pain dissipated. The witch told the queen that to finish the spell, she would have to bed her husband, and so she did. She climbed back into bed with him, rousing him from sleep, and there in the light of the moon, they made love, sealing the spell the crone had cast.

It was confirmed three weeks later, when the queen's period did not arrive, that she was with child. Elisaria spent the next nine months terrified that she would lose the baby, never telling her husband of that night under the moon. Never telling him of her visit from the witch he once sought.

The day their daughter was born, the sun and the moon aligned just so, that the world was sheathed in darkness. Within that darkness the child's silver eyes shone, her screams filling the castle corridors, and the air itself stilled. Watching. Waiting.

The queen was weakened. Her very blood hummed with tiredness, her legs couldn't hold her weight. It was a week before she even had the strength to hold the baby, a week before she felt the soft skin of the person she fought so hard to bring into this world. Three before she could move about the castle unaided.

Their daughter was a troubled baby. The servants would whisper of how her screams would fill each waking hour, going long into the night. Screams so piercing it was as if she was in great pain. But all the healers of the kingdom and elsewhere never found anything to be wrong with the child.

Over the next six years, their daughter's powers grew stronger with each passing day. At age three, when her first ability manifested, they were proud beyond words. She had gained the healing powers of their kingdom, the same power the king and prince possessed. But it wasn't long before more abilities developed.

The queen began to grow fearful of those powers. The day the princess made their son disappear was the worst of her life.

For two days, Elisaria thought she would have to grieve yet another child. But the girl brought him back, shaken and scared. The prince never spoke of where he went. Elisaria only held him tight in the days that followed.

They decided to keep their daughter from the public eye, scared of what might happen if they didn't. Her powers were unlike any they had ever known or heard of. Something even copious amounts of research couldn't help with.

Elisaria convinced her husband that seeking out the fortune teller was their only option, that she would hold the answers. Orilius was not so sure, for what she had told them before had been false. The queen still did not confess her truth.

The king agreed to seek her out regardless, in the hope she could ease their worries.

In the end, it did not matter. For fate had other plans.

1

THE PRINCESS AND THE BIRD

RAYLIN

The market goes quiet as Fee's warning call echoes from high above, hushing my heart.

Oh, crap.

I search the skies for him, but his snow-white feathers blend seamlessly with the clouds, making it impossible to spot him. Like he hears my thoughts, he dips lower and I catch a glimpse of the colours of the rainbow spreading through the tips of his wings.

Others are raising their eyes to the skies now, seeking out the screeching bird. A small child almost bumps into me, her eyes fixed above. Her mother pulls on her arm, dragging her from my path. "Watch where you are going, Franny," she says before giving me a small, apologetic nod, her eyes not meeting my face buried deep within the hood of my cloak.

Fee's calls become louder, more urgent. It's then I remember I need to move.

I place the trinket I'm holding gently back on the stall, turning towards the castle gates. Not wanting to cause a scene, I keep my feet moving at a steady rhythm, not too fast yet.

The castle grounds are bustling with people this afternoon, the hot sun bringing everyone from their homes to enjoy the market. I weave in and out of the crowds to avoid a collision. The castle gates are opened each day to welcome the market vendors and people of Sorrelle, but it is not often this crowded.

Rumours of the princesses of Aldros arriving at the castle have spread through the villages like wildfire. One from each of the nine other kingdoms have been invited in the hopes of winning the prince's heart and securing the spot as the next Queen of Sorrelle. Hence the busy market. Everyone's out buying dresses, or fabrics to make their own, in the hope they receive an invitation to the ball. Half of the men attending likely hope to catch the eye of a fine lady themselves. Fat chance of that happening. They will all be too busy making eyes at the one person who truly matters in all this.

Prince Malakai.

No one has told me all this specifically, but I have heard it as I pretend to browse the stalls, lingering at the ones I know gossip the most. It's amazing the things people say when they think no one is listening.

As soon as I make it through the gates, I ball the fabric of my cloak into my fists, lifting it to my knees, and start to run. My bare feet—filthy from this morning's trek to the market—slap against the cobblestone path. I have been tempted there by the shoe stalls, the rows of silk slippers, sparkling heels, and boots that lace up almost to your knees. However, each time I walk away empty-handed.

I like the feel of the earth beneath me, the way the grass kisses each inch of my foot or the way wet mud squelches between my toes. The cobblestones are not so kind; many times I have returned home with bleeding cuts and scrapes.

I break through the tree line, feet submerging into the soft, overgrown grass.

Fee swoops low, his large form flashing in and out between the breaks of trees. He makes a low caw, urging me on. We haven't had to do this for a long time; she never arrives in the middle of the day. I usually wake to her sitting beside me, stroking my hair, or to the smell of freshly made pancakes and warm golden syrup.

My heart slams against my chest, fists tightening against the fabric of my cloak. I need to move faster. I must be there when she arrives. I don't even want to begin to imagine how she'll react if I'm not.

I should stop doing this, stop leaving when I'm not supposed to. But from the first moment my feet touched solid ground those five years ago, something inside me flipped, and I couldn't stop. Every day that I can, I leave. I know it's not safe. If anything happened, how would she ever find me? But it is as if the wind calls to me, whispering my name until it can touch me. Caresses my skin with its words. Hopefully I won't need to sneak around much longer. Stars willing, this time she understands.

I reach the top of a small incline, pushing aside the pink-flowered shrubbery. I suck in a breath as my tower comes into view. *Home.*

The clearing around the tower spreads wide, filled with tiny white flowers that seem perfectly normal during the day, but by night they become something else entirely. They glow a brilliant silver, lighting up the trees surrounding the open space. Moon

Flowers, named as such for their resemblance to the moon's glow. The tower itself sits directly in the middle of the clearing, reaching high up, taller than the vast majority of the trees in the forest. Its dark stones are jagged and rough. One window sits at the top of the tower, looking out into the world beyond, a circle just wide enough to fit a person. I would know.

Of course, there is a hidden door, which can only be accessed if you share the same blood as the person who drew the magical runes in the first place. Which was not me. I never learned the magic needed to make my own. So, I have to escape the hard way.

Fee soars ahead, reaching home before I do. He flies straight through the window and into the room above. I stop at the bottom of the tower, my foot tapping against the floor impatiently.

"*Hurry*," I whisper to myself.

I step back as I see it, the rope hurtling towards the ground. Fee perches in the window and watches as I loop the rope around my hand and start to climb. This is when I wish I had boots. The sharp stone digs into my feet as I press them against the walls of the tower, wedging my toes between the cracks. I remove one hand from the rope and loop it up higher. Then the other hand. Over and over. The rope bites into my palms, pinching at my fingers as it tightens.

Almost there.

I am faster now than I was when I first started doing this, quickly learning I needed to wrap the rope tighter than comfortable to get enough grip. I would often slip, the rope sliding through my hands and burning me. It felt like it took hours the first time I climbed up and I wanted nothing more than to give up at the halfway mark. But that was forgotten when I left again the next day. Until I returned that night and had to do it all over again. Now

I welcome the pain; it is nothing compared to the torture of being imprisoned here.

It helps that the marks do not last long; my body soon heals them, my powers restoring me to full health. The power was gifted to me by the sun, blessed upon me at my birth, just like most royal children—those lucky enough to gain the gift of the old gods.

Unlike the other princes and princesses of Aldros, I am different. Along with the powers of the sun, I was gifted those of the moon. The dark and twisting gift it forged for me scared those who were meant to love me unconditionally. I feel those gifts within me now, cold and creeping, slithering for a way out.

I reach the window and grip the ledge, pulling myself in head-first.

She's not here yet, thank the stars.

I pull the rope up through the window, untie it from around my bedpost, wrap it in my cloak and shove them both into the darkness within me, the everywhere and nowhere, hidden safely from anyone but me. My personal void. They disappear from my hands as a cold breeze washes over me.

I change quickly into a clean dress, one of plain blue cotton, and throw the dirty one in with the others already soaking in the rose-scented water bucket. I dunk my feet in too to rid them of the mud caked along the soles.

I catch a glimpse of myself in the mirror beside me and gasp.

My hair is wild and windswept. I untie it from its braid and brush through it, untangling all the knots, which takes forever as it is so long. All these years of never having it cut, it now reaches my ankles. I re-braid it and throw it over my shoulder, the light brown colour catching the sun and casting golden streaks throughout.

Fee lets out a soft noise and I know immediately what's wrong.

He must go back in the cage.

He hates it inside there and I know exactly how he feels. A four-poster bed and a rug do not make this room any less a prison.

He swoops into the large cage that hangs from the ceiling.

"I'm sorry." I know the words do not mean much but it's the least I can say. He may not be here if it weren't for me. She brought him to me on my seventh birthday. A whole year after being here alone.

I was so happy. Finally, I had someone to talk to. Even if it was a bird. I did not stop for a second to think about how unfair this was on him, not until later. By then it was too late. He wouldn't leave.

She had plopped his cage down on my bed, not even voicing a 'happy birthday'.

"His name is Felix. He's yours now. A gift," she had said instead.

He was a lot smaller then, cowering in the corner of the cage, shivering. His pure white feathers emitted a rustling sound.

"*Felix*? What a peculiar name for a bird. I think I'll call you...Fee," I said to him while I stuck my finger through the bars, trying to reach him.

"Call him whatever you like. I cannot stay long. I have things to take care of."

My heart sank at that. A year had passed, and I wanted to go home. She had stayed for approximately ten minutes, before leaving Fee and me sat on the bed together alone. It was then I realised his cage didn't have a door.

The first time I used my magic to create an opening in his cage, I panicked and took it right back. What if he left me? He watched me with those big, deep brown eyes, a slither of hope filling them for the first time since he arrived five days prior.

"You won't leave me, will you?"

He inched closer, his cage shaking slightly from the movement.

He shook his head slowly, *no*.

Then that was that. We've been best friends ever since. I bet no one back home can say they are best friends with a bird. As he grew bigger, his cage grew with him. A spell cast upon it I assumed, but why no door I will never know. I think he's fully grown now. He and the cage have remained the same size for a while, ever since the colours appeared at the tips of his wings, all the colours of the rainbow. The blue is my favourite; it reminds me of the rich waters back home.

As I seal up the cage, the sound of shifting stone echoes through the tower.

"*Raylin*!" a sing-song voice carries up the spiral staircase.

I do a last-minute check, make sure everything is in its rightful place.

"Raylin, my dear." She smiles as she reaches the top floor.

"Hi, Aunt Genevieve."

2

Prince of Nowhere

Malakai

Malakai stretches out his fingers, stiff from the copious amounts of writing he has endured this morning. Letters to kings and queens, thanking them for allowing him the pleasure of introducing their princesses to Sorrelle.

He leans back in his chair, hands rubbing at his tired eyes. "I need out of this room," he says to no one but himself.

He slams his hands against the dark oak desk once as he stands, giving up on the task in front of him. The quills jump from their spot, the inkpot threatening to topple over. He winces, his body freezing, but it stills and rights itself. The letters are saved from his destruction.

If he had his way, there would be no need to write letters, for there would be no princesses arriving at the castle. At least not for the reasons that they are now. He has never met them, yet he already despises them, despises everything they stand for. His mother has forced his hand, and what better time than his twenty-first birthday. Only months until the big day, he doesn't have long to either find a bride or come clean to his parents, the king and queen, about his true reality.

A princess will not satisfy him. A princess is not what he wants. His heart belongs to a lowly servant. A boy with hair of russet, and eyes to match.

Malakai has been in love with Teddy for as long as he can remember. The boy stormed into his life when they were just children, his little voice capturing Malakai's heart as he told him he wasn't being very princely playing in the mud within the castle gardens.

Teddy's mother had worked in the castle a long time before the day she had to bring her son to work. Her sister, who usually watched him, had fallen ill. Malakai didn't get to speak to the boy again, but he would often watch him from his chamber windows as he walked the market square in the castle courtyard. He liked how the sun bounced off his bronzed hair. A golden sunrise, he thought. Malakai didn't understand his feelings, didn't know then that a boy could love another boy. He was only nine and his parents never spoke of such things.

It wasn't until he was fourteen, Teddy thirteen, that he sang a silent prayer to the stars above. Teddy's mother had gotten him a job in the kitchens. Of course, Malakai would find every excuse under the sun to visit, looking for things he did not need, or procuring food he did not want. He built such an odd collection of perishables that he would leave it out for the servants to take their fill when they tended to his rooms.

By the age of sixteen, Malakai could not imagine a life without Teddy in it. They had grown fond of each other over the years, sneaking off at every opportunity to spend time together in secret. Often they would go deep into the forest, the moon high in the sky, and they would spend hours there, telling stories and sharing their days.

It was there they shared their first kiss. Malakai became so scared of his feelings he didn't speak to Teddy for three months. He found reasons not to be in the castle, even going as far as to convince his father to take him to another island for a trip. It was on that trip that he met Glin and Dario, two men who were so open with their love—even if others did not accept it—that it opened his eyes to possibilities unknown.

He thought about Teddy in that moment, thought about how hard the past months had been without him. He went home immediately, rushing to Teddy's worn-down shack, hoping above all that he would forgive him. He did. Although neither were ready to tell the world, they could tell each other. Wrapped in Teddy's arms, lying upon his bed, Malakai whispered the three words that he had known all along. *I love you.*

Malakai rubs his fingers over the speck of island where he met the men that changed his life. The large painted map of Aldros takes up the whole left wall of his bed chambers. Ten kingdoms, all separated by time and ocean, fourteen smaller islands spread throughout.

The ten major kingdoms have their own kings, their own queens, each going by their own rules and ways of life. All of varying sizes and strengths. His kingdom, Sorrelle, is the biggest. The Kingdom of Salt and Ships. Or, more accurately, as Malakai likes to call it—much to his father's displeasure—The Fish Kingdom. Sorrelle had always been known for their fishing vessels, the waters surrounding it filled with the best fish Aldros has to offer. It isn't the most glamorous of places, not outside the castle at least, but it is home to many.

He didn't know how he felt about becoming king one day, overseeing a whole kingdom. He wasn't even sure it was something he wanted. There wasn't much choice in the matter; he had inherited his father's power. That, and he was the oldest heir, the only heir. He taps a finger to each of the kingdoms that will be arriving in mere hours—Thezmare, Zenick, Jalendia, Mirdoff, Faldova, Yendoth—recalling each of the powers they possess. He knew little about them, only the facts he was taught growing up. History had been his least favourite subject. Faldova had always fascinated him, however; how people could stand to live in the blistering cold snow all year round he would never know.

The weather in Sorrelle had been growing colder over the last months and he could barely stand it. Today was one of the few days of warmth remaining, and he was stuck inside his room with parchment and ink.

All things considered, Malakai should have deigned to learn more about the other kingdoms and their princesses before their arrival, but again, he despised them, so found no use in it. He had already decided to spend as much time as he could away from them. He was sure he could find other things to do. After all, the castle was unnecessarily large, with plenty of places to hide. He would have to attend the balls of course, but those were easy to sneak away from. He had been practising that his whole life.

There's a tap at the door and a familiar voice calls, "Kai?" It opens before he can answer.

"I'm in here."

"Preparing yourself, I see." Damien comes to stand beside him, hand resting on the pommel of his sword.

Malakai lets out a sigh, fiddling with the signet ring at his finger. "Do I really have to do this?"

"It might not be so bad... You might finally make yourself a friend."

Malakai turns to glare at the man beside him, the sun radiating off his golden-brown skin. "You're my friend, are you not?"

"I do not count. I am a lieutenant in your guard."

"You are still the greatest friend I have ever had." Malakai slumps in the chair beside his bed.

Damien rolls his eyes, smiling at the prince. "I'm the only friend you've ever had, Kai."

Malakai picks up a piece of paper, scrunching it in his fist. "Right. Because you're Mr Popular? Tell me again, did the other guards invite you to the tavern last week? Or the week before that? Or the one before—"

"Okay, okay. I never said you were not my only friend also."

Damien winces as the balled-up paper Malakai was holding hits him in the face. He simply picks it up from the floor and throws it into the waste bin on the other side of the room.

"He's popular, and he's got superb throwing skills. You're going to make someone a very happy woman one day, my friend." Malakai winks.

Damien walks toward the map painted on the wall, taking in its details, the royal family crests delicately painted beside each Kingdom's name.

"The sun god treats you well, you will be fine," he says now, voice low.

Malakai snorts. "If he treated me well, then I wouldn't have to keep such secrets from my parents. He would have given me a sibling, so I didn't have to become king."

In all his aggravation, he knew it was true. The god of the sun had been kind to his family. His father and he had both been fortunate enough to be gifted his power, a drop of warmth in their veins the day they were born. He feels that warmth in him every day, a softness inside him he could not live without. A power neither of them care to use often.

Just like all the royal families of Aldros, the power can be passed through generations, each kingdom having their own special gift. Though not all heirs will inherit the power, and only those that do can become an heir to the throne.

Sorrelle was blessed with the ability to ease others' emotions or rid them completely if they so wished. Malakai's great grandfather was generous with his ability to do so. He was also careless. He left people mere husks of themselves. When a person stops feeling a certain emotion, it sets their others into overdrive, trying to balance out what lingers inside of them. Many lives were lost by the sufferer's own hand. His son—Malakai's grandfather—was a lot wiser. He taught his child to be sparse with the gift, use it on only those who truly needed it. It was human nature to feel loss, to feel sadness, to feel anger. It was how one learned to be themselves. His child, in turn, taught Malakai these same pearls of wisdom, though still teaching him how to control and harness his ability.

Malakai had only used it a handful of times throughout his life. When Teddy's mother died, he had begged him to use the gift on him, to take away his grief. Malakai did not.

"The king's council wishes for your attendance in the drawing room. Last-minute details for the upcoming arrivals, or so I'm told."

Malakai sighs, dragging himself from the chair into which he had melted.

"Lead the way."

3

AS FRAGILE AS A FLOWER

RAYLIN

Genevieve lets the woven basket she's holding drop to the floor with a thump. Its contents bounce inside; a crisp green apple falls over the edge and rolls across the floor towards me.

"Food," she says with a wave of her hand towards the discarded basket. "I assumed you needed some. Although maybe not..." Her eyes scan the room, noticing the extra bits and bobs I have accumulated. "You really should stop doing that. You have no idea where these things are coming from. Someone will notice their disappearance."

She doesn't know the half of it; most things I conjure I keep tucked away in my void. She's right though, I have no idea where this stuff comes from. I'm pulling it from people's homes and hands for all I know. It wasn't as simple as just manifesting. The violin I conjured was proof of that—it was carved with another's initials, PMF. It didn't stop me from keeping it though.

The same could be said for my void.

When I send stuff there, I don't know where it is. It is everywhere and nowhere. A dark abyss made just for me.

When my brother and I first discovered I possessed the power to make things appear and disappear, we played around with it for hours on end. I was only four at the time, and we had no right messing with things we had no clue about. Reed was nineteen and knew better, but he did nothing to discourage it. He was always fascinated by my powers.

Reed inherited our father's healing powers, the power of our kingdom. My father rejoiced when I turned three and healed a bird that had fallen into our gardens. His joy didn't last long, when he found me a week later, giggling and floating above my bed. It was not normal for a person to gain powers outside of their family's own.

It only got worse as time went on and new powers manifested. Sometimes Reed and I would keep them secret, not wanting to scare our parents.

So, the day I figured out I could make stuff appear, I ran straight to him.

I remember it was raining, great big heavy droplets. We played in the study. Reed would give me random prompts and I would bring them to us. A piece of paper, a glass horse statue, a boat paddle, a carrot, the list went on. Before we knew it, a pile almost as tall as four of Reed had accumulated. That's when I figured out I could send it all back.

It took a lot of concentration, and I had already grown tired from using my power too much. I felt my eyes drift closed for just a second, then I stumbled but caught myself on the desk. All I remember was his voice, "Ray—" and poof, he was gone.

Reed was gone.

I tried to bring him back, tried with all my might. Nothing worked. I'm unsure how long I sat there, tears streaming down my face. The rain had cleared and the sky became dark. Then my mother's voice was filling the room, breaking through the silence.

"Raylin, my little moon. What's the matter?"

I couldn't tell her; my heart was breaking, and the tears wouldn't stop. They felt as harsh as the rain that had fallen earlier on.

"Where's your brother?" Her fingers tightened on my shoulders, her eyes grew wide.

I was showing her my memories. Another power manifesting so soon after the last. I didn't know then how I did it, I just knew I didn't want to speak but I wished I could tell her what I had done to Reed. She released me with a loud gasp, her hands flying to her mouth.

"What have you done, Raylin?" Her voice was quiet, scared. Was she afraid of me? "Bring him back."

"I– I can't."

I flinched as she grabbed hold of me.

"Bring him back now, Raylin." Her hands were too tight, I struggled in her grip. "Bring. Him. Back," she roared.

Then my father was in the room, pulling her from me. She sobbed into his chest as she told him what had happened. He stared at me, face blank and unblinking.

I didn't stop. For days after, when I wasn't sleeping to regain my strength, I was trying to make Reed appear. It was day three, walking through the castle corridors, when I felt it. Felt him. I grasped at him, reached out for him, thought of nothing but him.

Then there he was.

Reed stood several feet ahead of me. His whole body shook, trembling so fast he looked like he wasn't fully corporeal. A maid had run to fetch my mother and she burst into the room, pulling my brother into her arms. He stared over her shoulder, not quite looking at anything.

"*Home*," was all he said.

He didn't speak to me much after that. We didn't play with my powers together again. I asked him once where I had sent him. He shook his head slowly, and all he told me was that it was nothingness, black and empty. I didn't ask again.

Genevieve fiddles with the end of my long braid now. Twisting the loose strands between her bony fingers. "I need some more, Little Moon." I tense at her words, my mother's name for me.

She pays me no heed and reaches into her pocket to pull out four smooth, clear oval stones. Sometimes I think she only comes here when she needs a top-up. The stones seem unnecessary, as she has the power to borrow the abilities of anyone of her choosing.

I shouldn't complain, she's the one who saved me all those years ago and who has protected me ever since. She's not my real aunt, but she was there often when I was growing up, a close friend to my mother. She has mostly been good to me, but her patience is short, and now and then she will snap. Her mood seems good today, so I do as she asks and grip the stones in my hand, hoping to keep her mood pleasant for what I am going to ask. I cast the memories of what happened last time out of my mind.

The power trickles through my veins, ice sliding down my arm. The stones glow in my fist and my body sags with the release. I open my palm to reveal the four ovals now glowing a brilliant silver, much like that of the Moon Flowers outside.

Glowing with my power.

"Good girl," Genevieve says as thanks and takes the stones from me, placing them back into her pocket.

She hands me a glass of water and I grip the bedpost to keep myself from falling backward onto the soft mattress. I cannot sleep yet. I need to speak to her first. I sip the water and clear my throat. "Auntie?"

"Rest, child," she scolds.

"Not a child," I manage before my heavy lids threaten to close.

She takes the glass from my hand and lays me back on the bed. "Later," she tells me.

The last thing I feel is her hand caressing my cheek.

The room is dark when I wake; only the soft glow of candles in the far corner gives any light. I still feel weak, but my power has mostly restored. Nothing food and more sleep won't fix.

Aunt Genevieve sits in the large, worn floral chair by the bed. The fabric is a muted green, with over-sized yellow sunflowers scattered about. It isn't pretty, but it is the most comfortable chair I have ever sat on. It's where I spent most of my days, head in a book. Before I started venturing outside, that is.

She's watching me intently, her pale blue eyes not leaving my face. Slight wrinkles line her skin, showing her age. What was once black hair is now a dark grey. Her thin lips arch into a crooked smile, and she scoots herself onto the edge of her seat. I didn't notice earlier, but her body looks more frail than usual, her cheeks more hollowed out. But her skin still has a healthy pink hue.

"You look like her, you know." Her words seem loud in the quiet room. "Your mother."

My heart leaps. I am starting to forget what she looks like. It's been almost fourteen years since I last saw my family, and I miss them more with every passing day. I haven't seen their faces since I was six years old. Since the night Genevieve came for me when the sky had darkened. They had come, the evil souls who wished to take my power, take my life. Father had always warned me of what fear could make someone do. That is why they kept me from the world, hid my abilities. That night, my nightmares came true. The monsters under my bed had become real. If it hadn't been for Genevieve getting me out of Gavaria, bringing me here, I don't even want to think about what might have happened.

"You have your father's hair, his light brown waves." She smiles and I wonder when it was she last saw them. Was it recently? "But that's her crooked nose. Her pale, blue-grey eyes, though yours are more silver than blue. You even have the same *perfect* jawline."

She presses her thumb to my chin, her fingers resting against my neck as she takes in my face.

"I want to see them." The words are out before I have a chance to think them over.

Her hand tenses against my jaw. "That's not possible. You know as much."

"I'm almost twenty. I can protect myself now."

Her hand drops from my face and she throws her head back in a laugh. "Do you truly believe that? How would you protect yourself exactly? As soon as you use your powers, everyone will know what you are. They would come after you, they would do anything to get their hands on what you possess. They will *kill* you!"

Each word is filled with venom, poised to strike and kill.

"But you would be with me, and father. Mother. Reed would protect me."

She closes her eyes, and for a moment I think she is considering it.

"*Raylin.* We have had this conversation before. It's not as simple as that."

Her words are a knife to my heart. I don't know why I thought this time would be any different. I've lost count of how many times I've asked only to be met with the same answer.

"Please," I whisper.

"Your family and I have done everything in our power to keep you safe. If you leave now, that would all be undone. This would have all been for nothing."

"Why only you?" I shake my head. "I mean...Why haven't any of them been here? Why just you?"

"Again, Raylin, it is not safe. People could be watching them, waiting for them to lead them straight to you. Your family would not risk your life like that." I can sense her patience thinning, her words coming fast and clipped.

I need to quit while I'm ahead, not wanting another repeat of last time. I pushed her too far, begged on my knees to let me go home. She forced me to conjure a cane, then struck me hard on the back five times. It was the first time she had ever used an object to punish me. Usually, a hand to the cheek sufficed. Felix flapped so vigorously, his cage swung and rattled viciously enough to crack the ceiling where it hung.

I stayed in bed for three days straight, and even after then it hurt to move freely.

It's all I can do to nod. I understand.

"I will speak to your father." Hope fills my chest. "I am still doubtful."

She sighs, like this is harder on her than it is on me. She gets to leave, gets to see my family, speak to them.

I don't say a word. I just sit quietly, fingers fiddling with the hem of my dress.

"I cannot stay." Her words twist at my gut, hollowing it out. "I have matters to attend to back in Kignet. It may be a while before I can return."

She places her hand on my cheek, and I feel the rush of ice scrabbling to the surface. Her ability reminds me of a leech, but instead of blood, she takes powers. Not takes, exactly, but borrows. Hers to use as she wishes. The more she drains the longer she gets to keep them. It tires me to the core when she does this, but it never takes long for my powers to restore, usually only hours. When I was smaller, I would sleep for days, my body fighting to regain my strength. She knows now to let me rest between filling the stones and taking more of what she wants.

Fee lets out a piercing squawk from his cage, and I feel her body tense, but she doesn't lift her eyes to him. She never does. She pretends he's not even here when she comes. She lowers her hand then, his warning reminding her to stop feeding.

She places her cloak around her shoulders and heads for the stairs. "To the moon," she says, smiling over her shoulder.

"To the sun," I answer back.

"And all around the world," we say together.

Her footsteps descend the stairs and I sigh.

She made that up for me the first time she left me here. A small reminder of her love, that I wasn't truly alone. I was terrified. She told me to repeat it every time I felt scared, which was all the time in that first year. I was only six and didn't want to be alone. I had just been torn away from my home without so much as a goodbye to my parents. It was too late for that. I don't remember everything she said on the way here, all I remember is crying. But she told me the castle had been infiltrated.

People had found out about my powers, the strength and quantity of them, more powerful than any known person for centuries. So she took me somewhere no one would find me. Hidden away by magic in another's kingdom. I sometimes watch Sorrelle's people from the window, on their walks through the forest, blissfully unaware of what lies in front of them. They don't see me, don't see the tower. I tested sound before, but they don't hear that either. I called out as loud as I could, but their faces didn't show any sign of recognition. Even now when I head out to the main villages, I rarely speak to anybody.

I try, my stomach clenches, and I am lost for words.

I listen for the shifting of stones to make sure she's gone, then open Felix's cage. He hops to the floor and shakes out his wings. My fingers sink into his feathers as I stroke his head. He's almost half the size of me now, his head reaching my hips when I stand beside him. His wings double his size when he spreads them wide. I have never seen a creature like him. I conjured and scoured through countless books on the beasts of Aldros after he first arrived, but it was no use, he wasn't in any of them. His closest resemblance was to a phoenix, but where they are fire, he is snow. I tried asking Genevieve where she found him, but if she cannot look at him, then she certainly cannot talk about him. My question was ignored, and I went on wondering.

I find the apple that rolled from the basket earlier, polish it against the cotton of my dress. I take two bites and I am done, my body too weak to digest much food. I pass the rest to Fee and climb onto the bed.

"Goodnight, Fee," I whisper, and use the last ounce of my power to throw out a gust of air, blowing out the candles and sheathing the room in darkness.

4

First Time for Everything

Raylin

The sound of his voice wakes me.

I know he's not here. Just residue from my dream seeping into the world around me. I don't even know his name, but he enters my dreams each night, his voice a song to my soul.

The first time I saw him two years ago, the world slowed. His golden-brown skin shone in the sunlight, his hair matching the midnight black horse he sat upon. It was easy to peg him as a royal guard in those black leathers and the sword strapped at his hip.

It was another year before I heard his voice; not to me, the words are never to me.

I catch him watching me though, those cobalt eyes burning into me, taking in every motion, every glimpse they can catch beneath my hood. It is like our own little game; he will watch me until I acknowledge that I know he's watching me, then he will look away. Then I use that time to shove whatever I'm holding into my cloak pockets.

It is easy to steal from people who least expect it of you. Who's going to suspect a pretty young girl in an expensive velvet cloak of stealing? Surely she can afford whatever she wants? Little do they know I also stole the cloak. It's not that I need to steal, I can conjure just about anything I can think of. But where's the fun in that? And I take whatever fun I can get.

I hop off the bed and stretch high. The night's sleep has almost completely restored my powers. I can feel it humming through my veins. The morning sun shines through the window, casting a bright beam of light across the worn carpeted floor, promising another beautiful day. I fill the bathing tub a quarter of the way, painstakingly slow, filling smaller buckets from the kitchen sink and tipping them in. Then I step in and scrub clean, wincing at the cold. I keep my long braid hanging over the edge, stopping it from entering the water. It takes too long to dry and I am itching to be outside in the open air.

Felix is still perched on the end of the bed, eyes closed. I dress in a simple pale-yellow dress. It is slightly too short, procured when I was years younger and inches shorter, but it's the only thing clean enough to wear. The cloak is long enough to cover my bare feet anyway, and I never remove it, even when the sun is blaring. It is my safety net. I can hide deep inside, pretending people don't notice me. Although no one would recognise me; at least I don't think they would. Even before I left home, I had never travelled to any other kingdom and very few had come to Gavaria.

Even if they did, I was only six and would have looked highly different to how I do now in womanhood.

"I will leave without you," I tease, and Fee throws open an eye, just the one. "Quit *winking* and start *waking*."

I'm sure he rolls his eyes at me. Strange bird.

Moments later, the rope is tied to the bed frame and I am making my way down.

Fee flies overhead, swooping and dipping, stretching out his sleepy wings. We never leave without one another. Not once. Fee used to, of course, but he would never go far, staying within the confines of our little clearing. Up until five years ago, when I first decided to leave the tower. Now he only leaves when I do.

It took me days to muster up the courage the first time I exited this prison. I would drop the rope from the window, then proceed to sit and stare at it until I pulled it back up and stayed inside. I did this multiple times a day, then the third day arrived and Felix was fed up of my indecision. He sat at the bottom of the rope, refusing to move until I made it to him. We stayed amongst the Moon Flowers at first, then day by day we ventured a little further, right up until we made it to the castle; that was a glorious day.

We are walking through the woods, the rope safely tucked back away under my bed, thanks to Felix, when we come across our first destination: the circle bridge. We sit by the water for a while, and I dip my feet in, watching it ripple around me. The circle bridge is one of my favourite places to visit. It's not really as it sounds, not a circle at all. The bridge curves up and over, but the reflection in the water makes it look like a perfect circle.

Small pink flowers clustered at the bottom climb up the sides and spread out the further up they go, as if they are being blown away in the wind.

It's quiet this time of the morning, the birds singing in the trees the only sound. I never walk back this way; it gets busy later in the day. People have picnics and play in the water for hours. It's Sorrelle's most popular attraction.

When I get to the castle gates, they are already open, vendors already setting up for the day. It's a large area, and even with all the stalls, there's still plenty of room to roam around.

The stalls sit in a long line down either side of the entrance, and a large fountain fills the centre of the space. The rim of the fountain is wide and flat, and people often perch on the edge, resting part way around the market. A stone woman stands in the fountain, her face angled towards the sky, her hair and dress blowing backward, caught in a treacherous wind. Water sprouts from her hands in a high arc, a secret power only she knows about. The whole thing is polished to a brilliant white—blindingly so, if you stare too long on a sunny day.

I walk through the gates, running my fingers against the black iron, still cold, the sun not yet hot enough to warm them through.

After five years, the castle still takes my breath away.

Beyond the fountain rests a set of stone steps. Tall pillars reach high, holding up a roof that houses four stone gargoyles, so old now their features have almost completely faded. You can still make out the long snouts and sharp teeth of what they may have been before.

The castle stretches out around the whole perimeter, closing in the courtyard that hosts the market. The bricks are worn and yellowing, not as well taken care of as the fountain. Or maybe just a lot older. There are many windows, large and small. I wonder if the king or queen sits at one, watching the people of their lands laze around the market. Watching them haggle and buy goods. I wonder if they hear of the rumours that spread like a bad sickness. I've never seen any of them, the royals. They welcome the market with open arms, but I don't think for a second they have ever ventured out here and browsed the stalls themselves.

Guards have taken up their places around the grounds, standing to attention.

I don't see him, the one who plagues my dreams. Maybe he's off duty today.

The market is now in full swing, people lingering at stalls and grazing their hands over things they probably cannot afford.

I spot Felix in the distance, perched on the far corner of the castle, his favourite spot to sit and watch the world go by. I worry sometimes I bore him, pacing the market for hours, but he seems content enough. So that's what I do; for three hours I blend into the crowds, acting interested in one object while I pocket another. I don't need or want the things I take, but in goes a delicately carved wooden elephant anyway.

I'm hovering over a fabric store, contemplating trying to make myself a new dress, even though sewing has never been one of my finer skills, when the smell of food hits my nostrils.

My mouth is watering, and I am walking to the stall without much thought. On the table sit two large containers filled with warm sticky buns. I hold up a finger, gesturing to the man I want one. I reach into my pocket and conjure a coin, handing it over with a smile. The man eyes me from head to toe but takes the coin, testing it between his teeth before handing over the wrapped bun. It's delicious and I eat it too fast, my stomach seizing from the heat of it.

I rarely get to eat hot food. I was never taught to cook and every time I tried, the food would either burn or taste of rubber.

I walk slowly to the fountain and dip my fingers into the water, washing away the sticky residue. The bottom is filled with coins, thrown in with wishes that probably went unanswered. A gleam from the stall to my right catches my eye and I head over. I have already walked past twice today, each time eying a dainty silver bracelet, a little crescent moon dangling from the middle. One I have looked at many times before. I pick it up and take a larger necklace in my other hand, this one chunky and gold, a too-large green emerald set in the middle. This, I pop in my pocket.

"Hey, you!"

My heart freezes.

Not me.

But it is me. I catch him from the corner of my eye storming right for me. A royal guard. Getting closer with each step he takes. "Empty your pockets," he commands.

People's heads are turning this way, getting a good look at what the commotion is about. A hand grips my wrist, bony and unforgiving. The vendor yanks the dainty bracelet from my hand, her sunken eyes wide, her mouth a wrinkled frown.

"What did you take?" her voice croaks out, full of accusation.

I pull free from her grip, pulling my hood further over my face from where it has slipped back, hiding within its depths. I only hope she didn't get a good look at my face. Stupid of me to let any of myself show. I turn toward the guard. He's nearing, but not yet close enough to grab me. Luckily for me, he is coming from the castle's direction, so I do the only thing I can think of—run the opposite way, back towards the gate.

"Stop!" His voice booms all around, but I ignore him.

He's tall and wide and hopefully cannot run as fast as I can.

More guards are springing into action now, alerted by the sudden shouting and running. I weave in and out of the crowds, heads spinning towards me, but no one moves out of the way. They don't stop me either. I sense Fee is close before I hear him, and the panic in his shriek sets my heart aflame. I cannot get caught, for my sake and his.

I am all he has.

The gates loom ahead, close but not close enough. My feet pound against the stone, ripping and tearing with each bound. I glance over my shoulder, my foolishness causing me to stumble. I quickly regain my balance, and now I know five guards are chasing me down. Confusion crosses the faces I pass, curious as to what is happening. Then I'm out of the gates, thanking the stars there are no guards posted here today. All I have to do is make it back to the tower. Once I am hidden inside its magic, they won't have any way of finding me. Then I will just have to lay low for a while. The thought twists at something deep inside me—no more leaving the tower.

I am almost at the treeline when a hand grabs my arm and pulls me between two houses. I'm pushed face first into the cold brick, the roughness biting at my cheek.

A hard body presses to my back. Warm panting breaths against my ear. "I can help you."

His voice is deep and rough. A gasp escapes me. I know that voice. It's the same voice I've heard every night in my slumber.

"Please let me go." My voice cracks, giving away just how scared I am.

Fee shrieks above but I cannot lift my head to find him. Can he see me? Does he know I've been caught?

I struggle against the solid build, but he just pushes harder.

He reaches into my pocket, pulling out the ugly gold chain.

"Don't move." He releases me and moves away, his voice floating toward me from a distance. I go to run but my body seizes when I hear what he's saying. "I don't know which way she went. Found this over there, could be a diversion."

Wait.

He's helping me?

Fee has gone quiet. Listening to these strangers' words just as I am.

"Head back to the castle. Make sure this hasn't caused any other problems. Nige, Thomas, you two head into the forest, see if you can spot any sign of her. I'll scour the village. Keep your eyes peeled, boys."

"We don't even know what she looks like," one of the guards says.

"Blonde hair I think?" another chimes in.

"But we know what she's wearing. Look out for green velvet. *Possibly* blonde hair, we will get her." His words send a cold shiver down my spine.

I thought he was merely a guard, but he's commanding these men with authority.

So why didn't he drag me out of here and claim his victory?

My heart thumps against my chest and I struggle to take a breath.

What does he want with me?

5

Cages or Wings

Raylin

He's back in front of me, but my eyes have blurred and I can't make out his features.

My whole body trembles. I gasp for a breath that I cannot take. My throat constricts and the world spins around me. Reaching out for something to hold on to, my fingers connect with something hard and smooth.

"*Shit.*" His voice is far away but I know he's right there, a blurred version of him at least. "Take a deep breath. I'm not going to hurt you."

I try to focus on his voice but it's no use.

What is happening? Did he poison me? How could he have poisoned me? He hasn't so much as touched my bare skin. I would laugh at myself right now if I could just breathe.

"Hey. Hey. It's alright."

I grip whatever my hand is against. My heart thrashes so hard it feels like it will burst from my chest.

A flash of blue, something warm against my cheek, a hot rush upon my lips. Something soft and fleeting. It steals my focus, all my attention now on the hard press of another's lips on mine. Then suddenly I'm not gasping anymore.

The world stops.

Warm air rushes into my lungs and I bring my fingers to my mouth, a vacant feeling building against them. His face comes into focus and his eyes are wide with panic.

"I– I am so sorry. I didn't know what to do." His words fall from his mouth so fast I can barely make out what he says.

Cold air touches my skin as he takes a step back, distancing us.

He kissed me.

He. Kissed. Me.

"You can't do that." My voice is small.

"I know. I know. I didn't– You couldn't—" He gestures to me.

I realise then it's him I'm gripping. Squeezing the strap of his uniform, my knuckles white. I drop my arm and tear my gaze away from him.

I had never kissed anyone before.

Why am I not angry? I should be angry. But all I am is thankful. The air in my lungs is a sign of that. A breeze rushes past us and blows at the loose hair around my braid, strands that came free when running.

My hood.

He had taken down my hood.

He can see my face.

My hands clumsily pull it back up over my head. "I should go." I turn to walk out of the narrow passage we still stand in.

"Wait." He grabs my arm but let's go just as fast. "They will just keep searching for you, they won't stop."

Then I will have to stay in my tower where they won't ever find me.

The thought makes my stomach squeeze. I don't want to be stuck back there. These years of freedom have opened my eyes to everything I missed out on growing up. But what choice do I have? It's that or the prisons beneath the castle. I couldn't possibly tell them who I was, that my family would pay for all the jewels in the world to have me home instead. He senses my hesitation.

"There's another way, a way that doesn't involve you rotting in a cell."

I want to laugh. I know he means a cell in the castle, but my tower is just as much as a cell to me. When I don't talk, he carries on.

"Princesses from each of the other kingdoms are arriving in the morning."

This I already know, but what does it have to do with me? I cannot be sent from my kingdom when I have been in hiding for fourteen years.

"I could make it so you can join them."

My breathing slows; does he know who I am?

"You would have to pose as one of the princesses, of course. But you would be hiding in plain sight. The other guards would never suspect you."

His suggestion surprises me. I shake my head, just a small movement, not understanding. "That's a rather elaborate plan for a thief. Why would you do this for me?" I ask hesitantly.

"I don't know." He admits through a nervous laugh. "I guess– I suppose I just don't want to see a young girl like you be locked away for stealing an ugly necklace." The corner of his mouth hooks up in a half-smile.

He says young girl like we aren't the same age, but I can tell he's not much older, maybe a year or two. His answer feels half said, like there is another reason that he omits. I see it inside him, this thing that goes unsaid, unquestioned. I should ask, but I find myself in a quiet bliss of unknowing.

"And what of the princess I will replace?" Am I considering this? I can't. What if Aunt Genevieve returns while I am off gallivanting in the castle?

"I would send her home. Pay her kindly for her trouble, tell her the prince has changed his mind, or that he has taken a bride already. I'm not sure yet, I haven't thought it through."

It sounds to me like he has. Does he feel it? This thing between us; whatever it may be. I often find myself wondering if I made up all the times our eyes caught over the crowds of the market. If the dreams of him that found their way to me at night were simply that—dreams. Could it be more than that? Could it become more? I could just go for a couple of days. Genevieve has only just been, and she did say it would be a while before she returned. I have always wanted to see the inside of the castle, to get a glimpse of the prince everyone talks so fondly of. It would give me a chance to find out what the other guards know of the thief in the market—of me. It would give me a chance to get to know *him*.

Something stirs in my gut, unsure and cautious. I know I need to say no, get as far as I can from this guard, and away from the castle. But something inside me is screaming to say yes, fighting at that part of me who knows to say no.

What if Genevieve arrives early and I am not there? Would I feel her wrath like I have many times over the most miniscule things? I dread to think of how she would react over something like this.

I chew on my bottom lip. What am I doing? This isn't logical. I can't just take another princess's place and ruin her chances with the prince. I shake my head to decline but the word 'okay' comes out instead.

"Come with me."

There's no time for hesitation as he leads me further down the passage, between rows and rows of houses. Bags of rubbish sit outside back doors, stained white paint from window frames flake off in the breeze. He walks straight up to a small brick house. The door creaks on its hinges as he opens it, a gust of warm air rushes out to greet me. He pushes the door closed once we're inside and walks into an adjoining room. I hear water being poured and the *click-click* of a stove being lit. I stand awkwardly by a large oak cabinet, papers and envelopes scattered on top. I don't know what to do with my feet. I scoot them about, feeling uncomfortable in my own skin at this moment. I leave my cloak on, hood up, not wanting him to see my face. Although he's already seen it and will see it again by morning. Maybe this was a bad idea. Maybe I should just hide out in the tower with Felix.

Felix.

What was I thinking? I can't leave him. He's likely going out of his mind wondering where I am. I need to find him. I'm heading towards the door to the outside when the blue-eyed guard walks back into the room holding two mugs of steaming liquid.

"Tea?" he asks, a small smile lining his lips. They look plumper this close. I have only ever seen him further away and atop a horse. It was harder to take in the finer details then. But his eyes are just as blue, his golden-brown skin complementing them perfectly. He's tall too, taller than I imagined. He places the mugs down on a small table in the centre of the room and flops down onto the two-seater sofa, unbuckling his sword as he does. I shuffle forward and sit in the chair furthest from him.

"This is a friend's place. He's away for a few weeks, so you can stay here for the night. The princesses are arriving by first light so we will get you into the castle then."

Does he just have all the answers stored in that pretty head of his? He runs a hand through his deep brown hair, so dark it appears black.

I don't know what to say, so I don't say anything at all. Years of not speaking to anyone but a bird and my aunt haven't exactly taught me many social skills.

"Unless– Where do you live? Will you need to inform your family?"

"No."

Yes. Fee. If I can find him. But I cannot tell him that the only person I need to tell I won't be home for a few days is a bird.

"You don't have any family?"

Yes.

I shake my head. I don't exactly need to inform a family I will be gone for a while when I'm already gone.

"Are you hungry?"

Yes. "No."

I sense his smile, but I don't dare look at his face. He gets up and heads back to the room where he got the tea, a kitchen I assume.

My kitchen is my bedroom. My bedroom is my living room. My living room is my bathing room. I'm just grateful my chamber pot is behind a closed door, so Fee doesn't have to watch me use that at least. Not that he would; he even turns away when I strip to wash.

He's a real gentleman. Gentle-bird.

"Oh, I'm Damien by the way." He laughs from the other room. My eyes snap in his direction, my heart stumbles. What a beautiful noise. I find myself smiling as he walks back in and places a wooden board full of cheese, crackers, and bread down beside the tea I am yet to pick up.

"Do you have a name?"

"Ray—" The word is falling from my mouth before I even consider it. Silly girl. You can't tell him your name.

"Ray. Just, Ray."

Maybe Auntie was right. I was foolish to think I could make it in the big world when I cannot even talk to one person without almost slipping up and giving them my real name. Raylin isn't exactly a common name. Who knows whos heard about Princess Raylin of Gavaria. I don't even know what story my family spun for where I've been all these years. Or if people know I am not at home at all.

His smile is brighter than the sun.

"Well. Hi, Ray."

I pick at cheese and bread while he talks. Before I know it, the sun has set and the room has become dark. Damien lights a few candles and they flicker between us, encasing us in a warm glow. I watch as shadows scale the walls, moving to their own design.

"There will be six of you tomorrow. Three kingdoms have no princesses to send, so—just six."

"What will we have to do?" It is the first time I've spoken since I told him my name.

"Not much. Live in the castle. Eat food. You will be free to do whatever you please, within reason. It's more for Prince Malakai to get to know the princesses of Aldros, and hopefully choose one as his bride. Whenever that time may come." He smiles at me and fidgets in his seat. "But you don't need to worry. None of the princesses have been briefed on each other, and as far as I am aware, none have ever met."

"Do you know who I will replace?"

"You are probably most suited to Mirdoff. Your pale skin matches. She's the only living niece to the queen, and she holds no powers. So you cannot be asked to show off a gift you do not have."

"Why does the prince need help finding a bride anyway? Is he hideous or something?"

Damien laughs. "The king and queen want to unite Sorrelle with another kingdom. He's turning twenty-one soon and is not currently courting a woman. His parents are using this as an opportunity for him to do so. If you ask me, the prince is not keen."

"Right. But twenty-one is still young, is it not? To be married, I mean."

I know my brother was barely twenty-one when he was set to marry, but that was for love, not some plan our parents cooked up to gain an upper hand with another kingdom. I wonder if Reed ever married her, Amily. I remember thinking how beautiful she was the first time I met her, the vivid red hair cascading down her back, brushing against the pure white of her feathered wings. I only met her once, when her family came to visit our kingdom. I wasn't in attendance the second time, the night I had to flee.

The servants had been in a tizzy all day getting everything ready for dinner. My mother wanted everything to be perfect. Which meant me being in bed before they arrived. Things would have been more than eventful if a power had decided to manifest halfway through dinner.

"It is," Damien says now. "The king is ageing. He wants Malakai with a queen by his side when the time comes to pass on the crown."

He pulls something round from his pocket, a bronze chain hanging from it. He presses a button and it flips open, revealing a clock face. His eyebrows pull together, his features lost in thought. "I need to head back to the castle. I have a few things I need to work out for tomorrow."

I shift with unease.

"You will be safe here, I assure you. There's one thing...I will need your cloak. My guards will be on the lookout for it. I can dispose of it on my way."

"Oh."

Why hadn't I thought of that? I know he's seen my face before, even up close today, but revealing myself here, willingly, in front of him, makes my skin prickle.

I stand and gradually remove the hood. His eyes catch mine and we stand there for a moment, still and quiet. We don't take our eyes from each other as I blindly undo the buttons holding it closed. It feels strangely intimate. I tug it off my shoulders and hold it out in front of me. For a short time, I don't think he is going to take it from me, but he clears his throat and averts his gaze, taking the cloak from my hands. My pale-yellow dress clings to me, my bare feet on show. I am instantly regretting my clothing choice this morning.

"If not before, I will be back by sun up. Make yourself comfortable and sleep. Tomorrow will be a busy day."

With that, he departs, and I am left in silence, the only sound the beating of my heart, too loud in my ears. I give it five minutes before I grab a thick woollen blanket out of the basket by the sofa and wrap it around my shoulders. I am out the door, the chill breeze fighting its way through my layers as I head around the back of the building. The house is close to the treeline, and with the moon hidden by clouds it is so dark I can only make out their silhouettes.

I've never been out this late before, and the forest is darker than I would have ever imagined.

"Fee," I half-whisper, half-shout. "Felix."

I cannot see any sign of him in the darkened sky. No rustle of leaves when I call his name to indicate that he's close by. I try calling once more—not wanting to make too much noise—before I head back inside.

I find the bedroom; it's small, its only furniture a bed and a set of drawers for clothes. I curl up on the hard mattress and let my thoughts wander. The feel of Damien's lips on mine still lingers but I don't let myself dwell on it. He only did it to stop me from freaking out. Nothing more. I don't even remember what it felt like, just the warmth and the softness.

I breathe deep, willing my thoughts to ease, for my body to stop trembling. "To the moon," I whisper into the darkness, finding what little comfort I can. "To the sun, and all around the world."

I twist and turn in the bed, but try as I might, sleep doesn't find me for a long while.

6

THAT WHICH CANNOT BE SEEN

MALAKAI

"Tell me again," Theodore whispers.

Malakai smiles, his fingers running through Teddy's copper-brown hair. "I've told you this story a million times before."

Teddy beams. "I know, but I like the sound of your voice."

They keep their voices low, whispers carrying on the wind around them. Theodore's back is pressed against the grass, the chill creeping through the blanket they have wrapped around them. Malakai leans over him, their eyes connected and lost inside each other. It is dark this deep in the gardens, but it gives them the privacy they don't get elsewhere.

"The warrior princess was fierce, but she was not immune to the powers of love." Malakai smiles, his fingers leaving Teddy's hair and grazing down his ivory cheek. "The king waltzed into her life, changing it forever. She loathed him at first, this cocky, riotous man. She detested the way he always told his stories to anyone who'd listen. She would scoff at them and mock him. Make him the laughingstock of the party. Until one day, she did not.

"Without noticing, the warrior princess had fallen in love with the king, and the king had always loved her. His savage princess. She would never admit it, not even when she drew her last breath."

"But he would tell her each day, the first thing he would say upon seeing her, and the last."

"Are you telling the story or am I?" Malakai scolds teasingly.

Theodore only smiles, his lips pressing together as if to say he will keep quiet.

"The king would be in agony each time she went into battle, wondering if this would be the time his love would not return home. Each time she would berate him. How dare he think so little of her that she would not survive. He did not listen, his worries growing ever stronger. He had her a necklace made, one of blood-red stone, a pendant of power and hope. A way to keep her safe when he could not do so.

"The pendant worked, right up to the moment it cracked, its properties useless and void. The princess did not tell the king, so as not to worry him further. And it was then that she was shot through with an arrow, piercing her heart and breaking it in two. It left the king alone, him too now useless and void, never hearing those three words he longed to hear from her lips. *I love you.*"

"Who told you this story?"

"My father. I was infatuated with it as a boy, and he would read it to me each night. Stars know why, it is so sad."

"Maybe he knew one day you would need to know the importance of those words."

Malakai's finger shoots to Teddy's lips, his body freezing in place. The snapping of a twig sounds, echoing through the quiet. Theodore goes still under Malakai's weight, his breathing slowing.

"You really should be more careful," the deep voice rolls on the wind.

Malakai's body relaxes, pulling Teddy with him as he climbs to his feet. A shadow emerges from the trees, the moonlight bouncing off a sword.

"What are you doing out here? I thought you had the night off," Malakai asks Damien.

"There were matters to attend to." His face is grave. "I was searching the streets for a thief. Nothing you need to worry yourself with."

"Might I remind you I am the *prince*?"

"...Your Highness."

"That's not what I meant."

The corner of Damien's mouth kicks up in a knowing smile. He knew what Malakai meant, that these matters, a thief in his kingdom, are things he needs to worry himself with.

"It will be brought before the royal council at tomorrow's meeting," Damien says.

Right. The royal council meeting. Something Malakai would rather not have to endure.

Teddy's fingers unfurl from Malakai's, sudden cold air pushing through the gap. "I should get back to the kitchens. Tomorrow's breakfast needs preparing."

"See you tomorrow?" Malakai smiles.

"Always."

With that, Teddy leaves. Quiet settles round the two remaining bodies.

“I should go fill in Parello. He will want to know all the details.”

“Of course.”

Malakai stands alone for a moment, letting the breeze wash over him. Instead of heading toward the castle, he takes another path toward the stables. The area is dark, the stable hand long gone, and only two small, flickering lanterns placed by the wooden building give any light. The shuffling of hooves tells him that some of the horses remain awake. He enters quietly, the door soundlessly closing behind him. The horse seems to know he’s there before he even sees him. His snout presses up against the gaps in the slats, huffing as he sniffs.

Malakai unhooks the lock, opening the gate wide. “Hi, boy.” He runs a hand up his long head. The horse—Beebo—leans into the motion, shoving his head toward Malakai. His saddle has already been removed and is hanging on the wall. Malakai decides against using it and climbs onto the horse’s back. It’s not as comfortable, but they aren’t going far.

The night sky closes in around them as they move quickly to the edge of the gardens. The iron gate looms ahead, disguised by thickets and brambles, cloning itself as part of the wall. It is never guarded; Malakai thinks his father may have even forgotten it exists. He found it when he was just a boy, spending his days within the gardens of the castle, avoiding duties inside. Even then it was hidden; it took him days to discreetly snip at all the branches holding it closed. He never told a soul about it, not until Teddy. Even Damien doesn’t know of its existence.

Beebo’s trot becomes faster as they pass the gate, the need to be quiet not so important this far from the castle. They weave through the crops of trees, the darkness crowding them. The horse needs no guidance, he knows exactly where to go. A place they’ve visited together many times before. The cabin ahead grows larger as they gain ground. As far as Malakai knows, no one has ever lived here, not this deep in the woods. It was abandoned years before he found it, that much was clear, and it's in much worse shape now. The wood moss-covered and rotten, the windows in disrepair, the roof caved in.

Malakai dismounts as they come to a stop in front of the gloomy cabin. He had been afraid the first time he came across the abandoned place, a crawling sensation scaling his skin. But he finds peace here now, a comfort he cannot quite explain. He was drawn here the first time and every time since. A pull in his core urging him on.

He became obsessed, spent every waking moment thinking about each curve and crook of the cabin. He would pore over Sorrelle's history books for hours, looking for a mention of it. He never found one. He asked his father once, but he had simply told him what Malakai had first suspected, that it was just an abandoned house. He didn't believe that. *Couldn't* believe it. His mother would not speak of it, his questions ignored.

Looking at it now, he knows there is more to it. There has to be. He once searched for clues inside but came up empty, the place void of anything but its ageing wooden floors and walls. The only piece of furniture remaining is a rocking chair that sits on the deck, gently swaying in the breeze as if someone sits there, gazing up to the night sky.

Malakai suspects that there is.

There is a presence here, he has always felt it. A light touch on his arm, a soft caress through his hair, a whisper on the wind. The presence is gentle and kind, not one he should fear.

He used to venture inside on nights like this, sit awhile, alone but not. The wood has grown too weak through the years; the last time he climbed the deck, the wood splintered and cracked beneath him, giving way to his left foot, his leg caught in the sharp angles of the rotten planks. A jagged scar remains. Instead, he sits on the grass before the steps, legs crossed and eyes closed.

"I brought you something." He reaches into his jacket pocket, pulling out a small emerald wrapped in silk. He unfolds it and places it on the deck. He started doing this a couple of years ago—bringing gifts. He's not sure how, or who takes them, but they are always gone the next time he visits. Just insignificant things, single gems, diamonds. Jewellery from the market, small trinkets he finds interesting. He doesn't know why he started doing it. He was browsing the market in the castle's courtyard one afternoon when a small glass fox caught his eye. He instantly thought of this place, the force he feels here. The rest is history.

"It may be a while before I visit again." He sighs. "The princesses are arriving shortly."

A pressure rests on his shoulder, the weight of a comforting hand. There is no one there. Just that which cannot be seen. The presence knows more about him than anyone, more so than Teddy. There is nothing he keeps from this strange dweller, no secret left untold. He told it about the first time he scraped his knee as a child. The first time he handled a sword. The first time he was bested by another's sword—the last two both being in the same moment, at the training he had begged his father for. He told it about Teddy, the ever-consuming love he feels for him, but also the worry. The feeling of sinking when all he wants to do is stay afloat. He told it about the night he cried himself to sleep because he knew that love wouldn't be forever. It couldn't. He told it about every moment, past and present. He spoke until his voice grew hoarse. He cried with it, laughed with it, and felt peace with it. Yet, he cannot explain the feeling he gets while here, so he tells no one. A secret he keeps for himself inside his heart. These moments, precious and few.

The next thing Malakai knew, he was waking with a jolt. The sunrise had replaced the moon. Beebo's snout pushes into his neck, urging him to get a move on. He throws himself across the horse, his body straining in protest from a night on the cold, hard ground. The last words he says drift on the wind as Beebo shoots toward the castle like a rocket.

"I'll be seeing you."

7

A WOLF IN SHEEP'S CLOTHING

RAYLIN

The sun is already shining through the window when I wake. I jump from the bed as a thump sounds from the other side of the door. "Damien?" My voice is croaky.

"Yes, it's me," he replies before opening the door slightly. "Sorry, I didn't mean to wake you. We should be heading out shortly. When you're ready, put these on and meet me out here." He places a small bundle down by the door before pulling it closed.

I slowly make my way over and pick up what he left.

There's a blue cloak, not as soft as my green one, an emblem of two keys crossing over one another stitched in gold on the left side—Mirdoff's royal crest. Along with the cloak is a pair of suede slippers in matching colour. I shove my feet into them, they are slightly too big but I suppose I can't go waltzing into the castle barefoot when I'm posing as a princess.

Damien is pacing the floor when I exit the bedroom. He cannot be nervous. If he's nervous then I can't do this. Does he think we'll be caught?

"What's the matter?"

His head snaps to me. "What?"

"The pacing." I gesture to the floor in front of him.

"Oh. Nothing. It helps me think...Let's go."

We turn left instead of right once we leave the house, carrying on down the backs of houses.

"Everything is taken care of. Three princesses arrived early this morning, including the Mirdoff princess." He looks around, checking no one is listening. "I had her carriage turning around and heading back before anyone laid eyes on her. From this moment on, you will only be known as Princess Lena. Commit that to memory. There's not much you need to know. Your aunt and uncle rule over Mirdoff, they took you in when your parents and sister died in a boating accident ten years ago. You have an older cousin, Jameson, who inherited his father's powers, so is set to take over as king eventually."

I already know all this, the stacks of history books lining the floors in the tower made sure of that. I spent lots of time poring over them, taking in the details of each kingdom. I Wanted to be prepared once I made it back home. These are things a princess should know, would usually be taught growing up. So I taught myself. It also helped me learn to read, something I knew little of at the age of six.

"I've been assigned duties in the castle while the princesses are here. Anything you ever need, come find me."

He leads me around a side entrance and before I know it we are on castle grounds. We walk up a gravel path and head into the castle through a wooden door. We arrive in a large room, empty of belongings, the only other person a maid dusting the high corners.

Her head turns to us, her eyes going wide. With a quick curtsy she turns away, back to the task at hand.

Damien hurries me up a set of stairs and through another door. We stand in the centre of a long landing, a runner of blood-red scales the floor. At the end of the corridor is a curved archway, grand oak doors standing open. I can make out the shapes of plush chairs and a fireplace. There are six doors along the corridor, three on each side, spaced apart and all numbered. Odd numbers on the left, even on the right.

"Number three." Damien gestures with his head. "These will be your quarters for the duration of your stay here. Each princess will have her own room. The room at the end there is a shared lounge. Guards will be posted outside at all times."

We reach door number three and panic sets in.

Just a couple of days. That's all it will be. Keep my head low. Then head home. Simple.

Damien opens the door but doesn't step inside. I poke my head in; it's big. Excessively big. A young girl stands at the end of the bed, her back straight and hands clasped behind her. She doesn't look directly at us.

"This is Ella. She is your handmaiden while you reside in the castle. Anything you ever need or want, you ask her."

I step into the room, giving a small 'hello' to Ella. She seems startled by that. I'm messing this up already. Do royals not talk to their staff? I remember always playing games and talking with the maids in Gavaria, some of my fondest memories are with them; but I was simply a child then. Maybe things are different once you grow.

"Princess Lena." She bobs in a curtsy. "It's a pleasure to meet you, Your Highness."

"Ella, Princess Lena has had a rough journey to Sorrelle. Take good care of her. Lunch will be served at one."

Ella nods and then Damien is gone. I watch the door, silently begging for him to swing it open and return.

"Your Highness, a bath has been drawn in the other room. If you would like to get settled in I will be in shortly to wash you." She says all this with a huge smile on her face like it pleases her to be at another's disposal.

"That won't be necessary. I can wash myself."

"Oh. I– um, that's what I'm here for. It is part of my duties as your handmaiden."

I can see I have made her uncomfortable. She's probably trained for years for this moment. "Very well," I say and head to the door she gestured to.

A marble clawfoot tub sits in the centre of the room, big enough for two. Two matching sinks line the opposite wall. Who needs two sinks? The wall above them is a mirror—the whole wall. The chamber pot is in its own cubicle, out of sight. The room is far too large, more open space than not. The floor shines so well I can see my reflection in it.

The tub is almost overflowing with bubbles, steam rising, tempting me with its heat. I realise how excited I am to climb in.

I'm in the bath. Water higher and hotter than I've ever experienced. It's going to be hard to go back to cold, shallow washes after this.

Ella has scrubbed me clean and I now smell like apple blossom. She has my hair draped over the side of the tub while she slowly undoes the braid, detangling it as she goes. Her fingers tug and pull at the tangled mess, but never hard enough to hurt. She keeps quiet, her face set in concentration. Now and then her mouth opens as if she will speak, but she never does.

My hair is scrubbed, scrubbed again, conditioned, and rinsed in record time. My neck aches from the mass of it when it's wet, seeming to double its usual weight. Ella leaves me to dry alone at my request. A silk underdress is hanging on the back of the door and I step into it, the softness of it caressing my skin.

I look at myself in the wall of mirrors, my large silver-grey eyes staring back. My top lip dips low in the middle, slightly smaller than the bottom one. A pink tinge coats my cheeks and I'm unsure if it's caused by the warm bathing room or the embarrassment of being washed by someone other than myself. I cannot help wondering if things were different, could I be standing here right now as myself? As Princess Raylin Edler, instead of some impostor, stealing another girl's opportunity. Or maybe I would already be married, some kind boy having whisked me away before any other had a chance. That version of me could be in love, picnicking by the side of Gavaria's rivers, mountains and seas at our backs.

Maybe one day I will get that.

An hour later, Ella finally has my too-long hair dried. She tied it in a loose braid, then wrapped it in a low bun at the nape of my neck, pulling out shorter strands around my face. She lined my eyes in a dark grey shimmer, making my irises seem more silver, like two glowing moons have been placed where my eyes used to be. My lips are now a shade of soft pink. I do not look like me. She has made me someone else entirely. Ella helps me into my dress and stares at me, her forehead creased and brows drawn together.

"What is it?"

"They must have gotten your measurements wrong, Your Highness, the dress is far larger than it should be. They will all need readjusting."

She's right. But of course, they weren't my measurements to begin with.

The soft blue dress sits in a deep v down my chest; the colour reminds me of Fee's wings, of Damien's eyes. The long sleeves are made from a see-through material, showing off my arms. What I assume is meant to be a fitted bodice creases and balloons in all the wrong places. At my hips the skirts poof out and feathers line different sections, creating a wave right down to my feet. Ella pulls the bodice tighter from behind and wraps a ribbon of the same colour around my waist, making the dress look as it should. It is beautiful, more beautiful than anything I could imagine. It makes *me* feel beautiful. Ella smiles back at me from the mirror. I didn't even notice I was smiling.

"If Prince Malakai doesn't fall in love with you from the moment he lays eyes on you, then I don't know who will." She laughs.

Ella leaves me to see the seamstress about getting my dresses readjusted. Then my uncertainty sets in. My whole body tenses, I cannot breathe. I need air. I rush to the glass doors leading to a balcony, but they won't open. They are locked and there isn't a key in sight. I thrust open a window and sit on the bed, my hands balled into fists in my lap. I should have let them catch me, surely now if I am found out my punishment will be severely worse. Not only that, but Damien will be in trouble also. He may lose his position in the king's guard.

Damn it. Why can't I breathe?

I think of the brooch back in my tower and it comes to me easily. I rub at the smooth diamonds, focusing on nothing but that. My panting eases and my breathing steadies. My mother gave me the brooch the night Genevieve rescued me. I was refusing to go to bed, wanting to join in with my brother's engagement dinner and not understanding why I wasn't allowed. Mother unclasped her brooch from her dress and asked me to take care of it, told me she didn't want it getting lost. I held the small leaf made of diamonds in my tiny hand, staring at it until I fell asleep. It wasn't until Auntie and I arrived in Sorrelle, and she erected the tower, that I realised I still clasped it in my hand.

I pin it to my dress, over my left breast. A piece of my mother here with me to keep me steady. I can do this.

My breathing has returned to normal by the time Ella collects me, though my heart still beats a pace too fast as we make our way down the hall. Guards stand at the entrance of the corridor, but I do not see a sign of any of the princesses. We make our way through large rooms and up a set of stairs, people bow and curtsy as we pass; a gesture I feel at odds with. A guard follows close behind; he's large, his skin paler than mine, hair lighter. We arrive in an entry room where two large wooden doors are opened to a grand set of stairs leading down into what looks like a banquet hall. I spot Damien standing with four other guards by the door. His eyes flick to me but he straightens and keeps his focus trained elsewhere. The five princesses are already in the room, scattered about, not uttering a word.

"Places," a commanding voice comes from the front of the room.

The princesses and I are then guided into a line, one behind the other, waiting to be announced to the King and Queen of Sorrelle.

8

The Princesses of Aldros

Raylin

I am doubting myself again when I take in my surroundings. I stand taller and shake off my worry. It's hard not to be nervous when I stand out from the others.

The princesses are all so beautiful. How could I even compare?

I have to remind myself that I am a princess. I may not have been raised like one, wasn't taught the ways of being a royal, how to properly present myself among others, or how to behave and act, but I am the daughter of a king and queen, I mustn't forget that.

I mimic how the girls are standing, backs straight, hands clasped in front of them. Similar to how Ella was standing when I arrived at my rooms, similar to how she is standing beside me now. All the handmaidens are with their assigned princess, and all appear to be about the same age as Ella, fifteen or sixteen at a guess. Is this what they chose to do with their lives? Or, like me, was this the best option they had?

A booming voice echoes through the room from the top of the stairs, startling me from my thoughts. "Your Majesties, King Rorik and Queen Lucia, and His Highness, Prince Malakai, I would like to present to you six esteemed princesses of Aldros."

There is a pause. A silence of taut anticipation before the voice carries on.

"Welcome, Princess Kiyoko Ito of Yendoth."

The princess closest to the doors makes her way to the stairs. Her black hair is in loose waves down her back. Her oval eyes, tilted upward at the corners, are a deep shade of brown, stark against her porcelain skin. She wears a silk lilac kimono, covered in rose gold cherry blossoms. She strides toward the doors with the grace of an angel, disappearing down the wide stairs before us.

After a short while, the voice calls out again, "Princess Briar Theron of Thezmare."

This princess wears a dress of deep black, so fitted to her body I wonder how she moves. The straps are just two thin golden chains, showing off her slender arms and her sun-kissed skin. Her hair of orange flames is cropped at her shoulders, framing her soft face. Her eyes shine like a field of green on a summer's morning, contrasting the brown constellation of freckles across her nose.

The next in line is announced as Princess Soraya Alstone of Jalendia.

Her colourful dress isn't as skin-tight as Briar's, but a slit from floor to hip reveals a slender, muscle-defined leg—which emerges every step she takes. The dress is all bright colours and patterns. She's tall, her body curving in all the right places. Her skin a deep brown, her almond eyes a dark umber. Her ebony, fluffy curls sit in a halo around her head, framing her face.

She retreats down the stairs, the voice then calling out again to announce the next in line. "Princess Catalina Xaviera of Zenick."

Her skin is a lighter brown than Soraya's, a shade more similar to Damien's golden tones. Her thick, long black lashes frame her hazel eyes. Her cheekbones look like they were carved by the gods themselves. She doesn't wear a dress; instead, she struts forward in a pair of silk trousers that sit high up on her waist, a slither of skin between them and the silk blouse she wears tied in a bow at her back, both in crimson red. Her dark brown hair is swept from her face in loose curls, thin chains of gold drooping across her forehead. She's all sharp angles and no-nonsense.

"Princess Lena Nisim of Mirdoff," the man calls.

No one moves.

Damien clears his throat and my feet catch his cue before my brain does.

That's me.

I carefully make my way down each step, not moving too fast for fear of tripping on my dress. The King and Queen of Sorrelle watch me from where they stand at the bottom of the grand staircase. A pang of nerves shoots through me. What if they know I'm not who I say?

Seeing them here, the lines of age on their faces, makes me think of my parents. When I picture them, I see them as they once were, although the years would tell me otherwise.

The king's hair is greyed, the salt and pepper stubble on his chin an exact match. Even from here, I can see the wrinkles forming around his bright green eyes. His large nose and thin lips are very unlike his son's. The queen's frigid-blue glare bores into me with contempt. Her face is set in hard lines, her pink mouth in a pout. Her hair remains a sandy blonde, not yet grey like her husband's.

Prince Malakai stands beside them, not paying much attention at all. He fiddles with the signet ring on his finger, looking like he would rather be anywhere but here. He looks more like his father than his mother, though there are only slight similarities. His emerald-green eyes match his father, and his messy cropped hair is shades lighter than his mother's. I wonder if his father's was this colour when he was his son's age. His nose is more like his mother's, but not quite the same. His lips plumper than both parents. All have the same light skin.

There's a twist deep in my gut at the sight of him, a kind of familiarity, though I've never so much as had a glimpse of the prince before now. It makes me want to reach out to him, to grab hold and never let go. I tear my eyes from him, ridding myself of the feeling.

All three royals wear the colours of Sorrelle, a deep green—much like my beloved cloak—with gold stitching. The prince's suit is dishevelled and creased like he was late and dressed quickly.

I reach the bottom of the staircase and, remembering my manners, I curtsy. I may have forgotten if so many others hadn't done the same to me on my way here. The king's gaze snags on my mother's brooch, and I have to resist the urge to lift my hand to it, to hide it from his sight. A line forms between his brows but I am quickly forgotten as I rush to stand beside the four princesses. We wait as the last name is called.

"Princess Arabella Galdur of Faldova."

The girl that steps out reminds me of nothing short of a snow queen.

Her pale skin and hair, so blonde it could pass as white, glow in the beaming lights of the hall. She's short, probably the shortest of all the princesses, and she's all skin and bone. A petite little thing. Confidence radiates off her, her heart-shaped face stern.

Winter blue eyes stare right at the prince, no makeup save for the blood-red painted on her pouty lips.

This girl knows she is beautiful, and it shows. A braid loops from one side of her temple to the other, while the rest of her hair falls in loose waves over her shoulders. She wears a long-sleeved dress made of snow-white fur, stretching right down to her toes; the only skin showing is a thin sliver where the neckline dips between her breasts. She slinks across the floor, dipping low to the king and queen, then comes to a stop in front of the prince.

"A pleasure to meet you, Prince Malakai."

He takes her offered hand in his, pressing it briefly to his lips. "Right back at you, Princess." Malakai winks at her, the corner of his mouth lifting in a smirk.

I sense the others tense beside me. Arabella knows what she wants and she isn't playing games.

The hall we stand in is magnificent. The ceiling stretches high above our heads, a great golden chandelier hangs in the centre, the flames burning bright, casting brilliant white lights over the room, reflecting in each tiny diamond droplet that hangs from the spindles. Four smaller matching chandeliers sit toward the four corners of the room. To the left is a stained-glass window stretched from floor to ceiling. It depicts a vast sea, the skies a storm cloud grey, a large ship sailing the ocean, the waves rocking it to-and-fro. The walls are white, banners of deep green hanging from all available space, fine gold stitching in the crest of Sorrelle—a sailboat on curled twists of waves, depicting their famous fishing villages. Swirls and patterns in the same design are carved along the ceiling and down the pillars, dusted in shimmering gold.

Although the room is large, only a single table sits in the centre, long enough to seat us all, plus more. The table is set for nine, so

I gather it is just us for lunch. As we are directed to our seats, ten guards make their way down the staircase, joining the five already scattered about the room, their backs pressed against the walls, silent and still.

I hope to sit on the side of the table facing Damien, but I am placed with my back to him. I try to copy how the others sit but my hands visibly tremble with nerves, so I place them in my lap out of sight. The first course is swiftly bought out, a crusty bread topped with some kind of pâté. My stomach grumbles, alerting me that I have not eaten today. I only hope no one else heard it.

"So, tell us about yourselves," King Rorik's voice croaks loudly across the table, so clamorous they doubtlessly heard him on the other side of the castle.

I panic for a moment as the room remains silent, then the princess from Yendoth, Kiyoko, speaks up.

"I am one of five children. My older brother is ruler of Yendoth. We all inherit power of the bloom, so older sibling takes crown." Her voice is soft. "I will miss them, but I am very grateful to be here." She bows her head slightly, and the king smiles at her, all teeth and gums.

I try to think of what I know of Yendoth from my history books. It is mostly known as the Kingdom of Flowers. I read the lands are covered in cherry blossoms, each royal having the power to make things grow and thrive from nothing but a whisp of air.

"I, too, am one of five siblings," Briar speaks now, her voice filled with excitement. "Unfortunately, I was not lucky enough to inherit my family's power. Only my sister and one of my brothers have the right to claim the throne."

The king spouts on about powers, then castles and upkeep, not letting anyone get a word in edgeways. I am thankful; I would rather listen to him drone on than have to talk about a family I do not know.

I can't help but think of my brother, Reed, at this moment. Has he taken over as king? Does he now have children of his own? The history books always seem to come to an abrupt stop, never anything recent within. And Genevieve never tells me of my family, or anything for that matter.

The second course is brought out, and the smell offends my nostrils. I have to breathe through my mouth to keep from heaving. A bowl of dark liquid sits in front of me, something I can only assume is soup. Little pink creatures bob around the bowl, with skinny legs and curved tails. Beady black eyes stare back at me. I watch as King Orilius picks one out and pulls it apart, taking out the innards and shoving them in his mouth. Just a shell of what it once was sits on a napkin beside his bowl. Others follow his lead, but I sit and poke them around with my spoon, bringing the liquid to my mouth and taking tiny sips every so often to fake eating it.

I look up and catch Soraya spitting one out into her napkin, trying and failing to suppress her shiver. She catches my eye and we both close our mouths in a tight line, laughter threatening to escape.

I thank the stars when the meal is over and I don't have to pretend to eat the fishy soup any longer. I know Sorrelle is known for its fishing villages, but I can only hope I can avoid any more of the castle's fish delicacies on my stay.

Queen Lucia announces a ball tonight, one I already anticipated after hearing about it for weeks in the market. She says it's more of a formality to introduce us to their people. It's only fair they get to meet who will be their future queen. Once the table is cleared and the king and queen have parted ways, our handmaidens come to escort us back to our quarters.

I spot Damien leaving the hall through the main entrance with Prince Malakai. They talk to each other with ease, smiles and laughter being shared. It's odd to watch Malakai this way after not speaking a word at lunch.

Once back in our quarters, Kiyoko, Briar, and Arabella head into their rooms. The conversation was tepid on our way back, only Catalina and Soraya exchanging words. They make a beeline for the lounge at the end of the hall and Soraya twists her head over a dipped shoulder to me. "Are you coming?" Her accent is thick, the words curling over each other.

They don't wait for me as they stroll into the room beyond. Two guards stand at ease outside the archway.

I stand there, frozen in the hall for a moment, hand on the spiral doorknob to room three. I shouldn't, should I? Lunch went well, the king went on about himself and his kingdom at such lengths that no one had the chance to question me. But what if I slip up to these girls? Damien seemed to have got it right that none of them had met Lena, or I would have been found out before I even got the chance to enter the banquet hall.

The thought of being cooped up in yet another room makes my skin itch. The need to be around people overrides any doubts I may have. One look at Ella and I am making my way towards the girls in the lounge. The guard at my heels stops with the others at the door as I enter; there's something comforting in the fact that they do not come in here.

The room is warm from the golden flames flickering in the fireplace. The mantel is carved in intricate designs of petals and rosebuds. Above the fireplace is a large mirror, painted thinly with a sunset, just enough so that you can still see your reflection, the paints casting your features in reds and golds. The cream carpet is deep and fluffy, thick enough that I can feel it on the tops of my feet over my silk slippers.

Soraya has kicked off her heeled shoes and is scrunching her toes in the fibres, the whole of her dark brown leg now on show through the slit of her dress.

Two plush sofas and three enormous chairs sit in a semi-circle around the fire, all in the same shade of burgundy that matches the walls. The room isn't overly large, but it is homely, welcoming.

Both princesses beam at me. Catalina pats the seat next to her on the sofa. "Come sit, Lena."

I awkwardly sit beside her, sitting far enough away that we do not brush against each other. Her legs are curled up in her seat, her shoes also discarded on the floor.

"As I was saying," Catalina speaks to Soraya now, twiddling with the necklace that hangs around her neck, "you should come visit once all this is over. We have some of the most beautiful beaches in Aldros. White sand and water so blue and clear you can see each grain of sand beneath." Pride and joy seep from her words.

"You should come too, Lena. I have to say, it's a breath of fresh air meeting other royals besides my boring siblings." She laughs wholeheartedly, a little joke of her own, but I can tell she loves them and her kingdom dearly.

"I would love to," Soraya replies, "but alas, most of my days are taken, preparing to take over once Ma is ready. Being here is already stealing valuable time. But I will be sure to take you up on that offer once I can."

They both look at me expectantly, and I nod slightly, my lips parting, ready to say something along the lines of 'sure', when shouting from the corridor cuts me off.

"I do not need my dresses *altered.* I need new ones."

The high, sweetly malicious tone of it came from no one but Arabella.

"Oh, that girl. So spoiled," Soraya whispers.

"I heard her bitching this morning because her maid back home forgot to pack her favourite lipstick," Catalina adds in, rolling her eyes. "Kiss me pink." She puckers her plump lips, kissing the air.

Laughter breaks out of all of us. We are quick to hush our volume.

"Does it look like I need winter clothes! There is no snow here. I was sweating like a drowning fish at lunch in this fur!" Arabella's voice carries down the hall, further away now.

"That doesn't even make sense." Catalina shrugs.

"That poor handmaiden," Soraya adds. "Bet she's contemplating her career choice right now."

"Such drama," Briar says by way of greeting, jumping over the back of a chair and landing with a soft plop in the cushioned seat.

Her tight dress is swapped out for soft cotton trousers and a cream blouse, the only colour the bright orange of her hair. Up close her face is peppered in more freckles than I first thought.

"What's crawled up Miss Prissy Princess's arse?" she asks, running a hand through her short hair.

Just as she finishes her sentence, Arabella storms into the room, takes one look at us all, stomps her foot, turns on her heel, and storms right back out. We look at each other one by one, eyes wide and uncertain, before bursting into fits of giggles. Briar lets out a massive snort, making us laugh harder.

"Oh my stars," Catalina says, putting a tawny hand to her mouth, trying to stifle her laughter.

The commotion dies down, taking the tension in my body with it.

This will be easier than I thought. These girls are nothing like I imagined. These three at least. When our handmaidens enter the room, announcing it is time to get ready for the ball, I find myself not dreading it at all.

9

TO BE KING

MALAKAI

The lunch with the princesses went about as well as Malakai was expecting it would. His father prattled on for so long about himself and the kingdom—just as he had anticipated—that he didn't have to speak much at all.

There was nothing seemingly wrong with the girls, but he just couldn't shake the annoyance he felt about the situation. He is to choose one of them as his bride, to stand at his side and rule the kingdom along with him. It wasn't fair on him, and it certainly wasn't fair on the poor girl. He would never love her. Not how she would want him to. And what would it mean for him and Teddy?

Malakai wouldn't give him up. Not ever.

"Where are your thoughts?" the queen asks.

Tea splashes in the cups as the young servant girl tips the fine-china pot, the liquid steaming. Once done, she takes a step back, her head lowered, eyes trained down. A stance all the servants do in the presence of the royals. The queen dismisses her with a wave of a hand, her gaze waiting on Malakai expectantly.

"What do you think of them? The princesses?" Malakai asks his mother in return.

She takes a sip of tea, her fingers delicate on the cup. "Decent enough, I suppose."

Yes, because that's what we look for in a life partner, Malakai thought. *Decent enough.* Maybe that is all his mother thought he was worth. His parents were forcing him into this after all. They couldn't care much for his heart.

"The Yendoth girl seemed kind," she adds now, sensing his discouragement. "Maybe Arabella, though it will take her some getting used to the new climate if she were to move here."

Arabella. Faldova's princess. The Kingdom of Snow. He had watched the beads of sweat roll down her brow at lunch, her discomfort as she slyly dabbed at it with her napkin. Watched as she tugged at the thick fur of her sleeves, searching for some reprieve from the heat. If she suffered this much now, coming into the colder months, he would pity her in the summer. Malakai's mouth twitched at the thought of choosing her, just to watch her squirm. Then again, that is probably what she wants, to be chosen. He saw it in her eyes as she greeted him, the glint in them, the hope.

He loses all amusement at the thought. She would want children of her own. She would want someone to love her. And that was something he knew he couldn't do. He couldn't take that from someone.

But wouldn't that be what he was doing to whoever he chose?

The queen's eyes are trained on him, watching his every movement, like she can hear his thoughts. It was his turn to squirm.

"Yes," he says, "decent enough."

There's a tap at the door; it opens with the queen's blessing. Damien emerges from the other side, his face serious, stern. Not the face Malakai has become accustomed to. He gets to see the softer side of the lieutenant, a face he would not dare show in front of the king and queen. It took them a long time to come around to the idea of their prince son having a guard as a friend, and they don't even know half of what the pair get up to. Or the secrets Damien helps Malakai keep.

"Your presence is requested at the council meeting, Your Highness."

Malakai gets to his feet with a swift movement, plants a kiss on his mother's hand, before strolling out the door without so much as a word.

The room in which the meeting is being held is far larger than it needs to be. The space around the table planted in the middle of the room is empty, stretching out to each wall. The largest wall is painted with a map of Aldros, similar to the one in Malakai's own room. This one is more detailed, notes tacked to islands, pins sticking out of various places.

The wall behind the table hosts a rounded window, a view of the gardens beyond. The other wall is covered by a deep green banner, the crest of Sorrelle stitched in gold—a sailboat cresting the waves.

Heads turn to Malakai as he enters. Four bodies rise to their feet and bow low; the fifth remains seated, hands clasped atop the round mahogany wood. The king gestures to an empty chair at the opposite end of the table and Malakai sits without question. "Sit," his father tells the other council members.

The royal council of Sorrelle comprises five figures: the King, the Sword, the Seal, the Hand, and the Brain.

The role of the king speaks for itself, their commander, their leader.

The title of the Sword is given to the kingdom's best fighter; his role is to protect the king at all costs. He is on the front lines at all battles, the one all fighters and guards alike report to, the captain included. The man in question is quite terrifying if you ask Malakai. He is shockingly tall, muscles so large they bulge through his clothes. He's all dark features and hair. Malakai has never once seen the man crack a smile. He couldn't imagine someone like that by his side at all times. But for all intents and purpose, Bayard is a man not to be messed with.

There's a thump on the table, a stumbled sorry, a rustle of papers.

Noah Tambold. The Brain. Malakai never understood how someone as scattered as Noah could be the brain of the kingdom, the person responsible for all planning and strategy. The boy always has a book in his hand and looks like he never sleeps. Maybe that's what makes him so perfect. His brain is crammed full of wonders and smart thinking.

Then there's Lissa Shostakovich, the complete opposite of Noah. Organised and straight-backed. Her face is all sharp angles, lethal enough to slice a man's heart right open. The Seal. She oversees all correspondence to and from Sorrelle. A strategist in her own right.

Last, and very certainly least, the Hand. Remy Gardeviar. How someone can be so far up oneself, Malakai would never know. He is responsible for all duties in and out of court. And Malakai is sure the man thinks he rules over the king himself. His light brown hair is scraped back, his brown eyes trained on the king.

"Speak, Parello," the king says.

It is only then that Malakai notices the captain of the guard standing beside Damien, who remains in the room.

Parello bows. "Your Majesty, there was a thief within the castle walls late yesterday afternoon. My men tried to apprehend her, but she got away. I have stationed extra guards—"

"*She*?" Remy questions.

"Yes. As I was saying—"

"Your men couldn't catch a *girl*? Your Majesty, this is unacceptable. These guards need looking into—"

"Enough." The king's voice is harsh. "I expect you have your men searching for the thief?"

"Yes, Your Majesty."

"Very well. Keep the council posted. You and the lieutenant are dismissed."

Damien and Parello both take a bow before exiting the room, the door closing with a click behind them.

"Tambold, any news on the shipments?"

"They are on the way. Henford informs me the ships got held up at Yendoth, but they should be with us soon."

Malakai straightens. What shipments? Noah wouldn't be in the know about any of the usual shipments of goods. Malakai can tell by the stern look on his father's face now is not the time to question such things.

"Shostakovich?"

"I have letters from Quendore, Your Majesty. They are asking for aid."

"Whatever for?" Remy butts in.

Lissa raises her eyes to him, her lips puckering with annoyance. Her fingers are tight on the parchment in her hand. "Queen Presley writes to you herself, Your Majesty. She states their coffers are suffering and it won't be long until they are out of coin completely."

"Then why doesn't she raise her taxes instead of expecting handouts?" Remy rolls his eyes.

"If you would let me *finish*, Gardeviar." She clears her throat. "She says she cannot raise the taxes. Her people are already struggling, barely getting by as it is. They've taken on more work, but the coin isn't building up, too many repairs and finances to take care of."

Remy snorts. "Maybe if their so-called queen stopped cavorting with another woman, she could keep better care of her kingdom. A kingdom needs a *king*, not two—"

Remy is silenced by the king's hand, holding it palm out to him in protest. Malakai's limbs turn to stone. King Rorik rubs his finger along his lips, the signet ring he wears—identical to Malakai's—catching the light with the movement. His brows pull together in thought, his eyes lost somewhere else. His gaze moves to Malakai, eyes narrowing.

"What would you do?"

Malakai blinks, shocked. His gaze flicks to the others in the room, all of them staring in his direction. "Me?"

"Yes, you."

Remy leans forward. "Your Majesty, if I may—"

"You may not." The king's stare does not leave Malakai's face. "Son..."

Malakai shuffles in his seat, suddenly uncomfortable. His father has never asked his opinion on such matters before, usually shutting him down if he tries adding his thoughts in where they are not wanted. It was a rarity for him to even be in these meetings. The king had requested he start to join them occasionally, to get a feel for what he was in for, or so he put it.

"I would help them," Malakai says.

Remy leans back in his chair, his eyes almost getting stuck at the back of his head he rolls them so hard. "Of course you would," he snips.

"Why?" is all the king says.

Malakai is surer of himself now, more assertive. "They are in need. We have the means to help. If the boot was on the other foot, would we not want others to do the same?"

"They are backing us into a corner," Remy snaps. "They come to the largest kingdom in Aldros because they expect us to help. They think we will not turn them down. I say we do. We say yes to them, two more rise up. Then the same over and over until we are left with nothing."

"I have it on good authority that letters were sent to all kingdoms," Lissa adds.

"Even worse, they are trying to get as much coin as their grubby little hands can snatch."

It is Malakai's turn to roll his eyes at Remy. "Because they are in need."

"So they say."

"Enough," the king orders. "Remy is right. We do this, more come asking."

"Then we say no the next time."

"We say no now."

"Father, you're being unreasonable."

The king surveys his son. "A king cannot always be reasonable. You must think about the bigger picture. Sometimes choices are easy, and sometimes they are not. This is one of those times."

Malakai shoots to his feet so fast, his chair wobbles behind him, threatening to collapse. "I hope if we are ever in need, it is an easy choice for them also." He storms from the room, slamming the door behind him. Remy's muffled 'we wouldn't be in need' follows after him.

Malakai stares at himself in the mirror. His jacket of the deepest green and gold hangs from his shoulders, pressed neat and crisp, not a crease in sight. Theodore stands behind him, his simple tunic and trousers at odds with the prince's finery. He catches his eye in the mirror, a wicked gleam there.

"Do something for me," Teddy says.

"Anything."

"Get to know them."

Malakai closes his eyes, a sigh escaping his lips. "Anything but that."

Teddy's hand runs along Malakai's arm, a soothing touch. He tugs at him, turning him so they are face to face.

"I know it seems impossible, like you have no choice." He places a hand on Malakai's cheek. "There is always a choice. You can fight against it, or you can embrace it. Make it into something of your choosing."

Malakai huffs a laugh. Each time he tries to make his own choices they get shot down. Maybe this is something he can rebel against, not give his father the satisfaction of choosing a princess, let alone a bride. Theodore was right though. There doesn't need to be a fight here, not with the princesses themselves.

He watches Teddy closely, the twinkle in his eye. He didn't think he could love this boy any more than he already does. But there he goes, surprising him again.

"Can you look at each of those girls and tell me honestly that this is what they wanted? To be taken from their homes and made to compete for a prince's affections?"

Malakai's breath catches. He hadn't thought of that. He had been so consumed in his irritation of it all, it hadn't crossed his mind that the princesses might not want this either. He wouldn't tell Teddy that. He knew what he would say. Big ego, and all that. He shakes his head, a smile spreading across his lips.

"Anyone ever told you how smart you are?"

"All the time," Teddy teases. "Now, go enjoy your ball."

"Your wish is my command."

The ballroom is heaving with people, the noise drumming in Malakai's ears.

He hates these things.

His mother sits on the throne beside him, her back straight, her eyes narrowed on the crowds. The king whispers with the Hand, Remy, hurried words that Malakai cannot make out. He wonders if it has to do with the letters from Quendore, or if that matter is now squashed.

Malakai turns his attention back to the room, searching the swarm of bodies for Damien, who's missing from up here on the dais, replaced with Cadet Michaels. Malakai thought he would come to find him after the meeting with the king's council, but he was left waiting. Though he didn't mind, it just meant more alone time with Teddy. That's where his eyes linger now. On the copper hair at the back of the room. Those soft fingers carrying trays filled with glasses of liquid bubbles. The fingers that just hours ago were gliding over Malakai's bare chest.

Teddy makes his way across the floor, right toward a sea of white fabric. Malakai has to admit the princesses do look beautiful.

Maybe Damien and Teddy were right, it may not be so bad. He could get to know them. There's no harm in that.

He watches the Mirdoff girl—Lena, if he's correct in thinking—as she sips her champagne, scrunching her face as the bubbles tickle her nose. She seems at odds with herself, her feet shuffling on the spot, not seeming to know how to stand. She puts her arms in three different positions before deciding on one.

She doesn't seem to be uncomfortable in her clothes, as Arabella was at lunch, but more uncomfortable in this space, at this ball.

She and him both.

The others are more at ease, relaxed in this environment.

His eyes follow Teddy as he makes his way back to the kitchens. That's where he spots Damien, leaning against the far wall, his eyes lingering on the princesses. If he starts trying to set Malakai up too, he thinks he might just lose his mind. Or maybe it's not Malakai he is thinking of at all. There's a look on his face, something Malakai cannot quite place. He's never seen that look on Damien before. It's like the look a child gets at a banquet full of sweet treats.

Interesting.

10

A PHANTOM DANCER

RAYLIN

When I enter the ballroom, my earlier eases are washed away, replaced by a hammering of nerves.

The five princesses are at my side. We are all dressed in various degrees of white. My dress is flowing silk, little diamonds sewn into the skirt, giving a glistening effect. It is stitched tighter than before, the seamstress having already made a start on my clothes. I feel a twinge of guilt for her, knowing I will not be here long. Maybe I could get away with taking a few of the dresses with me.

Kiyoko wears a white kimono, flowers sewn in with a silver thread. Catalina has traded in her silk trousers for a poofy number, the skirts spreading out three-people wide, resembling a marshmallow. Briar's dress is similar to the one she wore this morning; it clings to her body, showing off every bump and curve. Arabella somehow got her unconventional requests answered. Her dress is still long-sleeved, but it dips low to her navel and cuts off just below the knee, fur nowhere to be seen. Soraya's dress is my favourite out of the bunch. It sits in a heart shape across her chest, the sleeves resting on her upper arms. The bodice is completely covered in diamonds, spread out and becoming more sparse as they reach the bottom of the skirts.

The ballroom is filled with people, more than I have ever seen in one space. Some sit at tables around the outskirts of the room, others dance to the lilting music. Hands clasp onto glasses of wine, sloshing around the liquid as they move.

High windows line each wall, though no daylight seeps through, the sun having set long before, welcoming the night ahead. The marble floor shines, beckoning me to slip in the heels I have been made to wear. I have to keep my steps small and shuffled to be able to walk in them. Servants walk the room, carrying trays with various liquids and foods. The smell wafts toward us, making my stomach grumble once again. Tall, skinny glasses are handed to us, a golden, bubbling liquid inside, and within minutes each person in the room is holding one.

I sip at it; it is an explosion of fizz. The bubbles shoot up my nose and I flinch at the sensation.

"Your attention, please," King Rorik's voice booms through the room.

He sits on a throne upon a dais at the head of the room, Queen Lucia on a matching one beside him. The backs of the thrones stand double the height of them, little sailboats and waves carved into the wood. The banners of Sorrelle hang above them, blowing in an invisible breeze. Prince Malakai stands beside the queen, his hand placed upon her shoulder. He doesn't look toward us. Instead, his eyes are on something or someone at the back of the room.

"We have invited you all here today to welcome our fine guests." He gestures towards us and hundreds of heads turn in our direction, whispers filling the room. "Within this group of princesses stands my son's future bride. *Your* future queen. Let's show them what it is to be part of Sorrelle. Let us show them what this kingdom is truly about. Let the drinking and dancing commence!"

A roar echoes across the crowd, cheering and thumping, shouts of joy, and the reverberating sound of glasses clinking together.

Then we are thrust upon it all, being dragged into the throng of dancing and cheering. I duck from a large man's arms, his stomach pushing against his shirt so much that his buttons are bound to burst. I squeeze through the narrow space between people, trying my best not to bump into them. An impossible task.

"Sorry. Sorry. Excuse me." I doubt they can hear me over the blaring music.

I've lost the princesses somewhere in the crowd. It's possible they are more attuned to this than I am. They've probably attended hundreds of balls growing up and know how to handle the hordes of bodies.

I spot an opening just ahead. As I am about to make a break for it, a hand grabs mine.

"Dance with me?" His warm breath is close to my ear, and a shiver works its way down my spine.

The voice is tender, full of something I cannot quite name. He spins me around and I am face to face with Prince Malakai, his smile tilted to one side, a small dimple a crease on his pale cheek. His emerald eyes are fixed on my face. This close I notice just how handsome he is. And again, I am hit with that familiarity, something palpable pulsating between us.

"You look like you want to be here less than I do," he says as he spins me in a dance.

His hand is against my back, pulling me close to his chest. His other hand holds mine by our sides. I don't know what to do with my free hand, so I place it on his shoulder, a gesture many of the other female dancers are doing.

Lucky for me he knows what he's doing; he moves slow, so his steps are easy to follow. Malakai is taller than me, so I have to tilt my head back to get a good look at him.

"Maybe I would rather be in bed with a good book."

He laughs loudly. My body tenses at the sound, not expecting to feel the vibrations of that very noise flow through me.

"Wouldn't we all, Princess Lena. Or at least with good...company." His smile fades at this.

"Why would you not want to be here? Isn't the whole point of this to find you a bride?"

I don't even know what I'm saying. For someone who usually struggles to talk to strangers, the words have no problem finding me now.

"My parents want to find me a bride. I, on the other hand, am perfectly content as I am."

"You seemed to like Arabella this morning."

Again with the word vomit. I blame the bubbly liquid from before. There will be no more of that while I reside here, that's for sure.

"You are mistaken." He leans in closer. "I was amused by her, yes, but not for the reasons you think. I have heard...things about her. I have a friend in Faldova who had many stories to tell when he visited here in the spring."

I can hear the mischief in his voice.

"What kind of things?"

"I'm not one for gossip. If gossip finds me, then I'm not inclined to turn it away, but I do not spread rumours. Rumours only get you in trouble." He winks at me, that smirk back on his face.

He's so close to me I can smell his minty breath, the orange spice of his skin. Malakai's eyes flick to somewhere behind me, glassing over like a lovesick puppy. He steps back from me, releasing my hand.

"Enjoy your night, Princess Lena." He salutes me and stalks from the room.

I look around to see what caught his eye, but all I see are dancing couples and growing crowds. No one else seems to have noticed his departure.

My hand still hovers in the air, resting on a phantom dancer. I let it fall to my side, quickly making my way to a table in the corner where I spot Soraya.

"These shoes are killing my feet," she says as I approach.

She's got her bare foot in her hand, hidden beneath the tablecloth, rubbing her thumb against the sole. "I saw you dancing with the prince." She wiggles her dark eyebrows at me.

"Oh, that. It was nothing." I fidget in my seat.

"You're not interested?"

"Oh, I– um..."

"Lena, relax." She laughs. "I cannot speak for the other princesses, but I for one am not at all interested in marrying Prince Malakai."

"You're not?"

"Not one bit. I am set to become queen of my own kingdom. If I had my way, I wouldn't be here at all. My mother encouraged me to come. If not for marriage, to explore a new land, meet new people." She sighs. "Besides, my heart already belongs to another." She's silent for a moment, a soft smile on her lips. A memory of her love fleeting across her features. "What about you? What brought you here?"

I don't respond right away and she searches my face for some truth behind my silence. "I didn't have much choice, I suppose." I smile, the lie easy as it isn't quite a lie at all. "So, this boy, what is he like?" I ask, moving the subject away from me.

"We're talking about boys, are we? My favourite subject." Catalina flops into a chair on the opposite side of the table, inviting herself into the conversation. Soraya carries on, not minding at all.

"He's tall, dark, and handsome. Just how I like them." She laughs. "But...that's not all there is to him. We've known each other all our lives, albeit very different lives. He doesn't come from wealth or royalty, but neither did Ma when she met Pa, and they had the best life together. Jalendia isn't all too strict on who you should and shouldn't marry. My kingdom isn't one for superiority."

"Had?" I ask.

"My pa died when my brother and I were young. It's just Ma now."

"I'm sorry," Catalina and I say in unison.

I don't think my heart could handle losing a parent. It hurts enough that I haven't been able to see them in so long, the memory of their faces growing more distant with each passing day.

"It's been a long time." She straightens her back and rubs a dark hand against her white skirt, flattening out the folds.

"My mother left when I was five. Just up and walked out in the middle of the night, leaving her four children behind. Not the same, I know, but I do know, on some level, how it feels to lose someone you love. No matter how much time has passed," Catalina says as she takes Soraya's hand in hers.

Soraya takes my hand in her free one. "And, of course, you lost your parents, right?"

My heart stills; I had almost forgotten. Lena was raised by her aunt and uncle. I give a small nod, hoping she will think it's just something I don't like to talk about. Her hand squeezes mine in understanding, her thick lips in a small smile.

"Well, enough of that." Catalina claps her hands, her dark brown eyes lined with tears. "I'm going to find myself a handsome young man to dance with. Wish me luck." She scans the crowd and floats off toward a group of boys not much older than us.

"Think I'm going to join her. Are you coming?"

"I'll be right over," I tell her, though I have no intention of joining them.

"Alright." Her eyes flick past me. "Though a handsome young man has already found you, it seems. His eyes have been on you all evening." She leans in and kisses me on the cheek before departing.

I twist in my chair to where she was looking, and there, by the garden doors, stands Damien, his eyes trained on me. He turns and exits the room, disappearing into the night.

I'm on my feet and going after him without much thought. I am drawn to him. Even before we met, those days in the market, our eyes would always find each other.

He's leaning against a large white oak tree. The branches hang low, concealing him in shadow. I glance over my shoulder. No one follows.

"It's going well...I think," I say to him.

His smile lights up his face, his cobalt eyes glistening in the moonlight. "You're doing great."

"I'm not doing much. The princesses are making it easier."

"Walk with me," he says, his head gesturing toward the depths of the garden.

We walk side by side, past bushes with pale yellow flowers that line the paths, towering high over our heads. The further we move from the castle, the darker it gets, the lights of the ballroom too far away now to light our path.

We come to a small opening. It's round, leading off in four different directions like we've come across the middle of a maze. There is a stone bench in the centre, surrounded by more flowers, but we do not sit.

"You look...like a princess." His eyes slowly scan me from head to toe, lingering for a moment before making their way back up.

"Ella did a good job," I reply, unconsciously touching my hair, which has been curled and pinned behind my ears.

"I don't think it's that." He shakes his head. "The prince– You're the only one he danced with before escaping the ball tonight. Did he say anything to you, Ray?"

It feels strange hearing my name here, somewhere where I'm not myself. It's even more strange to hear it from someone other than Genevieve, the only person I've heard my name from in fourteen years. Although my brother is the only one who ever called me Ray. But Damien cannot call me by full name as I did not give it to him.

"Don't call me that, someone will hear you."

"There's no one here. Just us." His arms spread to the side, gesturing to the emptiness around us.

That's when I see him. Fee.

He's perched on a branch of a tall tree watching us. I want nothing more than to run to him, hold him in my arms. But I cannot. What would Damien think if I started talking to a bird in the middle of the garden? He would think me mad.

I force my eyes away from my friend, and back to the man in front of me. "Prince Malakai didn't say much, just that he didn't want to choose a bride."

He starts to walk back in the direction we came, and I take one last look at Fee before I follow. I am comforted by the fact that I now know he knows where I am, that I'm okay.

Damien doesn't head directly to the party, but a side door further down. We enter a long corridor that I don't recognise. I have no idea why I put so much trust in him that I will just follow him around a strange castle, but I do. Servants pass us with trays of food and drink, and I remember I didn't get anything to eat. We walk up some steps, stopping in front of an unremarkable wooden door.

"This is the servant's entrance to your quarters. I will have to leave you here."

Why did he bring me here instead of taking me back to the party? Maybe he somehow knew I didn't want to be there. He opens the door for me and I step through.

"It's Lieutenant Reynolds, by the way, if you have to ask for me. A princess shouldn't be on a first name basis with a guard. Goodnight, Ray." He whispers the last part, his full lips in a smile.

"Oh, Lieutenant Reynolds," I call out before closing the door behind me, "would it be possible to get the key to the balcony in my room?"

"Of course, Princess Lena, consider it done." He bows his head to me.

An excitement rushes through me, this little secret we share, a better feeling than stealing goods from the market.

In my room, I change into the silk nightgown that has been laid out on my bed, and climb up onto the mattress, softer than a cloud, the covers so plump I sink into them. I think of the food downstairs in the ballroom and a platter appears in front of me. I can do nothing but hope it didn't just disappear from some poor, unsuspecting servant's hand.

There are rows of meats, light to dark, folded into roses, thin slices of cheese in different shapes and sizes, fruits of all different colours, and mini bowls of olives and nuts. I eat until my stomach cannot take one more bite, and I feel as if I will throw it all back up if I do.

I lay back on the bed, staring at the ceiling, letting the feel of this life wash over me.

11

AN ORPHAN FOR THE QUEEN

RAYLIN

I'm awakened by the door opening softly. My heart pounds in my chest from the nightmares that plagued my slumber. I don't have them often, but when I do they are fierce and all too real.

I was locked in a cell. No light save for a slither through a door at the end of the room. I was the only one there, all other cells empty. No one came when I screamed, no one came when I cried out for help. My hands were bleeding and broken from slamming them against the cold metal bars, from clawing at the dirty stone floor. My throat was rough and sore so that when I tried to scream, nothing came out. The pink dress I wore was so dirty and torn it was nothing but a ghost of what it once was. The smell of piss and burning flesh seared my nostrils and stung my eyes. Even now, in my wakefulness, I can smell it.

A steaming cup of tea has been left on the bedside table and I bring it to my nose in the hope of ridding the smell that clings to my senses. The floral scent washes over me, the dream becoming nothing but a hazy memory. Ella plods around the room, tidying things that don't need tidying. She enters a large room where dresses upon dresses are hanging, more hats and shoes than any one person needs. She emerges with a simple cotton dress, still more remarkable than anything I've ever owned, and hangs it by the dresser. It's pink, much too like the colour of the one in my dream, the neckline rounded with ruffles that hang over the breasts.

"There are no activities planned for the day. You are free to do as you please, but it has been requested that you do not leave the castle without a member of the royal family and a royal guard for the time being. Just a precaution." She bows low. "I have other duties to attend to if you will excuse me, Your Highness, but I will be close by if needed."

"Of course." I smile at her, waving my hand toward the door.

"Oh, I almost forgot. Lieutenant Reynolds asked me to pass this on." She reaches into her pocket and pulls out a bronze key.

I scramble off the bed, getting myself caught up in the blankets, and take it from her. "Thank you, Ella."

Once she has gone and the door is safely shut, I run to the balcony. The key turns easily with a small click and I swing the doors wide. Fee is already waiting on the banister and bursts into the room. I pull him into a hug, his soft feathers caressing my bare arms. I must squeeze a little too tight as he wiggles in my grip.

"Oh, Fee." I feel the cold wet of a tear on my cheek. I had been so caught up in everything happening yesterday, I hadn't realised how much I missed him until he was here in my arms. He must have been going out of his mind with worry.

"I am so sorry." I hold his head between my hands, the end of his curved beak pressed against my nose.

His eyes are glassy like they are on the verge of tears, and it makes me wonder if birds can cry. I tell him everything, every last detail. I'm not sure what he already knows and what he doesn't, so I assume it is nothing. I don't even truly know if he can understand me, but the way he looks at me, the different emotions flashing in his eyes, makes me think he can. I would like to think he can. He has been my biggest comfort these past years.

My best friend and I against it all.

"Maybe it wouldn't be so bad staying here. Just until the prince chooses his bride, then we could go home," I suggest to him. His head tilts sideways, observing me. "You will stay with me, of course, though maybe not in the room." I look around, taking in the surroundings.

The pale green walls, the large bed big enough for four in the centre of the room. The vanity unit is filled with products, a dresser by the even bigger walk-in wardrobe.

No. Nowhere to hide him here.

"But it will be perfect. You will get to be out in the open skies, then you can come back to me here and I can tell you stories of the goings-on in the castle." I feel that pang of excitement again at the thought of staying here a while longer.

Felix lowers his head, his eyes closed, and nudges my leg.

"I know, I will miss you too. But, well, I think I could like it here. I think I could have friends."

He places a clawed foot on my knee, raising his eyes to mine. It feels strange sometimes, the way he looks at me. His eyes seem almost more human than animal. I can see the understanding in his gaze, but also the pain. I don't want to hurt him, but this is the first time in forever I feel like I can be someone other than the girl confined to her tower.

Quicker than words can be spoken, he turns and flies from the room, disappearing into the cloud filled sky.

Once I am dressed, hair brushed and loose down to my ankles, I make my way to the lounge at the end of the hall. The room is quiet, however Catalina, Kiyoko, and Arabella are already seated around the low burning fireplace.

"Morning." Catalina raises her eyebrows at me, her lips pressed together in a smile.

"Good morning." Kiyoko bows her head to me.

Arabella remains silent, watching the fireplace intensely like she desperately wants to douse it with her mind.

I sit beside Catalina on the sofa and the cushion tilts my body closer to her. She scoots in beside me to whisper, though the seats are pushed so closely together, that it is probable the others can still hear her. "Where did you disappear to last night?"

"I just went back to my room. I wasn't feeling well."

"Hmm." She eyes me suspiciously, a small smile that doesn't quite show her teeth.

I feel eyes on me and look up to see Arabella watching us, her face giving nothing away, her eyes hard as stone. Her white-blonde hair is pulled over a pale shoulder and she twiddles with the ends nonchalantly.

There's a taut silence in the room, veering on the edge of being awkward.

These girls are all complete opposites, thrown together by consequence, and they don't know how to talk to each other. They may have grown up in similar backgrounds, in similar situations, but they have nothing in common.

Catalina and Soraya seem to be the only two with anything to talk about, or at least a thread of something to talk about. But I think that is just the way Catalina is; she seems so at ease at talking about anything and everything with anyone who will listen. But even in this room she remains quiet, catching my eye every so often and squeezing her lips together to keep the uncomfortable laughter in.

I think we all see this as a safe space. Somewhere even the guards cannot see us, cannot watch our every move. Briar enters, stilling in the doorway for a moment, her wide eyes flicking to each of us, probably thinking the room was empty for how quiet it is. She flops into the chair beside Arabella and gives her the widest smile.

"Ahoy, M'lady," she says in a mocking tone.

That's Catalina done for; the laughter erupts from her. Arabella fidgets in her seat, not making eye contact with anyone. The corner of her mouth twitches, but she holds back the smile. Soraya bursts into the room, closing the doors behind her, shutting us off from the outside.

"Harper, my handmaiden, is the biggest gossip," she says in greeting.

She squeezes herself beside Catalina on our sofa—even though there's a whole empty one opposite us—kicking off her shoes and fiddling with her dress.

"You can't lead with that then stay silent," Catalina urges her on.

"She's been filling me in on the juicy stuff all morning while she did my hair. It looks rather fetching don't you think," she says while fluffing her tight ringlets with her palm.

"Yes, amazing, it looks beautiful. But...the gossip." Catalina waves her hand, her whole body leaning in. It's a funny sight. A princess so eager for something to grasp on to and fill her nosy little soul. She would spin with excitement with all the things I hear down in the village.

"Right. She had all the usuals, who's doing whom, who's broken whose heart, mostly servant-related stuff. But then she got talking about the prince. There are a lot of rumours floating around about a mysterious figure who sneaks into his room some nights and will stay for hours. Other nights the prince will disappear himself, no trace of him in the castle, but he will be asleep in his bed come morning. Many of them think his heart is already filled with another's love. She was unsure if the king or queen knew, but it is unlikely. They would have put a stop to it by now, and we wouldn't have been needed."

Memories of last night flash through my head. Could this be why the prince is so reluctant to choose a bride? Because he already has his eye on another? He mentioned something about rumours, about how they get you in trouble. Does he know the servants suspect him? I'm sure he doesn't care if they do. They seem unbothered, and none have gone to the king or queen with this information. Or maybe they have, and that is why they are pushing him to choose a princess from another kingdom. Maybe they don't approve of his current attraction. Or the rumours could be baseless, and just that—rumours.

"Who is it?" Arabella is on the edge of her seat, her stare intense and fixed on Soraya.

"They don't know. She said no one has ever seen a face, just glimpses of the figure before the door is closed."

Arabella is the only one visibly bothered by this information, the only one who seems at all interested in marrying the prince. If the rumours are false, or even if they are not, then she may very well get her wish. She sits back in her seat and rolls her eyes as if the gossip is pointless if not every detail is unveiled.

We sit this way for hours, talking and laughing with each other. It feels good to be involved with something like this, the secrets I keep seeming easier to conceal as the time goes on. I don't say much, but it is still more than Arabella who doesn't utter a word. Kiyoko's whole body relaxes after a while, joining in the conversation more, talking about her family and her home, though her hand often rubs nervously across her porcelain skin. She talks about her parents, who died a long time ago. It seems to be a running theme amongst us, having one or no parents. Briar is the only one who still has both, and the real me, of course. But I cannot talk about Raylin here. Here I am Lena, and Lena's parents are dead.

I wish I could be myself with these girls, could make friends, go back home when this is all over, write to them and see them whenever I want. But soon enough I will be back in the tower, and they won't even know who I truly am. Maybe they will meet the real Princess Lena one day and wonder who I was. I will be nothing but a mysterious piece of gossip to them.

Soraya talks about her kingdom some, about the desert sands, the river that stretches on so long it takes multiple weeks to go from one end to the other. She's never done it herself, but she would like to one day. She talks about her twin brother with so much pride. He has become one of their fiercest hunters, something most children are taught from a young age, even herself. It is important to be able to use a blade and a bow in Jalendia, as most of what they eat is foraged or hunted by themselves. They are a small, independent kingdom, relying on no one but themselves and each other.

Catalina talks of her family, her beloved Abuelo who sadly passed away two years ago, her two older brothers and sister, with whom she is incredibly close. She mentions her father but doesn't speak much of him. She tells of the gift of transformation, how only the males in her family receive the gift, of how unfair it is.

The conversation goes on far into the evening, then one by one our numbers decrease, until only Soraya and I are left behind.

"So, who's the handsome guard?" Her thick accent rolls over the words, sounding sultry.

"Who do you mean?" I play dumb, though I know she means Damien.

"The one you snuck off into the gardens with last night, never to return. You forget I am the one who caught him staring, Lena."

I pick at a non-existent thread on the arm of the sofa.

"Just be careful. I hear the queen doesn't take too kindly to the less fortunate mixing with her kind."

"It isn't like that," I tell her, trying to convince myself more than her.

Well, it's not entirely false. I feel something when I am around him. Then again, I'm sure with a face like that, most girls do; his handsomeness could rival the prince himself.

"Well, you know where I am if it is...like that, and you need someone to confide in. I am not as big a gossip as I seem. Some secrets stay secrets." She looks at me, an emotion on her face I cannot quite pinpoint, almost like regret. "But some should not."

I left the balcony doors open. Just in case Felix decided to come back.

There's no sign of him when I enter my room and something twists in my stomach.

He will come back.

He wouldn't leave me completely. Would he?

What if he thinks I've chosen this over him? I wouldn't. I would choose nothing over him. I stand on the balcony, but there's no flash of white or the bright colours of his wings. A night chill wafts through the room, but still I leave the doors open, wanting him to know that I would never shut him out, of this room or my life.

I would give anything for him to be able to talk to me, tell me exactly how he feels. I've learned to read him pretty well over the years, the little actions and ways he has for telling me things, but there are times I want to know exactly what is going through his mind. Does he have rational thoughts? Or does he just think about worms constantly, the odd mouse he catches in the forest? I'm lost in thought—thinking about the time I fed him ice cream and he twitched for two days straight and I worried I had broken him—when Ella enters the room, giving me a start.

"Oh gosh, Princess Lena." She bows. "I am so sorry, I did not realise you were inside your rooms. Please forgive me."

"It is nothing to worry about, I was just thinking of a friend," I reassure her.

She comes closer, picking up a brush on her way, and sits just behind me on the bed, gliding the brush through my long hair.

"Your hair is wonderful. I wish I could grow mine this long."

"Why don't you?"

"It's not permitted for staff of the castle to have hair longer than their elbows. Shorter if you work in the kitchens." Her voice is soft but I can hear the disdain in her words.

"Do you ever think about leaving? Creating a life away from here?"

"Oh." She laughs. "I cannot. The queen owns me, just like many of the girls who work within the castle."

I turn to face her, not hiding the look of disgust on my face. "She owns you?"

"Please, don't think bad of her. She has done us a good deed. Lots of the girls here, myself included, are orphans, raised in the orphanage in the east villages. The queen pays kindly for the children once they are old enough to care for themselves. Not all of course, she would never have enough jobs for them all, but the ones who have proved themselves."

"What of the boys?"

"Those too. But they get taken to camps to train as guards and warriors. The money she pays Madame Lorelai goes towards taking in more orphans, so it all works out."

I cannot believe what I am hearing, children sold to the castle. How can these girls, these boys, think that this life could be better than being taken in by new families, raised in a proper household? The queen has warped their minds and it sickens me.

"There are more than you would think. Orphans, I mean. The sea is not a safe place, it sweeps through houses and destroys families during bad storms. Many fishermen have lost their lives out there. Women who see no other option, with their husbands gone and no money to feed their young, jump from the cliffs and the ocean swallows them whole."

"How old were you when you lost your parents?" I take her hand between mine, her fingers cold and trembling.

"Four. My father died at sea and months later my mother jumped in after him. The orphanage wasn't so bad. I had friends, Madame Lorelai was good to us. I came here at eleven and this is where I have stayed for the last five years, where I will stay until the queen decides otherwise." She smiles brightly.

She doesn't mind it here. It's all she's ever known, I suppose. But that doesn't always stop you from wanting more. I would know.

12

OPEN SKIES

FELIX

Danger.

Squawk.

Fuck.

Raylin.

13

THE EASE OF KNOWING YOU

RAYLIN

The sun blares down on us as we walk along a stone path to the stables.

Ella woke me this morning, beaming from ear to ear. Prince Malakai requested all of the princesses join him on a picnic. Most of my excitement came from the hope of maybe seeing Fee on our expedition. He still had not made an appearance since yesterday morning and it worried me. Our handmaidens dressed us all the same, a beige pair of riding leggings and a different colour blouse for each of us, cropped above our elbows, along with a pair of leather boots. Our hair was secured in a low bun at the nape of our neck, all but for Briar, whose hair was too short to do much with. Hers was instead in two braids, starting at her forehead, pulling all the hair from her face.

I have never ridden a horse before. The others were all so excited to get out of the castle and to be riding; they most likely grew up learning to ride and may have even owned their own horses.

I remember my father's horse, a great ink-black steed with mane and tail so dark it shone blue in certain lights. Father used to try to get me to ride with him, but I barely reached the animal's knees and would refuse. My fear was made much worse the day my brother fell off his horse, breaking his arm in two places. Luckily for him, he possesses the power of healing, so from then it was merely a great talking point for Reed at every gathering. If I could just conquer this fear today, once I am home, I can ride with them to my heart's content.

I just pray to the stars it isn't as difficult as I am expecting.

That fear smacks me in the chest as the four guards guiding us come to a stop in front of the stables.

Malakai and Damien sit upon two horses as big as my father's, both a deep red-brown, but where Damien's has a white tail and mane, Malakai's has black, each the opposite of their own hair. Malakai is dressed in riding gear, a deep green like his usual get-up. Damien wears his guard's uniform, sword at his hip. Six horses are saddled beside them, all in shades of brown with deep umber manes. Four more horses stand readied further back, presumably for the guards.

"Welcome, ladies. Sorry I didn't meet you for the walk down here. I came earlier for a run with Beebo here," Malakai explains, patting the horse lightly on his neck.

"You named your horse *Beebo*?" Soraya stares at him, her thick brows raised.

The prince's smile stretches across his face like he finds this just as amusing as she does. "Well, I did name him when I was four, so you will have to give me some slack. Not as bad as Satsuma,"—he reaches over to Damien's horse—"who I also named when I was four, if you are wondering." His smile never wavers. I can see he enjoys this, and he is like a whole different person today.

Arabella, Kiyoko, Briar, and Catalina are being assisted into their saddles by stable hands. Soraya reaches a long leg into the stirrup and swings herself up onto the horse with ease, and Malakai lets out an appreciative low whistle as he watches her.

I stand by my horse, idly stroking his mane. I turn, looking at our surroundings, for what, I don't know. Somewhere to run off and hide? A white knight to come and throw me up on to the horse?

I'm not even sure I want that. This one is smaller than the prince's but its height still terrifies me. A knight is exactly what I get anyway, or rather, a lieutenant. Damien's beside me in a heartbeat, one knee on the ground, his hands cupped together in front of me.

"Need a hoist up?"

I look around, but no one is paying us any attention. Even if they did, it's just a guard giving a princess a helping hand.

"I don't think I can do this," I whisper, shaking my head.

He looks at the horse then back at me, his eyes growing wide. "Oh. *Oh*. You've never ridden before?"

I shake my head.

"You'll be fine, I promise. Just squeeze your thighs to the saddle, heels down, and keep your reins short. I will stick close by. We won't be moving fast." He pastes an encouraging smile on his face, but it doesn't do much for my nerves.

What if I fall immediately? It will be obvious to the others I've never ridden. I close my eyes tight, placing my foot in Damien's hands. I feel him push up as I do, and I swing my leg up and over, gripping the saddle.

I've done it.

I'm sitting on the horse.

I cannot stop the smile that spreads on my face, and mouth a 'thank you' to him. If only my father could see me now. Damien pops my foot into the stirrup, pointing my toes up before walking back to his horse. I copy the action with my other foot and do as he said, squeezing slightly with my legs, scared to squeeze too hard in case of hurting the horse, or worse, scaring him into running. I let go of the saddle horn with one hand and grip the reins. I can do this. I'm doing this. Now if I just stay here all day I will be fine.

No moving, thank you.

Once we start going, I don't feel too unsteady. I wobble a bit with the first few steps but soon find my centre. We all trot in an unorganised huddle before spreading out more evenly. Damien does as he promised and sticks close by, barely three paces ahead of me. Two guards stay further upfront, the other two sticking to the rear—far enough away they cannot hear conversations but can keep their eyes peeled for any danger.

Catalina and Briar walk ahead with Malakai, presumably telling jokes of some sort if his laughter rippling on the wind is anything to go by. Arabella is close behind them, her head turned to the sky, looking at something I cannot see. I wonder for a moment if it is Fee, but I see no movement above. Soraya walks beside me, but one look at Damien, a teasing smile on her face, and she trots off ahead to walk with Kiyoko.

Damien slows down, falling back into pace with me. He almost doubles my height with his large horse and his tall frame. I am going slower than necessary, but right now I feel this is as fast as I can go. My horse is happy to stick to an un-hasty pace.

We head down a short path, through large gates, the stone walls covered in brambles and bushes, and straight into the forest. I recognise where we are as soon as we enter, having explored the forest hundreds of times the past five years. There is no obvious path this way, but I know further ahead we will cross a run-down, abandoned cabin, empty save for a rocking chair, its purple paint flaking off. That place always gives me the creeps. Even in the daylight it appears dark, the wind whistling through the broken windows like voices calling out to you, luring you in. The last time I ventured this far in, I was sure I saw shadows lurking inside. Waiting. If you avoid the darkness of the cabin and carry on the grass-flattened earth, you will come across the circle bridge.

"How are you finding your stay in Sorrelle, Princess Lena?"

"Wonderful, thank you, Lieutenant Reynolds. The castle is beautiful, from what I have seen of it anyway." I keep my eyes trained ahead as I talk to him, nervous to make any movements in case I fall from this horse.

"You haven't explored yet? It would be a shame to waste your days here held up in your rooms. The king's libraries are some of the best in Aldros, he prides himself on that. I hear you like a good book?"

My eyes flick to him, then to the prince. The only person I mentioned reading to was him, the night he whisked me into a dance at the ball. Does he talk about these things with a guard? Just how close are they?

I do like to read, and I have never been to a library before. If you don't count my stacks and shelves of books back at the tower, most of those being history books, probably not all that exciting. I did read tales of witches, dragons, creatures that would tear you limb from limb and drain your blood if you were so unfortunate to come across one. Gorks, they were called. I was only twelve when I read this particular one and had nightmares for weeks. Most of those I sent back, the initials on the first page, or the looseness of the spine, indicating they already belong to another.

Once, I conjured a book so old I dared not even open it. The pages were a darkened yellow, the leather it was bound in torn and frayed. Hands had touched it so often the words were faded and gone; only a large letter 'A' remained, barely visible on the spine. I'm not entirely sure how I came across it. I usually need some idea of what it is I'm seeking to conjure it, but I was thinking of another book and, for just a split second, I lost my focus. Then there it was, this heavy tome, in my hands. I sent it back without reading it. Something about it just felt...wrong.

"I will be sure to check them out," I tell Damien now.

"Maybe I can join you, show you around." My eyes flick to him but he's staring ahead. His throat bobs as he swallows.

"That would be...nice."

I'm unsure if he means it to be kind, or if all this lingering is just to keep an eye on me. He's the one who brought me here after catching me stealing after all. He probably has his concerns.

We walk past the abandoned cottage, the wind at ease today so no whispers greet us as we pass. Malakai eyes the building every few hoofbeats, and I'm curious now, wanting to know if he has sensed before what I have. The place is eerie and the air around it is colder somehow.

We make it to the bridge in record time and find a quiet spot close by. The four guards stay on their horses, spreading around the perimeter, enclosing us in a wide square. Damien stays with us, helping Malakai to haul off the bags strapped to their horses, laying down blankets, and spreading out the food. I'm surprised by the fact he didn't bring someone along to do it for him. Once done, Damien steps away a few paces but stays close by.

"Please, sit," Malakai says to us all, sitting on a piece of red tartan fabric himself.

We all gather on the blankets, sitting at odd angles and in no real order at all. Soraya pulls me down beside her, right in direct eye line of Damien, which she did on purpose no doubt. She kept throwing glances over her shoulder the whole way here, not so subtly watching us.

Light conversation passes around while we eat, Malakai asking how we like the castle, about our travels here, boring small talk. But he acts intrigued nonetheless. I cannot eat much, a sinking feeling in my stomach returning every time I think about how close we are to my tower. I would only have to walk over the bridge and through a copse of trees, and I would be there. I am in and out of the conversation once eating is done with, half there and half not.

When I hear mention of powers, my focus snaps into place.

"Yes, the power of the flame. Only my sister and brother were lucky enough to inherit it. Three of us not so lucky," Briar says in answer to something Malakai asked.

"What about you, Soraya?" he asks.

"You could say I was lucky, depending on how you look at it. I inherited my family's power, where my twin brother did not. But...I envy him sometimes. At times my power feels more like a curse than a gift. You try having the dead constantly in your ear; the screams are deafening."

"I can only begin to imagine."

"It's not always bad." She smiles. "I've helped many pass on. And the secrets...wow. The secrets, they can be...eye-opening." She laughs.

"Kiyoko, all your family have inherited the power of the bloom, right?"

“Yes, Your Highness.” Kiyoko bows her head, whisps of black hair falling from where it is tied.

“Please, call me Malakai. All of you. No need to be so formal here. Catalina, I’m sorry, I forget, what is your family’s gift?”

A chill trickles through me. He’s asking everyone. *Shit.* What was Mirdoff’s power? I rack my brain, thinking back to the history books, but nothing comes to me.

“Transformation. Into a jaguar, to be exact. Only the men in my family gain the gift. Sexist if you ask me.” She smiles, throwing a grape into the air and catching it in her mouth.

Please don’t ask me, please. Only five more kingdoms, not including Sorrelle, think, think.

Gavaria, my kingdom, I know has the power of healing. Faldova, ice. Quendore, their people are born winged. Genevieve’s kingdom, Kignet, can borrow the powers of others. But, Mirdoff, what is the last power?

“Arabella, I’m sure we all know yours, the Kingdom of Ice and Snow,” Malakai smiles.

“Then at least let me demonstrate.”

She picks up a half-empty bottle of red wine, holding it from the base in her palm. Eyes focused, her fingers turn a shade of blue as ice snakes up the bottle, the glass clinking and cracking. No one takes their eyes off it. Once the ice reaches the lip of the bottle, it makes a loud popping noise, before falling to the floor in chunks. Arabella looks up, a huge smile on her face.

“Well, there was no need to waste perfectly good wine, but...impressive. I love it,” Malakai tells her, his smile no smaller. “And yours, of course, Lena, is one reason my father has never invited your family to Sorrelle. The power to walk through solid objects.

I'm sure he thinks you will sneak in and steal all his heirlooms, but you yourself don't have the power, right?"

"Yes!" I say a little too enthusiastically now, remembering the power. Intangibility. Of course. I have many times wished I could develop the power. "I mean, yes, that's our power. But no, I did not inherit it."

I catch Damien wince slightly.

"And you, Malakai?" Briar asks.

"My father and I, we can ease the emotions of others with just a touch. It is not something we do often. We don't like to mess with things like that. But to know we can help in someone's time of need, it's comforting actually."

Talk soon subsides, the afternoon ticking by in what felt like minutes. Kiyoko shows off her powers by making hundreds of tiny pink and white flowers spring up around us. They sprout up from the ground from nothing, the petals opening delicately like butterfly wings. Malakai and Catalina begin to throw grapes at each other, trying to catch them in their mouths, cheering loudly every time they succeed.

Kiyoko and Briar lay in the grass, pointing out obscurely shaped clouds. I keep my eyes peeled for Fee. Still nothing. When the knot in my stomach doesn't diminish, I excuse myself and walk to the water's edge, a spot I have dipped my feet in many times before. I sit there, dipping my fingers into the water, when I feel someone sit beside me, and I assume Soraya has followed me over.

But it isn't Soraya.

Arabella's white-blonde hair has been removed from its bun and is now pulled over one shoulder. She takes her shoes off, carefully placing them next to her, and lowers her feet into the water.

"I've been watching you."

"That's not creepy at all, Arabella." I turn to face her.

"What is going on with you and the guard?" she says in a hushed tone.

"Not that it is any of your business, but nothing."

"Don't give me that." She rolls her eyes. "He hasn't stopped watching you all day, and I saw you leave with him the other night at the ball. I wouldn't say that's nothing."

She ignores the part about it being none of her business.

"Look, you're right, it isn't any of my business, and frankly I do not care. But the queen would. I have heard...things about her. What she does if someone goes where they shouldn't. I know we don't know each other, and I know you all think I'm not a very nice person, but I wouldn't want to see someone hurt over something as foolish as dallying with a royal guard."

"Well, thank you for your concern," I snip, "but I can handle myself just fine."

"Very well," she says as she stands, her face blank as usual.

"That's not true, you know. That I think you're not a nice person. I don't even know you."

Something flicks across her face, too fast for me to read. "If you play with fire, it is likely you will get burned."

14

RUNAWAY

RAYLIN

The sun is beginning to set when we climb back on our horses and head toward the castle. I find it easier on the journey back, my body easing into the comfort of being upon a horse. I stick to my slow pace but don't fear moving in the saddle.

Once back at the castle, most of the others have already headed back to our quarters. Prince Malakai has been called away on royal duties of some sort. Soraya leans back against a stable post, her mouth raised on one side as Damien and I arrive. We didn't utter a word to each other the whole way back, but he stayed close regardless, not breaking his promise from this morning.

"If you don't have someplace to be, I think I will take you up on that offer of seeing the libraries now," I say to Damien once our feet are on solid ground.

"Of course. Princess Soraya, would you care to join us?"

"I would love to," she chortles, sliding her arm through mine.

We follow Damien through the castle. It is only a short walk before we stand at a set of doors, floor to ceiling, made of solid oak. The gold carvings stand out against the dark wood. Two guards are posted there, one on either side. Damien gives a small nod to the chubby guard with a long black beard, then he pulls a crank, and a click echoes through the hall as the doors open gently, revealing a large room beyond.

I stifle a gasp. I have never seen anything like it.

Marble floors stretch out in the distance, tall archways lead into room upon room full of books. The ceiling curves up and over, little cherubs dance in an orange sky, round chandeliers hang low, casting the room in a warm glow. A spiral staircase sits at the far end, leading to another floor. More books than any one person could ever imagine line each wall, leaving no spot uncovered. Soraya's eyes are as wide as mine as we look around.

"This is the largest in the castle. There are two smaller libraries, more reading rooms really," Damien says from behind us.

"We have a library back home, but...nowhere near this magnificent," Soraya tells us.

I glide my fingers along a shelf, feeling each spine. One shelf is filled with books all bound in red leather, no names, just what I assume are numbers, but they look more like little lines, growing larger and changing shapes as the row goes on.

As I continue into the room, a bright blue spine catches my eye. I take it from the shelf and it creaks as I open it, the pages still crisp, like it has never been opened before let alone read. *The Adventures of Greta and Rinks.*

"You can take it to read if you like," Damien says over my shoulder. "The king would never notice such a book missing. I cannot even remember the last time he stepped into these rooms. He's not much one for reading."

I raise my eyebrows at him. "He does not read, yet he has one of the most beautiful libraries in all of Aldros?"

He huffs a laugh. "The king is a simple man. He cares about being the best, about winning, nothing else."

I place the book back in its place and carry on down the shelves. Soraya is nowhere to be seen, lost within the books herself. Damien grips my elbow, forcing us to stop.

"Do you feel that?" His voice is urgent, confused.

I shake my head, not feeling anything.

"It's like a hum, it feels...powerful." His head swings around, looking for the source.

The darkness within me reaches out, rushing to the surface with its icy claws. Is it me? Is it the power inside me he senses? I rip my arm from his grip.

"I don't feel anything," I tell him, stepping away.

My heart hammers in my chest as I scan the shelves, trying to act like nothing is amiss. I pick a book at random, not even looking at the name.

"I'm tired," I announce. "Will you tell Soraya I am heading back to my room?"

As I turn to rush from the room, Damien's fingers graze along my wrist as if they will clutch onto me, but they do not find their grasp. "Ray, wait. What is going on?"

"Don't call me that here," I snap, a bit too much venom in my tone. "I'm just tired. I will see you tomorrow."

Back in my room, I slam the door closed behind me, startling when I see Ella sitting on the end of my bed. She jumps up, curtsying low.

"Are you okay?" She looks down at my arms, eyes lingering there.

I realise I am clutching the book tight against my chest, my knuckles white. I feel the power inside me whirring. I haven't used it much the last few days and it is eager to get out. It must have been me Damien felt in the library, there's no other reasoning.

"I'm fine," I tell her, slamming the book down on the vanity unit. I walk towards the balcony doors and swing them open. "I would like these left open."

"Of course, Princess Lena, anything. It's just...it is meant to be cold tonight. Storms are brewing, and the air can get below freezing here by the sea."

"I like the cold."

"Of course." She bows her head and my heart squeezes.

"I'm sorry. I shouldn't talk to you that way. You are only trying to help."

She keeps quiet, her head lowered. I take a deep breath, my eyes scanning the sky. Where are you, Fee?

I spend the night pacing my room.

I released Ella of her duties hours before, telling her I was unwell and going to rest for the remainder of the day. My thoughts are all muddled; I cannot quiet them long enough to think things through.

If Damien grows suspicious of me, figures out I have powers, he could turn me into the king and queen. They could have my head for fooling them, for infiltrating the castle. These feelings I get when I am around him are...confusing. Looking into his eyes is like finding someone I thought I had lost. He is always there, by my side, like he is drawn to me as I am to him. But does he even feel that way or is it his moral compass simply telling him he should watch me, keep himself not far from me?

And Soraya, she has been so kind, pulled me into a friendship I could only dream of before. I feel deep down we could truly be friends. But once she learns I lied, will she even want to know me? Will any of them want to know me?

I'm not even sure if Fee wants to know me any longer. He has never been away so long. I only hope he is angry and not hurt. Angry I can handle.

It is past midnight when I decide to leave.

For myself. For the good of everyone. It will only hurt them more if I stay, the lie only setting deeper. This way it is a clean cut. I will leave while everyone is sleeping, go back to the tower, and stay there as long as needed. Wait it out. Not even Damien will find me there, hidden within magic.

I will simply vanish.

Part of me wishes I could climb aboard a boat and head back home to Gavaria, but what would my family say then? Would they too be mad at me? They have kept me safe all these years, am I truly willing to throw all that away for a silly mistake? That's all this is. A mistake. I should never have come here. Should never have left the tower to begin with.

I stand at the door, listening intently for any sound or movement on the other side. When I am almost certain no guards stand beyond, I crack open the door, just enough to see the dimly lit hall. Two voices drift down from the entrance to our quarters, far enough away that I cannot make out what they are saying. I slip off my shoes and tread on silent feet into the hall, pulling the door closed behind me with a *click*. Hurrying to the servants' door that Damien brought me to just days before, I creep through and it whines loudly as I close it. I freeze, closing my eyes, my hand still gripping the handle. No one comes.

I hurry down the hall, not entirely sure where I'm going. It's dark, only a faint orange glow from the other end. I make it into a large, empty room, recognising it as the one we came through the first day.

Then I am outside, standing with my back against a cold stone wall. Goosebumps spread across my skin. I should have put on a cloak. Just as Ella had warned, the night air is freezing. I feel like I've been dunked into frigid waters. Drops of rain fall sporadically, a low rumble of thunder in the distance.

The only high point in these conditions means very few guards man the castle grounds, and most are inside now. I see none on the path into the forest, so I duck and run, not brave enough to look around. Knowing the gate will be locked, and possibly watched, I go further down and use branches and brambles to heave myself over the wall, trying not to think too much about the thorns and sharp edges digging into my skin, knowing they will heal themselves in a matter of moments.

The wall is a hell of a lot taller than a horse. I brace myself as I drop down the other side, my knees screaming in pain as I slam to the floor.

Ouch.

Then I'm running...

Running.

Running.

By the time I make it to the tower clearing, the rain is falling harder. The thunder roars in my ears like a warning. Flashes of light cut through the sky like a blade into flesh. I am contemplating how I'm going to get into the tower when the rope drops from the window.

Felix! He's here.

I run harder, the cold air stealing my breath. The familiar bite of the rope tugs against my palms as I climb, faster than I've ever climbed before, the thought of seeing Fee willing me on. When I stumble through the window, I cry out, "Fee, I'm so—"

My heart stops.

Felix flaps in his cage, wings smashing into the bars, his squawks swallowed by a clap of thunder.

He didn't leave me. He's been trapped here this whole time.

"Where have you been?" Genevieve stands before me, her eyes narrow, lips drawn together in a tight line.

"I—" I am lost for words.

She grabs me by the hair, forcing me to my knees. The sky tears open and a bright light flashes through the darkened room, lighting up Genevieve's anger-ridden face, then gone again.

"I'm not asking again, girl." Her words are a snarl in my ear.

"I am sorry, Auntie..."

Then I tell her everything. I have no choice. Either way, my punishment will be dire. I tell her of the first time I left the tower five years ago, and of the many times after that. I tell her of the market, the things I steal there. Of being caught, of feeling like I had no choice but to go. Though I leave out the part of me wanting to. I tell her of Damien, of Malakai, the princess. All of it.

She releases me and I fall to my hands, my face wet with tears, my body dripping with rain.

"You've been escaping for five years?" She walks from one side of the room and back again.

"Y– yes."

"And these people you speak of, they believed you were truly the princess from Mirdoff?"

"I'm certain."

She taps her long black nails against my dresser, her features lost in thought. "You will go back."

"What?" I whisper. Disbelief rushes through me. She wants me to go back to the castle?

"The queen has something of mine, of my family's. It was taken from us a long time ago. You will make them trust you, and you will take it back. Understand?"

I nod. "What is it?"

"An obsidian pendant, the shape of a teardrop."

"What does it do?"

"That only matters if you get it." She takes my hand, pulling me to my feet. "Raylin, if you do this, you can go home. You can be with your family again."

I cannot stop the gasp that escapes me. "How will you know when it is done?"

"Come back here. You will be safe here until I return."

I thought she would be mad, that I would be punished. Instead, I have found a way out.

A way *home*.

"And Felix?" I ask, looking to where he sits, motionless now, watching us.

"He will stay with me for the time being. He will draw too much attention. Just until it is done, then you can take him with you."

"I will do it."

"I know."

She places a hand on my cheek and the bitter cold of my powers rushing to the surface shocks me, my body draining faster than usual, my power eager for release.

I stagger in place, my eyelids closing, then the black nothingness embraces me.

15

I HAVE A DREAM

RAYLIN

I wake to rays of sunlight warming my skin. I am sprawled out on top of the blankets of a large bed. The memories of the night before come rushing back and I shoot up, stick straight, looking around the room. How did I get here?

"Oh good, you're awake," Ella says as she emerges from the bathing chamber.

My head spins, squinting against the bright light.

"I have run you a bath, I thought you might need it." Her eyes dart to my legs before again resting on my face.

I look down and see they are covered in mud splatter, my dress too. Which has also dried stiff against my skin.

"Right," I say, feeling my matted hair.

Genevieve must have brought me here, but how did she get us in? And how did she know where to take me?

I shuffle off the bed and follow Ella to the bath. The water is deliciously warm, the room filled with the scent of strawberries.

"Should I even ask how this happened, Your Highness?"

"I think it's best if you don't."

She scrubs me clean and brushes the knots from my hair. Once dried, she helps me step into a violet dress, cut to the knees.

I spend the whole time thinking about the obsidian pendant. Stealing it won't be a problem. At least I don't think it will, in that I have experience. Finding it will be the hard part. The castle is swarmed with guards, so I can't just go snooping around searching for something that belongs to the queen. And I definitely can't go around asking about it. That's if she even still has it. Genevieve said it was a long time ago; what if she has lost it or given it away? That does not seem likely, but I have to consider all scenarios. Maybe Malakai would have seen it before; I could get closer to him, try to gain information. The most likely place would be with her other jewels, I suppose. So I should find out where she keeps them. Try to gain access somehow. I need a plan.

A knock sounds at the door, breaking me from my thoughts.

"Leave us," Damien's deep voice sounds through the room. I turn just in time to see Ella depart through the doorway.

"What do you think you're—"

"Where were you last night?" He stands by the door, a blank stare on his face.

"I was here," I lie, gesturing to the bed.

"No, you weren't. Ella told me you felt unwell, but when I got off duty I came by to check on you, Ray. You were not here." He steps toward me.

My heart beats so loudly, I fear that he can hear it. "I went for a walk, I needed air."

"You went for a walk in a storm?"

He strides closer, not stopping until he is in front of me. I stay seated on the bed, lifting my head to gaze up at him, staring into those cobalt eyes.

"Mhmm," is all I can manage.

"And if I ask the guards who were on duty, they will confirm?"

"No. They didn't see me."

"So you snuck past the guards?"

"There was no sneaking. I didn't want company, so I went through the servant's passage."

"Right." He narrows his eyes at me, then bends down so we are face to face, his hands on either side of me, resting against the bed. He's so close our breath entangles; he smells like apples and sunshine. We stay that way for what feels like hours, but it is merely minutes. Our eyes searching each other, our chests rising and falling to the same beat.

"Prince Malakai has requested your presence in his chambers," he says as he straightens, breaking our staring competition.

"Whatever for?"

"You will have to ask him that. I was only told to retrieve you."

A young boy, around the age of thirteen, with a head shaved to stubble, opens the chamber door when Damien knocks.

"Princess Lena, for His Highness," Damien tells him.

"Ah, Princess," Malakai says from behind the boy, pulling the door wide. "Please, come in, take a seat."

The room is enormous, triple the size of mine. Curtains sit open to a room of a higher level, a bed as long as the wall inside. A desk scattered in writing materials and books sits by a large window, looking out onto the courtyard, the market in full swing below. Toward the other side of the room, an unlit fireplace stands before a gathering of chairs, cushions large enough to take up the whole seat. I sit in the darkest green chair, placing the cushion onto my lap, a shield of sorts.

"Send for some tea, will you, Arnold," the prince tells the shaved-headed boy.

He closes the door, leaving Damien outside, then joins me, sitting in a chair closest to me and throwing his cushion to another.

"You do not need to look so nervous, you know. I don't bite." He winks. "I feel like I haven't gotten to know you very well. The others are...more outspoken."

"There is not much to know."

"Ah, I do not believe that for a second. I can see it in your eyes, the secrets they hold." His smile widens.

The door opening saves me. A boy walks in and sets a tray down in front of us, a pot of steaming tea and two fine china cups resting upon it. The boy's copper-brown hair falls into his eyes as he bows to us. He looks to be about the same age as me, slim, wearing a loose brown tunic and trousers. As he raises his head, he catches Malakai's eye and they both still for a moment. Malakai quickly averts his gaze with a wavering 'thank you'. Then the boy leaves the room on hurried feet.

"What was that?" I stare at him, wide-eyed.

"It's tea, Lena," his words come out strained. He clears his throat.

"No, not that, *that*..." I say, gesturing between him and where the boy was standing just seconds ago.

"I do not know what you mean. He is just a servant from the kitchens."

"I do not believe that for a second," I copy his words from before, raising an eyebrow at him.

He pours the tea and hands me a cup; the smell of Jasmine and Patchouli fills my nose. He doesn't answer, just stares toward the window and sips from his cup.

"Have you ever played cards?"

I shake my head as he pulls a pack from the table drawer.

We stay that way for a while, he teaches me a simple game, simplifying it further for my sake. It still manages to confuse me, and Malakai wins time and time again.

As we play, he talks about growing up in the castle, how he trained for a year with soldiers in the barracks, though it was pointless, as even if war came, his father would never allow him to fight. '*It is not as a prince does,*' he mimics him. He tells me of his lonely childhood, how he spent his days playing alone, his mother never having wanted one child, let alone two.

"It was forced upon her like she's forcing it upon me. What honour is it to become king if you cannot live a life of your choosing?" he says angrily, shaking his head.

I add in when I can; things that wouldn't matter no matter what kingdom I came from. I tell him of my best friend, leaving out the part about him being a bird. I tell him of a childhood of loneliness—much like his own—making him believe it was from losing my parents, not because I was isolated in a tower, inside his own kingdom for that matter.

I picture his face if I was to tell him right now that for the last fourteen years Princess Raylin of Gavaria has been trapped inside Sorrelle, wandering just mere feet from his bedroom window for five of those years. The thought makes me smile.

"What is it?" He smiles back, running a hand through his dishevelled white-blonde hair.

"Oh, nothing. Just...funny how two people can grow up so close by, but not have ever met."

"I would not say Mirdoff is close, but I understand your meaning." He breathes out a laugh. "I want it to be different. When I am king, it will be different."

"How do you mean?"

"There are ten kingdoms inside of Aldros, seven of us here right now, all around the same age, yet none of us have ever met before this week. I'm sure all our families have only met a handful of times, which seems odd to me."

"I suppose so..."

"I say we all make a pact, here in Sorrelle, not to let our futures be spent sitting in the same kingdom, day after day. I want to see all of your kingdoms, meet all of your families, and of those not here today. I do not want to live as my father has lived."

"I agree." I lift my cup in the air, to toast his own. "To the future. May the days be bright and many," I copy the line from an old book I once read, but it has the desired effect.

When this is all over, when I hand the pendant to Genevieve and I am free to go home, I will tell him, tell him everything. I just hope he can forgive me for my deception.

The corridors have darkened as I make my way back to my room with a promise from Malakai that he will take all the princesses on a tour of the castle tomorrow. My plan to find the obsidian pendant may be a slow one, but it's the best I've got. I cannot go sneaking around the castle trying to find it by myself; not that

I'm ever by myself. A pudgy guard walks close behind me now, following my trail since I left Prince Malakai's chambers.

"Where is Lieutenant Reynolds?" I ask him.

"On an errand from the king, Your Highness."

Helpful.

Ella's voice finds me before I am even fully through the door to my room. "I am sorry, Princess Lena. They wouldn't leave."

Soraya and Catalina jump off my head, bounding toward me.

"You've been alone with him all day," Catalina states. It is not a question.

"What happened?" Soraya asks, her face lit up.

I smile at them, my heart exploding. I have never had this, never had friends, people to get excited with. As much as I love Fee, it is not the same.

"Ella, would you mind fetching us some food, please." I take hold of Soraya's and Catalina's hands, dragging them to sit with me on the bed.

They squeal and tease as I tell them everything, keeping the awkward encounter with the copper-haired boy to myself. Their eyes light up when I tell them what he said about all of the kingdoms uniting. Catalina coos about how beautiful Prince Malakai's and my children would be.

"But it is not the *prince* she wants, is it?" Soraya knocks Catalina with an elbow.

"*Oh, Lieutenant Reynolds, ravish me.*" Catalina throws herself at me, and we fall back on the bed in fits of giggles.

Ella returns with another servant in tow, both carrying a tray of food. Thick slices of honeyed ham, chunks of potatoes—so crisp they crunch when we bite into them—and mounds of vegetables. The three of us gobble it down in silence, savouring every taste.

Once the trays are cleared, we lay on the bed, our faces to the ceiling. The sky turns a fathomless blue outside the window.

"What's your favourite thing about home?" Soraya asks.

"The boys." Catalina wiggles her brows.

"You're shameful," Soraya jokes, nudging her playfully.

"The smell," I say closing my eyes. "The scent of my mother's perfume as she kisses me goodnight. I can still smell it, if I close my eyes and wish hard enough."

I cannot wait to smell it again for real.

Soraya's fingers lace through mine, holding me gently. My ribs tighten at the gesture; it feels wrong to let her think I'm talking of a mother long-since gone from this world, not one I will see again shortly.

Catalina plays with the small charm dangling from her necklace. "The long walks on the beach at night," she answers seriously this time. "The stars twinkling in the sky, my brothers and sister by my side. Nothing but us against it all."

"The community. My kingdom may be small, but we are mighty. We are a family, each and every one of us," Soraya says proudly.

We stay there, in comfortable silence, soaking in each other's warmth. I close my eyes, and I am certain I can smell the vanilla of my mother's perfume.

16

TO NO AVAIL

RAYLIN

We wake together on my bed, draped in blankets placed there by Ella no doubt. She must have found us here, fallen asleep in our bubble of comfort. Truth be told, it was the best night's sleep I have ever had.

Soraya and Catalina leave with their handmaidens. Ella helps me dress for the grand tour of the castle that awaits. She braids my hair down my back, weaving delicate blue flowers throughout. I wear loose-fitting silk trousers and a blue blouse to match the flowers. I contemplate cutting my hair daily, getting rid of the heavy locks, but I know I will miss it; it is like an extra limb.

I meet the others in the corridor, and a guard leads the six of us down the hall and through another. Soraya quickly steps to me and loops her arm through mine. I do the same to Catalina as we reach her. Kiyoko and Briar walk side by side ahead of us, exchanging quiet words. Arabella walks alone at the front of the group. We are guided down into the main entrance hall, where Malakai and Damien already stand waiting.

"Good morning, ladies," Malakai greets us all.

Damien bows beside him, catching my eye on his way back up. Catalina doesn't miss the exchange, her arm squeezing tight against mine as she holds in a smile.

"I thought we could start at the beginning." Malakai gestures to the large doors behind him. "We'll make our way around the palace, stopping for lunch on the way."

"Sounds amazing," Briar tells him, pushing her fire-bright orange hair behind her ear.

We walk through room after room, nothing really of interest to me. There's only one place I want to see; the queen's jewels, wherever they may be.

We are in a dark room, larger than any before it. Podiums are positioned throughout, displaying various items. Heads of deer and bears are stuffed and hung on the walls. Fish mounted to plaques, little gold nameplates beneath them.

"...heirlooms collected and passed down through my family." I only catch the last part of what Malakai says.

Could it be here? The pendant, hiding in plain sight?

We make our way around the room, my arm still looped with Soraya's, Catalina now captivated by a golden glove. I check every podium, leaving no stone unturned. We admire a dagger, the hilt covered in coloured gemstones, the blade made from a blackened glass.

"Beautiful, isn't it?" Malakai says from beside me. "It was the first blade ever made for the first King of Sorrelle."

Soraya drags me to the next podium. "What is this?"

My heart beats faster when I see a delicate chain hanging in a display case. But it is not what I seek. The pendant is round, a deep crimson.

"It was my aunt's, my father's sister. It is said to be made with bloodstone and quite powerful indeed, once upon a time. It was damaged long ago, rendering it a useless necklace."

I see my in and I take it. "Your mother doesn't keep it with her other jewels?"

"No, after my aunt died my father wanted it kept on display in memory of her. Besides, my mother has enough jewels, too many."

"Will we see them today?" I push.

"Not possible. My mother keeps all her jewels locked in her vaults. Even my father is forbidden to enter. Probably in fear of him seeing how much coin she truly spends on them."

"Oh, that's a shame, it would have been nice to see her collection."

"Yes, I am always partial to viewing jewels." Soraya laughs.

A couple of the other girls have gathered around and are agreeing with us. I feel Damien watching me intently, his gaze full of questions.

"Well...I suppose I could ask her to give you a tour herself? But I wouldn't hold out too much hope."

The subject is dropped as we carry on our tour. I pay less attention now I know that the pendant is unlikely to be anywhere we go. We eat a lunch of warm rolls and beef stew packed with vegetables. I catch Damien's eye from across the room, his back against the wall. Caught in his stare, I completely miss my mouth with the spoon, dribbling hot liquid down my chin. I quickly grab my napkin, but it is obvious he sees the mishap as a laugh bounces from him, a cough soon following to cover it up. He recovers quickly as heads turn to him, standing stock still like nothing ever happened. I feel the warmth in my cheeks as they redden, and the corner of his mouth flicks up when his eyes find me again. I avert my gaze, looking down the table, catching Malakai also watching me, his mouth in a small smile. Briar soon catches his attention, and he tears his eyes from me.

When lunch is over, we walk about a room full of portraits of prior kings. I can see Malakai's hair in them, his chiselled jaw and emerald eyes, though his are a more intense green than any in the paintings. But that's where the similarities end.

A guard rushes into the room, causing the wooden door to bang against the wall. He whispers something to Malakai, and the smile is wiped from his face, replaced by something close to shock.

"Ladies, my apologies, but I am needed elsewhere." He goes to turn, but swings back around, unsure of himself. "Lieutenant Reynolds, I need you with me. Cadet Michaels, will you escort the princesses back to their rooms."

And with that, they are gone, rushing down the hall, Malakai's words to Damien hushed as they go.

"Excuse me, Cadet Michaels, was it? It would be a shame to waste the rest of this warm day. Do you mind showing us to the gardens?" Soraya may seem like she is asking, but there is an authority in her voice.

"Of course, Your Highness," the cadet says, bowing low.

It is only a short walk when we come to a set of double doors. Cadet Michaels and another guard follow us out, keeping their distance but not leaving us. We walk up the path and arrive at the small clearing Damien took me to on the first night here. This time we veer right, heading down a different path. We come into an open area, freshly cut grass extending out beyond and a narrow gravel path separating the two sides.

Statues stand to attention every hundred feet; much like the one in the fountain in the courtyard, these are made from a white stone, polished clean. The first one we pass is a small child carrying a basket of flowers in her hand, her leg kicked out in a flick behind her. The next is a woman, her toes in points and her arms stretched above her in a dance.

There are many, children and adults alike, all doing mundane tasks, frozen in time. A young girl sits, her legs tucked beneath her, a book in her hands, her face pointed to the sky, distracted by something.

"They are kind of eerie, don't you think?" Arabella's voice gives me a start. We had all been silent, too fixated on the statues.

"They so real." Kiyoko pokes the young reading girl in the face.

"Don't touch them, they might come to life and get you." Briar grabs Kiyoko, putting a raspiness into her voice, like a child imitating a ghoul.

"Ugh, don't, you're freaking me out." Catalina shudders.

Soraya shrugs. "I kind of like them."

"Of course you do." Catalina laughs.

"What's that supposed to mean?" Soraya lifts her hand to her chest, a fake look of offense on her face.

"I have to agree with the others; it's like their eyes are following me." I laugh, moving side to side.

"Your Highnesses, if it is okay, the sun is starting to set, I should get you back to your rooms. The prince would hate for you all to be out in the cold and dark."

"Think they are creeping him out too," Catalina mutters.

None of us protest, pleased to be escorted away from the statues.

The halls seem too quiet as we walk down them, no servants rush in and out of rooms, minimal guards stand around.

"Where is everyone?" Soraya asks, but the guards escorting us remain silent.

Something seems off. A blanket has fallen over the castle, muffling any sound. We walk past a small room, its door open to shelves of small glass bottles, the smell of herbs wafting out around us. A woman is rummaging around in a trunk, her thinning grey hair hanging over her face, her bony, wrinkled hands pulling out bottles of liquids in various shades. Her head lifts as she hears us pass; her eyes are sunken, dark circles lining them. She sneers and slams the door closed, causing glass bottles to clink together.

"What was that place?" I whisper to Soraya.

"A healer's station, at a guess."

The old woman's frantic rummaging concerns me. Is someone hurt? I could heal them quicker than her medicines, though revealing myself would come at a cost I'm not sure I'm willing to pay. But if they are seriously injured...

We get to our rooms and I step inside. Ella is already there, which is not unusual. What is unusual is her puffy, red-rimmed eyes.

I rush to her. "What's the matter?"

"It's the king, they are worried he won't make it through the night," she chokes out.

Oh no, that must be what had Malakai rushing off just hours before, what the healer was so caught up in doing. "What's wrong with him?"

"They're not sure. He was fine this morning. Then come lunch, he collapsed, and he hasn't woken since."

I am at a loss for words. King Rorik could die. My chest is tight. I squeeze Ella's hand and sit silently with her while she sobs. I'm unsure if her strong feelings are for the king himself, or on behalf of the queen, who she undoubtedly looks up to.

After Ella calms and leaves, I slink out onto the balcony, wrapped in my blue cloak. Few stars twinkle in the sky, the full moon casts silver light over the gardens below. I see a figure emerge onto the path, his white hair giving him away as the prince. He rubs at his eyes. I watch as his chest rises and falls in a heavy sigh. I am about to shout down to him, asking if he wants company, when the copper-haired servant comes up behind him, taking him by the arm and pulling him deeper into the garden, away from sight of the doors. Malakai sobs into his shoulder and I kneel to get a better look. The boy has Malakai's face in his hands and is saying something to him, but his voice is hushed, and I am too far away to hear. Malakai pulls the boy closer, their mouths mere breaths apart. They close that gap, falling into each other.

I gasp, my hand flying to cover my mouth.

"What are you doing?" The voice comes from behind me, shocking every nerve ending in my body.

"Oh my stars," I whisper-shout, swinging around. "You scared me."

"What are you looking at?" Damien cranes his neck, looking over my shoulder.

"Nothing, I– I thought I saw something. It was nothing."

"Why are you always acting so...peculiar?"

"Peculiar?" I raise my eyebrows.

"Yes, you are up to something. Like this morning, what was that? Why were you so curious about Queen Lucia's jewels?"

My breathing turns shallow, fist clenching at my side. "I like pretty things, that is all."

"I swear, Ray, that better be it. I cannot have you trying to steal the queen's jewels. She will have both our heads." He walks into my room and I follow.

"I am not a thief," I lie.

"You could have fooled me. You forget why you're here."

"That was one time." I mock a look of affront.

His laugh shatters my demeanour. "It was not one time." He steps closer to me. "Do you think I didn't see you? All those days in the market, slipping things into your pockets."

"What?" I step back, but he steps closer still.

"I saw you, Ray. Your quick little hands, your sly distraction techniques. The one thing you would only ever pay for was your food. I could never figure out why though. If you had coin for the food, then you had coin for the goods. So why steal them?"

"I don't know what you're talking about."

"Yes, you do."

He's so close now, our lips inches apart. My chest grazes him on every intake of breath. His cobalt blue eyes are staring into my silver-grey ones, taking in every blink, every flicker. This close I can make out a thin scar that runs across his full bottom lip. Before I realise what I am doing, I guide my thumb across it with trembling hands.

There is a sharp intake of breath, whether from him or me I am unsure. Then I'm off the ground, the muscles in his arms tense as he holds me close. My legs wrap around his waist, his fingers dig hungrily into my thighs as he grips me, pushing me back against the wall. Our eyes do not leave each other, we are glued there, staring into the endless depths as our breaths entwine. The butterflies in my stomach are somersaulting, doing tricks they have never done before, the anticipation driving them insane.

"Kiss me," I whisper.

Something like relief washes through me. I know now how much I truly want this. To be kissed, but most importantly, to be kissed by him.

He says nothing. His head tilts slightly, his lips brush against mine, slowly, softly.

I'm unsure of what to do, I have never done this before, so he silently teaches me. His kisses are gentle, patient.

It is my hunger that calls out for more.

I pull his bottom lip between my teeth, coaxing a groan from him. He closes his eyes, his body pushing hard against mine. I run my hands up his neck, into his dark hair. His kisses become demanding, his tongue roaming my mouth, caressing mine. I am thankful he is holding me because my legs are jelly, threatening to give way at any moment.

He pulls away, just slightly, his eyes searching my face before his lips crash into mine once more.

There is nothing.

Only him. Only this moment.

I fall into him, into the endlessness before me. The ice of my power surges, rushing like a tidal wave toward the bank.

I am nothing.

The entire world implodes. A catastrophic event.

Our lips part, I am pulled back into reality, my power laps at the surface of my skin, begging for more. We stay wrapped around one another, his hand cupping my face, his thumb rubbing against what is now, I imagine, my pink stained cheek.

"You are...magnificent." He smiles. "I have to go," he adds. "I do not want to, believe me." His eyes flick to my swollen lips. "The prince needs me."

I remember then, King Rorik. I nod, not certain I can even speak. I also remember Prince Malakai, out there in the gardens with the copper-haired boy. I don't think he needs Damien at all. Damien's lips find mine, one last time, a soft goodbye, then he is gone.

I flop onto the bed, my skin molten lava, my insides burning ice, a never-ending smile on my face. The memory of his lips on mine. My head feels light, the room around me out of focus.

There I fall asleep, still cocooned in that kiss.

17

ONE REGRET

MALAKAI

Teddy's mouth is warm on Malakai's. His lips soft. He loses himself in that sensation for a moment, letting it loosen the knot in his stomach, melting away the grief and worry that binds it. He lets the grip of Teddy's slender fingers against his arms ease the tension building inside his head. He lets the panic settling in diminish with the scent of fresh-baked bread and seasonings that cling to Teddy's clothes. He gives himself over to it all, succumbs to the boy before him, letting him take that burden for just a few moments. The reprieve makes his body sag, the fog clearing from his mind.

It's not just the worry for his father that claws its way through every thought, every breath. It's what's to come if something should happen to his father. The position Malakai will have to take. The duties he will have to uphold. He's not ready. He's not sure he will ever be ready.

He's selfish, he knows he is. The guilt of his thoughts build up like a wall inside him, keeping them hidden. His father lies unresponsive in bed, and he's fretful about becoming king.

When the guard brought the news of his father's condition, it wasn't panic for the man who raised him that came first, standing there amid the princesses. No, it was panic for himself. He hated himself for it. It was only when he laid eyes on his father that the reality of it hit him. His father could die. He looked so small on that bed, his arms relaxed by his sides, blankets pulled to his chin. The bags under his eyes had gone dark, purple-blue clouds bringing in a storm. His skin was pale, sickly. If it hadn't been for those details, it would have looked like he was simply sleeping. If he hadn't fallen to the ground in front of Malakai's mother and several servants, people may have believed that he was.

The queen had replayed what transpired over and over, to guards, to the healer, to Malakai. She had started telling the story through tears, her words breaking off and her voice trembling. By the last time she told it, her voice was distant, her eyes dry and lost. Malakai had cleared the room, placed guards outside the door. Then he held his mother until she felt ready to let go. They stood there for what felt like hours, just clinging to each other, his father stiff as a board beside them. Once she was safely tucked inside her room, Malakai came here, to find Teddy, to let his own tears flow.

The king's study is dark.

Malakai sits at the white ash desk, his fingers running along the edges. The moon blasts through the stained-glass window, casting blues and greens across the wooden floor. He hisses as his finger catches on a loose piece of wood, the point piercing the soft area around his nail.

He knows what must be done and he doesn't enjoy it one bit. There's a soft knock at the door as it opens. Lissa Shostakovich appears in the doorway, her long blonde hair tied in a braid down her back, her eyes still misted with sleep.

"May I ask why you are sitting in the dark, Your Highness?" she asks, closing the door behind her.

Malakai stands, moving to the other end of the room. There's the sound of a match lighting, the hiss of flame hitting gas, then the room is filled with a warm orange glow. "Please sit, Lissa."

He waits for her to take a seat before making his way back to his chair—his father's chair. "You're aware of my father's...condition?"

Lissa dips her chin in a small nod, her eyelids closing briefly.

"I need you to draft a letter to my uncle."

Shostakovich straightens, all sadness clearing from her features. "What would you like me to say, Your Highness?"

It is not a secret that many don't like the Lord of Sorrelle, that being the kinder way of putting it. Even the king himself has trouble finding common ground with his brother. Lord Jasper grew up angry and bitter that his younger brother was the one to inherit their family's gift. That their father favoured Rorik over him because of it. Malakai's father disagrees, says their father favoured him because he wasn't a spoiled brat. He treated their sister just fine, and she didn't have the power either. The three of them had a rocky relationship; Rorik got on far better with his sister, but even their bond was limited. He was consumed with duties and training, their father put him through the wringer. He would train with weapons until his fingers bled, he would train with books until his eyes bled. He didn't feel favoured.

"Tell him...everything. We cannot keep father's condition from him, there would only be fallout. Tell him we are running tests and will know what is wrong soon enough. Make it clear he does not need to come here. Under any circumstances. His presence would only make matters worse."

"Consider it done." Lissa rises as she says this. "He will be fine. He will pull through."

Malakai could see the hope shining in her eyes, the same hope reflecting from him. He gives her a small smile, but he's not sure he believes her words.

He remains inside the study a long while after Lissa departs, listening to the silence around him, the steady beat of his heart in his ears. When the sky outside begins to grow lighter, he finally pulls himself up. He doesn't go to his rooms; he goes to his father's. A chair is already placed beside the bed, likely from his mother having spent hours here during the night. He places his hand on the king's, his skin rough and cold.

"Father." Malakai gulps, blinking away the tears that burn his eyes. "You cannot go yet. It is not your time. I need you to fight. There are so many things I need to tell you, things I should have told you long ago." His throat catches, the tears falling freely now, no use trying to stop them. "I should have been honest from the start. I cannot marry any of Aldros' princesses."

Malakai hesitates, his leg shaking under where his arm rests. His father could not hear him, he's sure, so this would be like a practice run. To gain the courage for when his father recovers and he tells him for real. He could do this. His chest contracts, he tastes the sharp tang of blood as he chews on the corner of his lip. Then the words flow out of him, a melody he's been wanting to sing for a very long time. "I'm in love with a boy, father. You would love him too, I know it. I wish it." Malakai sighs. "I know it's not what you wanted for me. I wouldn't ever want to disappoint you, not in a million lifetimes. But this is who I am. And as wonderful and charming as those princesses may be, they are not what I want."

Malakai closes his eyes. Maybe Sorrelle doesn't need a queen. Maybe, instead, it can have two kings.

His father *has* always liked to acquire things others don't have.

Four days later, it is evident that Lord Jasper did not heed Malakai's words.

Malakai stands beside his mother under a stone arch, watching the lord's carriage pull up to the side entrance of the castle. Malakai cannot help but admire the horses that guide it, their coats bright white, a match to their mane and tail. Their bodies seem more muscular than a normal steed, their legs thicker, hooves sturdier. Their eyes shine an iridescent blue, a colour Malakai has never once seen on a horse before—or any beast, creature, or human for that matter. They are magnificent. Otherworldly.

They come to a stop inches from the queen and prince, their gaze fixed on the two. A stumpy man climbs from the carriage, grumbling and groaning about not being able to enter through the main gates. About the market stalls taking up too much space. He's shorter than Malakai remembers, or maybe he's just grown himself since the last time he saw his uncle. It's been, what, five years now? Malakai doesn't recall. He still looks the same: receding hairline, gut too large for his clothes, snide eyes, and twisted mouth.

"Lucia, lovely to see you again." He takes the queen's hand in his. Malakai is sure she cringes as the lord places a wet kiss there. His mother looks like she hasn't slept for years, the circles under her eyes darkening with each passing day, eyes are red-rimmed and swollen from the nonstop crying. Lord Jasper seems to notice this too, his gaze narrowing on her face. "And *you*,"—his focus turns to Malakai, a smirk on his mouth—"*little prince*."

Malakai doesn't give him the satisfaction of showing his annoyance. Instead, he makes himself stand taller, easily towering over the man, even at half his age. "Uncle."

"On with it then, what's wrong with that almighty brother of mine?"

The queen tenses beside Malakai. She wants the lord here less than he does. She knows his father would detest the fact he's shown his face. "The tests are inconclusive," she says now.

Jasper rolls his beady eyes. "I always did tell him his healer was useless. I should have brought my own, he would have had him back up and running in no time."

"He's not a machine," Malakai snarls. "And our healer is just fine. Father's condition is...unusual. The tests show he is perfectly healthy, but his body is slowly deteriorating, and he will not wake. He's in somewhat of a coma."

Jasper discards anything Malakai says, clapping his hands together once. "Well, in any case, it is a good job I'm here."

"And why is that, Jasper?" Lucia drawls, more emotion in her voice than Malakai had heard in days.

Jasper laughs like it should be obvious, that the queen was simply making a joke. "We cannot expect a child to run the kingdom, can we? No, I will handle things. The little prince can carry on with his usual dilly-dallying."

"I think you will find I am perfectly capable."

"Ah. Don't you worry, boy, Uncle Jasper's got you." He thrusts between the queen and prince, patting Malakai on the back as he goes. Malakai cringes at the lord's third-person reference.

If there is one thing Malakai regrets, it's sending that damn letter.

"He wouldn't want him here, Malakai." The queen has her head in her hands, her palms rubbing against her eyes.

Malakai stands beside her, frozen to the spot, not knowing what to say or do. "I'm sorry."

Queen Lucia rises at his voice, taking his hand in hers. "I did not mean that, it is not your fault." She shakes her head, tears streaming down her cheeks. "I cannot stop. I just want it to stop. I want him to be okay." She's spent the last four days this way, perched beside the king's bed, tears flowing. Servants would pass through the room, she would not stop. They would bring her food, she would not stop.

Malakai had tried everything.

Everything but one thing. Something he wasn't sure he wanted to do. Something he wished someone could do for him in these moments. His mother seems to know his thoughts before he speaks them. Reading something in his features perhaps, a wordless offer lingering there. She squeezes his hand, her eyes locking on to him. He cannot help his father, but maybe he could do this to help his mother.

Lucia nods with a shaking breath, her gaze never leaving him. “Do it,” she whispers.

Malakai kneels before her, a wobbling breath of his own escaping his lips. He hasn’t used his powers for a long while. When he reaches for them, he feels the warmth inside him stretch and moan with relief. He takes his mother’s hands in his own, his eyes closing slowly. His gulp fills the silence.

His power moves like a wave through his veins, embracing every inch of his being. He feels it move from him, capturing his mother in its thrall. He takes hold of that feeling, of her feelings.

He reaches inside, and he wants to scream.

He can feel it all. Every emotion she has ever felt. Every memory that clings to her. The softness of her love. The rage of her displeasures. The disgust, the terror. Her pride, regret, shame, guilt. Her hope. And the most consuming of them all, her sadness.

He focuses on that misery, homing in on it, careful not to disturb what else lay within. It’s the colour of a storm, a swirling grey threatening to consume all in its path. Malakai wraps it in the warm golden light of his power, holding it gently, soothing it. He doesn’t want to take it, not all of it. His body trembles from far away. In here, he is merely an echo of himself, a spirit. The storm grows quieter, decreasing in size, calming to a gentle rain.

He releases his mother’s hands, his chest heaving with wild breaths. He drops to the floor, his body not able to hold him. There’s a pause in his mother’s movement, and he’s worried he has done something wrong, took something he shouldn’t. But then she's by his side, holding him in her lap, her hand in soothing circles on his back.

Malakai forgot how much it hurts to take another's emotion. Her pain washes through him in bouts of agony, smashing against his own walls. Three deep breaths, and it dissipates, gone forever. He cannot just ease an emotion, he has to draw it into himself. It doesn't last long, it cannot take root, not without its original host. But the suffering is like no other.

He focuses on the silence.

His mother isn't crying.

They stay that way for a long time, the prince laying in his mother's arms. A boy once more, lost and in need.

18

WHAT ONCE WAS MINE

RAYLIN

The next week passes in a haze.

King Rorik remains in slumber, his body becoming thin and frail. Prince Malakai spends the majority of his time by his father's side, leaving us princesses to entertain ourselves. We waste our days roaming the castle and the gardens, none of us knowing what this means for our stay here, if we will be sent home with not so much as a goodbye, or if we continue as we are.

Things become clearer on day four when the king's brother arrives at the castle. He's shorter than the king, his belly protruding over his trousers, the buttons on his shirt barely holding on. He walks around like he owns the place, demands we eat dinner with him each night, putting me off my food when crumbs and sauces fall and soak into his dark beard. The queen and prince do not join us, hidden behind closed doors, grieving for a man that has not yet died. With their absence, there has been no word of visiting Queen Lucia's jewel vaults. The waiting makes me nervous. I have tried on multiple occasions to use my powers to conjure the obsidian pendant to me, but without knowing exactly what it is I'm trying to bring forth, it's no use, my power is obsolete.

To try to raise spirits, Lord Jasper announces a talent showcase, one involving the five princesses and me. He gives us two days' notice, telling us we will each show off our greatest talent in front of an audience. There was no conversation on the matter, no such thing as manners from this fulsome lord. He says it is for the prince, but I have no doubt it is for his own sleazy purposes. Repeatedly we have caught him staring, drool pooling in his mouth like a rabid animal. He doesn't seem all that bothered that his brother may be dying.

I have only seen Damien a handful of times through the week, only once alone. It was brief, he held my hand in his, our lips not getting to touch before servants were rushing through the room, cleaning up empty dinner plates. Prince Malakai has been making good use of his right-hand man, having him running around the castle like a headless chicken, taking care of business. But Damien doesn't mind; Malakai is not just someone he works for, he is also his friend, and his friend is in need. We take what moments we can, stolen glances and brushing of hands as we pass in the halls.

The morning of the talent showcase arrives in a flurry of activity, servants rushing to get the ballroom prepared for the evening ahead.

Nerves eat away at me as Ella pulls and prods, making last-minute adjustments to my dress. She wanted something new made for me, something special for tonight. The glimmering silver matches my eyes, covered in rows of tiny diamonds, right down to the flowing trail. It fits snug to my body, a narrow slit between my breasts to my navel, strapless to give my arms all the movement they need for my act.

I will play the violin, the only thing I know I am truly remarkable at. Up until I came to the castle, I practised every day on the one I had conjured as a young girl. I cannot use that one here, of course, having no explanation for where it came from if it appeared in my rooms, so I had Ella procure one for me. The body is made from dark brown maple, a white rose painted at its base.

Ella pokes me with a pin.

"Ow."

"Well, stop moving then," she quips.

"I'm not moving, you're just not being careful."

"I am too."

Ella spends a lot of her time here in my rooms, sometimes busying herself, sometimes not, lazing around with me late into the night. She tells me stories of the people who work within the castle, I tell her stories she believes are made up, but are in fact stories of my childhood. She has become a friend, a little sister. I can tell she feels the same, her face the picture of happiness when I comb through her dark hair, instead of her combing through mine. She teaches me how to apply makeup, how to properly fold clothes—that one I had to force out of her. By her own words, 'a princess should not know how to fold clothes.'

I step out of the dress and Ella rushes from the room without a word. She's in such a tizzy today, I have no clue why she is so worked up about this showcase. I, for one, would rather not be doing it. I have never played in front of anyone but Fee. Tonight I will be playing before a room full of hundreds of people. The thought alone makes my stomach twist in knots.

I pick up the borrowed violin and sit on the small metal seat on the balcony, running my fingers along the strings. I just hope I am as good as I think. Maybe I got so used to the sound of my bad playing, it sounded good to my ears. Because it *was* bad. The noises I could make with it the first time I played, even Fee deemed it necessary to be out of sight and sound while I practised. I hold the violin, turning it over in my hands.

My hand flies to my mouth, stifling the gasp that escapes.

In tiny letters on the base of the back, a carving I did not notice before. PMF. My heart thuds erratically in my chest. How is that possible? I conjure my violin from where it lays discarded in my tower. There on the base of my violin, a messier and larger carving, but the same regardless, the letters PMF. How could it possibly be, the violin I summoned all those years ago belongs to the same person who lends me the newer violin I now hold in my hands. Ella did not disclose who it belonged to, and for some reason, I never thought to ask.

I make a promise to myself to find out.

Hours later, I am scrubbed, dried, and sprayed with something that smells like lavender. My lips are painted in a red stain that gives them a slight hint of colour, my hair curled, half up half down, and I am zipped into my silver dress. I have to admit, I look spectacular. I have never felt as beautiful as I do right now.

"Wow." Ella stares at my reflection in the mirror. "I'm amazing."

We laugh together, but she's not wrong.

"Ella? The violin, who does it belong to?"

"Um, I'm not sure actually." Her brow creases. "I mentioned to my friend, Theodore, we needed one and he turned up with it later that day." She shrugs.

Theodore. The initials don't match, but maybe a family member? Another friend?

"Can you introduce us...so I can thank him."

"Yes, of course. He works in the castle actually, he will be about tonight."

There's a knock at the door and Soraya pops her head in before either of us can answer. "The others are– oh my." She steps fully into the room, taking my hands and spinning me around to get a good look at my attire. "If I didn't know any better, I would worry the moon had fallen from the sky and landed in this very room."

"You flatter me. But it is not I who is the most beautiful in the room."

Soraya's ice-blue gown pops against her dark skin. The high neckline and long, see-through sleeves cover most of her body, the skirts bounding out at the waist in elegant ruffles. Her hair is pulled slick at the sides, the loose fluffy curls piling down the middle of her head, from her forehead to the nape of her neck.

"You should see what I do with the dress later." She winks. "You ready? The others have already headed down."

"Let's not keep them waiting."

We walk arm in arm down corridors, Cadet Michaels leading the way. He's become part of our pack, always going where we go, often talking when he probably shouldn't. He's the youngest of all the guards here. I'm not sure how much protection he would truly be if we were in danger. His pudgy belly and legs probably wouldn't get him far.

We are led backstage to the other princesses, all doing last-minute preparations. Ella had my borrowed violin brought down while I was getting ready; it sits on a stand now, ready to be brought to life. I peep through the heavy green curtains hanging from floor to ceiling, blocking us from view of the crowds.

Tables have been set up around the room in staggered lines, making sure every person can see the stage. On the opposite side of the room, Queen Lucia sits rigid in her throne. I can see the dark circles under her eyes from here. Malakai sits next to her in his father's throne—his throne soon enough, I suppose—leaning to one side, his thumb and index finger rubbing at his eyes. Damien stands a short distance from Malakai, his hand resting on the pommel of his sword. A smaller, less extravagant throne has been set up beside the queen, where Lord Jasper now sits, his hand resting on Queen Lucia's arm, his whole body angled toward her, whispering into her ear, her face the picture of boredom.

Banners of deep green and gold hang from the ceiling, shimmering in the lights of the chandeliers. The *ding ding* of something solid tapping against glass rings out around the room, followed by Lord Jasper's voice.

"Gentle folk of Sorrelle, we are pleased to have you here today. As you may have heard, my brother, King Rorik, is unwell." He takes a deep breath, closing his eyes as if the words pain him.

Oh please. He's hardly mentioned the king since he arrived, let alone gone to see him.

"We hope tonight, we will lift the spirits of Sorrelle, along with helping my nephew, Prince Malakai,"—he waves toward him—"in choosing a bride. So, if you would please turn toward the stage to witness some of the most beautiful princesses in all of Aldros showcase their most prestigious talents."

The crowd applauds. Whistles and words of encouragement fill the room.

Kiyoko is up first. She walks onto the stage in darkness, then a spotlight floods over her. A trick of flame and mirrors. She closes her eyes, her arms spreading to the sides. The crowd has silenced, drinking in her every move. She brings her arms down, bending her knees in unison. As she rises, the sound of butterflies fluttering spreads across the room.

No. Not butterflies.

Flowers bloom across the edge of the stage, on tables, up pillars, and walls, their soft petals shivering open. They cover each and every surface, and before we know it the whole room is cast in shades of pink and white, the smell of spring invading our noses. The crowd goes wild, clapping and cheering. She bows low and exits the stage.

Arabella pouts. "Good luck following that."

"I have all the luck I need. I have the voice of an angel on my side," Catalina says, making Briar blush.

They head onto the stage together, the crowd quieting once more.

The duo part ways, Catalina heading to a piano at the side of the stage and Briar standing in the middle, the latter's coppery skin glowing in the beam of light. Catalina's soft melody cascades over the awe-struck crowd, casting them in her net. People visibly sink into their chairs as Briar's voice joins the music. Catalina wasn't wrong; Briar's voice is captivating, her high notes sending goosebumps across my skin. It's not long before roars of enjoyment are once again bounding through the room.

It's Soraya's turn next. She stands in the centre of the stage, a long wooden pole, flat on both ends, in her hands. Her face is tilted, looking out at the crowd through lowered lashes, a predator about to strike. She lifts the pole, slamming it down, once, twice, against the floor. Her hand reaches around her back, un-clipping something from behind, then her ruffled skirt comes away, revealing tight fitted shorts in the same ice-blue as her dress. She whips the skirt toward us with the pole as she spins, flipping herself backward, feet over head. I can barely keep track of her as she uses the pole to vault up, spinning and gliding through the air, every bit the huntress she is. She ends in a spin, crouching low to the floor, one knee bent before her, the other leg stretched to her side.

If I thought the crowd went wild before, it was nothing compared to now.

"That was amazing, Soraya."

I clip her skirt back around her as Arabella makes her way across the stage. She rolls her shoulders, her pale blue eyes scanning the crowd. Her eyes dart to us, so fast I would have missed it if I wasn't paying such close attention.

She's nervous.

I don't think I have ever seen her show any other emotions beyond arrogance and unimpressed. She readjusts the bow on her dress.

"You can do this," I half-whisper, in the hopes she can hear me. The way she straightens her back tells me she does.

A chilled air sweeps over me, goosebumps rising along my skin in reaction. Arabella's hands turn a shade of pale blue, her fingers twitch, ice creeps from her palms, growing longer, forming a pointed shape. Moments later she grips onto long blades of ice, two daggers in each hand. Mouths hang open in the audience, gazes of anticipation clinging to the knives in her palms. As swift as an archer firing an arrow, she throws them into the crowd, high above their heads. A blast sounds and the pointed ice blades burst into a million flecks. There is a collective gasp as snow falls through the room, a perfect show from our ice princess.

Arabella hurries from the stage, a small smile clinging to her lips.

"Last but not least..." Soraya squeezes my shoulder.

"Good luck," Arabella says sincerely, gaining a look from all of us. "What?" She rolls her eyes.

I grab the violin and bow, walking slowly to the X at the centre of the stage. My heart flip-flops in my chest. The crowd didn't seem quite so large and scary from behind the curtain. I place the chin rest under my chin, holding my arm out steady. The murmurs from the crowd throw me off balance, but I quickly regain my posture. My eyes find Damien, his cobalt gaze fixed on me. I suck in a deep breath, close my eyes, and begin.

I see myself alone with Fee in our tower. Sitting on my bed, as we so often did. The bow gliding across the strings of my violin, filling the space with music. I feel the vibration inside me, starting in my toes and spreading up, up, through my arms, into my fingers. I am not even sure what I play, I just let the music flow through me, pour out of me like water from a fountain. I feel freedom, I feel never-ending love, hope. I see an open sky filled with thousands of luminous stars. I let the hand holding the bow drop beside me as I finish, my eyes remain closed. The room is quiet, the only sound is my jittering breath.

My eyes fly open at the first clap, more and more joining in, everyone is on their feet, tears in their eyes. A weight clamps down on my chest. I rush from the stage, wanting to be away from it all. I feel like something private has been taken away from me, something I didn't even know I wanted to keep hidden. Soraya's fingers brush against my arm as I rush past, her touch too warm.

"Dinner will be served shortly if you ladies would like to follow—"

Cadet Michaels doesn't have a chance to finish his sentence before I run from the room, violin still gripped in my hand.

19

RISKING IT ALL

RAYLIN

I'm being stupid. I know I am. What matter is it that hundreds of people have heard me play? But still, I cannot seem to shake this feeling. I wish Fee were here. I want to know how he is. I can't imagine he's faring well in Genevieve's presence. It's obvious she is not keen on the bird.

I have my back pressed against a wall, my eyes closed, when voices from the room beyond rouse me from my thoughts. Whispers and urgent tones. I recognise one as Queen Lucia; she must have snuck from the show early.

"You think he was *poisoned*?"

"I do," the unknown voice replies.

"But you tested him, nothing was found."

"There is one thing I know of that could cause these symptoms, that can go undetected in the blood,"—there's a pause, a sucking in of breath—"Wraith Flower."

"No. It cannot be. Wraith Flower hasn't grown for decades, and never in these parts of Aldros."

"It is the only thing that makes sense, Your Highness. There is a test I can run to be certain. But you must know, if it comes to be true...there is no cure, not without more of the flower."

"Do it."

I round the corner seconds before the door bursts open. The queen and the bony, grey-haired woman I saw before in the healer's station exit, going their separate ways.

"I see you found my violin of acceptance."

I swing around, a shiver dancing along my skin as my eyes meet Malakai's bright smile, a dimple on each cheek. His white-blonde hair is no less messy than usual.

"This is your violin?" I hold it out as if it has burned me.

"Yes. See." He takes it, turning it over to show the small carving at the back. "PMF. Prince Malakai Foxwald."

This violin, the other one I have kept as my own for longer than I can remember, belongs to Prince Malakai. The universe really does work in mysterious ways.

"It was perfect, thank you."

"No, thank you. I don't think I could ever play it as hauntingly beautiful as you did tonight. It was truly magical, Lena."

He's looking down at me, I up at him, and something pulsates between us. His brows pull together as if he feels it too and it confuses him. It is as if we are two opposite ends of a magnet being drawn together, something inside us wanting to snap into place, to connect.

"How is your father?"

"Much the same. I worry, if he doesn't wake soon...his body is becoming weak, there's no telling how much time he has left. Yet still, they cannot figure out what is wrong..." He shakes his head, sadness in his eyes.

I wish there was something I could do.

Perhaps there is.

"Let me escort you to dinner." He holds out his arm for me. "I will not allow you to leave me to deal with my most gracious uncle alone," he says with a wink.

We are seated at a round table, the other princesses, Queen Lucia and Lord Jasper already tucking into their meal. Damien stands a little way off, watching us closely.

"*Are you okay?*" Soraya mouths to me. I bow my head in a small nod.

Malakai and I sit beside each other, the last two empty seats at the table, the queen on his other side, Briar on mine. On our plates, to my horror, is a fish—filling half the space, its head still attached—with steamed rice and carrots. I pick at the food, not feeling hungry with the beady black eyes staring up at me.

Lord Jasper drones on about changes he thinks should be made to Sorrelle. All the things he would have done if he had inherited the kingdom's power.

"The fishing villages do not need their taxes raised," Malakai sneers.

"Well, they make enough money, selling all those fish in the market. That's another thing, if I had inherited my father's power, you best believe that market wouldn't be happening inside castle walls. It's an—"

Queen Lucia slams her fork down on the table, cutting him off. "With all due respect, Jasper," she hisses through clenched teeth, "you do not have any power, physical or otherwise. It would be wise to keep your mouth shut. My husband is laid up in bed, unable to move, unable to speak. That is your brother, and if he should die, then Sorrelle goes to *my* son. Not you. Your opinion here does not matter."

Lord Jasper stares at the queen, his mouth gaping open, eyes wide. He regains control over his face, clearing his throat with a croaky cough, then goes about drinking his wine. Not another word leaves his mouth. Malakai takes his mother's hand in his. Her breath is shaky as she draws it in and out slowly.

"I think I am going to get an early night," she says to him, then turns to the rest of the table. "Forgive me for my outburst, ladies, tonight has been a pleasure."

"Lieutenant Reynolds, would you escort Mother to her rooms," Malakai calls out.

"No, no, that will not be necessary, I will check in on your father first. Enjoy your evening, son." She comes to a stop as she stands, as if remembering something. "Tomorrow. I will take you all to the jewel vaults tomorrow. If one of you is to wed my son, then you should see them. One day soon it could all be yours."

With that, she is gone. My heart thumps in my chest. This could be it, tomorrow I could find the obsidian pendant, my ticket home.

"Your mother doesn't reside with the king?" I hear Kiyoko ask.

"Not since his illness. The healer worried it would be contagious, but we've been around him plenty and are fine, so..." He shrugs.

I give it thirty minutes or so before excusing myself, feigning needing the restroom. I try to move quickly down the halls and up the stairs, my dress restraining me from moving as fast as I would like. The longer I am gone, the more suspicious they will become. I turn left for the royal chambers and pray to the stars that the queen isn't still inside. One guard stands outside the doors, his finger tapping on the pommel of his sword in boredom. I rush toward him, throwing as much panic as I can muster into my voice.

"There's an incident in the ballroom, the captain has called for all the guards to attend."

He looks at me with wide eyes, his head swinging toward the chamber door and back to me.

"Hurry," I pant.

Then he's running down the hall. I just hope he does not get there too fast, his captain having no idea what he is talking about. Although he should have words with a guard who would so easily leave his post. I was expecting more of a fight.

I crack open the door and a cool breeze rushes out to meet me. The room is quiet and dark, my prayers answered; Queen Lucia is long gone. Bayard, the king's Sword, is nowhere in sight. A warm glow from the candles placed beside the bed flicker across King Rorik's face.

The force of recognition of this man comes crashing down on me.

I take in his features, the differences I see in his aged face, from those of a small child looking at her father's best friend. I was only five the last time he saw me, so it's no wonder he did not recognise me on my arrival at the castle. For the better, I suppose, as I did not arrive here as the girl he once knew. The days I would walk the market, I would wish so hard that I would see him, a little part of my old life. I never did.

I place my hand on his cheek and memories flood my mind, my father and him, laughing in the study inside our castle, drinking a glass of golden liquid. His large arms pulling me into a smothering hug. His laugh as he chased me through the garden's wildflowers.

I never met Queen Lucia or Prince Malakai, but King Rorik would visit often, he and my father being the best of friends.

I hope they still are. I wonder if father has told him his own daughter resides in his kingdom, hidden from sight. I wonder if my father even knows in which kingdom I linger, or if that information belongs to Genevieve alone.

I reach out for my powers, my father's powers, Gavaria's powers.

Unlike my other abilities, ice-cold and unforgiving, my healing ability is warm and soothing. It rushes through me like a summer wind, reaching out to wrap itself around the king. My palm glows with a flameless fire against his cheek. It courses outward and consumes him, spreading across his body until there is not one inch untouched, burning bright inside the dark room. I guide it through him, drowning the poison within, snuffing it out with languished effort.

King Rorik's eyes fly open wide, the circles around them sunken and dark. He sucks in a heaving breath, coughing and spluttering as he does. I help him sit to regain himself. He's thinner than he was a week ago, his skin wrinkled and sagging around his bones.

"What happened?" he croaks out.

"It's okay, you will be okay."

He looks at me for the first time. His brow furrows, and he truly looks at me, seeing something he shouldn't see. "*Raylin*?" His face drops in realisation, his voice small. "Is it truly you?"

My lip quivers, no words come. His thumb rubs away a tear from my cheek that I didn't know had fallen.

"What are you doing here?" The voice comes from the door, causing us both to jump. "Father, you're awake!" Malakai rushes to his side. I stand, stepping back from the bed. "Damien, get Mother. Fast."

Damien rushes off without a word, looking back over his shoulder at me as he goes.

Malakai turns to me. "What happened?"

"I– I found him like this. I lost my way and heard him calling out. There was no one around, so I just..."

Rorik doesn't take his eyes off me, a deep crease forming between his brows.

"I should go."

"Lena...thank you...for not letting him be alone," Malakai says as I reach the door.

"Lena?" I hear the king say, confusion in his strained voice.

"Yes, Father. Oh, I am so happy to see you."

I head back to my rooms, forgetting the party that waits in the ballroom.

My skin feels prickly and hot.

My dress is too tight.

The halls are quiet, I don't pass a single soul. I storm into my room, knowing it will be empty, and shove open the balcony doors, collapsing to my knees.

Air.

I need air.

He knows who I am. It's only a matter of time before they come for me. Then what happens? The king wouldn't let them harm me, surely. He wouldn't chastise me for the lies. He may be angry, may tell my father, but he wouldn't let harm come to me, I am almost certain of that. Does he even know my family has kept me hidden all these years? Or did he still believe me to be in Gavaria, living amongst my family? I don't think the latter would be the case; he would have visited my father many times over the past fourteen years.

It hits me then. I don't know what anyone believes of the Princess of Gavaria, I do not know what stories my family spun, I do not know anything.

The cold air does nothing for my lungs, my chest tightening with every thought. I need to get out of this dress. I fumble with the zipper at my back but cannot grasp it. I frantically search my room for something to help, scissors, anything. Tears wet my face, my breath coming in shallow pants. Static fills my ears, drowning out any sound. I try again at the zipper, it's no use. I pull at the side, trying to tear the seam, nothing. My skin heats, a fire burning inside of me, fighting to get out. I fall to my knees, not registering the pain as they slam against the hard floor.

Fee. I want Fee.

The room spins, blurring to near-nothingness. I am falling, hands flying out to find purchase. I hit something hard, something smooth. A face appears in front of me, eyes wide with panic.

"What is it? What's wrong?" Soraya takes my face in her hands.

"Dress...off..."

She's quick, pulling the zipper down with ease, yanking the dress down, letting it pool around me.

"Fetch some water," she says to someone else in the room.

She pulls me in, a cold hand placed against my bare back, the other running through my hair.

"It's okay. *You're* okay," she whispers, rocking me back and forth like a child.

I focus on the feel of her, her cold, smooth skin, the smell of tulips mingling with the smell of sweat. Someone hands her a glass of water, Ella, her face full of concern. Soraya pulls away just enough to tip the glass to my mouth, small sips. I let my chest rise and fall in time with hers, matching the tempo of her breaths.

Once my breathing is semi-normal, she helps me to my feet. My body is barely covered by the thin slip I wore beneath my dress. She lays beside me on the bed, keeping my hand in hers.

"I don't know what happened," I tell her.

"I think it was a panic attack. My brother gets them too. I knew you didn't look right before dinner, I should have gotten you out of there."

"No...it's not your fault..." I don't know what to tell her, I can't reveal what happened with the king. Although she will find out soon enough.

"Do you want me to stay?"

"Thank you, but no. I will be fine."

"If you're sure." She climbs off the bed. "Ella, if anything happens..."

"I will come to get you, I promise, Princess Soraya," Ella reassures her.

It takes her the next five minutes to leave, hovering by the door, asking over and over if I'm okay. I have never had someone worry for me in this way. It makes my toes tingle, a ball of warmth spreading through my stomach.

"Where did you go?" Ella perches by my feet.

I shake my head, no excuse to save me.

She smiles. "King Rorik is awake."

"That's great." I am unsure if I smile back, my eyes closing, exhaustion taking over me.

"She doesn't need visitors, she is sleeping."

My eyes flutter open, seeking out Ella, who is standing at the door talking to someone in hushed tones. The sky outside is still dark.

"No, you cannot come in. If it is important, you can come back in the morning, *when she is awake.*"

I find myself not caring who stands on the other side. My whole body aches and I just want to sleep in this soft bed while I can. I pull the blankets to my chin and close my eyes once more.

20

VISIONS OF OLD

MALAKAI

His heart stops in its tracks. His father is awake. He's sitting up, and he's awake. Malakai cannot believe it. Is this real? Is he dreaming? If so then he never wants to wake from this moment.

After Lena left, he held the king so tight he thought he might break his ribs. Now he just sits staring at him, a beaming smile on his face.

He's okay. He's awake.

Though Malakai can tell from the look on his father's face he is groggy, confused, he probably has no idea what's going on. Queen Lucia rushes into the room, her haste almost causing her to fall. Damien is close behind her, but there's something in the way he looks at the king that Malakai cannot quite place. It's not relief, it's something else.

The queen drops to her knees beside the bed, holding the king's face in her hands. "I– you're—"

King Rorik's eyebrows inch closer together. He tries to speak, but his mouth is dry, no words come out.

"Water!" The queen shouts. It's not a demand, more a word she forgot, one that she is just now remembering.

The king drinks heavily, gulping the water down in great mouthfuls. Once he's done, Malakai takes the cup, refilling it and placing it on the stand beside his father.

"What happened?" King Rorik croaks.

Malakai's eyes flick to the queen, a silent confirmation of what they should tell him. *Not Jasper, not yet*, her eyes say back. "You took ill, Father. A week has passed in your slumber."

"A week," Rorik says quietly, his gaze drifting to his hands lying open in his lap. "The girl?"

"I told you, Father, that is Lena, one of the princesses staying at the castle, for me to choose a bride. Remember?"

His mother's head snaps to him, the question visible on her face. "Lena was here? With your father?"

"Yes. She found– I will explain later. It's not important."

Queen Lucia lets it go, for now. Her focus is back on her husband.

Awake.

The king coughs, dry and hoarse. He struggles to take a breath. Malakai grabs the water, helping his father to sip.

"Jasper is here," the king rasps. It is not a question.

"How did—"

"Because I know my brother. He would take any chance he could get to watch my downfall." He sighs. "And Seranay?"

Malakai looks to his mother, their worried glances reflecting one another. "Father, Seranay is dead. You know that."

Rorik hesitates, his eyelids shuttering, brows forming a tight line. He looks to the bedroom door, the open space beyond, as if searching for his long-lost sister. "Right. Dead."

"Your father needs rest, time for his mind and body to recover." The queen looks over her shoulder. "Lieutenant Reynolds, send for the healer, for food."

Malakai stands. "I will go with him. You stay with father, both of you need rest." He follows Damien from the room, briefing the two servant girls hovering outside on his mother's orders. They hurry off as if it's their life's purpose. Malakai supposes it is.

His mind wanders to Seranay, the aunt he never got to meet. The aunt whose blood pendant lies abandoned on a podium in the castle museum. She died when he was just a baby, but he heard tales of her. Her brave and eager spirit, a woman who had the world at her feet, only to have it all torn away in battle. Malakai once believed the story his father told him, of the fierce princess and the king, was about his aunt, but his father only laughed and shook his head. Malakai hadn't understood what was funny; the king told him plenty of stories about Seranay, so what was so different about this one? Still to this day, he didn't know who the story was truly about. Simply made up, perhaps.

Then there was the matter of the cabin, the spirit that lingers there. Was that Seranay? Is that the connection he felt? An aunt all but forgotten from his memories? It was a possibility. It was a question he had never been inclined to ask. The spirit was his, and his alone. He would not taint it by alerting others. But that left him with questions that had no answers. He wanted to know. He needed to know.

He didn't know many things, he realised. Looking back on his childhood, he was always laughed off, his questions discarded. The truths he wished to know, hidden.

"Kai?" Damien pulls him from his thoughts. "Are you okay?"

Malakai nods. "Actually, not really." He lets out a nervous laugh, lowering his voice. "I should be relieved, so why do I feel so...odd? Something isn't right."

"It's normal to feel apprehensive, Kai. You thought your father was on his deathbed, then suddenly, without warning, he's not." Damien cups Malakai's shoulder, squeezing it gently. "All's well."

"You're right. I'm being silly. Will you do something for me? Go back to the party, keep an eye on my uncle. I don't want him disturbing them tonight."

"As you wish."

Malakai flies through the garden, his feet barely touching the ground. He doesn't stop at the stables. It's illuminated, meaning the stable hands are still there, which means he cannot get Beebo without being detected. Instead, he runs. The night breeze whips through his hair, stings his eyes, but he doesn't care, doesn't stop. The hidden gate doesn't slow him down either; he tears through it at lightning speed, an ache in his chest pushing him on.

He only slows when the cabin comes into view.

He feels guilty sending Damien on a fruitless mission; if Jasper wanted to see his brother tonight, then he wouldn't let any guard stand in his way. Though Malakai hardly thought he would leave the party just to see the king. He had barely deigned to visit him since he arrived.

Malakai pushes the guilt aside. He had to do this, had to come here. He has to know. He barges into the cabin, not caring if the wood were to collapse beneath him. The presence wraps around him, warming him from the chill night air.

Malakai speaks into the emptiness, his voice lost in the dark, "Is it you, Seranay?"

The connection sags, the warmth parting with a swoosh from his skin.

It's not her.

There's a crawling up his spine, a sensation of danger, of pain, but it's not him in danger, it's the spirit, who they once were. There's a scream in the distance. It's not real, it's in his head, like a memory resurfacing. It tears from a woman's throat. She is scared. She is dying.

"I don't understand," Malakai whispers, "help me understand."

Something shimmers at the edges of his vision, an image, fuzzy, distorted. He can make out the wooden slats, a bed beneath the window, moonlight sneaking through in strips of silver. It's the cabin he stands in now, but it is not broken, not abandoned. A woman lays on the bed, her head thrown back against the pillows. Bodies stand around her, one clutching her hand, whispering in her ear. Malakai cannot make out their faces, they are missing, blank.

There's blood.

So much blood.

Too much blood.

Another scream erupts into the quiet, swallowing all sound. Then there's another. It doesn't come from the woman, it comes from—

Wood cracks.

Malakai feels the floor beneath him give way, but he doesn't move. He doesn't fall. His breath releases, the smell of rot filling the air. He lowers his head and gasps. The floor is gone, caved in from his weight, yet Malakai remains in place, standing on nothing, floating on air. That warmth has wrapped around him again, holding him tight. Not allowing him to be injured.

"Who are you?"

No one answers, he doesn't see any more images, the warmth doesn't leave again. Yet, something feels different. Malakai's heart beats slower, a gentle rhythm, a knowing rhythm. Like the answer lies within him. Like he's known it all along. But he doesn't know *how* to know. He doesn't know where to search for the answer.

He moves without warning, not of his own accord. The spirit guides him out of the cabin, down the steps, placing him with care on the grass beyond.

Then she is gone.

Malakai twists on the bed, squinting against the morning sunlight, turning away from the glare to the shadows it casts on the map of Sorrelle on the opposite wall. He had forgotten to close the damned drapes when he stumbled into his room last night. The party was well and truly over by the time he arrived back from the cabin, the castle quiet. He decided he wasn't ready to turn in, so instead he lost himself at the bottom of a bottle of golden liquid.

He hadn't slept for a week, and last night was no different.

His head thumps. An orchestra of amateur musicians settling in for the day ahead. He groans, yanking the blankets over his head, sheathing himself in darkness. The rush of the market below drifts through the open windows, alerting him to the time. He should have been up hours ago. He wasn't getting out of this bed anytime soon, not with the way his insides were playing round-abouts. Big ones that spin on an endless loop.

Bile creeps up his throat, his lips clamping shut at the feeling. He can do nothing but groan away the sensation. If he moves again, he doubts he could keep it down a second time.

"Stars have mercy on your soul," a resonant voice says from somewhere inside the room.

Malakai grumbles back, crying out louder as Damien yanks the blankets from him, letting in the too-bright light. He waves the cup he holds under Malakai's nose, the rich scent of coffee rising on the steam to meet him.

"Can't...move."

"Any particular reason you got blackout wasted last night? Alone, might I add."

Malakai scrunches his face, eyes still closed, as he wiggles up the bed, pulling himself against the velvet headboard. It was with no uncertainty that he knew who had told him. The guards would have seen Malakai flailing about the castle, probably under orders to keep watch and make sure he got back to his room in one piece.

How did he get back to his room?

He sips the coffee slowly, ridding himself of dry mouth. "No reason, other than I like the taste of whisky," he lies.

"Your father's five-hundred-year-old bottle of whisky."

Malakai winces. He had forgotten that specific detail. The evidence lay discarded by his bed.

Damien studies him, his eyes narrowing. "You're sure that's all it is?"

Malakai turns his attention to the map behind Damien, a sigh escaping his lips. He truly thought he had been right in thinking the spirit was that of his long-lost aunt, but he had been wrong. And he is still no closer to figuring out who it was. Maybe it wasn't even important, maybe she was nobody. His father had told him no one had dwelled in that cabin for decades. He had sensed before that it was a female's essence, but last night's hazy images only confirmed it. He knew she was the woman who lay on that bed, covered in blood, screaming. The screaming. Malakai stills, his mind moving faster than he can process.

There was another scream, right before the floor gave way. A scream that wasn't hers. It was new, small, ripping into the world.

It was a baby.

She was giving birth. Is that how she died? He tries to conjure up those images again, tries to see those faces. But it is useless, the faces are blank, the voices masked like they are underwater.

"Is this about the princesses again? I thought you were over that?"

Damien's voice gives Malakai a start. He had forgotten he was there. "No. No, it's not that. It's just..." Malakai wants to tell him, he does, but this has been his little piece of escape for so long that he cannot bring himself to speak it. Instead, he changes the subject. "What's the deal with you and Lena?"

It's Damien's turn to jolt, his face turning to stone. "Nothing."

"You cannot lie to me, old friend. I've known you too long."

Damien raises his eyebrows as if to say, *right back at you.* He opens his mouth to say as much, then, thinking better of it, he relaxes, a coy smile kicking up the corner of his mouth. "I like her."

Malakai smiles. "Five years, and I don't think I've ever seen you smile about a girl, not once."

"I've smiled about plenty of girls."

"No, you've smiled plenty about what you've *done* with girls." Malakai winks. "This is different."

"It is."

Something inside Malakai expands. Either he's happy for his friend, or he's going to throw up. He's not sure which. Oh, no. Definitely the latter. He scurries from the bed, racing to the bathing chamber.

He's pretty certain the entire contents of his insides explode from his mouth.

21

Secrets of the Castle

Raylin

The morning comes. No guards take me away, no one locks me up, no one shows any indication that they know what I did the night before. Curiously, it seemed even the guard I had lied to had not said a thing; though I have seen no sight of him since he ran from the king's chambers.

The corridors are filled with whispers and murmurs, each talking of the king's sudden recovery. Though I learn he still lays up in bed, weakened by his ill state. Maybe this is why he is yet to reveal who I am.

The princesses and I are led down a narrow passage by an elderly servant, her greying hair tied in a tight bun at her nape. 'The queen's handmaiden,' Catalina whispers from behind me. The passage is only wide enough to walk in a single row, but we soon enter a wider space, two large golden doors before us. Both doors are identical, carved with a small circle inside a larger one. Two robins sit beak to beak inside the smaller circle, fighting over a glittering green gem, both clutching to it with their claws. Queen Lucia stands before the doors, her hands clasped in front of her and a smile on her face. The colour has returned to her skin, her eyes seeming bluer than the days before. She is radiant in the knowledge her husband is now awake—mostly himself.

"Good morning, ladies. I hope you all slept well." Her smile reaches ear to ear. She doesn't wait for us to reply before carrying on. "Behind me lies Sorrelle's jewel vaults. I would ask that you refrain from touching where possible. But in any case, if you will wear these,"—she gestures to her handmaiden, who hands us each a pair of white, delicate satin gloves—"if the need does overcome you, they will keep the jewels and surfaces free from fingerprints and debris."

She turns her back to us, placing her hands around the larger circles on the doors and twisting; something inside the doors clunk as she does so. Her handmaiden hands her a small pin and she pricks her finger with it before handing it back. A bead of blood appears on her finger, which she smears across each of the green gems between the birds' talons. The gems soak up the blood, drinking it in, then they glow brightly in the dimness of the room. A click sounds, and the doors part slightly, showing a thin slither of the room beyond.

My eyes grow wide as the queen swings the doors inward.

The vaults are lit in brilliant white light. The whole room is made of mirrors, the floors, the walls, everything reflecting back at us. Rows and rows of crowns line the shelves, countertops below filled with glass hands wearing rings large and small, dangling necklaces and dainty bracelets. A headless glass mannequin stands in the centre of the room wearing a corset of diamonds, each held together by thin golden thread. It is completely translucent; you would have to be fearless, outrageous even, to wear such a piece.

A tiara catches my eye, delicate leaves cresting up into a point, a small emerald—matching the eyes of the prince—hanging from its middle. Queen Lucia leans over my shoulder, taking the tiara between her fingers. "You like it?"

"It's beautiful." I smile.

She lets out a little sigh, a small smile on her lips, and places it atop my head.

"Even more so now." She grazes my chin between her finger and thumb, twisting my head gently toward the mirrored wall beside us.

My heart slows in its beating. I never got to wear a tiara back home. They are more a statement piece among royal children, only worn at balls and royal affairs to show our place. Being only six, I had never attended such things. I begged my mother to let me wear one, but she told me to stop being un-princess-like. We should not beg.

The queen lifts it from my head, placing it back in its rightful spot. I still feel it, a phantom tiara sitting in its place. I catch Arabella's stare in the reflection, her face blank before she averts her attention back to the jewels around us. Queen Lucia walks the room, letting the others each try a piece of jewellery. I am the only one to wear a tiara, much to Arabella's annoyance, who loudly let us all know when the queen slips a too-wide ring on her finger and she scoffs, asking to try a crown instead. The queen simply ignores her.

I scan each shelf, searching for a certain colour and shape. Most of the jewels are brightly coloured, glinting in the bright lights. I almost miss it, masked carefully to the back of the room. One mirror is set forward, not connected to the main room at all. I check behind me, but everyone is busy with the sights before them. I slip silently behind the secret mirror, into a small, dark room. There are no fancy mirrors or floors beyond, only a dim light shining through from the room before.

A round table sits in the middle of the space, scattered with crowns and jewels with dark stones of black and red. And there, in the centre of the table, a clear glass case, inside which hangs an obsidian teardrop pendant.

My heart thumps loudly in my chest, echoing around my ears. I inspect the case, gently try to lift its lid, but it does not budge. The very air around it seems to vibrate, a warning to not try again. I quickly edge back out of the room. I know the pendant now, I know its curves and angles. I can bring it to me, I do not need to take it at this moment.

Back in my room, I sit cross-legged at the foot of my bed.

I concentrate hard on how the pendant looked. Its thin leather chain, the way the darkness seemed to move and swirl inside the dark stone itself. I try my hardest to bring it to me through the void, to conjure it out of thin air. But it does not work. Each time I open my eyes, my hands remain empty. Maybe the case it resides in is spelled somehow. I cannot just waltz back into the vaults, not without the queen. Not without her blood.

Would Malakai's blood work? Then even so, what excuse would I use to get him to take me? He wouldn't before, why would he now? There would also be no way of sneaking the pendant out with him breathing down my neck, not without being able to take it from its case easily.

I go through a mental list of my known powers, trying to think which one could help.

The void is useless in this situation. Air manipulation, healing, and being able to show people memories are also off the table. Levitation could be helpful, but it won't get me inside the vault, and I can only hang slightly above the ground as it is. There has to be something. I feel the depth of my power hum in my blood. I have not even begun to tap into what lies dormant inside.

A knock on the door distracts me from my planning. Malakai greets me with a smile, his messy hair standing on end more than usual.

"Take a walk with me, Princess." He holds out his arm for me.

I take it without much thought, always feeling relaxed in his presence. We walk down hall after hall, toward the lower levels of the castle.

"I hear your father is doing better," I pry.

"Yes. Thank you again, for being there."

"No problem at all, just in the right place at the right time, I guess."

"You are his guardian angel." He smiles. "Not that he remembers."

"What do you mean?" I ask, trying not to seem too eager.

"His memories are hazy. He remembers waking, there being someone there, but that is all." He takes in my face, mistaking my relief for concern. "Oh, we're not worried. His memory seems fine today. It is just last night's events that are...fogged."

"Well, in any case, I am glad to hear he's awoken mostly well."

"We just need to fatten him up again. Shouldn't take much convincing, he's hardly stopped eating today." He laughs.

We walk in silence for a short while, exiting the castle through the garden doors. The sky is dimming, shadowed in dark shades of orange and red. We turn left, leaving the path to the main gardens behind. He leads me through a thicket of trees with thin, white trunks, their leaves beginning to dry and turn orange and yellow. No one loiters in the gardens, and it hits me that this is the first time I have seen Malakai without a guard. The first time I have been without a guard. Apart from the times I have snuck off, of course.

"Where are we going?" I ask cautiously.

He stops suddenly, spinning to stand in front of me.

"Can I trust you, Lena?"

I stare at him, his emerald eyes searching my face, waiting for an answer. I don't give him one right away. I mean, I think he can trust me. But then, I keep this big secret about my identity from him, and I doubt he would call that trust. Could this be what this is about? Does he know who I am? Maybe his father told him before his memories became nothing more than a misted dream. But maybe not, I cannot give anything away.

I nod. "I believe so."

He bites his bottom lip, taking my hand between his trembling ones. "I think so too. I feel a connection between us..."

I nod again, knowing exactly what he means. I feel it too. I have felt it every time we are near. It is not romantic, more a feeling of safety, of comfort, like I've found something I once lost.

"I want to tell you something. Something no one but Damien knows. I am– stars, why is this so hard?" He smiles, shaking his head. "I have heard the rumours about me. I am sure you have heard them too, about the mysterious figure I sneak around with."

I glance down at my feet.

"Well, it's– it will be easier to just show you." He grabs my hand, leading me deeper into the trees.

I stumble on a branch lying fallen on the floor, but his grip on my hand doesn't let me falter.

"Malakai! Slow down."

He stops suddenly and I bump straight into his back, wobbling back a step.

We are in a small clearing surrounded by white tree trunks. Damien leans against one, fiddling with the pommel of his sword. The copper-haired kitchen servant, the one from Malakai's room all those days ago, the one I saw him with in the gardens, stands a little way from him, staring at us both. My eyes flick between the three of them, waiting for what is to come.

"Lena,"—Malakai walks towards the boy, taking his hand—"this is my boyfriend, Theodore."

Theodore.

Ella's friend that procured the violin. The one that belonged to Malakai. I cannot stop the smile that spreads across my face. I had suspected, after seeing them from my balcony the week prior, but I couldn't know for sure.

"No one can know," Malakai says, his eyebrows drawn downward in worry.

"They won't. Not from me."

Malakai's worry melts from his face, replaced by a toothy grin, dimples appearing on his cheeks. He runs to me, pulling me in a tight embrace.

"I brought *him* here for you." His head flicks in Damien's direction. "I see the way you look at each other."

My body tenses. "I don't know what you're talking about."

"Don't be coy. He is my best friend. I can read him like a book. That, and he tells me everything." He winks, and my cheeks burn at the memory of Damien's lips on mine.

I ignore him, leaning over his shoulder. "It's nice to meet you, Theodore."

"You too, Your Highness." He bows his head.

"Oh, Teddy, none of that. We are amongst friends," Malakai says to him playfully.

Theodore gives him a shy smile, their hands clasping together between them. They stay there, leaning into one another, whispering things I cannot hear.

"Hi." Damien's fingers brush the inside of my palm, sending jolts of electricity through my body.

"Hi," I say, turning to face him.

"I tried to come see you last night. Princess Soraya told me you had a panic attack? Your handmaiden wouldn't let me in."

"Soraya had no right—"

"I was worried about you."

"I'm sorry." I shake my head. "I was fine. Soraya and Ella were with me, there was nothing more you could have done."

"What happened? Was it to do with the king?"

"I'm not sure." I shake my head again. "No, just– everything I suppose. I hate keeping this secret."

"I know. It won't be much longer..." He lowers his head, closing his eyes.

"What's wrong?" I place my hand against his golden-brown cheek.

"What happens once this is all over? I don't want it to go back to how it was before, simply watching each other from a distance in the market."

"I don't want that either."

He pulls me into his chest, his arms gentle around me.

"You ready?" Malakai says, causing us to pull apart.

Damien gives a quick nod. "Always."

We arrive at Malakai's chambers, him and me side by side, Damien keeping close behind us, Theodore at the rear, a plan in our pockets.

"Your Highnesses." The guard by the door bows low.

As we enter, Damien stays behind, distracting the guard while Theodore sneaks in behind us.

"I don't want to be disturbed," Malakai tells the guard, shutting the door. "This is a lot easier when you have an accomplice."

He walks to the large bookcase against the back wall. As he pulls on a book, the whole thing shifts, revealing a hidden passage.

My gaze flicks between him and the space beyond.

"Follow the path down, you will come to a door with a white X. Damien will be waiting for you." He smiles.

"Have a good night," I say to both of them.

Malakai seals the secret entrance as I climb through, a dim light down the other end my only guide. I walk slowly, my hand running along the rough stone wall. I get to the door Malakai described, only passing two other plain ones on my way. I open it slowly, checking for anyone lurking. All I see is Damien, his smile blinding. I shut the door, which I see is actually a large painting of fishing boats sailing on a calm sea.

Damien takes my hand, the halls void of people, and we walk this way until we reach the servant's door to the princesses' quarters. There we say our reluctant goodbyes and I head to door three. My room is quiet, Ella having listened when I told her to take the night off. I barely have the door closed, when it creaks open and Damien slips in.

"I didn't want to leave you just yet," his voice is soft.

I run and jump into his arms, our foreheads pressing against each other, our warm breaths mingling. He kisses me hard. There is so much need in it, it makes my stomach twist. He walks us to the bed and we sit there for a moment, me on his lap, legs wound around him, not talking. He flings me around, throwing me gently to the bed. Slowly he unstraps his sword, placing it on the floor, the same with his dagger, then his boots. He leans back against the pillows, one arm out, and pats his chest with the other. I flick my shoes off with eagerness and clamber up to him.

I snuggle into the crook of his arm, my face angled up toward his. His arm wraps around me, his skin warm against mine. This time he kisses me gently, our lips discovering things about each other that words cannot. My hand finds his hair and a groan escapes his lips as I run my fingers through it.

"I like this," he says between kisses.

I murmur in agreement.

"Where are you from?" I ask once our lips finally part.

"A small island far from here. But in truth, I never really had a place I could call home. My father died when I was young, my mother...she didn't much care for me. She wasn't a very nice person."

His brow furrows and I can see talking about her pains him.

"I stood by and saw her do many terrible things growing up. As soon as I could, I got out of there, far away from her. I told myself I wouldn't be like her, I wouldn't let the people around me get hurt the way she hurt them."

I lace my fingers through his, squeezing gently.

"That, you do not. I may not know everything about you, Damien, but I know you are kind, selfless. You could have let me go down for my crimes. Instead, you saved me."

I look up at him, his eyes glitter with something unsaid, his smile a thousand suns burning against my skin. He kisses me once more, and again, I am lost in him.

22

ROYALS NO LONGER

RAYLIN

Ella's gasp wakes me. Sunbeams filter through a crack in the curtains, rays of morning light zig-zagging over the crumpled blankets. I feel the warm breath in my hair before I register what is happening. My eyes fling open, connecting with Ella's dark brown ones. They are wide, her mouth hanging open. Damien still lays sleeping beside me, our legs entwined. We hadn't meant for him to stay the night.

Two things happen at once. Damien lets out a soft moan, stretching up so his wrinkled tunic rises just so, showing off his toned body. Ella lowers her gaze, her cheeks blushing as she stares down at her feet. At this precise moment, Malakai walks through the open doorway, Ella not having closed it in her shock. He doesn't hide the smile that spreads on his face at the sight of us.

"Ah, there you are, Damien. Come, we have many things to do."

Damien shuffles off the bed, placing a final kiss upon my head, grabbing his things before following Malakai back through the door. Ella closes it behind them, turning to me, her cheeks now an even darker shade of pink.

"I want to know everything. But first, His Highness wants all the princesses ready within the hour. He feels terribly that you have all been cooped up here, so he is taking you on a trip."

We do just that. As Ella helps me get ready for the day, I spill all there is to know. Which isn't a huge amount, in all honesty. I leave out the two secrets in all this, Malakai's and mine, but I tell her about the stolen glances, the fevered kisses, how we held each other through the night. Ella coos and squeals in all the right places.

Once I am ready, we make our way to the courtyard with the others, all dressed in simple dresses, wrapped beneath cloaks to beat away the chill of the day. We are escorted to a carriage, where all six of us climb in—leaving the handmaidens behind—and are taken down a bumpy road to the fishing docks.

As we climb from the carriage, a boy around our age, in simple clothes, his messy white hair under a sailors hat, leans over the edge of a large sailboat. "Ahoy, ladies," Malakai shouts.

His clothes are still finer than most you see about the villages, but his royal garments are gone for the day. He looks at ease upon the boat, like this is where he belongs.

"You can sail?" Catalina calls to him.

"Of course I can sail." He winks. "Well, come on, we don't have all day."

As we climb aboard, I catch a glimpse of Damien, bent over, tightening the mainsail. Like Malakai, his guards' leathers are gone, replaced by simple trousers and a tunic, a dark navy cloak tied around his neck. He lifts his head slightly, looking at me through thick lashes, a smile tugging at his lips.

I follow Soraya to the front of the boat, holding on to each other for warmth as the boys get the boat moving. There are no guards aboard, just the eight of us, alone for the day. It feels thrilling to be away from the main castle, to be moving off Sorrelle lands. I haven't set foot on the waters since arriving here fourteen years ago, that being my first and only time to ever sail the seas at all.

There's a pang deep inside me, a guilt for leaving without Fee. He should be here with me, we should be doing this together. I remind myself he is safe. It wont be long and we will be together again; we will be going home. Together.

The air is cold, the wind pushing us speedily across the waters. Malakai and Damien remain busy, keeping us in a steady direction.

"Where is it we are going?" Briar shouts over the wind.

"Nuval." Malakai smiles. "Thought you ladies deserved a day away from all the nuisance of being a royal."

Catalina comes up beside Soraya and me, the light catching on the small charm of her necklace, which I realise for the first time is a paw. A nod to her family's transformation gifts. "I've been before; they have some of the best shopping a person could wish for."

"We're going to need it if we want to get out of this blistering cold." Soraya shivers.

Two hours later, we are docking at Nuval. I tuck my arms inside my cloak, trying to warm my frozen fingers. Few boats are anchored here, bobbing beside each other in the angered sea.

"Quiet today," Malakai observes.

"That's probably because you chose one of the coldest days of the year to come," Damien jokes back.

The smell of wood smoke and fresh bread fills the air, warming my lungs as we walk huddled together to the main town. Stone houses with tall chimneys spread sparsely along the streets, no real rhyme or reason to their order. We pass one with a bright yellow door, a small child sitting in the garden, plaiting her doll's hair. She looks up at us as we walk by, a serious expression on her young face.

Not much further up the street, shops of different sorts start to replace houses. I look into the window of one filled with hats, an old peeling sign stating, *On Your Head*, above the door. Next door, a shop with the most magnificent dresses in the window. A dress made of silky grey sits front and centre, the light reflecting off it creating all colours of the rainbow. My stomach twists at the reminder of Fee, the colours of his wings.

He's safe. I remind myself once more.

Other than the girl we saw on our way in, the streets mostly remain bare of people. Even inside the shops seems quiet, save for the workers.

"Where to first?" Malakai asks no one in particular.

"That one," Kiyoko says, pointing to a shop across the street.

The Scentuary.

The smell overwhelms all my senses as we walk through the door, making me feel a little queasy. Notes of rose, cardamom, citrus, leather, cedarwood, burnt sugar, and oranges—just to name a few—all hit me at once.

Perfume bottles line the shelves, and a small stand in the middle of the store with empty bottles has a sign reading, *make your own.* The other girls revel in the excitement of it all, spraying different scents on little card sheets, getting each other to smell them, although how they can tell the difference with so many scents filling the air I will never know. Malakai talks to who I assume is the store owner; a short woman with ebony hair, large round glasses framing her eyes.

The smell becomes too overbearing, so I step outside. I take a deep breath, sucking in the chilled air. I lean against the side of the building, the stone wall digging into my back. Pulling my cloak tighter around me, I watch as the dark clouds roll through.

"Are you okay?" Damien asks, placing himself against the wall beside me.

"Fine. The smell was just—"

"A little much?"

I nod. We stand in silence, close enough to feel each other's warmth.

"I got you something." He moves to stand in front of me and hands me a long, thin box.

I take the lid off slowly, not knowing what to expect. Inside is a dainty silver chain, a crescent moon hanging from the middle. My heart somersaults. It's the one I was looking at the day I was caught, I am sure of it. The bracelet I had looked at so many times before.

"Is this...?"

"It is. I got it the morning after we met...*officially*. I had seen you look at it a few times, curious as to why, out of all things, this is what you chose not to steal."

I didn't have a reason, most of what I took was ugly. Large, brightly coloured gems on thick, dramatic chains. Nothing I would ever wear. But this, something about it reminded me of my mother, her nickname for me, Little Moon. And something in that memory of her made me not want to take it, not want to steal something so precious.

"Put it on me?" He wraps it around my wrist, doing up the tiny clasp. His eyes are glued to mine as he lifts my arm to his mouth, placing a soft kiss on the inside of my wrist, right beside the small silver moon.

A beast inside me stirs.

I take a handful of his cloak in my fist and close the gap between us.

“Thank you,” I whisper against his lips, “I love it.”

He replies by dragging my bottom lip between his teeth, a smile lifting the corner of his mouth.

We are pulled from our embrace as the others pour out of the shop, all six of them carrying a blue paper bag, *The Scentuary*, stamped in swirling pink letters.

“I got you one,” Malakai says, handing me the bag.

“Thank you, you shouldn’t have.”

“Don’t thank him yet, you haven’t smelt his taste in perfumes,” Damien says, scrunching up his face.

“Hey!” Malakai punches him in the arm playfully.

We spend the next few hours shopping. Browsing shops filled with jewellery, clothes, shoes, everything and anything you could imagine. The dark clouds come in thicker and darker with every door we exit. We are just finishing up in the dim bookstore when the rain starts, splashing in thick droplets against the ground. It is coming so fast and heavy it is as if a sheet of frosted glass has been placed in front of the store.

“Excuse me, do you know of anywhere we can get shelter and some hot food nearby?” Malakai asks the frowning lady at the till.

“The Clumsy Crow tavern a few doors down. You best hurry though, he gets busy this time o’ day, people finishing up work and heading down to wet their whistle.”

With a quick thanks, we head into the cascading rain, running in the general direction the woman pointed, arms above our heads, not helping much in defending us from the rain at all. Damien takes my hand in his, pulling me faster. The tavern comes into view ahead, its brown, creaky sign blowing in the wind, old and faded with time. The words *The Clumsy Crow* are barely visible.

We push through the doorway, all dripping water onto the hard-wood floor. It is not an overly large place; a long wooden bar sits at the far end of the room, a small door leading to what I assume are the kitchens. Around the edges of the room are booths, long benches with flattened leather cushions on either side of rectangular tables. Scattered throughout are smaller circular tables, dotted with mis-matched wooden stools. There are torches mounted to the walls, creating a warm, dim glow. Most of the tables are occupied with customers, large tankards in their hands. Few women in attendance. A large man with black, greasy hair that sticks to his face watches us from a nearby table, sucking his tongue to his yellowing teeth. His beard is full of crumbs, his hands covered in black smudges of coal.

Damien pulls me a little closer when he notices the man's stare, his hand still wrapped around mine.

We remove our sodden cloaks, hang them by the door to dry, and take a seat in the only available booth, all squeezing in along the benches, four on each side. Damien ends up across from me, stretching out his leg to rest it against mine. Malakai is beside him, Soraya and Arabella also on their side. I sit closest to the wall, Catalina beside me, Kiyoko and Briar on the end.

A woman with sunken eyes and muddy blonde hair, falling in frizzy waves, approaches our table. "What can I get ya?" she says, a no-nonsense tone to her voice.

"What food do you offer?" Malakai asks.

"Not much. Ovens broke. Best I can do ya is..." she says, turning her head to look over at the bar, "dried boar strips and stale bread."

"We'll take it. And eight tankards of your finest ale, please."

"Sure thing." She walks off, not even a hint of a smile ever appearing on her face.

"Ale?!" Arabella whisper-shouts, her eyes wide.

Malakai shrugs, not an ounce of Sorrelle's prince in him today.

"We're royals," she whispers to him, "not common folk."

Her face screws up as she eyes everyone in the room. Malakai's laugh startles her.

"Today, dear, yes you are." He winks, causing her to scoff.

Catalina sits nudging me in the arm at the interaction, as if I am not sitting right here hearing it all. The tankards get set down on our table with a clang. I stare at the brown liquid; it smells kind of sweet and tangy all at once. So far since arriving at the castle I have gotten away with not drinking the wines passed around at meals and parties. Holding the glasses and feigning drinking them. Before the ball at Sorrelle, I had never so much as sipped alcohol, and I haven't dared a sip since that night either. The thought of being fuzzy and not in control of myself in the castle scares me.

I have read about people being drunk in books, and the idea of it seems not at all inviting. Here, though, I am not so sure I can get away with pretending to drink. But I am around people I consider to be friends, and I know Damien wouldn't let me say or do something silly to out myself, so I take a sip.

The bitter taste coats my tongue, leaving behind a fruity mix of flavours. The cold bubbles tickle my nose, and the froth pops against my lip. Damien smiles at me, forgetting himself as he leans over and wipes the foam from my lip, letting his fingers linger there just a little too long. Soraya and Malakai both catch my eye at the same moment, not holding back their smiles. Arabella is too busy sneering at her ale to pay any attention. The others beside me don't seem to notice either. Damien pulls his arm back, clearing his throat as if just noticing what he has done.

His eyes find mine, and there is not an ounce of regret there.

23

NO GOOD DEED

RAYLIN

By the time the third tankards have been sloshed upon the table, the tavern is a full ruckus of noise and laughter. A bard plays joyous tunes, filling the stale air with his words. Some revellers join in with uneven pitches, a bawdy song about a sailor wooing a maiden.

Our table matches the atmosphere of the bar, laughter, and chatter being easily exchanged. Even Arabella lets out a joke or two, the ale going straight to her head. I know, because it has gone straight to mine too. My body feels light, my skin warm, my head buzzes with static, nothing else matters but this moment. Damien's fingers are laced with mine beneath the table, and although we think we are being inconspicuous, I am sure the others notice we are both missing an arm.

Briar is dancing at the end of the table, her skirts lifting and twirling as she moves. There's a softness to her as she smiles, something free and uncaring blooming along her features. She pulls Kiyoko to her side, spinning her in place. She smiles but her movements are more rigid, her eyes flicking around the room, careful of who's watching.

Catalina glides to her feet, taking Arabella with her. The four of them laugh and dance to the music, Kiyoko relaxes, and it could be just the four of them in the room, spinning and swaying to the beat.

Damien's fingers squeeze gently against mine, drawing my attention to him. His gaze is piercing, taking in every dip and curve of my face. His smile is electric, sending shocks of heat through my body.

I don't notice the music ending, I don't notice the men approaching. It's not until I realise there is no more laughter that I feel something in the air has changed.

There are two men by the table, their clothes and hands covered in black smears. Their hair hangs loose around their faces, looking like they've not washed in days. One has a scar across his right eye, the colour of which is misted, faded substantially from the blue of his other one.

"How's about we borrow a couple of your pretty ladies for the night? You can't be needing all of 'em," the one with the scar sputters.

"I think not," Malakai says from where he's risen from his seat, standing angled in front of the girls.

"You talk posh, boy. Not from round 'ere, are ya?" the burlier man sneers.

Damien releases my hand, climbing to his feet, positioning himself beside Malakai, not to cut him off, but to protect him should something go awry. "We want no trouble."

"Then it won't be any trouble to let us take ya females, will it now?"

The scarred man wraps his fingers around Arabella's arm, tugging at her. Malakai and Damien both take a step forward, but before either of them can react, the man stumbles back, crying out, blood gushing from his nose.

"You *bitch*!" he shouts.

Arabella had swung back her arm without notice, fist connecting with the man's face. She shakes out her fingers, blood now coating her stark knuckles, though I am unsure if it is hers or the man before her. The burlier man makes to grab her, but Malakai is quicker; his leg comes up, shoving the man back with a leather boot to the stomach. The man stumbles, falling backward with a crash into the wooden table behind him. The occupants of the table jump up, dripping with ale. One grabs the man by the scruff of his tunic, bringing him to his height.

The scarred man, who now has a face coated in blood, mostly recovers. Wanting to help his friend, he throws himself at the man who grips him. They go flying into another table and it is then that all hell breaks loose in the tavern. Tankards are thrown, ale splashing up walls and bodies. Hot-tempered shouting sounds from all corners of the room. The man standing behind the bar hollers, pointing to us, who stand slack-jawed at the destruction.

Before he can make it to our table, we bolt through the tavern door, and make it part way up the cobbled street, rain lashing down on us as we come to a stop.

A strident laugh bursts from Malakai. Everyone else follows suit.

"You just punched a man in the face!" Catalina howls at Arabella, making her laugh harder.

Malakai speaks once we have all recovered. "There's no way we are getting that boat back to Sorrelle tonight, not in this." He gestures to the sky. "We need to find shelter."

Before long we have found our way to a small inn, all dripping wet once more. Damien pays for the two remaining rooms, and we make our way up the stairs, down the long winding corridor. Unlocking the first room, we make our way inside, Damien and I hand in hand at the back of the group.

The room is small, barely space enough for two people. The bed is a double at most, its thin sheets looking worse for wear. The only other furniture in the room is a small dresser and a blue-and-orange striped sofa, about wide enough for one to sleep on.

Damien tugs on my hand, gesturing with his head as he guides me from the doorway and to the other room. He quietly unlocks it and we slip in undetected, locking it behind us. This room is similar to the other one, the bed slightly smaller, the sofa an exact match, maybe a little more torn. The only light, that of the moon through the window.

Damien spins me around, pulling me against his warm body.

"Do you know how difficult it has been all night, not to pull you over that table and kiss you?" My cheeks redden at his words, my eyes darting to his lips, to the little scar across his bottom one.

"How did you get it?" I ask, running my finger along it.

He stiffens against me, his throat bobbing as he swallows. "A story for another time." He smiles, his hand snaking up the back of my neck.

No more words are exchanged, just his lips against mine, ridding me of all thoughts. He lifts me off the floor, my legs dangling in place, and carries us to the bed. He lowers me down until I am laying across the worn sheets, his body angled over mine, propped up on one arm. His other arm strokes up my leg, his soft fingers—softer than I would imagine from a guard—gently roaming higher and higher. He hesitates as he gets to the hem of my dress, scrunched up at my thighs. I nod, letting him know it's okay. They carry on their climb, ascending higher still. His lips kiss down my jaw, my neck, sending warm shivers through my body. My hands find his arms, squeezing and admiring the muscles beneath his cotton tunic. His fingers reach the band of my underwear, lingering there, drawing idle shapes on my skin. A knot inside my stomach unfurls, my back arching, begging him to move those fingers to the left, to touch what is mine.

An invisible bucket of ice water is dumped over us as a thump sounds at the door, followed by a voice.

"Damien, let us in," Malakai mumbles.

Damien's head lowers, his forehead resting against my chest, he lets out an exasperated breath.

"Go away, Kai," his voice is rough, full of need.

"One room isn't big enough for all of us. We need both."

"We should probably let them in," I whisper reluctantly.

He lets a sigh out through his nose, planting one last kiss on my lips and straightening my dress before going to the door.

"Thank you, it's freezing out there," Malakai charges into the room, Arabella right behind him.

"Just you two?" Damien checks around the door, but no one else is there.

"Yeah, the others all camped up together, so it looks like we're stuck with each other," he says, a goofy smile on his face. "Let the girls take the bed, we will snuggle up on the sofa and keep each other warm," he adds, falling back against said sofa.

"Sofa is fine, but I am not snuggling up with you. And don't even think about stealing all the blankets."

Arabella and I climb into the bed, my body still tingling from all the places Damien touched. The thin sheets barely do anything to keep off the chill of the room.

"If it stays this cold, then I will certainly be snuggling up with Lena," Arabella says, shocking me into a smile. She lets her guard down once a few drinks are in her. She has become surprisingly pleasant.

I listen to the breathing in the room grow heavy with sleep, Malakai letting out very un-royal-like snores, while I stare at the ceiling.

Tonight felt like a dream, one that I don't wish to wake up from. The easy laughter between friends, the soft touch of an incredibly attractive man, one I know I am growing feelings for, blooming like delicate flowers deep within. Thoughts of telling him my true identity niggle at me. He already knows I'm not who I pretend to be—that being his idea. Could I tell him I am Raylin, Princess of Gavaria? If I am correct and he feels the same way I do, I expect I should not be worried.

Perhaps he will come back with me. Meet my family, join our kingdom, there we will not need to hide how we feel, we will not need to be a secret. My only obstacle now is the pendant, I just need to figure out how to get it. I need a plan. Today has been a distraction, thoughts of stealing the wretched thing banished from my mind. I cannot let that happen any longer. Malakai has trusted me with his secret, maybe I can trust him with mine. But stealing from his family is a whole new game, one I don't anticipate him being up for playing.

The boat rocks against the churning waves, taking us home. Golden sunshine illuminates Sorrelle's castle as we near, a backdrop of clear blue sky stretching out as far as the eye can see. A chill still clings to the air, a light mist floating around us.

"Where did you disappear last night?" Soraya finds me pressed against the rails, looking down below at the sea.

"To bed, why do you ask?"

"Because I heard Malakai pounding on the door after he left our room."

My cheeks burn, I know they have turned a deep pink. "We kissed. Damien and I," I admit.

She raises an eyebrow, a smile stretching across her plump lips. "And? How was it?"

"Well...it wasn't the first time."

Her mouth drops open. "You kept that to yourself!" she says a little too loudly, causing Briar and Kiyoko to turn to look at us.

"Shh." I nudge her. "I will tell you everything later, away from prying eyes and ears."

We arrive in Sorrelle, the journey longer than the day before without the strong winds pushing us faster. The carriage takes us swiftly back to the castle, where we are greeted by our handmaidens, escorted to our rooms, washed, and dressed in clean clothes. I am thankful to have the grime of the inn scrubbed from my skin; even the sheets on their beds felt filthy.

I spend the long afternoon in my room, pacing the floors, treading onto the balcony and back indoors more times than my fingers can count, simply trying to come up with a plan to get the obsidian pendant. I have been over it time and time again, and still, no new ideas come to me.

It is when we are called for dinner, one the royals will be attending, that a thought unfurls, one that may or may not work at all. All I can do is try.

Hope.

We are guided to a smaller dining hall, much the same as the larger banquet hall we attended on our first day, the one we have eaten in most days on our stay. The walls and ceilings are lined with white and gold, hanging from them, the tapestries and banners in the deep green colours of Sorrelle, the sailboat crest stamped upon them.

King Rorik sits at the head of the table, looking much better in the days after waking. His cheeks are still slightly sunken, but the colour of his skin seems normal, his eyes brighter. The eyes I purposefully avoid.

Lord Jasper sits to one side of him, quieter than the man I have come to know, now knowing his place with the king in attendance. Prince Malakai sits beside Jasper, fiddling with his cloth napkin. Queen Lucia sits on the other side of the king, her back straight and gaze focused. I make a beeline in her direction, securing the place beside her, everyone else scatters around the table, taking their seats. I look to the guards standing on either side of the room. I spot one of them as Cadet Michaels, the other I am not familiar with. Damien is nowhere to be seen, which makes what I am going to do that bit easier.

Dinner consists of roasted lamb, fluffy mashed potatoes, and steamed long beans. The sound of cutlery clanging against plates is the only sound in the room for a long while.

"Where did you sneak off all night with our fine guests then, Mal?" Lord Jasper asks, a smile quirking at the side of his chubby mouth.

"Firstly, that is not my name. Secondly, how is that any concern of yours?"

"Just curious is all." Lord Jasper stares him down, the face of someone trying to get another in trouble.

"All night?" Queen Lucia chimes in.

"I just took them to Nuval for the day, Mother. The weather was bad, so we couldn't get home."

The king's eyes whip to his son's face, something like annoyance, maybe concern on his own. "*Nuval*? Of all places, you took them there?" King Rorik's voice is harsh, worn out.

Lord Jasper slyly smiles into his food. Malakai goes rigid beside him. Jasper knew exactly where we were. Knew exactly what he was doing questioning Malakai on it at this precise moment.

"It was a lovely day, the shops there are beautiful," Soraya says, seeming to try to ease the king's worries.

He ignores her. "You know how dangerous that place can be. Look what happened last time."

"Last time was my fault, Father. We are all here, aren't we? We are all safe, nothing bad happened."

My gaze flicks to Arabella, who keeps her head down, pushing food around on her plate. Something bad *could* have happened. Almost happened.

"What happened last time?" Catalina asks.

"Last time," King Rorik sneers, his eyes not leaving his son, "he was attacked. They stole all his gold, his clothes. They do not care if you are royalty. They take what they want. When they want," he spits, angry at Malakai or the people of Nuval, I'm not sure. Both, conceivably.

"And that is why this time I went free of my royal attire. We all dressed accordingly, no royal crests giving us away. I was careful with flaunting coin. We kept safe. I promise." Malakai doesn't meet his father's eyes, staring down at his half-eaten food instead.

"You are a fool," King Rorik grunts.

"What would you have done? Haul them up in this forsaken castle day after day? Drive them insane with boredom? Oh, that's right, that is what you are doing."

"I would not have taken her there! Somewhere she can get hurt!"

My brain stutters, I fidget in my seat. *Her.*

Everyone stops moving. Glances of confusion pass around the table.

"Her?" Malakai shakes his head, his brow creasing. "What do you mean, Father? Who?"

All the anger has melted from the king's face. Left now is nothing but a blank stare. "Them," he corrects himself, turning back to his food, finished with this conversation. For now.

Malakai looks to his mother, concern showing on both their faces. They think him still recovering, they think his mind is still foggy. I know otherwise. I am the *her* he spoke of. He remembers, so why isn't he telling?

Everyone slowly eases back into quiet conversation, cutlery again clinking off china plates. Servants have fled the room, knowing too well they should not be around for what transpired here. I use this opportunity to offer more wine to Queen Lucia, setting my plan in motion. She holds her glass as I pour.

I focus my energy, reaching for that frosty power inside of me. It rushes up to welcome me, happy to be at service. I send a small jolt through my arm, down to my fingers clasped around the bottle's neck. The shock of it bursts the bottle into a hundred tiny shards, scattering across the table, on dinner plates, on the floor, all over The Queen and me.

Queen Lucia stares down at her arm, trying to process what happened.

"Oh my stars, I am so sorry." My mind is focused as I grab a napkin and pat it at the blood swelling on her arm, multiple scratches oozing thick, sticky red.

"Enough!" She shakes me off, removing herself from the table.

The king follows her.

Servants pile in the room, sweeping the floor and clearing the table, the food now inedible. While everyone is occupied, I lean down, reaching up my skirts and tucking the bloodied napkin in the band of my dress.

My heart races. Galloping a thousand beats a minute.

I regain my position, intent on helping, when I spot Lord Jasper watching me from over the table, a twisted smile on his lips.

He doesn't know what I am up to, but it is clear, he knows I am up to something.

24

A FRIGID ENCOUNTER

MALAKAI

Dinner had gone worse than expected. Malakai had hoped to keep yesterday's trip quiet, knowing his father wouldn't have been keen on him taking the princesses so far from the castle, and particularly not to Nuval.

He wasn't sure how his uncle had found out; he had made certain Damien only chose a few of his trusted guards to know their whereabouts. Leave it to his uncle to sniff out a rat. Malakai cannot understand why the lord is even sticking around. His father is recovering as well as they could expect, the exception of that curious slip up at lunch. Malakai had a bad feeling about that. Was the king referring to his sister? He had thought her alive when he first woke. But Jasper wouldn't care about that. He must be up to something for him to still be here. The same reason that brought him here in the first place perhaps, Malakai just had to find out what that reason was.

His attention snaps back to the princesses before him as they arrive at their quarters. He hadn't meant to walk them all the way back here, his mind had been elsewhere. He makes to apologise for his father's behaviour but, thinking better of it, he closes his mouth. Why should he apologise for something that wasn't his fault? There was no logical reason for his father's reaction. Malakai had travelled to Nuval plenty of times since the mugging. It hadn't even been all that bad in the first place, they hadn't hurt him, simply taken his coin bag. And his favourite dagger, that's what Malakai had been most vexed about.

"Oh," he says, "I almost forgot, Father was going to announce it at dinner, but I suppose I shall do it now. With my father's recovery and my birthday nearing, we thought we would begin the festivities in style. There will be a midnight carnival arriving at the castle in the next couple of days. I do hope you will all join us in celebrating."

Briar gapes, her eyes round. "Wait...you don't mean *Baron Bean's Midnight Carnival*, do you?"

"Yes, that's it."

Collective gasps go around the group.

"*The* Baron Bean, is coming here?" Catalina squeals, her and Briar clasping hands in excitement.

"You've heard of him then?" Malakai smiles, thoughts of his father buried deep.

"Heard of him!? He runs the best carnival in all of Aldros," Briar exclaims.

"I heard there's a man who can swallow snakes whole. Living, breathing snakes."

"I heard there's a woman who can transform into a cat."

All the 'I heards' passing about the group indicate none of them have seen the elusive Baron Bean or his carnival. It was the same for Malakai. Though come to think of it, he had never heard anyone be completely sure of anything when talking of the greatest carnival of all time. It was almost as if it was all a hoax, a strange rumour spread throughout Aldros. It made Malakai wonder if anything would appear on the night the carnival was set to arrive.

Malakai leaves the girls there, their excitement following him down the corridor as he goes. He makes it to the second floor, managing to avoid being followed by a guard. By now, most think Damien is by his side, which he normally is. But the meeting about to take place doesn't call for Damien's presence, for any guard's presence for that matter. It would be rather inappropriate.

He leans against the wall, the painting of a gilded lion beside him, its jaw wide in a roar. He checks both ends of the hallway before pressing a hand to the frame. A soft *click* sounds, the painting parting with the wall just slightly. Malakai slips through, entering the dark, narrow passage behind. The door to the right is slightly ajar, indicating his lover is already inside. He steps over the threshold, the soft warm glow of a lantern greeting him. Teddy stands before him, smiling wide, wrapped in the pale violet blanket they left behind before.

Save for the lantern light, the rest of the room is dark. No windows or doors for light to seep through. The room is thoroughly cut off from the rest of the castle. Unless you know of the secret passages, there is no way in or out. The room is small, the wallpaper peeling from the walls, the carpet worn and aged. A small sofa sits against the nearest wall, a stack of books and parchment opposite—all coated in a thick layer of dust. Malakai had never been inclined to rifle through said piles, so he didn't know what they held.

He could only assume the room was a hiding place for the first king, him being the one to build the passages. He was a curious man, though many others would choose to use the word mad. The stories Malakai had read always painted him as paranoid; he was always sure someone was out to get him. Hence the passages, he needed comfort, a way to hide from the rest of the world. Then, over time, the passages were forgotten, left to dwell between the brick walls. That was until Malakai stumbled across one.

Almost all the corridors in the castle have one, some interconnected, some not. It had taken Malakai an age to find them all, marking them out on a map as he went. He rarely uses the map now, remembering which paintings hold which rooms. There was the odd occasion he would find something interesting, a relic of some kind, something, too, lost over time, forgotten. Sometimes these objects would be a clue, leading him to other places within the castle. He thought maybe the first king of Sorrelle left them there to remind himself, or maybe he knew one day another would find the passages, and these were gifts, strange and unimportant for the most part.

"You took your time," Teddy says now, wrapping the blanket around the two of them, bringing them chest to chest.

"I am here now, aren't I?"

Teddy lets out an appreciative groan, his lips finding Malakai's. "I missed you yesterday," he whispers against them.

Malakai replies by pushing their mouths together harder, devouring Teddy's breath. The blanket drops to the floor without a thought, their hands exploring each other's bodies. Teddy pulls Malakai's tunic over his head in one swift movement. His gaze lingering on his bare torso. "I don't think I can ever get over these muscles."

Malakai huffs a laugh, pulling Teddy back to him. He shivers as Teddy's hands glide up his body, his soft baker's hands gently pressing against him. Within breathless moments, they are both down to their underwear, bodies crashing together. They blindly fall to the sofa, ignoring the puff of dust that bursts into the air.

Malakai's hand lingers on Teddy's waistband, waiting for his blessing before slithering beneath and taking grasp of the hardness within. Teddy gasps, back arching at the movement. The kisses become ravenous, begging for more. It is all Malakai can think about. More. More. He nips at the soft skin of Teddy's neck, his hand moving faster against him, the moan of pleasure that escapes him undoes everything that Malakai is, everything he once was.

He flips Teddy over, spitting into his own hand for that sweet lubrication, and enters him from behind with enough conviction to command an army. He thrusts into him, gently at first, then harder, harder. His breath turns ragged, hitching with each thrust of his body. He reaches round, taking Teddy in his hand, taking them both to the brink of euphoria. Teddy's knuckles turn white as he grips the back of the sofa, his soft moans turning Malakai to molten liquid.

They move as one, bound and unbroken.

Nothing matters but this moment.

Nothing matters but Teddy and him.

Forever. Always.

Malakai's lips are hungry and wanting, exploring the extensive line of his partner's neck. Malakai's hand pumps at Teddy's cock, coaxing moan after moan of pleasure. "Say my name." His words are rough, filled with need.

"Malakai," Teddy rushes out between pants and groans. "Malakai."

It is his name falling from his lover's lips which undo him.

There is not a word for what he feels in this moment, bliss too small of a feeling, even euphoric is not enough. They move together, the world shattering around them, the very pillars of the castle crumbling to dust. Absolute ecstasy fills him, so much that it tips over the edge. Fireworks blaze and explode beneath his skin, leaving behind sparks of light.

Malakai bellows with delight, Teddy's elation not far behind. Their hands clasp together, squeezing as they fall over the edge as one before flopping in a heap against the sofa.

Resting against Teddy, Malakai draws lazy circles on his back, steadying his breathing with each hitched breath. "I am yours. Forever."

"As I am yours."

Malakai cannot keep the smile off his face as he makes his way back to his room. His heart is full, beating not for himself, but for Teddy. Theodore. His love. His king.

He vows at that moment to tell his parents everything. He wants to share this love, not hide it away. Something this magical should never be kept locked in a box, tucked away from the world. It should be celebrated, cherished. It would if Teddy was a woman, and it shall even now. Malakai promises that to himself.

He is so lost in the clouds; he doesn't even notice the smirk of the guard's face at his door. He enters obliviously into his rooms. Unaware of what awaits him. It's only when he takes the steps to his bed chambers that he sees the surprise.

His eyes bulge from his head, the smile wiped from his face. He stops, foot hovering above the floor. He looks behind him, sure this is some kind of joke. Then back to the body decked in white on his bed.

Her milk white legs are bare, corset tight, cinching in her tiny waist. A see-through chiffon is thrown delicately around her shoulders, her white-blonde hair cascading like a wave over the pillow.

Her eyes are closed, red mouth soft, lips parted slightly. Her breathing deep, her chest rising and falling in long strides. Malakai whispers, confusion lacing his words, “Arabella?”

Her eyes spring open, her gaze latching on to him like she knew he was waiting there. She gets to her knees, shoulders back, chest out, head slightly tilted as she looks at Malakai through lowered lashes.

“Wh– what are you doing?” Malakai stutters, running a hand through his dishevelled hair.

“Let’s not play pretend. You know as well as I do that we are the best suited. So let’s just stop this whole facade and get on with it. Choose me and send the others home.” She crawls toward him on the bed, never breaking eye contact.

“Arabella, I—” There are no words, Malakai remains frozen as she comes toward him. He cannot help but feel bad for her. This beautiful woman throwing herself at him. Begging him.

She slides off the bed, one leg in front of the other as she saunters toward him. Her hands rest on his shoulders, one sliding skilfully down his chest. She reaches the bottom of his tunic, hand reaching beneath, running over his defined chest. Malakai’s first thought is, *Stars, her hands are cold.* His second is that he needs to stop this before she embarrasses herself. More so than she already has.

"Arabella, you need to stop."

"Do you not like it, Your Highness? Do you not find me worthy enough for you?" Her voice is low, velvety.

"No!"

Her hands fall to her side, her posture slacking, swaying as she takes a step back. "Oh."

"That's not what I meant. You're worthy, just not for me—No, that's not right. Any other prince would be lucky to have you, any other man. But I'm not, it's just...Oh for stars sake. I'm gay, Arabella. I'm– I'm in love with a man."

Malakai takes a deep breath, releasing it slowly. He's never said those words to anyone before. Sure, he introduced Lena to Teddy, he has told Damien about him. But not once has he used *that* word, not once had he felt the release of pressure that the word held on his chest.

Arabella is a statue, still enough to be one at least. Malakai's not even sure if she breathes, eyes wide and staring.

"Say something."

Her lips part, the only indication she hears him. Within a blink, realisation takes over. She gasps, hand flying to her mouth. Her arm curls around her middle, her ears turning a bright shade of red. "Oh my." She laughs nervously.

Malakai spots her cloak thrown carelessly across the chair. The white is stark against the deep green. He grabs it, carefully draping it around her shoulders, giving her some form of reprieve.

"I should go." She swallows, a flush spreading across her cheeks.

Malakai reaches out to her, stopping her before she can leave. He takes hold of her arms and she lowers her head, avoiding his gaze. With a gentle nudge of his fingers against her chin, he tilts her head to look up toward him. She seems smaller at this moment, cowering in on herself. This courageous, formidable woman, shattered by mere words.

Malakai keeps his tone warm as he says, "Don't ever beg for someone else's love, Arabella. You do not need to. I have watched you since you arrived here, and you are not what you pretend to be. You may fool your kingdom, you may fool everyone else, but you cannot fool me. I have been pretending my whole life to be someone else. I see right through you."

Tears pool in her eyes, her features softening. "I'm sorry," she whispers.

"Do not apologise. You came after what you wanted, that's something I never could do. But do not throw yourself at any man. Anyone deemed worthy of *you*, would not allow someone so beautiful to wait. So I am sorry for making you think otherwise."

Malakai stumbles back as she throws her arms around him. His arms wrap around her, holding on to each other as if they've never been held before.

"Will you stay?" Malakai smiles down at her, beaming as she smiles back, a simple nod in answer.

They spend hours on the bed, sharing fruit dipped in melted chocolate that Malakai had delivered to his room. The bananas are Arabella's favourite, something they don't have back in Faldova, the climate too cold.

"It wasn't always bad," Arabella says, a sad smile on her lips. "When my mother died, Father lost a piece of himself. But he had me, and we were enough for each other to get through it. His every ounce of attention was mine." She looks out the window, a crease forming between her brows. "That went away when he met *her*. I was only eight, but I knew right away who she was deep down. Now I live in a castle with an evil stepmother and stepsister." Arabella laughs. "It sounds like something from a storybook, but that's truly how it was. She would pit my father against me, and our relationship frayed until there was almost nothing left."

Malakai's warm hand squeezes her cold one, a comforting touch.

"I was a stranger in my own home. My stepsister, Freyja, is older than me, and she would get to attend the balls, wear the crowns. But little old me? I would be scolded for trying. I realised in the end that, if I wanted to stop them from walking all over me, I had to become like them. I had to play a part.

"It is why I wanted this so badly, why I wanted *you* so badly. I thought if I could just get someone with all this"—she waves her arms in a circle—"at his feet, then I could prove I am more than what they thought. I could secure my place as the next Queen of Faldova."

"But surely that is already yours. Freyja is not your blood, she would not have your gifts."

"No, but Anya is pregnant. Well, by now she's probably had the child in my absence. If that child has the gift, I know Anya will do whatever it takes to steal the kingdom from me."

"We won't let that happen, Arabella. You are the rightful heir, and I will do anything in my power to help you. You have my word."

"I don't think the word of a prince will be enough."

"What about the word of a king?"

Her eyes go wide. "Would your father truly help me?"

"Not my father. Me. Father said as soon as I choose a bride, we will have a coronation. He will pass his crown to me."

"But...you don't want a *bride*, Malakai."

"No. But maybe I won't have to."

25

A WAY IN

RAYLIN

I'm standing on the balcony of my room, watching the sky turn a sorrowful blue, when Soraya speaks from behind, having let herself into my room. My gaze flicks to my mound of pillows, the cloth napkin with Queen Lucia's blood tucked beneath.

"Don't suppose that handsome lover of yours has shown you any secret passages around the castle?" She leans against the wall by the door, fluffing up her dark curls.

"He's not my lover."

Her eyebrows hitch up a fraction. "But he has shown you secret passages?"

"Depends on where you want to go." I eye her suspiciously.

"Don't fret. Just to the kitchens, we have a mission."

I take her through the servant's door and down the stairwell. Not too certain which way to go from here. We turn a corner into a well-lit corridor and both spot the guard at the same time, scrambling back into the room, our backs against the wall.

"What exactly is our mission?" I whisper.

"Food, booze, whatever we can get."

"What in the stars for?"

"A celebration of life, of course." She peers around the corner, dragging me out when she sees it's clear.

We move quietly, looking for any indication of the kitchen. We are having no such luck when voices drift toward the corridor, getting closer and closer with each breath. I grab the bronze handle of the door closest to me, taking Soraya's hand and yanking her inside with me. I don't see inside the room before we are enclosed in darkness. It is pitch black, not even a speck of light seeping through the cracks in the door. I feel utterly alone. My heart ricochets in my chest, that giddy feeling exploding in my stomach. It's not like it matters if we get caught really, we will just be escorted back to our rooms. But this...this is the thrill I became so keen on when stealing in the market. The thrill I get when Damien kisses me. Adrenaline pumping through my veins.

A clink sounds from behind me.

"I think we found one of the things we seek." Soraya's voice comes from far away.

There's a scrape of metal against metal as she pulls open the curtains, moonlight flooding the room. Case upon case of glass bottles adorn the space, some reaching high above us.

"Looks like we found the king's liquor room."

She pulls a short, wide bottle from a wooden crate, amber liquid sloshing inside. She goes to another crate, pulling out a similar colour liquid, this one more red, the bottle twisting in on itself in the middle.

She cradles the bottles beneath the layers of her skirts. "Let's get out of here."

We make it back to our rooms without incident.

"Today is the anniversary of the death of Catalina's grandfather." Soraya shrugs. "She usually has a big family gathering to remember him, but I guess getting drunk with us will have to suffice."

We gather up Kiyoko and Briar before making our way to Catalina's rooms. She welcomes us with open arms, then excuses her handmaiden—a short girl with cropped blonde hair—for the night.

"I will be right back," I announce before I am fully in the room.

I knock on door number five, Arabella's room, but there is no answer. I knock again; silence.

The bottles of liquor Soraya and I procured are passed about by the five of us. We all lounge on the plush purple rug at the end of Catalina's bed, sipping from the bottles, having no glasses to decant the liquid into.

"Sorry, this is all we could get," Soraya says.

"This is perfect, having you all here is more than enough. I sent my prayers to the stars earlier on, not my usual offering, but my Abuelo is sure to have heard them, even from so far." Catalina smiles, swigging from the twisted bottle.

"To Catalina's Abuelo," I say, holding the other bottle aloft. She clinks hers with mine and we proceed by all swigging from each bottle.

The amber liquid burns my throat as it goes down, sitting in my stomach like burning lava. I pace myself, not wanting my head to become fuzzy too fast; I have another mission later on tonight.

The minutes tick by, turning into hours. The conversation gets louder as the liquid in the glass bottles decreases. I am unsure how the exchange got to where it is now, but all eyes are on me, anticipation twinkling in each of them.

"So...has it been anything other than kissing?" Briar interrogates.

I shake my head, my face going hot.

"Ugh! I am so jealous." Catalina throws herself back against the rug. "That man is a piece of art. I can just sense the rippling muscles beneath all those clothes. It's a crime that he doesn't walk around stark naked."

I grab the pillow from beside me and throw it at her. Before it can hit her, she grabs it, placing it behind her head, her smile wide.

"You're despicable," I tell her, not hiding my laughter.

"It's not *my* fault. Sorrelle hasn't exactly been offering the boys up on a silver platter. The pickings are slim."

"Is there someone back in Zenick you have eyes on?" Kiyoko asks her.

"There are a lot of *someones* in fact." Catalina winks and Kiyoko's eyes turn wide. "Turns out there aren't many restrictions when you are the powerless, youngest in a long line of powerful siblings."

"What about girls? Have you...kissed any girls?" Briar says, fiddling with the bottle in her lap.

"I haven't. But that's partly why I'm here. My sister is not married, yet Prince Malakai isn't quite to her tastes. The main flaw being that he has a penis."

"Have you?" Soraya asks Briar, who shakes her head slowly.

"I have never been kissed before," she admits, "so I am unsure who or what I like. I find both males and females attractive enough."

"Could be that you like both. My brother does," Soraya says, her shoulders lifting and falling.

"Both," she whispers, almost to herself, contemplation crossing her features. I don't miss the way her eyes flutter to Kiyoko, lingering there for a moment.

"So, how is it, with him?" Catalina's eyes twinkle.

"It's...like magic. Like that rush inside you get when you use your powers, the way your toes tingle, the way your heart sets alight." I realise too late what I have said. "Or...the way I've been told powers feel." I laugh it off.

Soraya's gaze lingers on me a moment, something in her face that causes my heart to stutter. Fortunately, the others do not pay attention to my slip up and Catalina raises the bottle high in a toast. "To making friends and copulation."

To making friends, we all say in unison, leaving out her last statement.

We remain on the floor, succumbing to slumber one by one. Catalina was the first to fall asleep, midway through a sentence, unsurprisingly. Kiyoko and Briar went next, the intoxication causing their heavy lids to finally give in, curled next to each other on the plush rug. Finally, Soraya's breathing becomes heavy, the steady pace of her inhalations filling the room.

I lay there for a few minutes, making certain they are all asleep, then I slink from the room, careful not to tread on fingers or toes. I make quick work of going to my room and grabbing the napkin, still laying beneath my pillow. Two guards remain at the main entrance to our chambers, so I follow the path I had taken Soraya along earlier. Instead of turning right down the staircase, I go up.

The castle is quiet, everyone sleeping or tucked away safely in their rooms. I avoid guards at their posts, and few roam the corridors at night, which makes my work easier.

Before I know it, I am down the narrow passage and standing in front of the large golden doors to the queen's vaults. My heart jumps, every nerve ending in my body standing to attention. I copy Queen Lucia's movements from the days prior, twisting each larger circle until I hear a clunk from within.

Now the harder part.

I grip the bloodied cloth between my teeth, pulling tight on either side, tearing the cloth in two. I wet the larger spots of blood on both parts of the cloth with my saliva, the only thing I can think to do without diluting the blood too much. My heart pumps too loudly in my ears, drowning out everything around me. I press the now-wet blood to the green gems set between the hummingbird's claws.

Please work. Please work.

Nothing happens. I keep the rags pressed there anyway, pressing harder.

When nothing continues to happen, my arms sag to my sides, an exasperated sigh escaping between my lips. The chances of it working were slim to none, but I still had hope.

I turn to leave when a soft click calls out to me.

I freeze in place. If I move, it might not be real.

I arch my head over my shoulder, and from whatever miracle I have been granted, the doors have parted slightly, a slither of darkness within. I creep inside, pushing the doors to behind me, making sure not to close them fully. Reaching deep within, I call for my kingdom's power, for light. A soft glow emanates around me, my very skin glowing within the dark. Shadows dance inside the mirrors as I make my way to the back of the room, heading straight to the hidden place beyond this one.

There it is.

The obsidian pendant. More beautiful than it was before.

I call for it. Willing it to come to me. Nothing.

I go to my knees before it. Placing my hand against the cold glass case, like so many times before with Fee's cage. I ask the cage silently to let me through, to let me touch what resides inside. The glass responds by refusing my request. The spell on it is unlike anything I have ever known, almost as if it has its own subconscious.

I think for a moment, asking it again to let me inside, but it gives the same answer as before. I try to force the cage off, nothing. Try to shatter it with my power, nothing. Try to shatter it with my fist, but all I get is pain.

"What is it you want?" I ask.

It does not answer.

If force will not work, then I will try a different method, one less likely but my only option now.

Keeping my hand pressed firmly against the glass, I show it love. I show it memories of my brother. My mother. My father. Of Fee, soaring beside me as we race through grasslands and waters. I show it the things I keep hidden, my feelings, my sorrow, my joy, my fears. I show it my tears, my heartbreak, my smile, my laughter.

I also show it things that have not yet come to be.

Me, returning home, wrapped in the warm embrace of my family, of my kingdom, willing it to give me that which will help me get there.

The glass surrenders.

It does not create an entrance; instead, my whole hand slips through, like the glass cage is not truly there at all.

The world slows as my fingers graze the pendant, lifting it from where it hangs. It moves easily with me through the case. When

I place my fingers against the glass once more, it has returned to a solid. I hear a voice, not audibly, but inside me, not my own, something other, wishing me good luck.

I flee the vault, securing the doors behind me, the pendant tucked in the bloodied cloth, clenched between my fist. I'm through the passage and barely down the corridor when a voice stops me in my tracks.

"And where do you think you're going at such a late hour, *Princess*?"

I contemplate throwing the pendant into the void for a split second, but I am too worried I won't be able to call it back, so I tuck it into the deep pocket of my dress, praying to the stars he doesn't spot my movement as I turn to face him.

Lord Jasper stands before me, head cocked to the side, his smug smile making me want to punch him in the face. His jacket has been abandoned, but he still wears his too-tight trousers and deep green shirt.

"To my room, Lord Jasper."

His smile widens. I take a step back as he takes one closer. "In that case...where have you *been*?"

"I don't see how that is any of your business."

"I make it my business when you are sneaking around the halls of my family's castle. Stealing the blood of my brother's wife."

He takes two steps forward, I take another back, only a small step before my back is pressed against a wall.

"You may have the little prince wrapped around your finger, but you do not fool me."

He steps close enough for the tips of our shoes to touch, his face barely an inch from mine. I turn my head to the side as his large nose comes into contact with my cheek.

My breathing picks up.

"Give it to me," he says, keeping his voice low. His breath is hot on my skin, the smell of onion lingering on his words.

"What?" He cannot know I have the pendant. How could he?

"The napkin."

Relief washes through me, but still, my heart thumps hard against my chest. I consider giving him the cloth, its purpose complete. But if I do, he can take it to the king, he would have evidence of what I have done. If I play him off as foolish, there is no proof. His word against mine.

"I have no idea what you are talking about," I lie, my voice coming out shakier than I intend.

His dumpy hand slams against my chest, shoving me hard against the wall. "Do not lie to me!"

My vision blurs; it is not Lord Jasper before me, but Genevieve. Her body pressed too close to mine, yelling at me to know my place, to behave. Her arm as it swings, lashing my back with a cane. Her fingers as they coil around my hair, grabbing and pulling as she throws me to the ground.

Tears fill my eyes.

He is not Genevieve. I owe this man nothing. He has no right to touch me.

"Get...off....me," I struggle to get out.

His smile widens, his hand pressing harder where it rests on my chest.

Something in my stomach uncoils, a chilled fog extending a hand, if I should so need it. I leave it there, not wanting to give myself away. Yet.

"You think me stupid? Is that it?"

I ignore him, flinching as he slams his fist into the wall beside me, letting out a roar of anger. He makes to reach into my pocket, and without a moment's thought I shove a palm against him. A dark unrelenting force shoots from me, knocking him back further than anticipated.

"You do not touch me." My voice doesn't sound like my own, raw and filled with command. "Do you understand?"

Fear grips him, freezing him to the spot. His eyes are wide and unblinking. Slowly, he nods.

"You will not speak of this. Of me."

I run as fast as I can back to Catalina's room, not caring if the guards see me. I sneak back into my spot, laying my head against the soft rug. All the girls remain undisturbed.

I do not sleep. I cannot sleep.

My heart thrashes in my chest, my body shaking uncontrollably, the ice of my power swirling through my veins, begging for more, begging for release.

I do not concede.

26

Midnight is upon us

Raylin

Two days pass. Lord Jasper doesn't utter a word of that night. If we happen to see each other, which is not often, he lowers his gaze and makes haste.

I keep the pendant close to me at all times. The morning after taking it, I clasped it around my neck, the stone cold against my bare skin. Within mere moments it felt wrong, something dark and powerful withering inside. It weakened me, like it was stealing my very essence. So instead, I choose my outfits carefully, being sure to pick the dresses with the deepest pockets, tucking the pendant inside. I bide my time, waiting for the right moment to make my move. To leave the castle undetected, find Genevieve and be free.

Truly free.

I will come back once it is done, tell Damien everything. Tell Soraya everything. Tell Malakai. Maybe not right away. But I will. I must.

Ella stands behind me, getting me ready for the night ahead. The sun slowly sets, leaving behind a blue so dark it appears almost purple. The carnival is due to arrive at midnight, which is apparent with a name like *Baron Bean's Carnival of Midnight*

Madness. I am told from the moment they arrive to the moment they leave, it is a spectacular event. Anyone and everyone will be there, which I decide is the perfect time to sneak away. The main gates will be open, giving me ample opportunity to pass through without question.

Ella sets my wavy hair loose down my back, pulling sections from my face and pinning them to the back of my head with a little contraption: a silver moth with wings in intricate detail sitting below a thin circle of metal, little branches sprouting off it to the sides. She loops my hair through the circle, securing it in place with a long thin stick made of the same metal. It is beautiful. My dress is a simple, pale pink silk, a low neckline that folds and flows between my breasts. It sits close to my body, loose enough around the bottom to give me plenty of movement, although no pockets, so the obsidian pendant is tucked safely in my cloak hanging by the door.

We still have time to spare before midnight, and I want to spend some time with Ella before I leave. I think I will miss her the most. Her laugh. The way she hums as she does my hair, the look in her eyes she gets when she sees what great work she has done on me. But most of all, the feeling I get when I am with her, a little sister I did not ask for, yet somehow need.

"What is your favourite thing to do?" I ask her.

She eyes me through the mirror, fiddling with my hair, a gleam in her eye. "I should probably show you, rather than tell you. Words could never be enough."

"Then show me."

She holds my hand tight as she races us through servant corridors. Workers pay us no attention as we go, used to Ella's easily distracted nature, I assume. We exit the castle by a narrow black door, straight into the gardens beyond. We are in a closed off area, a place I have never seen—the main doors to the gardens I have been through many times before are nowhere in sight—but she doesn't stop as we go deeper, no real path to follow. The sound of something sharp scraping on mud meets us through the thicket of bushes and her grin goes wide as her gaze flicks to me.

Ella pushes aside branches and leaves, creating a space within a bush for us to pass through. We stand in a small clearing, only the silver light of the moon upon us.

A large beast is chained to an even larger tree, the thick chain looped multiple times around the trunk, a wide piece of metal locked in place around the beast's back foot.

"This is Nasima," Ella whispers, so as not to spook the creature.

I step closer, taking in every detail. The face, beak, and talons are much like that of an eagle. But the body, a lion through and through. It's larger than a horse, with remarkably large wings cascading over its back, indicating that it is a female.

"A gryphon." I take another step closer. "But how is she here? I thought they were native to Kignet."

Genevieve had told me about the magnificent creature that roams her homeland as a child, the creature that represents her kingdom, stitched into each banner and flag. I spent the weeks that followed delving into books looking for any morsel of them I could. I was incredibly fascinated with the beasts. One of the few creatures known to man to have such a mix of different animals within them. Only the females have wings, letting them fly through the skies. They are said to mate for life once they find a partner; if one were to die, the other would never search for another, they would live alone forevermore.

"It was found within Sorrelle's forests around five years ago, thought to have lost its way. She's been here ever since, us servants care for her. I am unsure if the king even knows she still lives, he didn't think she would last a week."

The creature lifts its head to me as I get closer, her pitch-black eyes fixed on my face. I stretch out an arm, lowering my hand to her and bowing my head. I feel a huff of warm breath against the back of my hand as she sniffs.

"*Lena!* Be careful."

I open my eyes to find the gryphon has moved silently, now towering over me. She breathes in slowly, her chest rising and falling in great huffs. Then she simply turns and keeps on digging her talon into the mud. I stroke her neck, and she lets me.

"She's beautiful." The word feels inadequate. "Why do you not free her?"

Ella shakes her head, her eyebrows pulling together in a question she does not ask. "We worry she won't be able to find her way home, that she will be captured or, worse, killed. At least here we can care for her, give her a good life."

"Being caged is not a good life."

"You're right." Ella's words are short, a sadness to them. "It is not."

I look at her, really look at her. For all this bravado she puts on, and for however much she may look up to the queen, she is still a girl trapped within her own home. We have that in common.

However, I have a way out.

I cannot stop my feet from shuffling as we stand on the castle steps, waiting in the cold for the carnival. In just a few meagre moments it will be here. The atmosphere is running high with excitement. The five princesses, Malakai, Lord Jasper, and me, are behind King Rorik and Queen Lucia, who stand hand in hand two steps in front of us. Damien and a regiment of guards linger further behind us, readying to patrol the courtyard, no doubt hopeful to enjoy the festivities themselves when they can. The gates remain closed, crowds of people piling behind them, waiting to enter.

As the bell tower chimes midnight, a blinding flash of light envelops the space before us. In the blink of an eye, it is overtaken with music and light.

The carnival has arrived.

Tents in various sizes of deep blue and gold spread through the courtyard, the roofs sloping up into peaks, little golden flags perched on top. Twinkling lights cascade down each tent like blinking stars, lighting up the night. From here I cannot see much else. There is something resembling a cage part way, but what resides inside I do not know. A man steps toward us, a tall hat upon his head matching the blue of the tents. His face is young, but his eyes are old and knowing, flecks of silver in them glinting in the starlit night. He wears a black tailcoat, the back stretching most of the length of his legs, black trousers, and shoes so shiny you could probably see your reflection in them. His skin is dark, his lips tilting up in a grin. He leans forward on a black and gold cane—the handle, the head of a lion, carved from diamond—bowing low to all who stand before him. As he rises, his gaze snags on me for a moment, freezing in place before landing on the king and queen.

Catalina squeezes my arm, her voice low. "It's him. It's Baron Bean."

"Welcome, one and all!" His voice booms out across the courtyard, soft yet lethal. "I invite you to join us for a night you will never forget, at Baron Bean's Carnival of Midnight Madness!" He takes a step back, spinning on his heel and disappearing in a cloud of smoke.

A cheer sounds out around the courtyard, and at that exact moment the castle gates are flung open, the crowds stampeding through impatiently.

"Go, enjoy yourselves," King Rorik pronounces.

Malakai grabs my hand and I grab Soraya with my other before he pulls me into the throng of people and tents. It seems we all had the same idea, as I turn my head and see us all in a long line, a paper chain of friends.

Damien catches up with us as we reach the first tent, never keeping Malakai too far from sight. A sign on the tent reads, *The Wisp*. We all step inside, unshackling each other from our grips.

It is like stepping through a portal, the inside much larger than it first appears. Chairs of deep blue sit in rows, a path through the middle. We choose a section toward the back and take our seats. I notice him then, a man perched high on a pole, balancing precariously on one foot. His whole body is covered by a thick, black one-piece suit, a smooth white mask of plastic over his face, no holes for his eyes, mouth, or nose. I don't take my eyes off him, watching, waiting for what will happen.

As the tent fills, he screams. A blood-curdling scream that sets the hairs on my arms on end. All eyes are on him as he takes a step forward, dropping into the air before being enclosed by a dark mist, then reappearing on the floor before us. The dark mist,

I see more clearly now, are shadows. Each one is in the shape of a person, attached to him like they are all his own. He does some more tricks, disappearing and reappearing throughout the crowd, enclosing people in shadows before making them appear elsewhere in the room. He ends on a high, his power surging through the room as he shrouds everyone in that black mist. Every single chair is empty, yet not, before we all appear again. He bows low as everyone claps.

Although he has no face, as he rises, I am certain his eyeless gaze lingers on me for a breath.

The next tent we enter is filled to the brim. We stand by the entrance and watch as two identical girls hang from bars on the ceiling.

"Chio," one shouts as she hurtles through the air.

"And Chiy," the other one calls as she does the same.

They catch each other in mid-air, twisting in a cannonball until they land feet first on a mat below them, hands still clasped. Chiy, or maybe Chio, throws the other back up. She catches the bar again with ease and swings as her twin grabs hold of her feet, sending her back through the air.

"I'm going to take a walk," I tell Soraya.

"I will come with you." She loops her arm through mine, and we leave the tent together.

We walk past a tent with the flaps wide open, a man inside throwing knives of flame through the air. Another houses a woman dressed in a puffy jacket and trousers of white and red, her face painted white, dark downward eyebrows and a slash of red across her lips. We watch as she plays the banjo, jumping from foot to foot as a man in a chair beside her nods off. Then she bends down, whispering something in his ear.

His eyes fling open and he starts to dance, hopping from foot to foot just like she was. Her voice is filled with joy and amusement as she tells the man to bend down and touch his toes; he obliges. Then again when she tells him to slap himself across the face. We move quickly from the tent, not wanting to be caught in the thrall.

"Why do they all have such unusual powers?"

I have only known of powers to come from the ten kingdoms, and only the royal families to possess them. It is odd to see such things beyond what we are taught. I was made to believe I would be hunted if people knew of my strange abilities, but here are others, those who do not come from the rule book. They are not hunted, they are celebrated, they are loved.

"There is said to be a time when anyone could possess powers, a time when there was one ruler for all ten kingdoms, and all in between. A place you did not have to be a part of the royal line to have such gifts. I never really believed in such things before,"—Soraya laughs softly—"but tonight, I cannot deny it."

"Where have you read such things? I have scoured history books and never once have I heard of such a tale."

"I speak to the dead; they all have stories to tell."

I laugh. Of course.

A cat sits before us, watching us as she licks her paw.

"Hi, little one." Soraya bends down to pet her.

She soon pulls her hand back, straightening to her proper height, hand tucked to her chest, as the cat transforms into a woman. Her long black-and-white hair hangs over her shoulders, covering her naked body. A feline smile creeps across her lips as she looks toward me, a purr emanating off her, before walking away without a word.

Soraya shudders. "So creepy."

I look over my shoulder as someone shouts our names, to see Damien, Malakai, and Arabella running toward us. "Wait up!"

"Oh my stars, a house of mirrors! We must go in," Malakai says as he reaches us, on the move again before he fully stops.

We enter the house of mirrors, and it truly is what it states. It is disorientating and reminds me of the mirror hiding Queen Lucia's extra room in her vaults, but there are hundreds of them, all set at different angles. I lose the others much too quickly.

Despite the mirrors, it is dark in here, as if they swallow light instead of reflecting it. Just when I think I've found a way, it turns out to be a dead end. I twist and turn, looking for someone, anyone. But all I find is myself staring back at me.

"Damien?" I call. "Soraya?"

There are no answers, like the mirrors suck in all noise as well as light.

I hesitate as I turn a corner, seeing a flash of blue ahead. I follow it, then see it again from the corner of my eye, but it's gone just as fast as I can turn. I stand still, staring into the mirror before me. There it is again, a shot of blue. But not in the room. In the mirror.

I put my palm against the mirror, waiting for it again. This time it lingers, hovering there. It has no shape at all; it writhes and thrashes in the air like it cannot escape, this blob of blue nothing. Faster than I can avoid, it shoots toward me, flying out of the mirror and crashing full force into my face. It moves across my cheek, slithering toward my ear. It stings my fingers as I try to remove it. I have no such luck—it is wet and cold as it slides down my ear canal. Baron Bean's voice sounds nearby and I whip around, looking for the source.

"Find the one with hair of green fire. There you will find what you seek."

I still. The voice did not come from a person, it came from my head, from that thing, the blue light. But why would he send me a message? And why in this manner? It could be possible it wasn't meant for me at all. But it feels like too much of a coincidence. That light followed me, got to me when I was well and truly alone.

I rush from the house of mirrors, that thing inside me guiding the way. The others aren't here, they must all still be inside.

Although I am outside, I need air. I need space.

I move quickly along the path, deeper into the lines of tents. There is a pull inside me, leading to where, I'm not sure. I follow it blindly, dipping in and out of groups of people.

It tugs and pushes, urging me on faster, the feeling dissipates completely when I stand before a tent, this one different from the others. It is draped in black silk. The very air around it is still, quiet, waiting patiently for an untold secret. Something cold trickles along my jaw. I wipe at it with my fingers, to see the same strange blue of that light, of Baron Bean's voice, this time dimmer, its colour faded and used.

I am where I need to be, I know that now.

I take a deep breath, sucking in the frigid night air, then step across the threshold of the tent.

27

THE SUN AND THE MOON

RAYLIN

Inside is dark, the only light a warm glow from a candle in the centre of a round table, placed directly in the middle of the tent. This one is small, unlike the ones I ventured into before. Two dark, high-backed chairs sit opposite each other at the table, both empty save for the black silk that hangs down the back of each.

A book lies open on the table, little symbols etched on the pages. If they are words, I cannot read them. A skull is beside the book, bloodied tears falling from the sockets where its eyes would be.

I am alerted to movement from the corner of the tent, two bright green glowing orbs advancing around its edges.

"I have been waiting a long time for you, Raylin." The voice is a purr, a soothing caress to my ears.

The shock of hearing my true name sends a prickle down my spine. "Who are you?" I ask.

The green orbs glide closer, and I realise they are not orbs at all, but eyes, large eyes, belonging to a woman with pale skin, the undercurrent of grey tinting each pore. Her dark pink lips pout as she tilts her head to the side, as if reading something written upon me. Her stare is indestructible, boring into me as if she is the hunter and I am the prey. Her deep blue hair hangs to her shoulders, flames of green blowing in a non-existent breeze; the colour matches that of her eyes.

This is who Baron Bean meant for me to find.

"Who am I?" Her voice is a feather, brushing against the softest parts of my skin. "Some call me Mystica. Others, Spiritus. Maga. Meretrix." Her face turns to a sneer. "But these are not names meant to entice. They are insults. Spoken by the scared. The spiteful. I do not recall my true name, the name given by a loving mother. My friends, they call me Constantine."

"How do you know my name?" I ask her, my eyes not leaving her face.

She circles me, her feet floating slightly off the ground, toes pointed. "I have always known you, child. Long before your mother came to carry you. Long before your parents came to visit me."

"You've met my parents?"

Her lips tilt up into a smile, not one of joy, but one of knowing, one filled with secrets and truths.

"Gavaria was a beautiful place, but still your mother's eyes were filled with sorrow. She wanted so desperately for another child. Her loss ate away at her heart, blackening it with each bite."

She glides across the room, closing the book on the table and placing it in a faded leather trunk.

"She did not think twice when she drank the witch's silver potion. Nine months later, you were born, tearing and screaming into the darkest hour, wrapped in the witch's magic. You see, you were born within a collision, the sun and moon aligning just right, encasing the world in black. Oh, how the old gods fought over you."

I watch her, words failing me. All I am able to do is stand frozen to the spot.

"The Sun God wanted to gift you with his light. He could sense the goodness inside you. The Goddess of the Moon had other plans. She grappled against her brother, forging into you the powers of them both, leaving it up to you what you might become. It was not the first time, and I suspect it will not be the last. Petulant, foolish beings."

She moves closer to me, lifting my hand in her icy one.

"Your power is endless. A scale tipping this way and that, each fighting to break free and become the victor. You are either destined for greatness...or great evil. There is no in-between."

Constantine drops my hand, moving effortlessly back across the room.

"When you trapped your brother within your darkness, the scale tipped to black. When you figured out how to release him,"—she waves her arm in front of her, moving in an arch from left to right—"brightness lit up that black, tipping the scale back to a middle ground. You have spent your whole life since tipping one way or the other. More often than not, you lean toward the dark. But each time that woman steals your power, the scale evens out, confusing it into submission."

I shake my head; her words sink in slowly. "Genevieve," I whisper. "She doesn't steal them, I give her consent."

She tips her head back in a laugh. It is not small and gentle like her voice, it is brash and raw, accusing and wrong. "You cannot consent to what you do not know. Do you ask why she needs your power? Do you ever ask *yourself* why it is that you cannot go home, Raylin?"

Of course I had asked. The first time she asked to borrow my powers, I asked her. It was for her kingdom, to restore it to its full strength. To replenish her lands. Something inside me squirms. That was fourteen years ago. I had not asked since. I just...I thought...I don't know what I thought. I had let her take and take without a moment's hesitation. She had saved me, cared for me, it was the least I could do to repay her. As for going home, I knew that answer. It has been brandished in me time and time again.

"Because of my power, it is not safe," I tell Constantine, not feeling so sure now.

Her eyes fill with sadness, a sigh escaping her as she moves toward me once more. "The truth lies within you." She places her hand on my chest. "You simply need to unlock the door."

"What do you mean? *Please.*" My chest tightens, tears fill my eyes.

"I cannot give you all the answers, Princess of the Broken. My vision forbids it. I can only guide you. But be warned, there are those who deceive you."

"Who?" I ask desperately, willing for any information I can grasp.

"One way or another, them all. Some will help you. But your power, it is destructive. It will turn those who love you against you if you are not careful."

"Please..."

Her icy fingers sting as she gently wipes away a tear rolling down my cheek. "Your future is not yet written, there are still things yet to be determined. There is one thing for certain...that which you cannot control will be your undoing."

Waves crash against my skull, drowning me in a vast sea.

"I must bid you farewell. Many things await you, Little Moon."

The words plunge into my heart, the name my mother uses for me a sharpened knife. I don't want to go, I want to stay, I need answers.

"The king's libraries are vast, are they not? There are many shelves you did not get to explore on your last visit; it would be a shame to leave here before you do." She looks to me over her shoulder. "Do not let the truth scare you. Embrace it, follow it. I will say no more, I have already said too much."

I leave her tent, my head swimming. The waves sink me further and further into their depths. I veer around the backs of tents, keeping out of sight of anyone who will stop me. I head to the libraries without much thought, my plans for leaving with the obsidian pendant abandoned. This is where she wants me to go, this is where the answers lie.

What do Baron Bean and Constantine know that I do not? I think of the looks the faceless man and the cat lady gave me earlier tonight. Could they all know? Is that why they are here?

Something Constantine said hits me like a boulder to the chest.

Princess of the Broken.

What did she mean by that?

Two guards man the castle entrance, but I pass easily, them knowing my face by now. The corridors are deserted; everyone is still outside enjoying the carnival, so I make it to the library in record time, pulling the lever with great effort. The doors open just wide enough for me to squeeze through.

I stand in the middle of the room, turning in circles, having no clue where to start.

Do not let the truth scare you. What truth? What should I even be seeking out? I think of the hum of power I felt the last time I was in this room and head to where I was standing with Damien that night, but there is nothing here. It feels ordinary, nothing reaches out, there's not a thread of anything, just air.

Embrace it. Follow it.

I spend countless minutes walking along the rows of shelves, running my fingers along the spines of each book. I am in the history aisle, doing just that, when I feel something. It is not strong, a whisper, something strange. A murmuring from within. The feeling weakens as I walk further down the aisle, just beyond my grasp. I test it by walking backwards to where I just stood, the feeling growing stronger. I bend down, running my fingers along the spines of books on a lower shelf and the feeling dissipates. Then I climb the ladder hooked onto a higher shelf, and there the feeling intensifies. The swirling cold of my power calls out to something once lost. I let it guide me, my arm enraptured in ice, shooting forward toward a dark red book, almost knocking me from the ladder. Once the book is in my grasp, the power fades, its work done.

The book is frigid, solid, more like I am holding a block of ice than paper bound in leather. Swirling black letters on the front display, *The History of Gavaria.*

I have read the history of my kingdom before, but this is different. This book is slightly larger, a deeper red. I try to open the cover, but it is frozen shut, the same with the pages. I take it to a small desk at the end of the room, place it down and stare at it, not knowing what to do.

I rest my open palms flat on the book. The rush of cold wind spreads through me and goosebumps break out across my skin.

Open.

I will the book to allow me inside, to show me what secrets it holds. But when I try to lift the cover, it does not budge. Footsteps sound down the corridor, louder and louder, coming toward the library. In a panic, I grab the book and shove it into my void.

It remains in my hands.

My heart thumps too loud. Why did that not work? A similar magic to what was on the case holding the pendant? But it doesn't feel the same. The magic on the case felt more alive, otherworldly. This magic, the magic binding the book feels familiar; it feels more like the ice swirling in my veins.

A thought comes to me then, on the same beat as a voice echoes off the library walls.

"Lena, are you in here?" Soraya calls out.

I stay hidden deep within the stacks, legs pressed against the deep oak desk I sat at moments ago. I cannot see her right now. I cannot see anyone. Not when my thoughts and my heart are going a million miles per hour. Who knows what might slip out of my mouth.

I wait for her footsteps to depart and fade away back down the hall, guilt tearing at my insides. I tuck the tome inside my cloak, clutching it to my chest, and head back to my room. Inside, I lock the door, not wanting to be disturbed. I sit on the floor at the end of the bed, crossing my legs in front of me, placing the book in my lap. If I am right about this...

Instead of calling inward for my magic, I call beyond.

I wrangle outward with an invisible leash, willing the magic around the book to come to me. Like a nervous dog, the power inches closer, rubbing its snout against me as if to see if I am trustworthy, to see if I am friend or foe. I extend a drop of my power, the power so similar to itself.

At first, I think it will cower and hide, wrapping itself back around the book tighter. Instead, it grips on. Clawing at me to come in, to return home from where it was once torn.

I let it.

A gasp escapes through my lips as ice flows through me, wrapping around my very core in an arctic fist. The power blends with my own and I am not able to discern between the two; they are one and the same. How did it end up here? What was it protecting?

I unhurriedly lift the hardcover of the book. The pages are thick and luxurious, the colour not quite white, but not quite cream also. I sift through the words, all facts I have read before, things I learned long ago. The previous kings and queens. My great-grandmothers and grandfathers. The feud with Quendore and eventual reconciliation. Deaths. Births. Everything familiar to me.

I flip through faster, waiting for my eyes to snag on something I do not recognise.

And when they do, time folds in on itself, the ticking of a clock coming to a stop, the whisper of the wind quieting, my heart stilling in my chest.

The lost princess...

I stop reading, flipping back a couple of pages to start at the beginning, my heart in my throat. The title page stares back at me, so unfamiliar, so daunting, I feel it cannot be real.

The Kingdom of the Broken.

28

WRITTEN IN THE STARS

MALAKAI

Malakai clutches Arabella's hand as they race through the mirror maze, their laughter drowning out all other sounds. They had eaten mounds of fluffy pink spun sugar, and it had gone straight to their heads.

They burst out of the exit, straight into the cool night, not waiting for the others as they zoom off to the next intrigue.

Malakai's eyes go wide as he leans close to the cage. The bars, crafted from translucent black glass, tower over him, the width as wide as two of the erected tents. Inside lie three creatures, undisturbed by the hubbub of the carnival—or what Malakai first thinks is three creatures. The pair lean closer, getting a good look at the beast that sleeps within.

Malakai has never seen anything like it, didn't know something so unusual could exist. The main body and head are what looks like a typical lion you would find in Jalendia, this one as white as snow. Curving from the lion's back is another head, this one nothing like a lion. Its snout is longer, drenched in dark scales and spikes. It's what the wings on the creature's back must also belong to, the scaled webbing tucked close to its side. Curled into the lion's mane is another head, pointed teeth poking out of its mouth. This one is attached to a long body, or what could be a body, as it also acts as the lion's tail. This, too, is covered in scales, a vivid green and blue.

"What is it?" Arabella gasps.

"That, my child, is something you do not want to be getting so close to." The voice comes from behind, giving Malakai and Arabella a start.

The man before them could have stolen the very stars from the sky and placed them in his eyes, the way they sparkle and flicker. He staggers toward them on his lion head cane, which resembles what dwells in the cage at their backs.

"Baron Bean." Malakai nods.

Baron Bean takes the brim of his tall hat between his fingers, lifting it as he bows low. "Your Highnesses," he says, voice smooth as honey. "I see you found my chimera. Magnificent, isn't she?"

"Not the word I would use. *Terrifying* would be a better choice." Arabella shudders.

"Ah, only if she decides to eat you." He winks.

Malakai takes a step back from the cage at that, and gazes at the beast inside. "Where does it come from?"

"To answer that, I would need to know." Baron Bean pokes his cane through the bars, gently jostling the beast in the leg. It shuffles but does not wake. "Where do any of us come from? A time or place? No one is certain."

"What's that supposed to mean?" Malakai asks.

Arabella looks at Malakai, eyebrows high on her head. *He is insane*, she seems to say, without uttering a word.

"Sometimes things remain hidden until they are needed. Until they have a purpose. Sometimes they are hidden for so long, people forget about them altogether. But nothing is gone forever. Fate will work her magic, even if that magic is just guiding a lonely boy into stumbling upon a lost secret."

Malakai freezes, his blood running cold. Baron Bean's smile has become knowing. But how? How could he possibly know about the passageways within the castle? Arabella's confused gaze flicks between the two of them, yet she doesn't ask the question she so longs to ask.

A fizzing noise sounds and Baron Bean snaps to attention. "I must be going. But just remember, when secrets find you, it is for a reason. Follow it." With that and a flash of white light, he is gone.

One of the beast's eyes open, one belonging to the larger scaled head. Its slit pupil dilates, twisting its head to look over at where they stand. It watches them with malice, unmoving. A shiver travels up Malakai's spine, a feeling of absolute dread growing inside him. At the beast. At Baron Bean's words. At everything here tonight.

"Let's find the others."

"Gladly."

The others are nowhere to be seen at the mirror maze. While looking for them, they bump into Catalina, Kiyoko, and Briar—the latter two hand in hand, pale fingers wrapped around bronzed ones—at the tent marked *Vincent Death.* Underneath are words reading, *to stop your death, first you must know how you will die.* It doesn't do anything for the unsettling feeling building inside Malakai's chest.

None of them have seen Lena, Damien, or Soraya, and agree to help look for them. They are just walking away when a voice calls out to them, "Arabella!"

Soraya and Damien are running toward them, looking panicked. "Kai! What in the hell, where did you go?" Damien says as they reach them.

"We've been looking everywhere," Soraya adds.

Arabella crosses her arms, her hard exterior again taking over. "We've been looking for you."

Catalina scans the group, her left brow hitching up. "Where's Lena?"

"She's not with you?" Damien's voice catches.

The feeling of dread inside Malakai grows and grows, spilling over the edges. The floodgates open, and it all comes crashing down, wiping out his every sense, swallowing his every thought. It is all he can see, all he can hear, all he can feel.

Something isn't right.

The very air grows colder, snaking along his skin.

Something is wrong.

He's the only one who seems to feel it, the only one it is affecting.

"We need to find her," is all he says.

Damien catches his gaze, just briefly but long enough to know something is up. He scrunches his brows, face concerned. Malakai only shakes his head subtly. Damien takes this as answer enough, saying, "Let's split up. It will be quicker."

"Soraya, Catalina, Arabella, and I will go inside," Malakai commands. "Damien, the gardens. Kiyoko and Briar, stick to the carnival. She can't be far. Meet back here in an hour."

Soraya and Catalina rush ahead, entering the castle before Arabella and Malakai reach the grand steps.

"Something's not right," Malakai announces quietly.

Arabella searches his face. "What is it?"

"I don't know. Something just feels...off."

She bites her bottom lip, eyes scanning the crowds behind them. "It's weird, isn't it? That she would just leave like that."

Malakai nods, unsure of what to say. "We will find her. Come on."

They make their way through the castle corridors, Catalina and Soraya nowhere to be seen. The feeling in Malakai's chest doesn't dissipate; it remains, cold and unyielding, tormenting him. He fiddles with the signet ring on his finger as they weave in and out of rooms, calling Lena's name.

Every room they enter is dark, unoccupied. Someone enters the corridor from up ahead, but Malakai cannot make out who it is, not until they move closer.

"Not enjoying the carnival, little prince?"

Malakai should have guessed. The short stout frame could belong to no one else.

Lord Jasper.

"We just wanted some alone time," Malakai says, taking Arabella's hand in his. Better that his uncle thinks this of him than anything other.

Arabella plays along, bringing her body closer to Malakai, giving the sneering man a hard look of her own. Jasper runs his beady eyes along the pair, his lip curling in a smirk. "You chose well, boy. She's a fine specimen." His gaze lingers on the bodice of her pale blue gown.

Malakai angles his arm so it is in front of her, blocking some of his uncle's stare. "If you do not mind, we would like to be on our way."

Jasper steps aside, creating a path ahead, the smirk never leaving his face. "Be sure to tell your father. We were starting to think there was something wrong with you. After all, you spend an awful lot of time with that lieutenant."

Malakai freezes, his body seizing.

Arabella squeezes his fingers. "Ignore him."

He swallows audibly, his jaw clenching to stop him from saying what he wants to say. Something he will come to regret. He knows what the lord thinks about people like him. It's why he would never want his uncle to be present when it finally comes time to tell his father. He knew the things he uttered about his own sister, that Seranay deserved to die for what she was, for who she loved. And he also heard his father's silence at those statements. That was why it had taken Malakai so long to even begin to decide to tell him.

If his father felt the same as Jasper does, it would break him. If his father didn't defend him when people said those things, it would break him. Seranay hid who she was her whole life. It wasn't until her death—when her so-called best friend couldn't hide it any longer—that everyone found out the truth. Malakai hadn't even been born then, yet still, he has to hear the things they say about her all these years later.

He sucks in a breath, forcing his feet to move forward, ignoring his uncle's hateful words and the laugh that follows them. Arabella doesn't let go of his hand, and he doesn't want her to. He needs the feel of her skin on his to ground him, to keep him from turning around and introducing his uncle to his fist.

They search for longer than an hour, but it is no use. There is no sign of Lena anywhere. It's the same thing the others say as they meet back in the throng of the carnival. All but Damien.

"Maybe he found her?" Catalina says. "They could have been a bit preoccupied to return?"

Malakai shakes his head. "He would have let us know. He's probably still searching."

"Maybe we should wait for her to come to us. She's safe within these walls. When she wants to be found, she knows where we are," Soraya says, though somewhat unsure.

Those words, *when she wants to be found, she knows where we are*, do something funny to Malakai's stomach. The words are too similar to what Baron Bean said about fate, about things remaining hidden until they are needed. He fiddles with his signet ring. "You're right. But I cannot stomach any more of this carnival. I'm heading to my room."

Malakai sits on the sill of his room, staring down into the courtyard, the carnival still heaving with people. He could not sleep even if he wanted to.

He finds the enormous cage, the beast dwelling within, clearly visible from up here. It's not sleeping either. It is pacing, its heads twisting in opposite directions, searching, but for what, Malakai does not know. Would rather not know. He catches a shadow out of the corner of his eye, someone emerging from the line of tents, a cloak of deepest black pulled far over their face. He watches the figure as they cross to the beast's cage, not minding their way, not moving for anyone. They place their arm through a gap in the bars, handing something to the creature, placing it directly on its large paw.

Malakai leans closer. No one else seems to see what is happening, no one pays any attention to the figure beside the cage.

The beast stares intently at them with all three heads, and if Malakai had blinked at this moment, he would have missed it. The creature nods each head in unison, a quick flick and over. The figure turns toward the castle, arms reaching for its hood.

Malakai stops breathing.

They pull back their hood, revealing a stunning feminine face. There is something cold about it, something old. But this face isn't old, it is young and smooth, it is strange. Her hair seems to have swallowed the night sky itself, dark and unforgiving. Except for those streaks of green; they almost seem to flicker and burn.

She angles her head, and there is no mistaking it. She's looking right at him, two sets of green eyes connecting over a sea of bodies.

Malakai gasps, a shuddering breath forcing its way into his lungs.

The woman's lips curl into a smile.

A knowing smile.

A deadly smile.

29

ALL AT ONCE EVERYTHING IS DIFFERENT

RAYLIN

I don't breathe as I steadily read the words.

I have turned to stone. Unmovable. Solid.

The air around me has gone cold, but I do not feel it.

The pounding of my blood in my ears the only indication that I still live.

I read it again. I don't want to believe the writing on the page, it is a trick, a sick game someone is playing.

Blood coated the floors. The bodies were strewn about the dining table. Food lay cold and uneaten. The servant who had found them was taken away, her eyes blank and distant. It was a mystery as to how this happened; the king had guards aplenty. A mystery, that is, until the castle was searched. Servants lay dead in the kitchens, in their beds, in corridors and royal rooms. The guards' quarters were much the same.

Abnormally, there was no blood. The bodies were tested, and no poisons resided in their system. It was as if a powerful force had swept through and simply stopped their hearts.

The same could not be said for the royal family.

Tears wet my face. Blurring the pages before me. I squint through them, carrying on.

Among the bodies lay the King and Queen of Quendore, their daughter, Princess Amily, 19, and their youngest son, Prince Cornwell, 8. Their middle child, missing, was later discovered to be safe back home—left with her uncle—with an upset stomach.

The Queen of Gavaria, Queen Elisaria, lay nearby in a pool of her own blood, her throat cut deep and clean. Curiously, King Orilius was found further away, slumped against the far wall, bloodied handprints painting the stones.

Missing were the King and Queen of Gavarias' children: Prince Reed, 21, and Princess Raylin, 6. The kingdom was scoured for weeks, but neither were found.

Speculation spread far and wide, the mysterious events capturing the whole of Aldros. There are stories, rumours spread by those who worked within the castle, that the young princess possessed many magical abilities, ones that have not been known for many moons. For fear of what she may be able to do, she was shunned by her family, kept locked away in her room.

Another source explained how when she worked in the castle two years prior, Princess Raylin, in a fit of rage, made her brother, Prince Reed, disappear, only to bring him back days later. This was the turning point for the family. They minimised staff, left the castle grounds less frequently, and the princess was seen less and less as the years went on.

From then on, the prince feared his younger sister. Before, they were close, but after, he would shy away if she entered a room, was never seen alone with her, and rarely deemed it necessary to speak to her at all.

So, on that dreadful night, when death plagued the castle, the two royal children were blamed.

Stories spread of how Prince Reed lost his mind, killing his future bride, Princess Amily, her family, and his own. The tales vary; some say he acted out of fear, others that he did it for gain, that he was jealous of his sister's power, wanted it for himself. The whys and hows change as the stories go on.

Sometimes Princess Raylin is the chosen evil. Her anger at being hidden away causing her to murder the entire castle, sending her brother back to where she once hid him, then disappearing herself. Some do not believe a young girl of six would have been capable of such things, that it was an outsider who tore the castle apart, taking both the prince and the princess in their clutches.

Only one thing always remains the same as the years go by—the pair were never to be seen again. Searches were undertaken in each kingdom, each isle, mountains, and landscapes explored. Apart from the odd reports of sightings of one or the other—which always turned out to be fruitless rumours—there was not a single clue as to what happened to them. To this day, people talk of the mysterious events that went down that night in Gavaria.

Some believe them to be long dead. Others believe Prince Reed to have perished, but that the lost princess is out there, her power growing. That one day she will return home and bring Gavaria back to its former glory. That the broken remnants of a kingdom long-abandoned will one day be restored.

Lies.

All of it. Lies.

I slam the book closed with a resounding thunk.

Reed would never hurt me. Would never hurt our family. They are not dead. They cannot be dead.

Genevieve would have told me. But...My heart slows, my stomach drops. This night, the night in the book, it was the night Genevieve brought me to Sorrelle, the night we left Gavaria for the last time. I work through my memories. What was it she said? She woke me up, she was panicking, there was someone in the castle, mother had urged her to get me out, someone was coming for me. For my power. Is that what happened? Did they die protecting me?

That cannot be right. Genevieve has seen them, she has spoken to them.

The book is wrong. Maybe that is why it was spelled shut, to stop the wrong information from getting out. But why not just get rid of the book? Why not correct it?

I cannot think straight.

I scramble to the balcony, breathing in the chilled air. I focus my attention on the low rising sun, a speck advancing on the horizon. The deep pink of the sky. The soft waves of the ocean. I rub the small crescent pendant of my bracelet between my fingers. My mind relaxes, the tangle of thoughts easing away.

Now I can think logically, I don't see how any of those words in the book could be true. Reed would never hurt our family. He would never hurt Amily. He certainly did not steal me away or hurt me. The only part I can count as true was what I had done to Reed, but it wasn't out of rage, it was an accident. I was a four-year-old who should not have been messing with powers she knew nothing about. Reed knew that, my family knew that. But they also knew it was hard for me. I was not good at controlling my powers. They would manifest so often I was never sure which to learn first. There was no one to teach me, no one to help me. Even now, sometimes I feel my power slip. Just like with Lord Jasper the other night, nerves and fear get the better of me. Those, too, I sometimes cannot control. Was never taught to control.

I need to see Genevieve.

I need to go to Gavaria. I need to go *home*.

I check the obsidian pendant in my cloak pocket. Still there. I cannot risk being seen. Being followed. I make quick work of going down the servant's passage, passing through the large empty room, and heading out of the side entrance of the castle. The small gate is closed, but not locked, and no guards linger nearby—something that registers as odd, but I do not dwell on it. I go as fast as I can through the forest, cursing myself for not changing out of this damn dress. It's loose around my legs, but not loose enough to run.

The abandoned cabin is silent as I pass, too silent. It's as if it watches me, eager to see my next move. My heeled shoes cause me to slip on fallen leaves and twigs, so I kick them off, leaving them behind, forgotten in the long grass.

I am over the bridge and almost through the thicket of trees to my tower's clearing when I hear the voices, both so familiar to me.

"Well...where is she then?" The anger seeping from Genevieve's words stops me in my tracks.

"We looked everywhere. I assumed she had come back here. She's had the stone for a few days."

I move forward slowly, slipping between two thick tree trunks. I crouch, peering through the gaps in the leaves. For the millionth time today, my heart somersaults.

Damien stands before Genevieve, his leather guard uniform tight enough to show each bulge of his muscles. He has his arms crossed against his chest, but his face gives away no emotions.

"You need to find her," Genevieve sneers at him.

Does he know Genevieve?

If this is a nightmare, I want to wake up now. Too much has happened, my head is dizzy with information that doesn't make sense. I pinch myself, praying to the stars that I will wake up back in my bed at the castle, sunlight pouring on my face.

I do not.

"I don't see you looking. Hanging around this forsaken tower isn't much help, is it, *mother*." Damien spits the words at her, but it is me they hit, shooting into my chest like an arrow. Swift and true.

Mother.

Mother?

I grip the tree to steady myself, the world before me swaying to a song I cannot hear. I have no time to think through what I am about to do. I step into the clearing, moving toward them with languished strength.

"What is this?" Both their heads whip to me so fast I worry they will snap their necks.

Damien's cobalt eyes are stunned as he takes me in. His face relaxes as I stumble closer. When neither speaks, I ask again, "What is going on here?"

"Raylin! I have been so worried about you." Genevieve rushes toward me, pulling me into a hug. I stand rigid. I do not hug her back.

Damien just stands there, staring, not uttering a word.

A squawk startles me. It's only then I notice the cage placed on the floor beside where Auntie was just standing.

Fee.

In seconds I have released him, not needing to touch the prison bars around him. He swoops out, stretching his wings before perching atop the cage. His deep brown eyes roam over me, checking every inch of my body. Then he settles a look on Damien, not moving from his stare.

"Did you get the pendant?" Genevieve asks, cupping my cheeks in her hands.

My eyes flick to Damien, then back to her. She already knows, so why bother asking? I nod. She stares at me, waiting for me to hand it over. "I don't have it on me," I lie.

Her eyebrows furrow, her eyes narrowing. "Just hand it over, child. I am not in the mood for your games."

"I want answers first." I step back, removing my face from her grasp.

"Answers about what?" She rolls her eyes, as if I am a bothersome child, asking her about trivial things.

"About why *he* is here." I gesture to Damien and he fidgets where he stands. "About why he lied to me. I want to know exactly what is going on here. I want to know what the obsidian pendant does. And I want to know why a book in the castle of Sorrelle says my whole family is dead!"

Genevieve freezes. "Dead?" she says, shaking her head. "Whatever do you mean?"

I gasp. I see it in her face. The lie. She knows. The woman that has raised me for fourteen years, the woman who I thought loved me, protected me, knew all along that my family were no longer in this world.

"Just hand over the pendant, Raylin, and you will be able to see them." Her voice is calm, but a storm rages inside of me.

"NO MORE LIES!"

Before she can step back, I grab her face like she has done to me hundreds of times. I grab for the darkness at my core, sinking my teeth into it as I tear through her mind. The world around us slows. Damien makes to rush toward us, but his movements are averse, as if time has come to a stop.

The air around Genevieve and me twists, folds in on itself, darkening and coiling in a maze of destruction.

I am no longer standing in the clearing of the woods.

I am marching down the corridors of my castle, the castle in Gavaria. I turn my head to the mirror on the wall; I am no longer myself, I am Genevieve. But not as she is now, the wrinkles not yet on her face. Her black hair is smoother and straighter down her back. I am her, but younger. Fourteen years younger, to be exact.

But I am not here exactly, I am watching through her eyes. Watching as she makes her way toward the banquet hall.

Watching her memories of the night everything went to shit.

30

MEMORIES DO NOT DECEIVE

RAYLIN

Genevieve's toes tingle as she sends a blast of power out around her. It slithers off in different directions, around corridors, upstairs, stopping the hearts of everyone it encounters. She keeps it from seeping into the banquet hall, a shield of power wrapping the walls in a warm hug. There's also a barrier of protection around the room of a small sleeping child, around my room.

A few more steps and the doors are thrown open, her hands never having touched the handles. Confused faces turn to her from around the table. My father, King Orilius, stands instantly. Gavaria's maroon banners hang low from the ceiling, fine stitching of golden hands beneath a glowing sun. A symbol of healing.

"What is the meaning of this?" he says, his eyes narrowing on her, on us.

The sound of his voice sends a shiver down my spine. Or Genevieve's spine; I am unsure whose feelings I am experiencing, they seem to meld together as one.

Genevieve swings her arm out, slamming my father back down in his chair. Holding them all in place as they struggle against the invisible bonds. The fear in Father's eyes is like an arrow to the heart, but it is no match for the anger that bubbles up inside us, spreading like a disease.

The next second passes in slow motion. My eyes slash across Amily's throat, her hands fly up, squeezing as her blood pours from the wound we have created, burbles from her mouth as she tries to breathe, tries to scream. She goes still, slumping to the floor as our hold on her is released, eyes still wide with terror.

The Queen of Quendore's scream rocks the room. Reed's pale blue eyes are fixed, staring down at his bride to be.

The King of Quendore is next, then his queen, both going out the same way as their daughter, falling in puddles of their blood.

So much blood.

The little prince stares at us, at Genevieve. I thrash for her to stop, but it is no use. She doesn't know I am here. These moments have already come to pass, there is nothing I can do to stop them now.

"Enough of this!" Father's voice booms out.

She does not listen.

Prince Cornwell visibly shakes, his cries for help going unanswered. Genevieve hesitates. I feel it deep within her; she's never killed a child before. That hesitation is soon ground away by the need for power. Cornwell's body jerks as she stops his heart, killing him instantly, that small mercy she could bestow upon him. His little body flops against the table, his face falling with a clatter onto his dinner plate.

We stalk across the room, my family's cries and screams filling the open space, my mother's pleading sobs louder than the rest.

We come to a stop in front of Reed, still pinned with the magical force to his chair. Genevieve's hands, my hands, find Reed's throat, squeezing tight as the tears roll down his cheeks, his eyes wide with fear. His body spasms, unable to fill his lungs. I scream internally along with my mother. I can feel his skin against mine, can feel the movement of his body. But no matter how hard I try, I can't stop. She won't stop. The smell of piss enters my nostrils, his body losing control. The veins in his forehead bulge, threatening to burst. I don't want to see, I cannot watch him die, but I cannot avert my gaze as life drains from him, his eyes closing as he falls to our feet.

Mother's screams go quiet, her head swinging around the room, just now realising they are alone. No one is coming to save them. *Raylin*, she mouths to my father. The realisation hits him then and his skin pales, every emotion leaving his face.

"This is what this is about." It is not a question. "Power. Control. You would destroy two kingdoms for your selfish gain!" His shout echoes off the walls.

Genevieve smiles in return, her power slicing across my mother's throat, silencing her forever. Blood splatters across Father's face, but he does not seem to notice as his voice booms out.

"Raylin! Run! Get out!"

It is hopeless. My room is too far away, I would never hear my father's last words to me. But I do now. I hear them now, I hear as he fights for me with the last of his strength, fights with whatever he has left.

"Please, Genevieve, you do not need to do this. Spare me. Spare Raylin. You can take her power, you can have it, I do not care, just please do not hurt her."

We lean in close.

"You weren't saying that the other day when I asked. When I came to you for help to save my kingdom. Your exact words were, *you will not ever lay a finger on my daughter.*" She laughs and my father flinches beneath us. "You think me stupid? Is that it? I let you live, you have me locked away for good. But if I kill you"—Father thrashes against his invisible chains—"then I am as free as a bird in the wind."

Her hand lashes out, grabs the dagger from my father's belt, and plunges it into his stomach, once, twice, three times, then twisting the hilt for good measure. He fights for breath, sputtering on air as he tries to force it into his lungs. We turn and leave him there, his whimpers travelling after us.

The castle is silent.

31

Fading

Raylin

I wrench my hands from Genevieve's face, slumping to the ground, the damp of the grass seeping through my silk dress. I cannot breathe through the sobs that tear from me. I gasp and heave. My throat constricts, nothing goes in or out.

A warm hand curls over my shoulder. "Ray?" Damien's voice undoes me.

"Do not touch me," I spit, pulling myself away.

I stare down at my hands. I can still feel their blood. I can still feel Reed's body struggling beneath me.

Reed.

No.

No, that cannot be right. Something is wrong. That book is wrong. Genevieve's memories are wrong.

Reed wasn't supposed to be there. His body was not supposed to be there. And my father. His body was not found with the others, yet we left him slumped in his chair at the table all the same. Was he not truly dead as she walked away?

"Where is he?" I scream at Genevieve as I get to my feet, my voice raw and painful.

She stumbles back a step, her eyes fluttering in confusion. "Who?"

"Reed."

"I– I do not know." She shakes her head.

"You're lying."

My power swirls inside me, threatening to break free, to tear the world apart. I try to grab hold of it but it slips free of my grasp. The air around us turns to ice. I do the only thing I can to stop it.

I turn and I run.

Fee's screeching follows me overhead.

"Ray, wait," Damien calls after me, but I pay him no heed.

I try to focus on the pounding of my feet against the ground, but the bitterness of my power still lingers on the surface of my skin, refusing to leave. I reach inside for that warmth, for the power of the sun. I cannot find it. My anger is too palpable and raw, feeding into the darkness.

I grab the obsidian pendant from my pocket, squeezing it in my fist until it cuts at my skin. The damn thing is the only reason I am here. The only reason I have seen all I have, the least it can do is help me now. I trip on a branch, falling to my knees, my attention fixed on what is in my fist rather than what is in front of me. I throw the pendant into my void, wanting to be rid of it. But more so, not wanting Genevieve or Damien to have it.

The blood swells in my palm where the pendant sliced at me. I reach for the brightness inside, willing it to heal me. Nothing. It pays me no attention.

I keep running.

Running.

Not fast enough. I pull at the side of my silk skirts, tearing them up the length, giving myself more freedom to move. I catch a glimpse of Damien from behind, gaining on me now, and will myself to go faster, to get away. I am afraid of what I will do if he comes too close, afraid of what my power might do.

I'm unsure of where I'm going until I arrive at the base of the castle. I stop once I'm through the doors of the garden and in the ballroom. What should I do? Do I go to my room? I don't think I can, I cannot lie about who I am any longer. I need to find Malakai, someone I think I can trust.

Heavy panting comes from behind me.

"Ray. Please." I swirl around to find Damien standing there, sweat coating his golden-brown skin.

"Why? So you can lie to me some more? So you can trick me again?"

"It wasn't like that, Ray, I promise." He runs a hand through his dark hair, closing his eyes. "I...I didn't know who you were at first. Not until after I had already gotten to know you. I didn't know my mother's involvement with you, I still don't understand now. There are no excuses, I know that. I should have come to you once I found out, but..." He takes a step closer.

"I don't know what to believe," my voice cracks, tears break from my eyes.

"You can believe *me*, you can trust *me*." He takes another step, his arm reaching toward me. "I would never hurt you."

I nod.

I reach out, placing my hand in his. He pulls me against him, his arms snaking around my back and holding me tight. The tension between us melts and I relax into him, breathing in his familiar scent.

My power rushes up to meet him, barrelling toward him like an avalanche.

I gasp as he holds me tighter. As he steals my power.

NO.

An icy blast bursts from me, knocking him backward. A shattering sounds as his body slams into the glass windows.

He rises from the floor, blood dripping from his nose. He wipes at it with the back of his hand. The smirk on his face tells me all I need to know: he played me again. He comes toward me, reaching for the dagger at his side. I grab at everything I have, willing every last drop to help me. The scream tears from my throat as I send out another icy blast, this one stronger. The very air around us ripples in waves. A loud crack fills the room, the splitting of marble wall.

Damien staggers but keeps his balance, his eyes dart behind me, then back to me, a bloodied smile on his face.

"Guards!" His voice is thunder to my ears.

I flinch. I know he can sense my confusion, can see it on my face. What is he doing?

"What have you done, *Lena*?" His eyes are fixed behind me, but his smile never falters.

I turn to look over my shoulder, understanding washing over me.

My heart stops.

No.

The sound was not marble at all. It was bone. It was a skull cracking open. It was a heart breaking. It was a life ending.

Ella lies motionless on the ground, her eyes open and distant, blood leaking from the gash in her head. I run to her, dropping to my knees with a thud. My hands hover over her face.

"No. No. No."

I reach inside for that brightness again, demanding it heals her. Save her.

I find only darkness.

I lift her into my lap, gently stroking her face. "I'm so sorry," I whisper, my tears mingling with the blood on her clothes.

My mother's voice roars in my head, the fear that gripped her the night I trapped Reed. *What have you done, Raylin?* The grip of her fingers against my tiny shoulders. *Bring him back.*

I cannot.

There's a rush, a clamour of leather boots against the marble floor, alerting me to the guards' arrival. I do not turn.

"Lock her up," is all Damien says.

Someone bends to take Ella from me, another set of hands against my shoulders, I think someone says my name. Not Raylin, Lena.

"Do not touch her!" I have no control as the blast leaves with my words, knocking them all away.

My tears do not stop as I grip on to her body. I cannot leave her, I need to undo this. I keep searching for the warmth of the healing power inside me, but it is not there, it is simply gone, it has left me. They've all left me, and it is all my fault. I am alone, and it's all my fault. I scream, releasing the frustration, releasing the anger, releasing the sorrow, releasing my power.

All I hear is static, all-consuming, pulling me down, down, down.

His voice pulls me back. That thread of connection snapping me to attention.

"Lena?" My head whips to the sound of Malakai's voice, the hurt in it.

A deep gash spreads from his ear to the corner of his mouth. He presses a hand to it, then brings it back down to examine the blood. His eyebrows pull together as he looks me over. Hurt and confused.

I injured Malakai.

I killed Ella.

Constantine was right. She told me my power was destructive, she told me I would turn those who love me against me. And now I have.

I am too stunned to notice as the guards pull me away from Ella, my gaze fixed on Malakai's. I do not resist as they cuff my hands in metal chains, do not struggle as I am led to an underground cell, do not fight as I am left there, utterly alone.

Hours pass in this windowless room. All cells are empty except for mine. No guard remains here with me, but I think at least two stand outside the main door, up the steep set of stone steps. Their voices drift down every so often, words catching in the wind and passing me by. Because there is a wind in here, a freezing draft drifting through, causing my whole body to shiver uncontrollably. There's no cloak to keep me warm, just the pale pink silk dress that Ella chose for me—torn and blood-stained now.

From what I can tell, I am deep underground. I heard mention of the prison cells in my time at the castle, but never found out exactly where they were located. Black mould clings to the stone walls. Damp lingers, the floors slick and moist. Rust covers the small bed frame, the thin mattress brown and musty. The cell bars are the only thing untouched by time, the black glass-like material strong and impenetrable. It reminds me of the obsidian pendant, discarded in my void.

I lay curled in a ball in the middle of the floor, the cold and wet seeping through the thin silk. I am thankful for it; the more I suffer for what I have done, the better.

The sound of Ella's head cracking against marble plays on repeat, a song I don't think I will ever be rid of. Every time I close my eyes, I see Malakai's face. The terror behind his eyes, the betrayal written across his features.

I stare into the dark, unblinking and unmoving.

I am a fool.

Those I trusted have deceived me. Those who trusted me I have hurt. I deserve to be here, I deserve to rot away to nothing.

"To the moon," I whisper into the silence, but I do not finish the words that used to comfort me, and there is no one here to whisper the rest back to me.

I have no one now. Genevieve made sure of that. All these years, I truly believed one day I would go home and be reunited with my family. But all along there was no family to go back to.

Reed. A little glimmer of hope flickers inside me. Could he be back in Gavaria? Waiting there all these years for me to come home, hiding from the outside world until we are together once more. Maybe he's out there looking for me.

Something inside me stirs, a longing ache working its way through my bones. I need to get out. I need to find him. I scramble to the bars, gripping them tight. "Hey! I need to leave! Let me out!" I shout, my voice hoarse. I slam my palms against the bars over and over. "Let me out!"

The door opens with a creak, the clunk of large boots hitting step after step echoes around the room. And then he comes into view, his smile coy.

Damien.

He tuts, shaking his head as he walks towards me. "No need for that, Princess. We're all friends here."

"You are not my friend," I spit at him.

"No. I suppose I'm not. But then, you don't have many of those now, do you?"

I reach an arm through the bars to grab him, but he takes a step back, smiling. He grabs my exposed wrist and twists it sideways, pinning me face-first against the bars. I let out a cry of pain as he pushes harder.

"Try that again, *Princess*, and I will put you back in chains."

The man before me is nothing like the man I have come to know. There is no hint of that gentle and kind Damien, just this ruthless, wicked man.

"What do you want from me?" I ask, tears stinging my eyes.

"I want what I have always wanted...to be stronger than my mother. To beat her to the punchline." The smile leaves his face. Releasing my arm, he steps back, careful not to touch the mould slick walls. "Not everything I told you was a lie. My mother isn't like yours. Never was. The only thing she has ever loved is power."

"She loved me...I thought she loved me."

He laughs at this. "Sorry to break it to you, but she never loved you. Merely what is inside of you."

"She loved my father."

This much I knew. I saw it in her eyes many times, the longing there.

"We don't kill the people we love, Raylin." His voice is serious, coated with something I cannot name.

My heart gives a little jump. I loved Ella, and I killed her. I cannot look up at him. I cannot move. My body feels weak, painful.

"She killed my father, you know? Poisoned him with Wraith Flower. I watched as he died slowly, the poison eating away at him. Weeks it took. Weeks I had to watch my father die. Do you know the effect that has on a child?"

"Wraith Flower?" I shake my head. No. How? "It was you. You poisoned King Rorik."

"Yours truly." He bows.

I struggle to keep myself upright, gripping onto the bars. It occurs to me now, watching this ruthless man, this cannot be the first time he was willing to kill.

"And Princess Lena? Did she suffer the same fate?"

"Not exactly. But the princess never made it home, no. You gave me no choice. And again, when you lied to that guard when you couldn't help but save the damn king. You killed him. You made me kill him. I couldn't have them asking questions, Raylin, you almost ruined everything."

His smile infuriates me, but I'm slipping, falling.

"You may want to let go of the bars," he says, watching me crumble before him.

I let go, stumbling back, catching myself before I fall. "What–what is happening?"

"Obsidian." He pats the cell, sending a vibration all around me. "It absorbs power. Leaches it from your very core. Much like Mother's and my ability, but where we simply borrow, obsidian will take all you have, every last drop, and only then, when you have nothing left to replenish, will it stop. You will be powerless. Why do you think Mother wanted that pendant? You didn't really think it was a family heirloom, did you?" He laughs.

Oh my stars.

"And the best bit...while trapped in a cage of obsidian, your powers will be suppressed, suffocated, they will not work. The first king's paranoia was a blessing in disguise. There is no way out for you here." He smiles, narrowing his eyes. "Not unless you hand over that pendant to me. Only then will I consider letting you go."

"Never," I gasp.

"Very well then." He turns, the sound of his footsteps disappearing up the stairs, then silence as the door creaks open and closed.

I am alone once more.

32

THE DEAD TALK

MALAKAI

Malakai stands frozen. He doesn't understand. People float around him, but he doesn't see them, his brain doesn't register who they are. What they are doing.

He doesn't feel the pain that lances through him, cold and deep.

There's blood on his hand. His blood.

There's blood on the floor. Not his blood.

He touches his face again, the thick red liquid there. It saturates his clothes, turning the deep green of Sorrelle an even darker shade.

Someone's shouting orders, their voice coming closer. Their words are a jumble of letters and sounds. His mind is mush. His brain has been put in a bowl and scrambled until nothing makes sense. There is one word that floats whole, but its meaning has been changed, turned into something else.

Lena.

Malakai's unsure if he tries to move or if his body gives up on him. He jerks forward, the ground rushing up to meet him. He's prepared to hit the hard marble when he suddenly stops. There's a pressure on his waist, an arm, he thinks. His back is pressed against a warm solid body, their shouting urgent.

"I can take him," a tender voice says.

There's movement, a shifting of bodies, a flash of white hair, he's afraid he is about to fall again, when he's pressed into a smaller body, their arms wrapping around him tightly. They stumble, shoving him up with full momentum. Then there's another set of arms, these stronger. Together they keep him steady. "Thank you," the first voice says.

"Can you move your feet, Malakai?"

Good question.

He tries, but his legs don't want to cooperate. At least, he thinks he tries.

The world spins, blurring beyond recognition. Shadows grow in the corners of his vision, closing in on the space before him until the world goes black.

Calendula, lavender, and honey fill the air. The scent from the healing salve Malakai became accustomed to as a child. The healer would apply a thick layer to every cut and graze he would get while playing. Malakai knew no fear, he would jump from great heights, explore places he probably shouldn't, play with weapons he *definitely* shouldn't, but there was always the salve.

Malakai's eyes flutter open slowly. His first thought is that he's not in the ballroom any longer, he's on his bed inside his room. He tries to rise, but a hand presses lightly on his arm, a voice says 'steady.' He recognises the voice as the same soft tone of the one who helped him before, the same small hand resting on his arm. He knows that voice. A voice he's grown fond of these past weeks.

His gaze lands on Arabella, her hair a tousled mess, curls tangled and frayed. The whites of her eyes are bloodshot, the blue more vivid than usual; she's been crying, he notes, from the tears staining her cheeks.

"I hope those tears weren't for me." Malakai rises so he is face to face with her.

"Of course not. You got blood on my favourite dress."

Malakai laughs, a sound he wasn't sure he would be able to make. Though it doesn't last long before he is wincing in pain, the side of his face tight and sore. He touches it, feels the sticky ointment, the small stitches holding the wound together.

Arabella takes his hand in hers. "Don't touch it, it will get infected."

"How bad is it?"

"It could be worse. On the bright side, once it's healed, you will have that rugged warrior look."

"Stop making me smile."

"I was worried about you, Malakai. Why did she do it, why did she kill that girl?"

Malakai swallows, his mind scrambling for information. "I– I don't know."

The door flies open without an announcement and Soraya comes through just as fast, a whirlwind of ebony skin and thick, bouncy curls. Her piercing gaze pins Malakai to the spot. "Good, you're awake. The royal council has gathered for a meeting, you need to be there, you need to hear the lies your friend is spinning."

Malakai's thoughts are a mess as he enters the council room, the sunlight beating through the large window doing nothing for his pounding head. If the pain is from his injury, or the tale Soraya fed him on the way here, he does not know.

All heads turn toward him as he crosses the threshold, the doors swinging open wide. No one says a word as he saunters toward the only available chair, taking it as if it's his stars forsaken right. Which he supposes it is, being the future king. He deserves to be in this meeting as much as any other person at this table. More so.

His father watches him from the other end, his face blank of emotion. Malakai has always struggled to read this father, always admired his strong will of not letting others know his thoughts. Malakai schools his features into that same unreadable expression, watching his father all the same, daring him to command him to leave. He only lowers his chin in a short nod, before turning his attention back to the guard Malakai interrupted.

Damien.

Remy Gardeviar speaks up beside Malakai, his words clipped, frustrated, "So what you're saying is, you let a thief get away, and not only did you let her get away, you let her infiltrate the castle, pose as a princess, let her be alone with His Highness, and poison your king."

Malakai startles, his eyes catching his father's for a brief moment. Why doesn't he look more worried? More shocked?

"Yes," Damien says, lowering his head. "We cannot apologise enough for what has happened. But I assure you, once I discovered her game, I took action. Only she was stealthier than I had anticipated. She stole my knife, and that's when Prince Malakai interrupted."

Malakai feels the burn of each set of eyes boring into him, looking at the laceration Lena caused. It wasn't a knife, that he knew for certain. The cold tingle of magic fading beneath his skin was more than enough evidence of that.

"And the handmaiden?" Remy asks, his tone telling Malakai that he doesn't believe Damien's story one bit.

"As I said before, in the wrong place at the wrong time. The thief shoved her, all there is to it."

Remy mutters something low under his breath, masking the sound with the rifling of parchment. He hands Damien a blank sheet. "Write it all down, every last detail."

Damien looks to the king, who nods, the only confirmation he needs to be on his way, parchment in hand.

"Noah, find out what people know. The servants know more than any in this castle, talk to them."

"Yes, Your Majesty." Noah Tambold jumps from his chair, scurrying toward the door.

"Remy, I need you to make arrangements for the servant girl. I am of the understanding that she had no family, one of my wife's orphans I expect. Discover any friends she may have had, they can help you with the funeral arrangements."

"A funeral for a servant?" Jasper pipes up, scoffing at the very idea.

"Jasper, you may leave. The meeting is over," King Rorik drawls.

Once they have left, the king, the prince, and the Seal are all that remain.

"Tell me," the king says quietly.

Lissa Shostakovich shuffles in her seat, pulling her blonde hair over one shoulder. "She never arrived back home. No one in Mirdoff has seen or heard from Princess Lena since the day she left for Sorrelle."

Malakai watches as his father closes his eyes, a slow, steady breath leaving his lips. He's realising what Malakai already knows, what Soraya had already told him. Lissa's words just set this truth in stone.

"She's dead, Father."

"We don't know that for certain," Lissa says.

"We do. And I know who killed her."

The king's eyes snap open, fixed on his son. "How? Who? Was it the girl?"

Malakai shakes his head, again trying to read his father, curious as to the worry that underlines his words, the worry that flicks momentarily across his features. "Lieutenant Reynolds. Damien. My friend."

"I would like a moment with my son, Shostakovich."

Lissa gathers her things, muttering something, a look of horror on her face as she scurries from the room.

"You are certain of this? These accusations are not something you—"

"Spare me the lecture, Father. You think I would say such things if I was not certain?"

King Rorik rises from his seat, eyes trained ahead, and jaw set in a tight line as he makes his way across the room. He decants a golden whisky into two glasses, passing one to Malakai, downing his own before speaking. "You know this how?"

"The Jalendia princess, Soraya. Her necromancy gifts. The real Princess Lena came to her late in the night, telling her everything."

"Why now?"

Malakai doesn't answer. Instead, he walks to the door and knocks once. It opens, a guard ushering in the princess who waits beyond. Soraya curtsies low to the king. "Forgive me, Your Majesty, but I feel it necessary that I am here for this."

"As do I, Princess Soraya. Please, come. I want to know everything."

Within moments, the three royals are sat huddled at one end of the table, the door firmly shut. Soraya's eyes flick hurriedly to the empty seat at her side, concentration lining her face. Listening, Malakai realises, to whom, he does not know. His father asks his question again, "Why now?"

"Sometimes it is not easy for them, the spirits." Soraya's words roll off her tongue, her accent thick. "They can become attached to their place of death, living their nightmare over and over, suffering day after day. Some stay that way forever, others make peace with the fate they are dealt, break through those horrors. Many make their way to people like me, a guide to help them cross over if they so wish."

The king fidgets in his seat, feeling uneasy at the words. "And this is what Princess Lena did? Found peace?"

"In a way. You have to understand, the spirit world does not work the same as ours, their version of time is vast. Think of it as being enclosed in a pitch-dark room; the eye can see nothing, there are no sounds, you do not know if minutes have passed, days, weeks. Years even. For them, it is the same. Lena died mere weeks ago, but for her, she has re-lived her death hundreds of thousands of times, which alone can drive a person to insanity. When I say they make peace, what I mean is they make do. There's very little choice when it comes to death, Your Majesty.

"But yes, Princess Lena broke from her death spell, with help from another,"—a glance to the seat beside her—"and made her way to me. She did not have far to come, as I remain here, where the spirit world claimed her."

"How did he do it?" Malakai asks, voice low.

Soraya watches him. "You're sure you want to know?" Malakai nods, eyes never leaving her face. "He stared into her eyes as he pulled her own cloak tight around her neck. He watched as the blood vessels burst, coating the whites of her eyes in red. He watched as her body flailed, as the last breath left her body. Then he stayed that way, not releasing her until he was sure he was dead." She turns to the king. "That is what she has been reliving, his face. That is why we are certain it was him. But your son was mistaken on one thing. That man is not Lieutenant Damien Reynolds.

"His real name is Caspian Velor, the Crown Prince of Kignet."

33

THE FACT OF THE MATTER

MALAKAI

King Rorik slams his hands against the table. "We have been fools." This is the fifth time in ten minutes he has divulged the same statement.

Malakai hasn't uttered a sound, the words spinning around in his mind. The Crown Prince of Kignet.

Five years. For five years Damien—no, Caspian—has lived in this castle, five years he has been Malakai's closest friend. All the while, it was all lies. Malakai goes over every moment, every word spoken between them, trying to work it out, nothing makes sense. "But why?" he finally utters.

"Of this, I am not certain." Soraya breathes deep through her nose, tilting her head to look at the empty chair beside her once more. She nods once, confirmation of some silent words. "I do have a theory. Not so much a theory, as a timeline of events. It started fourteen years ago, the night Gavaria fell."

"Raylin," the king says, understanding in his voice.

"The Princess of Gavaria? What does she have to do with this?"

Soraya looks to the king, her eyes narrowing. "You knew?"

He nods, a look at his son, not hiding the regret that sets on his face. "The girl in the cell is not the thief they pretend her to be. She is not the one who poisoned me with Wraith Flower. She is the one who saved me from it. She is the missing princess, Malakai."

Malakai's heart thumps loudly in his chest, his eyebrows crashing into each other. He opens his mouth to speak, but struggles to form a thought. "She– They– I– I don't understand."

"Queen Elisaria's spirit came to me on my first night in Sorrelle," Soraya says softly. "She revealed to me Raylin's true identity. She had been looking for her daughter all these years, roaming these lands. She could sense her here, yet she could not find her. She suspected magic of some kind. She knew the person who had taken her would go to any lengths to keep her hidden. The same person who went as far as to kill a whole castle full of people to take her in the first place."

"Who?" the king demands. Though Malakai knew he must already suspect.

"The Queen of Kignet. Genevieve Velor. You were not the only ones fooled by a Velor; she had played the part of best friend to the Queen of Gavaria for many years, doted on their children. But it was all for power, a hunger inside her. The same hunger I expect her son has. The same reason he is after Princess Raylin.

"It wasn't until that night that the veil was lifted, and Elisaria found her long-lost daughter, here in this castle. Along with everyone else, she did not know who Caspian was; she thought him Raylin's saviour, someone who had broken her from Genevieve's clutches. She thought her daughter was finally saved. She thought her safe here, with you."

"It was all for their own gain," the king whispers to himself. "They all died for nothing. What I do not understand is what was Damien's play? He was simply a guard, he had no interactions with the girl other than that of duty." The king doesn't miss the look shared between Malakai and Soraya. "Tell me."

The pair remain quiet for a moment, their gazes locking, both wondering who will be the first to say the words. Malakai takes a breath, his lips parting, but Soraya beats him to the punch. "They were...having relations, Your Majesty."

King Rorik's eyes grow wide, his head flicking between the two before him, words stuck in his throat. Malakai reaches out a hand, resting it on his father's arm. The king brushes him off and rises, pouring another glass of golden liquid, this one larger than the last. He knocks it back in two gulps, fingers rubbing at his brow.

"Princess, I would like a moment with my son."

Without hesitation, Soraya gathers herself and departs, leaving the room in silence.

"As far as I am aware, he never hurt her. He has deceived us but I don't think he would—" Malakai cuts himself off, the words he would utter devoid of meaning. *I don't think he would ever hurt her.* He killed an innocent girl. Malakai has no clue what he would or wouldn't have done. It occurs to him then, Damien—Caspian, doesn't know that they know. To him, his plan is still in motion. Did he mean to get Raylin locked up? Isolated from everyone, alone? There were many times they were alone together, but it would have been too obvious then, for a princess to go missing from the castle. But a thief from a cell, maybe people would turn a blind eye.

Then why did he bring her here to begin with? Why did he make her play this part? There must have been something else, another secret. It doesn't make sense. He could have stolen her away from...from where? Where has she been all this time? Malakai's head swims with questions, more and more forming from the depths.

"There's something else." His father's voice is low, unsure. Malakai stays quiet, watching as the king paces the window. "This is not how I wanted you to find out, but I feel it important you know. Now more than ever."

Malakai's thoughts vanish, a shiver working its way up his spine at his father's tone, goosebumps prickling his skin. "What is it?"

"Your mother...This is hard to say. I..." The king comes to a stop, closes his eyes, his hand resting flat against the wall.

"Father—"

"Do you remember that story you loved as a boy? The one about the king and the warrior princess?"

"Of course, but it couldn't be about Mother, the princess dies at the end."

"It is not. But it was about me. I loved another for a long time, Malakai. I still do, I think about her every day. Every time I look at you."

Malakai's breath catches in his chest, his heart skipping over a beat. "I don't—"

"The ending wasn't quite right, I changed that for your sake. Too young to understand, or I too scared to tell you the truth. Your mother has wanted to tell you many times. She loves you, Malakai, more than you will ever know. But...she is not your true mother. She is not the one who birthed you."

Something clicks inside Malakai, two puzzle pieces coming together, an answer to a question that has long plagued him. "The cabin," he whispers.

His father nods, a single tear escaping his eye. Malakai watches as it rolls down his cheek, a reflection of the one on his own face. "Your mother, Lucia, and I, we may love each other now, but there was a time when, well, when I was a fool. I strayed. I met a woman who took my breath away, my heart along with it. Her brother warned me, told me it was a mistake to ruin what I had for his sister. He knew her better than anyone, knew she was not one for love. But still, I tried.

"Then there was a time when I didn't have to try anymore. I wasn't married, I wasn't committed, in the sense I did not have a queen. And I wanted her to be that, I wanted her by my side. For a while, I thought I may get that. Get her. Then she disappeared."

Malakai stays quiet, watching the emotions spread along his father's face, emotions he has never seen his father display in company before. He focuses on his words, soaking them in. Waiting.

"Months passed—eight to be exact. I had word from her brother that she was safe. I knew then that she had left me. I was lost and confused. I married Lucia in that time, had given up hope for her return. Then one night, her brother came to me, urgent and worried. I raced with him to that cabin, my healer with me. They had barely made it to Sorrelle in time, but there she was, in the place we would often spend time together, hidden from the rest of the world. Our private sanctuary. But now that sanctuary was covered in blood, filled with her screams.

"And then, there you were. Your tiny hand wrapped around my finger. My world was filled with light, with joy. But it was all ripped away in an instant."

"She died," Malakai says through tears.

"She died," the king repeats. "She had lost too much blood, she was weak." Rorik's eyes go distant, staring out into the dimming sun outside the window. "She held you in her arms till the very end, said words to you that she had never uttered to another soul. '*I love you, Malakai.*'"

Malakai fiddles with the signet ring on his finger, the matching one to his father's. She had tried to show him, tried to tell him. She had conjured images of his birth in his mind, but he hadn't understood. He hadn't been back to the cabin since that night. There was something about what she had shown him that scared him. Maybe deep down he had known, known what she was showing him, known that the connection he felt with the spirit that lingered there wasn't just nothing, wasn't just a coincidence.

His mother. She was his mother.

"Who was she?"

His father places a hand on his shoulder. "Someone brave. Someone strong. A force of nature, a storm of wild determination. Her name was Adira, and she was my best friend's sister. She was the Princess of Gavaria, son. This is why I am telling you now. That girl locked in our cells, Princess Raylin, she is your cousin."

Malakai gasps. He knew then what he had felt each time in her presence, that tug of recognition he had each time he looked at her, a bond like no other, of blood, of family. "Does she know?"

"No. This was a secret we kept close to our chests. Your mother chose to stay, chose to raise you as her own. Orilius agreed."

"We must release her. We cannot let her rot down there."

"In due time, son. She is safer there for now, just until we find Genevieve and the boy. If we go to her now, it will alert them. We have to let them believe they are winning, let the rest of the castle carry on as they are."

"You cannot mean that."

"It is the best option we have right now. I won't let her be taken, not again."

Malakai understood his father's reasoning, he did, but that did not mean he couldn't speed things up a notch. And that's why, as he and Arabella make their way down the corridor, he goes over the plan again in his mind.

Find the liar. Play him at his own game. Lock him up. Throw away the key. Release his newly found cousin. And live happily ever after. Simple.

Okay, he knew it wouldn't be that simple. There was a web of lies to unfurl, angry, grieving people to console, and answers to questions he was unsure if anyone knew.

That could all wait. He couldn't let Raylin stay down there much longer. It had already been days, and stars knew what she was going through down there. He had once heard screams so pained coming from those corridors that he hadn't dared go down them for years. Cousin or not, she had become a friend in her time here, one of the rare few he truly cared about, and he wouldn't see her hurt. No more so than she already was. No matter what she had done. He knew there must be an explanation to it all.

Malakai thought Damien—Caspian, would be a difficult man to find, lying low perhaps, but that was not the case. A brief interaction with a cadet told Malakai all he needed to know, and when he and the snow princess entered the small library—more of a reading room, few books lining the walls—they found him perched upon a chair, a book open in his lap.

Malakai feels all the more foolish upon seeing him. How he had ever thought this man a simple guard, he doesn't know. His rich, golden skin seems to glow under the soft, flickering lights of the room, his deep black hair framing those piercing blue eyes. He has the look of a royal, holds himself as one, straight back and crisp words. He could see why Raylin had fallen for the liar so fast, sank into his words, believed each one he uttered. Malakai had not exactly been opposed to the union, pushing the two together at every chance he got.

"How are you feeling?" Malakai takes a step toward him, a look of concern on his face.

Caspian raises his eyebrows. "Me? You're the one who got hurt."

"Simply a scratch, my friend." Malakai gives him a small smile, playing oblivious to his schemes. Arabella remains still beside him, face stern, nothing changed from her usual public demeanour. "I know you were fond of the girl, it cannot be easy."

"No. It is not." Caspian takes a deep breath, sadness taking over his face.

Malakai cannot help but wonder if he truly did grow feelings for Raylin. He certainly looks genuine. But then he had over these five years, when in fact it all meant nothing to him. It was all a game of cat and mouse.

"Your guards are on the case, right?" Malakai fiddles with a loose thread on his jacket. Caspian nods, brows inching closer. "Do they know anything yet?"

"I told your father all I know, Malakai."

"No new leads then?"

"I don't know what else there is to find out. She was a thief, she was caught, and now she rots."

"You would let her rot for simple thievery?" Arabella spits, too much venom in her words. Malakai shoots her a look: *calm it.*

"It's not that simple. And it is not my choice. If she was caught before, then no, I would not let her rot. She has committed treason. She has infiltrated the castle. So now, yes, she must rot. Either that or face another kind of punishment."

Malakai stiffens. He couldn't mean execution. They hadn't used that as a form of justice in Sorrelle since before he was born. His father wouldn't allow it. Malakai wouldn't allow it.

Caspian pulls the round bronze watch Malakai has seen many times before from his pocket. "I must be going, I have matters to attend to."

"We shall come with you." Malakai makes to follow him.

"That would not be appropriate. I have a meeting with my commander, then guard duties to fulfil. That reminds me, Malakai, you should have a guard posted with you at all times, just until things have settled."

"You're right. I will find Cadet Michaels. I'm sure he will be willing to oblige."

Caspian nods once before abandoning them in the small reading room.

"Was that your grand plan? Talk him into confessing." Arabella rolls her eyes.

Malakai sighs, looking her over. "You think so little of me, Bella?"

"Do not call me that, I hate it."

"Yeah, it didn't sound right. And to answer your question, no. I just wanted to talk him into leaving, so we could follow him, smartarse."

"So then why are we still standing here, dingbat?"

Malakai shoves against her playfully. Taking her hand in his, he drags her to the far wall, to where a painting of his grandfather hangs, the green eyes matching his own. With a click, the painting springs forward, revealing a faded wooden door. They climb through silently, walking blindly through the dark.

"What is this place?" Arabella asks.

"There are secret passages all over the castle. The first king was a paranoid man, he wanted an easy escape were he to face an assassination attempt. In the end, he was killed by his son, so maybe he had a right to be paranoid."

"How awful."

"But how wonderful for us."

Arabella makes a disgusted sound, catching Malakai clean on the shoulder as she swings out her arm.

"Ow."

"So you truly believe he is going to his commander?"

"Oh, stars no. There are only a handful of places he could go from my grandfather's reading room, three of which I know for sure he wouldn't be heading. So that leaves the cells or the garden. I'm taking a gamble."

"He wouldn't be foolish enough to go visit her, surely."

"That's what I'm counting on."

Malakai comes to a sudden stop, Arabella nearly crashing into his back. A soft click sounds and light floods the narrow passage. Back in the main castle, they get a glimpse of Caspian as he exits into the garden and Malakai lets out a relieved breath. He wasn't sure if he had made the right call.

They wait barely seconds before going after him, keeping far enough back that they have time to take cover should he turn. Arabella clings to Malakai's arm, nails digging in. Malakai lets her, the feeling easing his nerves.

They are off castle grounds when he hears Damien's voice. It gives him a start, gut wrenching at the idea of being caught, knowing what his former friend is capable of. Thoughts of Soraya's words come rushing to him, images of Damien draining the life of an innocent princess. He shakes them away when he sees who Caspian is talking to.

The woman looks to be about the same age as his father, fine wrinkles lining her face. Misty blue, serious eyes bore into the boy before her, grey-black hair falling to her shoulders. She wears a cape of deepest purple pulled tight around her, body shrouded from the chill air.

"Well, where is she?" the woman hisses.

"She used her magic, Mother. They saw. If I wanted to keep my identity hidden, I had no choice but to lock her away. I can get to her, I just need time."

Genevieve. This was Genevieve. The woman who killed Raylin's family. The woman who has kept her hidden from the world all these years. Here, in Sorrelle. Malakai had secretly held out hope for his friend, hoped that Damien had been true, that these years had changed him, that he had changed him, Raylin had changed him. But seeing him here, with her, his hope evaporated. Raylin's power was all he wanted, and he's working with his mother to get it.

"Time is up." Genevieve scans the trees. Malakai and Arabella press themselves further into the spiked bark. "Come, I fear the forests have ears."

"Where?" Caspian asks.

"Home."

Malakai nearly misses it, only turning in time to see the dark shadow curl around the pair, hiding them from sight. Within a blink, air swallows the shadow, Genevieve and Caspian with it. Gone. The space they stood empty.

"What now?" Arabella whispers.

Malakai turns to her, chewing on his bottom lip.

"Now...we defy the king."

34

When All Is Lost

Raylin

I'm unaware of how much time passes.

What feels like days could be hours, what feels like hours could be days.

There are no windows, so there is no sunrise, no blue skies, no twinkling stars. It is only darkness. I counted the minutes between one visit from a servant to another—all of whom dump a large bowl of water and a chunk of stale bread beside my cell—but their visits are not consistent. It took twelve hours from Damien's departure before the first servant arrived, another fourteen for the next, only nine by the third, then I gave up, too weak to focus on anything but staying alive.

Five servants have passed through in the time I have been here, not a single one looking toward me. How can I blame them? Ella was their friend, and I took her away from them.

No one else visits. I had hoped Soraya would come, but as the time ticked by, I realised no one was coming for me. I understand. Who knows what Damien has been telling everyone. The story he's spun to paint him as the good guy. He is far from it. If I could just explain to them, tell them who I am, tell them what happened that night, maybe they could forgive me.

The thought of Damien twists my stomach. How could I ever have trusted him? He talks of Genevieve as if he isn't just like her. Hungry for power, not caring who they hurt in the process. What I don't understand is why he has been in Sorrelle for so long, yet never approached me. Not once. We first laid eyes on each other two years ago, why not come after me then? Follow me back to the tower and take from me what he wanted. Did he even know who I was at first? He must have. There would be no other reason for him to be here. The Prince of Kignet, posing as a guard for five years, right under the noses of the royal family.

I wince at the hum of power in my blood, now replenished and eager for release—it doesn't understand it will not work here. I tried several times, reaching toward my void and begging for warmth, for a cloak, for anything, but it was no use, Damien did not lie. For once. I would do anything for a change of clothes, the pink silk I wore to the carnival now torn and filthy, more a scrap of material than an elegant dress. I close my eyes and focus all my energy on the one good that came of all this—I got Fee out, he's free. I hope he flies from this place, gets as far away from here as possible. Far away from Genevieve. I could never live with myself if he gets locked back inside that cage. If I get to live at all.

Without even a bucket to piss in, I have to relieve myself in a corner. The smell of stale urine clings to the air, dried to the stone floor. If I thought the prison of my tower was bad, this is one-hundred times worse. I tried avoiding the musty bed, but after my first sleep on the ground, when I awoke to my body as stiff as a board and screeching in pain, I gave in. The bed isn't much better, I can feel every dip and curve of the frame through the slither of a mattress, but it isn't cold and wet, and that's about as much as I can ask for in here.

I haven't moved for several hours. I lay still on the bed, staring at the mould on the far wall; if I squint hard enough it looks like a horse grazing in a field of green.

The door creaks above, a servant's footsteps making their way down the stairs. It is fruitless, my bread and water from the last visit still sitting outside my cell untouched. Urgent whispers carry down after them, and a voice snaps back. I move then, recognising that voice.

"Raylin?" the voice calls out.

Then Arabella is standing before my cell, her white hair dull in the darkness, but her pale blue eyes glimmer. I stare at her, sceptical if she is real or if I am hallucinating.

I decide it's a hallucination. Arabella doesn't know my real name. My shoulders slump.

"We're here to get you out," the fake Arabella says.

We? There is no one else with her. I'm even more sure now that she is a figment of my imagination. Why my mind would make her up, and not Soraya, or even Catalina, I do not know. Her eyes dart toward the stairs and back to me.

"It stinks in here." Her face scrunches up.

That's more like it. Much more Arabella.

Her eyes dart toward the stairs again, her foot tapping urgently against the floor, echoing around the open space. A low whistle sounds through the room. She grabs hold of the large obsidian lock and it doesn't take me long to realise what she is trying.

"Your powers won't work. It's obsidian," I say, leaning back against the bed. "That, and you're not real."

"I'm not real? What? Oh, for stars sake, just stay back, will you? And you might want to cover your ears."

She homes in on the lock, ice slithering from where she holds it, extending up and up, her fingers turning a pale shade of blue. A misty fog unfurls, like breath seeping from your lips on a cold day. She trembles as she grips the lock tighter, her knuckles turning white from the force. Cracks pierce through the quiet, sparse at first, then growing in quantity, quicker and quicker. A bang splinters through the room, the sharp sound penetrating my ears.

I should have covered them.

The lock is now in thousands of tiny shards, scattered around the floor. Arabella swings the cell door open. "Come on," she hurries me.

I do not move. I just stand, staring at her.

She grabs hold of my hand, pulling me toward the steep steps. I look over my shoulder, back to the rank cell below.

The door at the top of the stairs swings open on its rusty hinges before we get there. Tears threaten to fall, but I do not let them. Soraya and Malakai stand there, urging us on. Together we run down a short corridor, into a small, overcrowded room. Furniture is stacked against the walls. Sofas and tables turned upside down. Boxes piled high. The curtains are drawn closed, blocking out any light, only a small slither coming from the closed doorway, barely illuminating our shapes.

"Is this really happening?" I say, my voice small.

Malakai takes my face in his hands. His eyes are sad, red streaks overtaking the whites, and he gives a small, slow nod. The slice I made across his face is still there, red and raw, sewn up with dozens of tiny stitches. My fingers hover above the wound, my bottom lip quivering, more tears threatening to break free.

Malakai pulls me into a hug, his chin resting on the top of my head, his fingers woven through my matted hair.

"I do not know everything, Raylin, but I know enough." His words release my tears. I stand there sobbing into his chest, breathing in his ocean scent.

"How?" I whisper.

"My father." He turns slightly, looking to where Soraya and Arabella stand, their eyes on us. "And Soraya."

I pull back, my eyebrows stitching together as I look at Soraya. She gazes at the floor.

"I knew who you were..." she says, "are—the whole time. I'm sorry. I didn't want to frighten you. I wanted you to come to me yourself, tell me your truth."

When I don't speak, she carries on, sensing the question on my lips. "Your mother. She spoke to me that first night, in the ballroom. She has been with you this entire time, Raylin. She is proud of you."

Her power. Of course. She can speak to the dead.

My mother is dead.

"My brother. Have you spoken to my brother?" Soraya simply shakes her head and the tiny spark of hope in my heart burns brighter. There is still a chance he is alive.

"As wonderful as this all is, we don't have much time. Put these on." Arabella hands me a soft pair of cotton trousers and a matching tunic.

"And Damien? Where is he?"

I strip out of my silk dress, not caring that I stand before them in just my undergarments. Malakai casts his gaze to the ceiling, giving me as much privacy as he can in such a tight space. My skin is dirty, but the clean clothes help mask the smell of the filthy cell that lingers on me.

"Gone," Soraya says. "We assume he fled back to Kignet, but we cannot be certain."

"Kignet. Then you know? That he is not who he says."

"We do," Malakai says, looking back to me now I'm fully clothed. "I need you to know, Raylin, it wasn't just you he betrayed in all this, and you have my word we will make him pay. His mother too. What I said before...this is why it is important for us all to know each other. If we did, the Prince of Kignet wouldn't have been able to fool us as he has."

I knew Genevieve had a son, had heard mention of him long ago, in a life before this one. Though in all these years she had never spoken of him. Not so much as a name of the one she birthed had fallen from her lips. I had learned it once, in Kignet's history books, but the name evades me now.

"His real name is not Damien, is it?"

Malakai shakes his head. "Caspian."

"If he is gone then why do the guards keep me locked away?"

"They do not know who you are. Caspian fed them lies, told them you were some thief they tried to capture weeks ago. That with...what happened the other day. Father thought it best not to reveal who you were just yet, he was hoping to clean all this mess up himself. But I cannot let this go on, I cannot let you dwell down there any longer. If he comes back—" Malakai shakes his head.

I know they weren't lies, but I don't tell them. Maybe that doesn't make me any better than him, but I cannot have them thinking worse of me.

"It wasn't your fault, what happened to her..."

The sound of heavy boots against stone floors carries through the door, then the shouting commences.

"What happens now?" I look to Malakai.

"We get you out of here." He and Arabella head toward the door, but he turns before it opens. "But, Raylin, promise me you will come back, once all this mess has been dealt with. There are things you need to know. Things I need to tell you."

I nod. "I promise."

They storm through the door, Malakai's commands heading back toward the prison. Soraya grabs hold of my hand, exiting the same way. We head up a tall set of stairs, landing in a corridor I recognise. She turns, taking us toward the main entrance of the castle.

"Wait," I say, dropping her hand.

"The others have taken care of the guards; it will be okay."

I look over my shoulder. "I know a better way."

It's not long before we are standing before the magnificent creature hidden deep within the gardens. Soraya eyes her with unease and the gryphon eyes her right back.

I wonder if she knows what I have done to Ella. Wonder if she has noticed her absence these past days. As I lower myself, Nasima turns her head to me. I kneel before her, bowing low to the ground. As I rise, I ask her the only thing I know for certain that I need. That I want.

"Will you take me home?"

She cocks her head to the side, then sinking low, she copies my gesture, giving her answer. *Yes.*

"But she is restrained?" Soraya says, more of a question as to how than a statement.

I smile at her, my nerves more than likely showing on my face. My power is ready and waiting, hovering near the surface as it has done since that awful morning. I focus it, sending it out like a spear toward the chains that prevent the gryphon from flying. The metal breaks. The cuff is still closed around her leg, but I didn't want to risk injuring her.

She steps toward me, ruffling out her wings. Then her roar breaks through the quiet, the anger and humiliation like an arrow through the world. A swoop from above catches my attention.

"*Fee,*" the word comes out on a relieved breath.

He waited for me.

I climb atop the gryphon, her back lowered for me. Just weeks ago I was terrified to ride a horse, now I am about to fly across the skies on a damn bird.

"Don't be a stranger," Soraya says, stepping back.

Nasima's back legs bend, gearing to pounce. As she bounds forward, her wings push against the air, lifting us from the ground. I grip around her neck in a tight embrace, my eyes squeezed closed. My stomach descends as I feel us gain momentum. Fee's squawk sounds close by. Slowly I open my eyes, afraid of what I will see.

We are high above the castle, the whole of Sorrelle in view, its people no more than pinpricks against the landscape.

I am free. Finally free.

But at what cost?

I have no family to go home to. I am leaving my friends behind.

I consider changing directions, going someplace else. But my heart won't let me. I need to see Gavaria, I need to see my home. And I need to satisfy that need of knowing if my brother waits for me there.

35

Truly Free

Raylin

We fly for hours, Fee sticking to my side, as he always has. A light mist of rain coats my skin, my clothes, setting the cold into my bones.

We bank lower, dipping beneath the clouds, and Gavaria comes into view.

It's quiet. No smoke filters out the chimneys. No sign of people dwelling in the streets. There are no flickering candles in the stone houses, no whispers of bedtime stories, no laughter of the drunk from the tavern, no iron torches brightening the dimming sky. Nothing. An empty, desolate kingdom. A husk of what it once was.

The castle still stands tall, although worn to time, chunks of stone broken and fallen to the floor. Nasima lands at the foot of the bridge. The water surrounding the palace soothes me, bringing back memories of when Reed and I would play along the bank, seeing who could throw sticks and stones the furthest.

Always him, of course.

He would laugh at the way I would throw, mock me with no reprieve. He tried to teach me many times, and though I got better to some degree, I liked to lose, liked to hear the laughter burst out of him when my stick would go no further than a foot in front of me. I throw a rock in now, not holding back as it flings from my fingers, skimming across the water, then sinking to the bottom.

I stare toward the castle, taking in the smooth, grey stone and the broken windows. My breath catches; I am a child again, being called home by one of many servants telling Reed and me that dinner is ready. I never left, Genevieve never took me away, I grew up here, my family wait for me inside.

Impatiently, I bolt across the bridge, scared and alone, heading straight toward the castle entrance. The large wooden doors seem smaller now somehow, or maybe it's just that I am taller, older. I force them open with eagerness. They are stiff, groaning as I push them. My bare feet slap against the white stone floor as I run down the long corridor. The furniture is thick with dust, cobwebs hang from the ceiling and walls. Vines creaking through cracks. My legs buckle as I barge through the banquet hall doors. I catch myself before I hit the floor, clutching the bronze door handle.

No one lives here.

Reed is not here.

My insides shrivel, condensing to half their size. The long table stands before me, chairs scattered around in an unorganised mess. Dark stains mark the floor, a spot for each person who lost their life here that night. My eyes travel around the room, landing on the spot I seek. The same dark stains cling to the far wall, the place *The History of Gavaria* said my father was found.

I make my way there, running my hand along the muddied spot, my fingers catching on a dip in the wall. Barely visible along the faded stone, a small rune is carved. A circle with two lines diagonally through it.

My father had a secret door. A door only his blood, my blood, can open.

A crisp wind envelopes my hand as I conjure a dagger, a simple blade with a worn wooden handle. I slice it across my palm, blood swelling at the surface. The shifting of stone fills the silence as I wipe my blood across the rune.

I step inside. It is cold and dim, a soft light hanging in the centre of the room, a little orb of magic, never diminishing. The place is untouched, layers of dust coating the crowns, jewels, and trinkets. A golden crown and tiara sit on velvet red pillows beside each other, both with wine-red oval diamonds embedded along the band. A matching pair. Tiny gold stitching on the pillows indicates who these belong to: Reed on the crowns, Raylin on the tiaras. A king and a princess. I had never seen them before, Father must have had them made ready for when Reed would be crowned king. He was excited for Reed to take over, he was so proud of him, of everything he had accomplished.

I move to the other side of the room and my foot connects with a discarded piece of paper, folded hastily, my name written across the top, smears of dark, bloodied fingerprints covering half the page.

I open it tentatively, my heart hammering in my chest.

My dearest Raylin.

I do not breathe as I read the next paragraph. Telling me of everything that happened, of what Genevieve had done. All in my father's handwriting. This is why he had been over here, this is why he had been in this room, all while bleeding out. She left him there, gasping for breath. She thought he had died as she walked away, but he held on, just long enough. Why did he not heal himself? I don't understand. I get my answer as I keep reading, the words becoming harder to make out, wobbled and drawn out like he was struggling to keep from parting this world.

My power is failing me, my wound too critical. With my last breath, I will pray to the stars for you, my daughter. I do not believe she will harm you. Her need for power will not allow it. What I do believe is that you will one day find this letter, and you will know how much your mother and I loved you. How much your brother loved you. Everything we did was for you. You see now what happens when someone seeks out the power within you. We were wrong to keep you hidden. You must be stronger than them. You must be stronger than us. Do not hide away and cower from your power, Little Moon. Fight for it. Show them who you truly are. For you are my daughter. You are the Queen of Gavaria.

Father.

I cannot stop the tears that fall, the cry of pain and loss that tears from my throat.

It is all true. Everything I saw was true. She killed them all. I am all that is left.

I stumble back into the banquet hall, my power a raging wind swirling around me, wrapping me in a blanket of darkness and ice.

I cannot breathe.

With the letter still gripped in my fist, I fall to my knees. I hear Fee's call from above as he swoops low and lands beside me.

"Leave," my voice cracks.

He inches closer, but I turn my face away from him.

"Go away, Fee," I cry.

Still he comes closer. But his presence isn't a comfort, it is a knife to my heart. This is all my fault. Everything that has happened is because of me. If I was never born, if I never brought these forsaken powers into this world, my family would be alive right now. Ella would be alive. Princess Lena would be alive.

I only get people hurt. Get them killed.

My power is a raging storm, wisps of darkness rupturing from me like flashes of lightning. I don't try to control it. I let it break from me, powerful and unwavering.

It relishes the freedom.

"I said, *GO!*" My voice booms like thunder, not entirely my own.

Felix flinches, but he listens. By choice or command, I am unsure, but he flies from the room, leaving me to wallow.

The power gathers inside me faster than it can escape, nothing but ice in my veins, the darkness taking over the remaining light.

Do not hide away and cower from your power, Little Moon.

I will not hide any longer. I will not be afraid. For them, for my family, I will be strong.

My power agrees, pulsing to our mantra.

Revenge. Revenge. Revenge.

I implode inward like a dying star.

But I am not light, I am darkness. I am everything I once feared, everything they will fear.

A scream tears from my throat, deafening and unafraid. The power ripples out of me in waves, cascading through the room and pushing at the walls, the ceiling. I scream again, the power ripping from me, smashing against the castle. The floor beneath me rumbles as the ceiling blasts off in chunks of jagged rock. The walls crumble in pieces to the ground.

My power doesn't stop there.

My body arches as the darkness flows, spreading across the kingdom and destroying everything in its path, the noise thunderous and raw. My power sends images to me along an invisible thread, connecting us as one. I watch as it rips through empty homes, claws at abandoned carriages, smashes through the villages as if they are nothing. As the adrenaline courses through me, I give in to the thrill, more addictive than any I have felt before.

The moon shines down on me through the broken roof, watching me proudly. It pulses against the night, celebrating its victory. For I have succumbed to its temptations, banishing the light inside me.

My power slows, its job finished. My hands find the floor and I stay there, panting on my hands and knees, my skin tingling and alive.

I catch sight of the bracelet at my wrist, the crescent moon dangling there. It clatters to the floor as I tear it off. Broken. As I rise, I find myself in the mirror before me.

Me, but different. New. I smirk at my reflection.

My light brown hair—the hair that once matched my father's—has gone, turned a midnight black. My eyes shine brighter, more silver than ever before, the colour rivalling the moon. My power dances around me in shadows, slithering along my skin. I pull all my hair over one shoulder, the braid loose and frayed. Without much thought, I grip it in a fist, and slice through it with the blade I conjured before. It swooshes down, falling on the tips of my shoulders. I take in the person who now stands before me, accepting her. Accepting me.

This is who I truly am, Father.

Chill wind whips through my hair as Nasima carries me through the skies.

After having washed clean, changed into the tight leathers I found in my aunt's former rooms—a woman I never met, but often heard stories of as a child—I emerged from the castle. Felix was nowhere to be seen. The gryphon had waited, curled in a ball by the water's edge. She happily let me climb upon her, taking off when I gave her our destination, on a promise that I will soon set her free. There is just one thing I need to do first.

We land in the large clearing in Sorrelle, the Moon Flowers twinkling in the night glow. Nasima lets out a huff as I lean my forehead against her large head, her feathers soft as I run my hand along her side.

"It's time for you to go home," I tell her. "You're free."

She steps back, her eyes skimming over me. Then she pounces, her back legs springing her up and over me. I watch as she disappears into the night, before turning my focus to the task at hand.

Without much effort, I tear the magical shield around the tower down and the very atmosphere seems to shudder. The tower stares back at me, as if asking if I am okay.

No, not really.

I run my hand along the sharp bricks. How could I have been so foolish to believe Genevieve all these years? Even after the day I first left the tower, nothing bad happened to me, yet I never questioned her. I still trusted her completely. I could have fled then. Fee and I together could have sailed from Sorrelle, gone far from this place. All of this could have been avoided. Damien—Caspian, would have never had the chance to pretend to save me. Princess Lena would have kept her life. I would not be standing here right now, ready to destroy the only place I ever really knew as home.

Gavaria always had a place in my heart, but it was my family I longed for. This...this tower, I lived most of my life here. I grew up here. Everything I have learned and accomplished has been here.

I step back, putting distance between me and the building before me. Genevieve once stood here, fourteen years ago, and erected this place with nothing but the materials beneath the ground, her borrowed magic raising rock and stone. Now I shall return them.

I will never come back to this forsaken place.

My power does not rush as I reach for it. Instead, it glides through me, does not need to urge me to use it any longer. It knows I am willing, knows I have chosen the bitter cold over the soothing warm within me.

The tower sways as my darkness climbs it, wrapping it in shadow. The earth below trembles as it swallows each falling stone, welcoming them back. A droplet of rain wets my cheek, the dark clouds above me threatening more. The tower splits, chunks of rock falling faster now, my shadows helping tear them away one by one. I thought I would be sad, but as the ground swallows the last of the tower with an ear-splitting groan, I feel nothing but relief.

Emptiness surrounds me. I am all that remains in the clearing; the place seems smaller now. Even the Moon Flowers have abandoned me.

I conjure a cloak, a deep green like the one I owned before. I never did find out what Caspian did with mine.

The forest stays silent and still as I make my way through, the same path I have taken many times before. This time I cut my journey short, heading through a small gap between trees further up from my usual spot. I weave through the darkened houses, the lights out, the silence of people sleeping inside.

The rain trickles down gently, dampening my clothes. With my hood pulled far over my face, I move on quick feet toward the docks. I enter a tavern that sits on the outskirts, hoping to find what I'm looking for. Sailors fill the tables, tankards in hand, their voices mingling. I take a seat in the far corner, gesturing to the wench for an ale. I stay beneath my cloak, hiding the fact I am a woman in a bar full of men. I close my eyes, my power scanning the conversations around the room, listening to the one name I want to hear.

Kignet.

And there it is. The place I want to be. Need to be.

I zone in on that table, three down from me, four men sit there, all nursing tired eyes and large drinks. They are dressed similarly, yellowing tunics, deep umber trousers and vests, and leather boots. Their great white wings pit them as residents of Quendore, a place where not even the royals possess powers, but all are born with feathers at their backs. A place with which my kingdom was to be aligned, through a marriage of their princess and my brother. A marriage that never came to be.

One winged man in particular catches my eye, his dark leather coat covering most of the length of his body; he has a tattoo of a flying dove on his neck. His ashy hair hangs loose around his dirty face, his eyes the colour of honey, bright against his tan skin, something he likely gained working long days on the ship. The fraying bandages wrapped around his hands tell the same story. His face is hard, serious, like he carries the weight of the world on his shoulders.

His voice is deep, commanding, as he talks to the other sailors. They listen intently. Their captain maybe? I sip at my ale as I watch through lowered eyes, taking in everything they say. Mostly things I don't understand, ships being something I never found interesting enough to trawl through books about. They are going to Kignet, and that is all I need to know. That, and how the hell I am going to get on their ship in the first place. They scuttle out at the tattooed sailor's orders, crates to load and a ship to ready, he tells them. He remains seated for a while after they leave, fingers tapping against his metal tankard, wings tucked in tightly behind him as to not let them touch anything.

Once he leaves, I wait a breath, not wanting to arouse suspicion by moving too fast after him. I turn on the street, empty. Where the hell did he go? I move silently, eyes flicking this way and that. I round a corner before I am slammed into brick, a hand around my throat.

"What do you want?" the tattooed sailor snarls. I stay silent. His fingers squeeze tighter. "Why were you watching me? Who are you?"

He yanks down my hood, his eyes scanning my face, eyebrows furrowing together. I take advantage of his confused state; my leg strides up, my knee connecting with the delicates between his legs. A yelp escapes him as his hand comes free of me and he keels over. I may have just ruined my chances of getting on his ship, but I will not let him lay his hands upon me without consequence.

"Do not touch me," I snarl.

"What the fuck? Are you crazy?"

I watch in silence as he collects himself, coming up to his full height. He's taller than me, older—but not by much. His stance is cautious now, ready for a fight might there be one. His eyes roam my body, taking in the leather-bound leg now peeking from my cloak, the blade strapped to my thigh.

"What's a pretty thing like you doing lurking around a sailor's tavern this time of night?"

"I need safe passage to Kignet."

The corner of his mouth flicks up, his eyes glistening. "And why should I help you?"

"Honour? Respect? Loyalty to your pride? Whatever helps you sleep at night."

A laugh rolls off him. "Indeed. I think I could spare room for one more. Not sure how my men will feel having to share their rations. Maybe you should bunk with me."

His gaze roams over me again, that annoying smirk on his face.

"I will do just fine."

"I'm sure you will." His eyes flick again to the dagger at my thigh. "Do you have a name?"

"No."

"Mysterious. Lennox." He holds out a hand; I do not take it. "Promise not to knee me in the balls again, and I will set you up with a bed and a hot plate." He turns, grinning over his shoulder, waiting for me to follow.

"I don't make promises I cannot keep."

He huffs a laugh. "Yeah, you'll be just fine," he says, stalking off toward the docks.

36

Distant Shores

Raylin

The ship looms before us, large and wooden, too many sails to count. I know it is his simply because of the statue that sits at the prow. A winged woman, facing off into the distance, her assets carved to immaculate detail, long wooden hair hanging over her breasts.

Lennox guides me past sailors, all loading crates upon crates onto the various ships. They eye me as we make our way onto his ship, but no one questions us—questions him. I do not let their stares bother me; I keep my back straight, my hood down, my now short, darkened hair swaying in the breeze.

"We have a stop to make before we arrive in Kignet. It will be a few days at minimum, weather dependent."

I was hoping for less, but without many options a few days will have to do. I could have flown Nasima there, it would have been quicker, but I wanted something a little more inconspicuous. I want the element of surprise on my side.

Lennox stops at a worn wooden door far below deck, the light blue paint chipped and peeling. He knocks once before a girl answers, her fair hair hanging limp, her eyes sunken, a wary expression on her face.

"We have a guest. She's not to be touched, understand?" Lennox's voice is stern, more command in it than moments before.

The girl simply nods, opening the door wider for me to enter. Bunks line the walls, three beds high, most occupied by girls of varying ages. All have curious expressions, staring down at me like I am a strange creature they have never encountered. I turn to question Lennox but the door is already closed, he is already gone. The room is small, with beds taking up the majority of the floor space. It's plain, one overstuffed unit of clothes, no possessions to show who the room belongs to. The fair-haired girl points to a vacant bed, then to me. Mine. Okay then. They all remain silent, watching as I undo my cloak and toss it onto my new bed. A collective gasp sounds as they spot the dagger against my thigh.

"You cannot have that here. He will have your hand," the girl on the bed closest to mine says, her brown hair covering most of her face.

"Who will?"

"Captain Lennox, ma'am," she says.

I smile. "Then it's a good thing Captain Lennox already knows I have it. And if he knows what's good for him, he will try to take no such thing."

Their eyes widen and they look at each other, a silent conversation fluttering between them. One by one their faces seem to settle, relaxing slightly. Though their gazes still flick to me, they do not seem so cautious, so worried. None of them have wings, I notice, so they are not Quendore natives.

"I'm Beth," the brown-haired one says, smoothing her hair back from her face, her skin a warm-beige.

"I'm Raylin," I tell them, finding no use in hiding my name now. I will not hide any longer.

If they recognise the name, they do not say. Instead, they take turns telling me theirs, Felicity and Annika—rich-brown-skinned twins—share the bunk by the door, along with a pale girl who calls herself Ash, her voice barely a whisper, her arms tucked into herself, shaggy mahogany hair falling over her face. The fair-haired girl I first met—Sadie—occupies the bed above mine, and Beth shares her bunk with two others—Naomi and Harper, both dark-haired and chalky skinned. Each of them are beautiful, though their eyes are distant, sunken, and full of horrors. What I see in them twists at my stomach.

"Why are you here?" I ask Beth, the only one who seems willing to speak with me, but my eyes flick to each girl, working them out.

"We...We're..."

"We are their playthings," Annika says, her voice thick with disgust.

Ash flinches at her words. My eyes linger on her a moment, before speaking again, "What do you mean?"

"The days on the sea can be long, often with no land breaks. The seamen, they use us for their...needs." Sadie keeps her gaze lowered as she says this, ashamed of herself, of what they do to her.

"They fuck us and throw us away, is what she means to say." It's Felicity that speaks this time.

Heat spreads along my skin, my chest tightening. Their needs. My jaw strains from where I clench it. What right do these sailors have, to keep these girls here against their will, force them to do things they do not want to do, all to please themselves?

The ship lurches, steadies itself out, the gentle motion rocking us. We are moving.

"Captain Lennox is a fair man. When he said you will not be touched, he meant it. He won't let them do those things to you," Beth says, mistaking my anger for them for worry for myself.

I shake my head. "And what about you? All of you. If he is a fair man, why does he let them do those things to you?"

"If he didn't let them, they would do it anyway," Ash whispers from where she is curled up on her bed, knees to chest.

"This way he can control them," Beth adds.

Sadie seems to see the question building inside me: why doesn't he set them free?

"We have nowhere else to go. That's why we are here, orphaned girls with no home and no family. If it wasn't for the captain, we would be dead on the streets. It may not seem like a better life, but some of the men are kind, some just want company, nothing more. They are just as lonely as we are."

"Here, we have each other," Harper says, gaining smiles from all the girls.

The fire inside me mellows out but doesn't completely disappear. Just like the queen with her servants, Lennox has these girls believing that this is the only path for them, the only life worth living. They do not know they can make their own fates, all they need to do is fight, to believe in themselves above all else.

Ella wanted more, she could have been more, and I took that chance from her. I will not let these girls be bound by the same destiny.

My sleep is restless, plagued with dreams of mountains of red, slick with blood and bodies, the sound of screams tearing through the black sky. There are flashes of faces, men and women I do not know. There's a clang of swords, the whoosh of arrows, a throng of bodies fighting for their lives. A man with white hair and silver eyes calls my name, reaching out to me desperately. There's a child, her red hair falling loose over her shoulders, slumped in a wheeled wooden chair. Blood coats her head to toe, her white wings now red, her eyes unseeing, already gone from this world. There's another before her, light brown golden hair, eyes pale blue. His scream rips out my heart, shredding it with its claws, tearing chunks off with its teeth. It is raw and broken.

I shoot up in bed with his name on my lips, "Reed."

I pant, my breathing ragged. My skin is slick with sweat, bitter and persistent. The room is dark, the girls all soundlessly sleeping in their beds. I gather my cloak—still clad in my leathers—and pad out onto the deck, thankful for the low rising sun and the crisp chill. Few sailors linger up here at this hour, most not yet risen for the day, and those that do pay me no heed. I let my fingers glide along the railings, wiping at the sea mist that coats them, breathing in the ocean air—the smell reminds me of Malakai. I try not to think of him, as with him comes the memories of others. The memories of things I don't want to dwell on at this moment. I just want to be here, in the middle of this vast sea, unbroken and unafraid.

"You couldn't sleep?" His voice sends a shiver up my spine.

Lennox stands beside me, his eyes trained on the ocean before us, the rustle of his wings familiar, comforting. Though its not *his* wings I long for.

"My dreams were not pleasant," is all I say.

"Ah. I know the ones."

His face is blank, unreadable, though I do try. I could let my power slither into his mind, look at the things that lurk inside, learn what he knows, the hows and the whys. Instead, I ask, "Why do you keep them here?"

He knows exactly who I mean. His gaze flicks to me and back again to the ocean.

"This is their home." I watch as his throat bobs. "I don't like it. Knowing that they may not like to do the things they do, there is only so much I can prevent. I don't force them to stay. But they know if they left there's no telling what would happen to them. The world is not a nice place."

Shadows pass over his eyes as he lands them on my face, scanning me over. "I don't touch them," he says, as if to reassure himself. "I wouldn't."

I don't respond, just stare at him, taking in the pained look on his face. More sailors clamber onto the deck, voices filling the quiet. Sails are raised, ropes are pulled at various locations. The seamen closest to us try their hardest not to stare, their eyes flicking our way through lowered lashes.

"Join me for dinner tonight." Lennox smiles. It is not a question.

I run a finger back along the ship's railing before turning and walking away, throwing the word over my shoulder, "No."

The day passes in a haze. I encourage the girls to venture with me out to the decks, something they tell me they very rarely do, not wanting to be a burden while the men work. We spend the afternoon sitting on the cold wooden planks, surrounded by the shouts and bellows of the sailors. If they care we are here, they do not say. They barely even look in our direction. From orders from their captain, or for the dagger strapped at my thigh, the shadows I now let dance around my skin, I do not know. The girls do not ask about it either, that darkness around me. They watch them, but they keep their mouths shut, glad of the protection it grants them in my company.

There's a calm silence, no words flow between us, but it is not awkward, it is comfortable, safe. Their faces are relaxed as they breathe in the salted air, letting the cold breeze wash over them. I remember feeling this way before, at the castle, with Soraya and Catalina by my side. Not that there was ever much silence with Catalina. I am grateful these girls have this. If nothing else, they will always have this.

We watch as the moon replaces the sunset, the oranges turning to a soft blue before we head back to our room. I listen to the girl's chatter while I lay on the bed, staring at the mattress above, picking at the worn wood of my dagger. A knock sounds at the door. The girls go rigid, dread filling the room. Sadie is the one to answer, opening just a crack to peer out. She stumbles back as the door is shoved open, landing on her backside.

"You," the man at the door spits, finger pointing up toward Ash in her bed.

I'm on my feet, helping Sadie to hers and guiding her to stand behind me. Ash's whole body is trembling as she scoots to the edge of the bed, eyes darting around the room, seeking help. Annika steps forward, putting herself between Ash and the dark-haired sailor. He's taller than her, skin slick with sweat and dirt. If his muscles are anything to go by, then he is strong as well as tall, his face sharp and stern.

"Wouldn't you rather something a little more...rough and tumble, tonight?" Annika purrs.

The man eyes her steadily, looking her up and down. "I prefer them quiet and submissive. Now move." He shoves Annika from his path, annoyance coating his words.

The others remain silent, curling in on themselves. They cannot do anything but watch this scene play out in front of them.

"She's not going with you." The words leave my mouth without a second thought.

"Excuse me?"

"I said—"

"I heard you, but I don't care who the fuck you think you are. The captain may have brought you onto this ship, but you have no power over his crew. You keep your mouth shut, or I'll shut it for you."

Ice.

I feel nothing but ice as I step forward, the chill of my powers creeping through my veins, flickering along my skin. "Are you sure about that?" I ask the now wide-eyed man.

My powers slither out to him, shadows pinning him against the wall.

"What in the stars are you?" he chokes out.

I smile as a scream is cleaved from him, that coldness inside me reaching into him, clawing at his very essence. I let it do its thing, not needing to be controlled now I let it go free, just a small coaxing from me is enough. A gathering of seamen stand beyond the open door, all with panic on their faces, some shouting things I do not register. I will not let another man cause more harm in this world.

There's a slender hand on my shoulder, a soft breath close to my ear. "It's okay," Ash says.

But it's not okay. It will never be okay.

I push harder, forcing another scream from the man before me. This could have been Ella. If the queen hadn't taken her in, she could have been forced into this life, men just like these putting their filthy hands all over her. I will not let this man take any of them. Not tonight. Not while I am here. And not ever again.

"Leave them be." Lennox's command comes from the doorway, but he's not talking to me, he's talking to his men.

I release the man and he rushes from the room without so much as a glance toward us. Lennox doesn't take his eyes off me, something like curiosity on his face. He's not afraid, not like the men behind him who scuffle off, pushing at each other to be the first to leave. He steps back, a smile on his lips as he pulls the door closed.

37

FORGOTTEN THINGS

MALAKAI

It has been days since Raylin escaped. At least that's what Malakai let people believe; he didn't hide his involvement exactly, but he did not voice the truth either. Nor that of the princesses.

It has been days since the very ground shook beneath them. Days since the air seemed to echo with despair, a bitter cold shifting in from the west. From Gavaria. He didn't know exactly what had caused it, but he knew enough, he knew it was her. And there was nothing he could do.

It hadn't taken long for the truth of Raylin's identity to spread through the castle. With help from the princesses and whispered words to their handmaidens, they had done exactly what Malakai had hoped. He suspected the whole of Sorrelle knew by now. Malakai spent his days in royal council meetings, where he wouldn't utter a word, his gaze far away, his mouth firmly shut. Watching. Listening. He knew his father suspected it was him who exposed the truth, yet he didn't ask, didn't question Malakai.

He spent his nights in his room, Arabella by his side. He hadn't seen Teddy in those days. The guards had become warier, the truth of Damien coming to light among all else. It hadn't felt like the right moment to tell his parents either. Malakai missed his love, but with extra guards posted on every corner of the castle, there was no way he could risk seeing him.

He longed to go to the cabin, to see *her* again. His mother. But that hadn't been possible either. So instead, he told Arabella everything. His whole story, beginning to end. And she listened to it all, quiet and contemplative. She held his hand, stroked his hair as he rested his head in her lap, whispering the harder parts.

She knew him now better than anyone ever had. She knew all his secrets. It felt good, Malakai thought, to share these things, be open with another. They lay together now, curled up on the bed, face to face, hand in hand, fingers laced through each other.

"I don't want to leave," Arabella whispers.

"I don't want you to leave," Malakai whispers back.

His father was sending them all home. The princesses were to leave come dawn. Malakai had felt the sorrow in his gut at the king's request, felt it again now, lingering, undeterred. He knew once they left he would be utterly alone, his nights filled with darkness and nothing more. There would be no more Arabella to light up those evenings, to soothe his aching heart.

It was selfish, he knew that, but it was selfish on both of their parts. They had grown to depend on each other, to find solace in each other's company. It wasn't just his needs and wants that desired to keep her here though, it was for her sake too. He knew once she arrived home she would have to mask her true self once more, hide who she was, who she is. Be treated like an animal by her own family. She couldn't be who she is with him, kind and thoughtful, her heart big and all-consuming.

A tear slowly rolls down her cheek. Malakai catches it with his thumb.

"We could marry," he says seriously. "If you are my queen, then you shall remain here."

Arabella smiles, not a full smile, just the soft curl of her lips. "No, Malakai. That is not the answer, and that is not what I want for you."

Malakai's heart breaks once more. "This is stupid," he says, turning on his back. "How did everything get so messed up?"

"I want to ask you something."

He turns his head to her but remains on his back.

"I've been trying to remember, but it is as if something fogs the memories." Her brows pinch together, forehead creasing. "Do you remember anything from that night? Not what Raylin did, but before. At the carnival, do you remember anything?"

Malakai raises a brow. "Of course, why would I—" His words are cut off by his thoughts. He sits up, heart smashing into the wall of his chest.

He doesn't remember.

Why doesn't he remember?

Arabella raises beside him. "You don't, do you?"

Malakai opens his mouth to speak, the words fail him.

"I can recall it arriving, the tents, the lights. But everything else is blurred, confusing."

"There was...a cage?" Malakai says, unsure. He can picture the bars, as dark as night, but not what lurked inside. What was inside?

"I think he spoke to us. Baron Bean," Arabella tells him, though she doesn't seem quite certain herself.

Malakai could remember a man, not what he looked like, but how his presence felt. How he felt in his presence. He was made of stars. No, that couldn't be right. People aren't made of stars.

Green flames.

Malakai remembers green flames.

But he doesn't remember a fire.

"I thought maybe it was me, just trying to forget. But I spoke to the other girls and they don't remember either. I think this is what they do, some kind of spell. It would explain why no one ever has a straight story about their time with the carnival."

She's right. Malakai thinks to the day he told the princesses of the events to take place; it was all hearsay and he had just assumed none of them had ever seen it for themselves. But what if they had, they just couldn't remember? Why would Baron Bean make people forget? It didn't make sense. Without being able to remember what he saw, there was no way of knowing what the ringmaster was trying to hide.

Malakai didn't like the thought of someone messing with his memories. He had had enough of people messing with the lives of others. He was done with it. There must be a way to get their memories back. It was like Arabella said, it was more like a fog, as if someone had poured water over an inked parchment. The details are there, but they are smeared, unreadable, leaking into each other.

They just need to find a way to reverse that process, to fix what has been done.

A short while later, Malakai and Arabella stand in the room behind the lion painting, mounds of parchment and leather-bound journals before them, dusted with age and forgotten.

Malakai didn't know why, but it was as if the room had called to him, seeking him out. The painting of the roaring lion felt eerily familiar, but not in the sense that he had seen it every day as he walked the halls, no. More as if he knew such creatures, met them perhaps, though he had never come across such an animal in his life.

"You think the answer could be here?"

Malakai eyes the stacks, some towering above them, others half the size. There was no rhyme or reason to their order, not that Malakai could see. The pages were yellowed, fragile with age. He picked up the rolled-up parchment closest to him, pulling the soft green ribbon holding it in place. He unravelled it slowly; the words were faded, barely legible. In the corner was a name, *King Julius Foxwald*. The first King of Sorrelle.

Malakai runs his finger over the name. The rest of the words are unimportant, simply the man's thoughts, his ideals. There's nothing that jumps out to Malakai as odd.

"There's something. I can feel it."

Saying the words out loud seems to set the feeling in motion. The sensation is unexplainable, like a whirring mist inside him, seeking out something lost. And though Malakai didn't know yet what that something was, he could sense it lurking here in those towers of words, something the first king felt important enough to keep hidden here. Baron Bean was said to roam these lands long before the first royal was appointed, and if this was true, maybe they met, maybe King Julius wrote something of him in these journals, wrote of the carnival, of all unknown.

Or maybe it could be that Malakai was going as mad as people thought the first king to be. That the rumours of said king were true, and all that would be here was rambling nonsense and words that did not matter.

But Malakai couldn't believe that. Wouldn't let himself believe that.

King Rorik, Queen Lucia, and Prince Malakai stand in the courtyard, the early morning sun casting shadows along the stone floor, reaching out toward the castle gates. The king and queen said their swift goodbyes to the five remaining princesses, apologising for the abrupt return to their homelands.

Malakai's goodbyes were not so quick; he hugged each princess, wishing them well. Then the carriages rolled out, and one by one they exited the palace grounds, the sound of horses' hooves growing quieter the further away they grew.

One, two, three, four, they went, until all that remained was Arabella, wrapped tightly in Malakai's arms. He could feel her shallow breath against his neck, the prickly cold skin of her arms, the soft fur of her dress.

"We will see each other again," he whispers.

"You promise?"

"I promise."

She pulls back from him, her ice-blue gaze filled with sorrow. With a deep breath and not another word, she climbs into the last carriage.

Malakai watches it long after it's gone, a space in his chest where she once was.

If someone told him just weeks ago that he could feel like this over a girl, he would have laughed at them. How absurd. Not once, but twice, in a matter of days, had part of him been torn away by a girl. It wasn't the kind of love he had with Teddy, nothing could come close. Maybe not even like the love he felt for Damien, though now that love was so torn and battered he could barely remember how it felt to be whole. He wouldn't even say it was the same as how he felt for his mother and father. This was something new, something unknown.

He had many different kinds of love inside him, he realised, some shrouded with anger, some with sorrow, others pure and undiluted. He knew to keep each one close, to cherish every happy moment, every piece of hurt. If there was one thing his power had taught him, it was that.

Malakai turns to his parents, their faces kind and loving, and like a switch flicks inside him, he knows what has to be done. What he had been wanting to do for so long now. He lets his mind clear, lets the courage take over his very being.

When Malakai was a boy, he craved danger, craved that feeling you get while rushing to the edge of doom, of the blood pumping hot around your body, your heart beating double time.

Walking along the cliff edge one day, he heard other boys from the village daring each other to jump, and while none of them would, Malakai emerged into the clearing, running at full speed. The boys' eyes had bulged from their heads. And that is all Malakai saw as he dove from the edge of the cliff, his heart thundering in his chest so hard he thought it may burst forth. When he hit the water, pain emanated through his body, but then he couldn't feel it any longer. Just the soft rush of the water, the bubbles rising around him. At that moment, he felt free, alive, just the darkness of the sea below him. He floated there for as long as his body allowed him. Until his lungs burned and his brain screamed at him to resurface.

When he finally did, he made the trek back to the spot where the boys had stood. Only to find it utterly empty. So he turned, and he ran, and he jumped.

All he had was that feeling.

That was how he felt right now, standing before his parents. All he needed to do was run and jump. There he would find that feeling. He would be free, he would be alive.

"There's something I need to tell you."

38

FATE IS A BITCH

RAYLIN

The following night, I walk down the narrow corridors of the ship, heavy bag in hand. It thumps against my leg, the contents clinking in the quiet. The only other sound is the sloshing of water from outside. I narrow my eyes in the darkness, trying to see the way with no lights to guide me. I get to the door with the word *Captain* carved into the worn wood. I do not bother to knock. With a gust of my power, it swings open with a thud.

Lennox sits behind a desk, leaning back in his chair, his wings draped behind him, a scroll in hand. His room is small, larger than the one I currently reside in, but still small. There's a bed to my right, blankets strewn across it, messy and unmade. To my left is a small shelving unit, filled with books and knickknacks. A dim light hangs from the wall behind him, a flame flickering in a lantern.

Neither of us utters a word as I stalk toward him, his eyes boring into mine, gold burning into silver. My arm protests at the weight of the bag as I lift it, slamming it down on the desk before him. He raises an eyebrow, leaning over and peering inside. He pulls out a sizeable golden coin, the etching of a hand on one side, the words *custodire et sana* on the other. Protect and heal. The coin of Gavaria. The coin I pulled straight through my void from the vaults of my kingdom.

"You will drop them off someplace safe. Leave them with the coin. Take some for yourself, payment for doing this for me."

He keeps his eyes on the piece of gold, twisting it between his fingers. He knows I talk of the girls, the only ones on this ship I care to save. I can only hope I can trust him in this.

"Should I ask where you got this, considering you boarded my ship with nothing but the clothes on your back?"

"You could ask, doesn't mean I will tell you."

"Consider it done. But I will take nothing." He throws the coin back into the bag. "It is theirs, all of it."

I nod, turning to leave.

"Wait." There is no command in his voice, only urgency.

I stop, staring at the open doorway beyond. Something in his voice makes my chest tighten, sensing the loneliness hidden beneath. The same loneliness I have felt my entire life.

"Why are you doing this? You barely know them."

"I will no longer let another suffer at the hands of the cruel people in this world."

His breath shudders, his gaze fixed on the books lying open before him. "The suffering is what makes us who we are. Without pain, without sorrow, who would we be? It took me a long time to realise everything happens for a reason. Fate is a funny thing. But she knows what we can handle. She also knows when we need a little guidance."

"Keep telling yourself that and maybe one day you will believe it."

"If it wasn't fate that brought you onto this ship, to these girls, along with your sack of coin, enough to give them all new lives, then what was it?"

I huff a laugh, shaking my head at him. *Fate*. Is that what he truly believes this to be? Was it fate that killed my family? Was it fate that kept me alone in a tower for fourteen years? Was it fate that broke me beyond repair? Was it fate that stole my life away? No. It was a friend. An auntie. Someone I should have been able to trust.

"It was the greed of others that brought me here, Lennox. Nothing more."

He gets up from his chair, moving with a cool calm towards me. "I think there is more." He comes to a stop inches from me. "I think you are standing here in my room because this is where you were meant to be at this precise moment."

The silence of the room is deafening. My swallow is loud in my ears. His honey gold eyes shine brighter, glowing in the dim light. Ice slithers along my skin, my shadows following in unison.

"And why is that?" I whisper.

"It is not clear. I have been trying to connect the pieces, figure it all out. But I think you and I have the same enemy...*Raylin*."

My body turns to stone. My words stick in my throat. I shake my head, just a slight movement. My power comes to attention, readying itself.

"It was your eyes I recognised. The brightest of silver. I had only ever seen one person with those eyes before. Fifteen years ago, when I visited her family's kingdom with my own. I don't think I could ever forget those eyes."

Realisation floods me. Fifteen years ago, when Gavaria was still my home. When Reed's girlfriend and her family came to visit. My five-year-old self was obsessed with the little boy's wings. He was seven, refused to play with me, so I followed him around until he gave in. Mother had been reluctant to let them stay, worried about what my power could do. It was pure pride on her face when we got through the three days without incident.

"Lennox."

He smiles. "I'm wounded that you forgot me."

"It wasn't me that night. You must know that."

"I had hoped. Everyone was so angry, the things they said..."—he licks his lips—"but I believed, in my heart I knew it couldn't have been you. But who?"

The silence spreads between us. We don't need to utter the words to know what we speak of. What night I mean. The night both our families were killed. His cousins. His aunt and uncle. I'm only glad he was not there.

"It does not matter. Soon it will not matter."

A crease forms between his brows, concern on his face. "You must let me help you." He takes my fingers in his, his touch warm.

I smile, closing my eyes, letting my shadows release further, surrounding us. "I do not need your help," I say softly. "I will not risk anyone else's life."

The ship stills, our destination reached. I let go of that small part of my old life, letting his fingers fall from mine.

"What of your brother?"

I shake my head. "I do not know."

"Come find me," he urges. "Once you are done, come to Quendore. I will tell Presley all I know, but she will want to hear it from you. We can clear your name, Raylin. We can help you find Reed."

Presley. Amily's younger sister. Now the Queen of Quendore, I assume. Their history books were likely spelled, just as Gavaria's had been, as never a word was mentioned of the family's deaths. Hidden by someone who did not want me to know the truth. Hidden by my own magic.

"Goodbye, Lennox."

I weave through sailors unloading crates from the ship, moving swiftly. The docks are uncrowded, the moon already high above. I round a corner, my boots skidding on soft sand.

Kignet stands before me in all its glory.

The view takes my breath away. Palm trees line the long pathway, casting shadows over rows and rows of sand-coloured buildings. Shops, tea rooms, taverns, boutiques. I had seen sketches in the history books, but nothing compares to the real thing. The streets are filled with people, the night air still warm and humid, the weather the opposite of Sorrelle this time of year. Further in the distance, I can see the silhouettes of pyramids. There are hundreds of them scattered across the island, large and small, their golden-capped peaks reaching high toward the open sky.

I start to regret my choice of leather clothing, my skin beneath becoming slick with sweat in the heat. I have no idea how long my journey to the castle will be, and I have packed no provisions to keep me sustained, too eager in my quest to think about such trivial things.

I have only walked a few steps when I come across a man sitting in a fold-out chair, cotton robes down to his feet. His skin is golden brown, like many from Kignet. His hair and eyes are a deep brown.

He looks at me, a friendly smile lining his mouth. "Need a ride?" he asks, his accent thick.

I look to the animals in a row beside him, each one tied to a wooden post. I have never seen anything like them. They are taller than horses, their legs longer, knees nobblier. Their necks are longer too, curving outward into their large heads, which are a similar shape to a horse, though their features are much larger. Bulging eyes with thick long lashes, flat noses, and wide mouths hiding large yellowing teeth. The closest one's bottom jaw swings side to side as it chews a mammoth leaf. Their bodies are covered in thin, short hair, but they have no mane, and their tails are rope-like.

A few of them sit, their legs tucked beneath them, their eyes closed. As well as a wooden saddle, they wear brightly coloured, patterned fabrics, spread over a sizeable hump.

"Please." I nod to the man.

He helps me climb on to the large animal. I sway as we make our way down the path. No cobblestones or bricks are anywhere in sight, the ground completely covered in sand. I try to sit up straight, holding on tight as I bob about in the saddle, the animal tossing me to-and-fro as it clambers toward our destination. The man doesn't speak with me. He occasionally mutters words in a language I don't understand at the animal I sit upon, tugging at his reins to hurry him along.

Smiling and laughing faces pass me, conversations drifting on the wind. I wonder if their smiles will be replaced soon. Instead, tears will wet their cheeks, their lives rocked by the news of the falling of their monarchy. The murder of their queen and prince, right beneath their very noses. The same injustice their queen bestowed upon my kingdom.

I cannot lie, I am delighted at the thought. Just picturing their faces as I release my wrath on them, my power ripping away their lives, thrills me.

The darkness that surrounded me in the days prior is quiet, hiding from sight, but I still feel it there, vibrating along my skin. It, too, is thrilled to be untamed.

The animal comes to a stop at the edge of a beach and I slide off from where I am perched, conjuring and handing the coin of Kignet to the man. He gives me a short nod before going on his way.

I slip off my black boots and bury my toes in the golden sand. It is warm and gritty as it moulds to each curve and crevice of my feet. I relish the feel of it. The beach is quiet compared to the streets at my back. Straw parasols lay abandoned in the sand, done with after a day of lounging in the sun. I watch as gentle waves lash along the shore, the white foam cresting the now wet sand. It is beautiful here. Peaceful.

I think I could spend my life here with the ocean as my companion. Somewhere like here at least. I have already decided I will not go back. The world can wonder what happened to Princess Raylin once more. That girl is gone. Dead. Her kingdom destroyed. Broken by my very hands. There's nothing left for me there. I will go somewhere new, be someone new. I will leave it all behind, banish every memory of what I once was.

But that life can wait. First, I need to finish what I came here for.

Revenge.

39

To save oneself

Raylin

I turn from the beach, leaving my boots discarded on the sand. The desert ground is warm, but not unbearable to walk across barefoot. It feels good to let my feet free again, to let them connect with the earth. It makes me stronger, more connected to my surroundings.

I let my power release, the darkness slithering along my skin, cooling every place it touches as I walk the path toward the large beige palace, taking it in now for the first time. I turned my gaze from it on the ride here, not quite yet ready to acknowledge what I would be doing.

I know what I want. But it doesn't mean it will not be hard.

Genevieve may have killed my family in cold blood, but I spent fourteen years believing she loved me. Believing she was protecting me from the evils of the world.

Turns out she was that evil. But those feelings do not just vanish, they are embedded in my very core, and no matter how hard I push them down, I still feel it there, worming its way through my heart. I had been a gullible fool. I ate up every lie she spun. Gave her everything she wanted. Weakened myself every time she deigned to visit, let her soak up every ounce of my power. I never questioned her, never wondered what it was she wanted my power for.

Stupid, foolish girl.

Her son is no better. Caspian played with my heart; my feelings for him had grown strong in such a brief time. But they weren't for him really, they were for Damien. And deep down I know they aren't the same person. Damien was nothing but an act. He was not real. I had been falling for a fictional man. I will have to remember that as I am ripping out Caspian's throat. He is not Damien. He never was.

I kneel before the palace. Its turrets reach high, scaling up into pointed arrows. The roof is rounded, curving over in large semi-circles. The windows are covered in intricate patterns, making it hard to see through. I can make out the shapes of people—servants and workers going about their business.

"Come to me," I whisper, sending my words out with a burst of power.

My darkness moves around me, wisps of shadows dancing over my skin, readying themselves for what's ahead.

It's not long before she hears my call.

Genevieve walks out of the large entrance doors of the castle, her face blank and unfazed. Her long black dress cascades down her legs, pooling at her feet. She seems older somehow, or maybe I had just imagined her younger, my mind filling in the creases and wrinkles she's gained over the years. But my love for her has depleted; now I am seeing her through new eyes.

Caspian is not far behind, stepping out beside her, he too having heard my call. The guard uniform I have seen him in many times before is gone. He dons a velvet suit of deep purple, silver stitching lining the cuffs and collar of his jacket.

The corner of my mouth flicks up in a small smile at the sight of him. He looks nervous as he takes in my new look, his eyes darting over the shadows that whip around me. We stare at each other as if seeing one another for the first time.

I suppose we are.

"Have you come to return what belongs to me?" Genevieve says, her voice serious.

I laugh. A loud, earth-rattling laugh.

"You are a fool, child."

"I was a fool for a long time. But no longer."

Genevieve smiles at this, shaking her head. "It will destroy you. The darkness. You will lose yourself bit by bit, just like the one before you."

I stare at her, my eyebrows pulling together. I recall Constantine talking of another the gods fought over, but what does Genevieve know of it? "The one before me?"

"You think you were the first? The dark and light have fought before, inside another. Long before either of our times."

Caspian's wide eyes lock on Genevieve, questions written on his face. His mother keeps many things from him.

"What happened to them?"

"He lives." A smirk lifts the corner of her mouth. "My family made sure of that. They didn't know then what I know now. They didn't know what obsidian could do. The power it could give us."

"That's why you wanted the pendant. You were going to strip me of my powers." This I had already guessed when Caspian revealed to me what the obsidian bars of the prison could do. "Then what?" I ask, my shadows growing impatient around me.

"I was going to reunite you with your family, of course."

Caspian goes still, his eyelids fluttering as he continues to stare at his mother. Secrets upon secrets unravelling inside that pretty head of his.

My heart thumps heavily against my chest.

She was going to kill me.

The ear-splitting screech that sounds above startles the three of us. Genevieve's head snaps to the sky, searching the dark for the bird she will not find. The truth of what I just learned overcomes me, and I use this moment of distraction to hit my first mark.

I splay my palm out in front of me, focusing that darkness within, and fire it out like an arrow from a bow. I hear it whizzing through the air before it hits Genevieve clean in the shoulder. Her body jerks back at the unexpected hit, her eyes wide with panic. She blinks once, slowly, her glare not leaving my face.

I ready myself with another arrow of shadows, but it stills inside me as a flash of white and colour bolt past.

Fee barrels straight into Genevieve, his claws tangling with her hair as she yelps and bats him away. Caspian throws his arm out, a gust of his own borrowed power knocking Fee away. Felix swoops up and back, somersaulting in the air before diving back into the sky.

Genevieve storms toward me, Caspian hot on her trail. Her hair is a mass of tangles and bunches, her eyes wild and cruel. "I should never have given you that damn bird. I should have killed him when I had the chance."

"Killing an innocent bird is a bit excessive, don't you think?" I say.

Caspian smiles, finding something amusing. They stop only paces from me and Genevieve holds out her hand.

"Give me the pendant, Raylin. Put yourself out of this misery. You don't want this power, what use is it to you?" Her face softens but I still see the anger there, hiding behind her features. "Your family is gone, there is no changing that. But if you do as I ask, you can have a family again...you will have us."

I may have fallen for it mere days ago, may have sank into her words, wished away the pain inside. But I see the lie written all over her face. She doesn't want me—why would she? There isn't anything in the whole of Aldros she would not say to get what she wants. She thinks me stupid, desperate. I don't need them. I don't need her. I already have the only family I could ever ask for, the only family I need, and he's up there in the sky. By my side at every turn, every obstacle.

I reach into the void and pull out the obsidian pendant. It dangles in my hand as I hold it out before me. "This is what you want?"

Caspian tenses beside her, as if he is going to pounce and grab the stone from my hand.

"Good girl," she says.

As she takes a step forward, I take one back. Her head cocks to the side as if surveying a wild doe she is worried will scraper at any moment.

"Felix!" I flick my wrist, throwing the pendant as high as I possibly can.

Fee dives down, grabbing the shiny black stone in his waiting claws.

Genevieve's face hardens, every last ounce of kindness she had pasted there vanishing in a matter of seconds. She bounds toward me, her hand connecting with my throat. I do not panic as I struggle to take in air. Instead, I smile. She is thrown back with a blast of my power, the ice-cold of it pushing her away. A shadow shoots for her, causing her to stumble where she stands.

I rally up a ball of dark energy inside me, aim, and let it fly.

She grapples beside her before it can connect, pulling Caspian into the line of fire. It gets him in the gut like a fist of iron and he doubles over with the force. His eyes are wide with shock, hurt, as he rights himself. He doesn't set his stare on me, it's on his mother. The woman who just used her only child as a human shield.

"You—" His words fail him.

Genevieve shakes her head, as if not quite believing what she has done herself. This woman's cruelty truly knows no bounds. There are no limits to what she will do to survive.

Caspian reaches into his pocket, pulling out a small, glowing stone. I recognise it as one I use to fill with power for Genevieve. The light flickers out as he absorbs what dwells inside, letting it fill him, course through his veins. The hurt is gone from his face and all that remains is anger, disgust. He bares his teeth as he lashes out with that borrowed power, aiming right for Genevieve.

I do not hide my surprise as I watch, son against mother. Out of all the scenarios I pictured, this was not one of them. It was always them against me. Pure evil against raging revenge.

His lashes strike hard and true, whipping her across face and body, blood seeping from the wounds.

"You never loved me." Caspian's voice is raw, untamed.

The only thing that comes from Genevieve is gasps of pain, too stunned to do anything but try to get away. She trips as she stumbles backward, falling to the sandy floor, her arms perched behind her, holding her aloft.

There is a moment of silence, a break in Caspian's attack. The trees still, the very air seems to stop and wait, an audience to what will happen here tonight.

"Don't..." Genevieve whispers.

Then she too is silenced.

The blood pours from her throat, her black satin dress now a sticky mess. Her eyes go blank as she slumps to the ground. My stomach twists, satisfaction curling around the sadness, merging into one. Caspian stares down at her, unmoving. I cannot help but feel sorry for him. No matter how awful she was, she was his mother, she died at his hand, and he will have to live with that.

For a few moments at least.

I feel bad for him, but that doesn't mean I will spare him.

I feel it before I see it. A ripple of power hurtling toward me. Then his head turns toward me, a smile lifting the corner of his mouth.

He may be sly, but I am quick.

I let my power loose and it crashes with his, slamming into each other in a thundering clash. He sends out another blast of power, this time hitting me. The pain radiates up my arm, but I ignore it as I send one back. My shadows move wildly around me, wisps of black smoke cascading over my body.

Fee is soon down beside me, beckoning to a call I did not send. He launches himself at Caspian. He doesn't make it. The blast hits him, knocking him to the ground.

NO!

I am unsure if I say the word aloud as I run to him, my mind filled with fog. His wing twitches as I lay a hand on him. His large body splayed out on the desert sand. His little un-bird-like eyes flutter.

My heart breaks.

40

DEATH A DARKNESS

RAYLIN

No. No. No.

I cannot lose anyone else.

I feel the tremble of my bottom lip, but I force the tears away. He's not gone yet. I can fix this. I reach inside, looking for any hint of my father's healing powers within me. All I find is darkness. I fight for it, begging it to come. *Please.*

It's gone.

Everything good in me is gone, vanished when I chose revenge over all else.

But what if it's not?

Caspian. He used a stone I had filled when that power still lived inside me. I look at him. His face is unreadable.

"Help him! Please."

He doesn't move, doesn't answer. Just stands there, hands in his trouser pockets, as if he is standing on the side lines of some royal ball, not watching as my best friend dies.

I feel Fee's heart weakening beneath the palm I keep placed on his chest. It is beating too slowly, barely keeping the blood pumping through his veins.

"Caspian, please," I beg.

Something flickers in his eyes. Something I cannot read.

"If there is anything good still left inside you...help him. You don't have to be like her. You can be different. You can be the man I knew. He was kind, he was good."

"He was not real," is all he says.

It is no use. He doesn't have to be like her, but he is. There is no denying it. He is her son through and through. Him above all else.

"Give me the obsidian stone and I will do it," he says now.

"I– I don't have it. I don't know where he put it." I shake my head.

"Find it."

"He doesn't have time!"

"Then I cannot help you."

A single tear rolls down my cheek. "I will do it." I say it fast, not questioning myself. "Help him, and I will do it. You can take my power. I don't want it." The tear falls from my chin, landing on Fee's crisp white feathers.

Caspian contemplates my words, his gaze skimming over me, taking in every inch of my form. He opens his mouth to speak, but all that comes out is a rumble.

No. Not from him. From the ground.

Then again.

Caught up in the commotion, I do not realise right away that the soft beating beneath my palm has stilled. When I do, I cannot swallow. My mouth is dry, my own heart threatening to stop.

"He's gone," I whisper.

Caspian takes a small step toward me before thinking better of it and remaining where he is. I scramble back, remaining on the floor. The tears flow freely now, the painful sobs breaking from my chest.

Caspian only watches as I fall apart.

The ground rumbles again. There is a flash of light, so bright it blinds me temporarily. I shield my eyes, trying to peer between my fingers at the scene before me.

Fee's body is cocooned in clouds of bright white, hovering in mid-air. The clouds dance around him, concealing him from view. I squeeze my eyes closed as they flash once more.

When I open them, there are no lights. There is no body. Fee is gone. Instead, a boy stands in his place. A man really, my age, or slightly older. He is completely naked; I can see every inch of him. Every muscle, every dip and curve of his toned physique. His hair is a mess of black curls, hanging in his face, no longer than his ears. He wears a look of confusion, his thick brows pulled together as he takes in his surroundings. He is handsome, devastatingly so. And when he looks at me, those eyes pierce my soul.

I know those eyes.

They are the same deep brown eyes I have looked into every day for the past thirteen years. The same eyes that have comforted me without words, that have looked to me for reassurance. The eyes that have encouraged me, supported me. The ones that have been there through all the good, and the bad.

They are Fee's eyes.

I suck in a breath, not realising I hadn't taken one for several moments.

"Hello, brother," Caspian drawls.

All my attention darts to him.

There's no time to ask questions as the earth rumbles once more. Louder and more aggressive. A cracking sound fractures the silence. Then another, and another. The very floor splinters around us. Fee is beside me, helping me to my feet, still not uttering a word.

An explosion sounds in the distance, and we watch as the sand bursts from a pyramid, shattering its golden cap. Black puffs of clouds filter from its peak like smoke from a chimney. Not smoke. Shadow. Darkness. Something so similar to the power inside of me, I can feel it, that pull of likeness.

An ice wind hits me hard in the legs, knocking me down. Another to my chest sends me flying backward, my head thudding against the ground. My breathing becomes ragged and painful. Damn it. I see a flash of deep purple as Caspian rushes toward his castle, fleeing the fight and the destruction of his kingdom.

The ground continues to shake as Fee sits beside me and takes my hand. I force my eyes open as my head becomes light. I don't want to stop looking at him.

"Hi," he says, his voice deep and raspy.

I smile at him, gripping his hand in mine. He blurs, then there are three of him and I scrunch my eyes, trying to rid the roaring in my head. The world shivers, shaking at the corners of my vision. I feel a cold prickle along my skin. My eyelids are heavy as they drift closed, this time I cannot stop them.

41

Nowhere But You

Felix

Felix digs his fingers into the crumbling stone of the window ledge, a fire in his heart, an ache in his bones.

How was it that his entire world had come apart in a matter of weeks? How was it that now he was free, all he longed to do was be back in that tower, his feathered wings by her side? There were days in the past years where all he wanted was to be human, to have hands once more. To run those very hands through her hair, to place them gently on her face, wipe away the tears that formed in her eyes. But now, how he wished to be a bird again, to be back in those skies, keeping her safe.

Yet here he stands, human, watching a bronzed sun lower in the distance. And all along, the girl he longs for lay behind him, sleeping in her childhood bed; drapes of pink and purple fabrics drifting down round her. Yet, this is not the girl he knew, this is someone different, a girl with a blackened heart. She had slept for two days, he had cleaned the blood from her head, the dirt from her skin, he had even changed out her leathers for a silk nightgown he had found. Felix had lost count of the times he had checked her breathing, checking she was still with him.

The weight of something solid hangs heavy in his grip. He brings it to eye level, not sure what to do with the thing now. The obsidian pendant dangles from its leather chain in his clenched fist, seeming to swallow all light.

He pockets the pendant carelessly. There's a part of him that wishes he had left in there, in Kignet; a part of him that wishes he had truly died there, that the curse hadn't lifted and saved him. But that would be too easy, too simple. He bites down on his lip hard, the tang of copper filling his mouth.

Raylin shuffles from behind him and he turns as her eyes flutter open, two glowing moons staring back at him. He's moving toward her without much thought, but his legs are not his friend, too long he has not needed them, and he stumbles.

She's at his side in an instant, hands clutched around his arms, keeping him aloft.

"I need to get the hang of having legs again," he jokes, though the words come out too serious, too rough.

She helps him to the small sofa on the far side of the room, and no words are shared as they stare into each other's eyes. Felix watches as Raylin plays with the hem of her nightgown, her brows drawing together slightly, just now realising she doesn't wear the leathers from before. He had left her in them when they first arrived in Gavaria, flying in on another bird she had saved, but when it was apparent she wasn't going to wake any time soon, Felix had changed her tentatively, avoiding letting his fingers laze too long on her supple skin.

"What did she do to you?" Raylin asks softly, her words a mere whisper.

Felix takes a deep breath, eyes finding hers.

"I'm not going to pretend that you don't know what it is like to be trapped, Raylin. We were both in that tower together, day after day, suffering beyond measure. But with you, sometimes it didn't feel like suffering, sometimes it felt like I was where I should be."

Felix stops, the words sticking in his throat. The pressure of them building in his chest.

"But every moment I spent inside a body that was not mine...It is unexplainable. It was torture." He shakes his head, his gaze going to the sky through the broken window.

"Genevieve is not my mother. She may have created me, carried me inside her, but she was not my mother. She gave that up the day I was born, when she knew for certain I didn't share the same dark tones of her husband's skin."

Raylin takes his hand in hers, squeezing gently. The sensation of her skin on his sends shockwaves of heat through his body.

"I was raised by a servant and her husband. She would often take me to work with her within the castle and I would even play with Caspian, neither of us knowing what we truly were to each other, not right away.

"I think Caspian must have somehow found out. He started asking questions. One's that raised a lot of my own. Genevieve, of course, never spoke a word to me. Not once. She acted like I didn't exist. Until one day, just a day after I had asked my mother if I was truly hers, Genevieve showed up at our door. I was alone. I knew when I saw her, knew the truth. I didn't need her to tell me, but she did anyway. I thought she was going to kill me. Instead, she cursed me, and brought me to you."

"Why did you never leave? You could have found a way to break your curse, to be free."

"How could I, Raylin? I knew who you were from the beginning. I had heard stories of you, of your kingdom. They were tales they would tell us to keep us in our homes, horror stories they spewed to keep us from misbehaving. I couldn't just leave you there. Then, after a short while, I didn't want to."

Something settles on Raylin's features, something Felix doesn't want to see there, something he cannot comprehend.

"You should go." Her words scatter across the wind, pulling at Felix's heart, plunging like a knife. He doesn't say a word, just watches her. She lowers her gaze, not wanting to see the hurt on his face. "I need you to leave. There are things I need to do, things you shouldn't have to be a part of. You have suffered enough."

"And what if I don't want to leave?"

"Then I will. There is no choice, Fee."

"There is always a choice. You don't have to do this. He may deserve it, but you do not have to take this path. You do not have to be like them. Caspian gave you that choice when he took his mother's life. Now it is your choice to take a different path."

She shakes her head, looking to the ceiling, blinking away the tears that threaten her eyes. There is no going back, Felix realises. She's already made her choice.

She was going to leave him. But without her, he was simply a lost soul, not a coin to his name, not a place to call home. There was nothing for him.

He didn't even truly know who he was. He had spent so long as something other that he had lost all sense of who he once was. There is no purpose beyond what he knows, beyond who he knows. Raylin is his purpose, his guiding light. But now that light has dimmed, dematerialised, threatening to extinguish all together.

They walk together to the kitchens, Felix absent-mindedly makes her food, searching amongst the abandoned tins for something salvageable. The beans stick to the bottom of the pan, burning to a black crisp. They pick at what he could save, though neither really eat. He is just trying to draw out these last moments with her, keep her here with him that little bit longer in the destruction of her kingdom.

He doesn't know what he will do once she's gone, but he knows that she will leave, knows there is nothing he can do to keep her here. He will make peace with that, and he will wait. There is nowhere else for him to go but here.

There's nothing for him in Kignet. Nothing he wants anyway. Nothing for him anywhere. Nothing but waiting. Waiting for her.

She will come back to him. He knows her heart better than he knows his own. He knows the hate that lingers black and cruel inside her, knows the anger she is feeling. Because he felt it once too.

The day Genevieve knocked on the door of his parent's small home, that hate flooded him like a fiery tempest. He knew then what he hadn't been able to work out before. He knew the woman before him was the one who birthed him. And he knew she wasn't there to claim him.

It wasn't fear that froze his limbs, though he was scared—it was outrage, unrelenting and unforgiving.

Her lip had curled, a cruel and vicious gleam in her eye. "You have no one to blame but yourself," she had said matter-of-factly. "You went snooping, asking questions that shouldn't have touched your lips."

"Caspian knows too," was all he could think to say.

"*Prince* Caspian thinks he knows a lot. But if there is one thing that boy can do, it's keep his mouth shut. You, on the other hand...*tut tut*."

She bopped Felix on the nose, a wave of heat blasting through him, knocking him to his knees. He fought against the pain slicing him, but he was only eight, and the woman before him was powerful and strong. He clambered to his feet, but with a hand to his shoulder, he was down again.

"I won't say a word," he cried.

"No. You won't."

She placed her palm to his forehead, and the pain was like no other. His insides squirmed and tightened, his very blood boiled to near combustion. He screamed. Bright, burning white light flooded his eyes and he squeezed them closed, but it was useless—the light was coming from inside of him.

He screamed again but all he heard was the screech of a bird.

Then there was no pain. There was no burning. There was no light.

He tried to speak, but there were no words. He opened his eyes, and he almost wished he hadn't. Everything was different, colours more vivid, objects larger than they had once been. Genevieve was larger, towering over him like a tidal wave. He tried to stand but only fell.

Genevieve laughed, shaking her head.

It was then he noticed the wings. The snow-white feathers falling beside him. What had she done?

Three days he thrashed wildly in the cage, praying to the stars for release. She kept the cage in her room. There she would watch him, wings slamming against the bars of his prison. She would not speak, only watch.

Caspian had come to him once. He had been brave enough—or stupid enough—to poke a finger through the bars. Felix bit down so hard the boy screamed, he lashed out at the cage so vigorously that it swung from the hook, landing with a crash to the floor. Still, there was no reprieve from his torment.

Day four was when he gave up hope. It was also the day Genevieve carried him through shadows to a tower so tall it could touch the clouds. Or that's how it seemed to Felix in that moment.

That was when it all changed for him. When he met *her*.

Fourteen years have passed and he still remembers that day like it was only yesterday. The look in her silver-grey eyes, the smile that spread so wide across her face he feared her cheeks may splinter and crack.

He thinks of that face now as he walks Raylin back to her room, so innocent and young. Thinks of the smiles she has given him over the years, each one more beautiful than the last. His gut twists at the thought of not seeing that smile again, the notion too painful to handle. Felix tucks a small piece of Raylin's newly short hair behind her ear as they stand in the doorway to her bedroom.

He doesn't say a word as his hand falls from her face, wouldn't even know what to say if the words could find him. So he simply turns and leaves her there, sorrow passing across both their faces. Her voice reaches him as he descends the corridor, a word so soft he would have missed it if he hadn't been listening so intently to her breaths. *Goodbye.* He doesn't utter it back, for this is not goodbye, simply, *see you soon.*

42

Home

Raylin

I watch out of the open window as the darkness twists on itself, shadow upon shadow colliding and renting the very air apart. I lean closer, my breathing slowing. The curtains beside me flutter in a silent breeze, the room behind me darkening.

Something stirs in me, something forbidding and raw that is not my own. A whisper beckoning me to come, to follow its wordless call.

The shadows turn to something solid, something tall and harrowing. A dark form stands in their place, the hood of their cloak pulled far over their face. Although I cannot see their eyes, I know where they look, for they are staring right at me. A long, white arm extends from beneath the cloak, a lengthy, bony finger straightening and curling, calling me forward.

I'm not afraid as I slip on a cloak of my own and move quietly through the crumbling corridors, making my way toward the gardens. Something about the figure feels familiar, soothing.

I rush outside, the urge to be close to this mysterious person pulling me along. The arctic air stings my cheeks, but I do not care. Nasima lays sleeping by a splintered tree trunk, her chest rising and falling slowly. I know now how we got back here. She came for me. Another loyal creature I do not deserve.

A man stands before me, his bony fingers having pulled back his hood to reveal himself.

His skin is dirty, streaks of mud and blood all over his face. His hair is a pale silver, wisps of it falling down his neck and face. His eyes are the silver of the moon. A deep V sits between his eyebrows, like he's spent his life in a rage of anger. He is young, yet not. His face shows no sign of wrinkles, of ageing, he's only years older than me. Yet, there is something behind his eyes, something I cannot place. A distance of time.

His plump lips pull into a smile at the sight of me. Black mist curls around him; my power jumps forward to greet it. There's a click within me, two magnets snapping together, eager to become one. Our power is one and the same. Born from the same darkness. Gifted by the moon goddess.

This is the one Genevieve spoke of, the power her family had captured long ago.

"It was you...you are what tore from the pyramid upon her death."

"And you are what released me."

I shake my head slightly. "It was her son."

He takes my chin between his lengthy thumb and index finger, lifting my eyes to his. "Without you, it would not have been possible. I have waited a long time for you, Raylin."

I do nothing but stare at him, a serene calm washing over me, nuzzling into me. He steps closer, not moving his hand from my face. My heart beats a little faster, taking in his rugged features.

"Come with me," he says, his voice filled with want. "Together we will be unstoppable. We will be free of their torment and capture. We will make them pay for what has been brought upon us. Together our power will be incomparable, undefeated."

I don't need him, but there is something inside me that *wants* to go with him, that longs to be near him. Our powers writhe about us, weaving around each other like children playing. I feel the possibilities, the strength we could have together.

I step closer to him, taking his free hand in mine. His smile stretches. "You will not regret this, my queen."

There's a pull as his power wraps around us, shielding us in utter darkness. It closes in, blocking out all light and sound. I feel him pressed against me, his coldness seeping through my cloak. My stomach churns as we are pulled through nothingness, the empty darkness around us taught and endless.

I do not question my decision as we travel through nowhere, everywhere, his little pocket in the world beyond. But I do wonder if I can do this, if what I thought was merely a void is truly a pathway to other places, a space in which I can step and wander. I want to ask him. I open my mouth to say his name before remembering I do not know it.

Klaudius. My name is Klaudius. And yes, you can.

His words are not spoken aloud, but I hear his voice clearly as if they were. Something else I was unaware I could do.

There are many things you do not know about your power. Many things I can teach you.

We come to a sudden stop, the darkness around us stilling and dissipating. My stomach is in knots, bile rising in my throat. The crisp air bites at my lungs as I breathe deeply, trying to help the nausea pass. Klaudius steps away from me when he is certain I am steady on my feet.

A gasp escapes my lips at the world around me. Gloomy rock mountains as far as the eye can see. We do not stand at their base, but at eye level with their tips; some of them at least. They are all in varying sizes, some smaller, some reaching out to the sky, but all jagged and dark. There are no forests, no wildlife, only the vast rocky darkness. The same sullen rock surrounds us. We are standing inside one of the mountains, an enormous cave swallowing us.

I know this place. A place many do not dare to tread, a place few have returned from. Written and known throughout history as nothing more than the Black Mountains.

I turn to Klaudius; his smile causes a shiver to crawl up my spine. Where before I found him comforting, now his features show nothing but calculating madness.

"Welcome home." His voice rebounds around the empty space, returning to me once more.

Welcome home.

EPILOGUE

The darkness closed in around him. His eyes fluttered open in the black nothingness.

He was dead.

His life was taken by someone his family trusted. His bride's life was taken. Were they here with him? Wherever here was. Could this be what the afterlife is? It didn't feel like it. A place in between perhaps.

His eyes roamed the space, but it was nothing but a dark abyss.

The familiarity of it flooded his body like a dam.

No. No. Not again.

He knew this place, had been here before. He wasn't dead at all. It didn't make sense. His throat was still sore from where Genevieve's hands had squeezed, the tenderness making him wince as he brought his fingers to his neck, swollen and bruised. How could this be? Impossible. He had felt his life drifting away. Felt the tightening of his chest as he tried to draw breath. He didn't understand.

He tried to scream, but no sound escaped. His throat constricted from the pain.

There he stayed, frightened and alone, in the looming dark of his sister's void.

Outside the days drew on, the months, the years. But in here, time did not exist. He did not age, stuck at twenty-one forever. There was no need for food or water, sleep or rest. His body remained as it once was, the muscles lining his arms and chest did not atrophy. His light brown, shoulder-length hair did not grow, nor did the stubble on his face.

Reed didn't know how long had passed, nor did he know his sister still lived.

After days of screaming, once his throat had healed, he gave up hope. In his heart he truly believed Raylin had perished that night, along with his family. Believed she was punishing him. For what, he couldn't quite remember. For abandoning her, he guessed, in those years after she first trapped him here.

This was his life now. Stuck here, frozen in time. Though how he longed to return to the things he left behind.

He often spoke to voices that were not there. Whispers whizzing through the dark like an arrow. Sometimes they sounded like his sister, her, but older somehow. He would call out to her, but she never spoke back. The others he did not recognise at all.

Other times he would imagine things, objects that were not real. Jewels that had no purpose and were terribly ugly if he had to admit it. Instruments and books, clothes and trinkets. It was rare he would hallucinate the same thing more than once, though some things stayed, finding a home here with him. It was not up to him what would show and what would not. Many times he tried to focus, willing his mind to think up certain things, but it never worked.

His favourite was a dark green cloak. A simple thing, one of the rare items that would come and go often. It smelt of flowers and the ocean, bringing him a great deal of comfort. The scent washed over him like a warm hug. Something familiar, yet not. He would hold it tight and breathe it in, until one day it was gone.

He missed that smell.

The abyss was endless. He would spend countless time walking, walking, and walking. But no matter how far he strode, he always ended up right back where he started, surrounded by useless items.

It was in that darkness that he heard her scream. A blood-curdling sound, one of pain and sorrow. He felt the ripple of magic tear through the void, washing over him in a brisk wind.

She was alive.

Raylin was alive.

He screamed back, screamed until his throat grew raw, calling out to her, begging her to release him.

Nothing happened. She could not hear him.

His manic laughter echoed through the void.

The void laughed back.

It seemed darker now. If that was even possible.

Within the emptiness beyond, a flicker of light appeared. A soft, warm glow floating before him. It grew larger as he moved closer. He reached out a hand and it shuddered under his touch, warm and welcoming.

"Hello," Reed croaked.

The sun's power did not reply.

Acknowledgments

First, thank you, the reader, for finding this book and deciding to read it. Though I'm sure your ever-growing TBR warned you against it. I hold these characters close to my heart, and it is with the utmost delight that I get to share them with you.

Scott, for being my greatest encourager, for helping me to follow my dreams, for standing by me, and for being the greatest love of all.

To my boys, Xander and Leo, though your constant interruptions for snacks and the rising noise levels never made it easy, I wouldn't have wanted to do this without you. Watching you, Xander, create your maps and stories alongside me, has made this all worthwhile.

This wouldn't be a thank you if I didn't mention my soul mate and hype girl, Beth. Not a single thing I do is a failure in your eyes, and for that, I will always be grateful. Without you, I don't know what I would be today.

My mum, June, for bringing stories and books into my life and never letting them leave. My dad, Les. My sisters: Tara, Michelle, Lana, Darla, and Nina. My brothers: Jason and Harry. And to all the people who have shaped who I am today. Thank you for giving me the memories and experiences that will no doubt push through in my storytelling; and for creating a world where my imagination was free to run wild.

The rest of my family, big and small. There are too many of you to name, the list would go on forever, and no doubt I would forget one, but I appreciate you nonetheless.

My editor, Jess, thank you for going above and beyond, and for helping me make this story what it is today.

Thank you to all those who have taken this journey with me, from my beta readers to my arc readers, the friends I have made through the book community, those in my writer's group—with a special shout-out to Hayley for being in all four of those categories—and those who are blissfully unaware they played a part in helping me learn everything along the way.

You all matter.

Made in United States
North Haven, CT
01 May 2023